FANNIN'
THE
FLAMES

PARRY

"EbonySatin"

BROWN

FANNIN' THE FLAMES

a novel

ONE WORLD–STRIVERS ROW

BALLANTINE BOOKS

NEW YORK

Striver's Row
An Imprint of One World
Published by The Random House Publishing Group

Copyright © 2004 by Parry A. Brown

www.ballantinebooks.com/one/

Cataloguing-in-Publication Data is
available from the Library of Congress.

ISBN 0-345-46907-0

Text design by Jo Anne Metsch

Manufactured in the United States of America

First Edition: June 2004

10 9 8 7 6 5 4 3 2 1

To all my girls

Nicolle
Michelle
Shanelle
Krystal
Krysten
Symoni
Nierah

〰

Always remembering those who perished
September 11, 2001, serving others:

Firefighter Gerald Baptise
Firefighter Vernon Cherry
Firefighter Andrew Fletcher
Firefighter Keith Glascoe
Firefighter Ronnie Henderson
Firefighter William L. Henderson
Firefighter Karl Joseph
Firefighter Keithroy Maynard
Firefighter Shawn Powell
Firefighter Leon Smith
Firefighter Coleman Tarel
Firefighter Richard Vernon

FROM THE HEART

A s always, I must first give honor and thanks to my Lord and
Savior, Jesus Christ. To God for the many talents and
never-ending blessings He has bestowed upon me. I
wish always to exalt Him in all that I say and do.

In May 1999 I had the privilege and distinction to be introduced
to the South Central Region of the International Association of
Black Professional Fire Fighters. My dear friend Lloyd Nelson insisted this was a group that would appreciate my work. In my zeal
to become a best-selling author I jumped at the opportunity to be
exposed to more than one hundred people in one place. I had no
idea this meeting would change my life forever. To say a mere
thank-you to Lloyd for this experience seems so inadequate, but to
the man I've come to love like a brother I express my sincerest gratitude, not only for the introduction but for all else you do for your
big sister.

To the past president Ted Holmes and the current leader, Johnny
Brewington, I wish to thank you for your endorsement of this project since it was only a bright idea. Freddie "Silk" Jackson, my protector and friend, thank you for always watching after a sistah.
James Hill, my airport buddy and constant encourager, you'll never
know how much your friendship has meant. My gurl and die-hard
fan Angie Wilson, thanks for hanging out and helping me understand how the organization works. To the grandfather of the
IABPFF, Joe Hughes, thank you for the many hours you spent
telling me the story of how it was. I would surely like to express my
special thanks to Brent Burton for all of your help and showing me
the African American Firefighter Museum in Los Angeles.

When authors give their work to advance readers, we can only hope that the feedback we receive is on point. Anthony Penn, I thank you for teaching me about the County of Los Angeles Fire Department with so much love and patience. Your wit and humor still has the corner of my lips turned up. I hope I've made you proud to be the lead technical advisor for *Fannin' the Flames.* Lloyd Nelson, I have to thank you once again, for painstakingly going through every line of the manuscript and helping me keep it real. Nicolle Brown, as honest as any daughter could be, you are a very talented reader. You hit it right dead center where the changes needed to be made.

To Glynda Ard, my best friend and confidante, who kept me going when I just didn't think I could finish, thank you for screaming at me when I felt like quitting.

Thank you, Melody Guy, for believing in this project and for your unwavering patience. Portia Ophelia Cannon, I could never have brought this story together without you. Your creativity rounded out the story and got me over that horrible hump I guess every writer faces at one point in time. You're the best agent, friend and supporter I could ask for. Thank you, Cheryl Bistany, for giving me the 411 on neurological injuries. The members of Los Angeles County Fire Department Station 122, I thank you for the experience of a lifetime. Spending twelve hours with you has forever changed the way I look at a fire truck.

Last and most assuredly not least, thank you to all my friends and family who love and support me throughout all that I do: my daughter Michelle Brown; the love of my life, Neville Abraham; my sisters, Mary McClain, Lorraine Sims, Jacqueline Naylor and Beatrice Johnson; my niece and very capable assistant, Chanté Sims; and my very special friends Don and Wanda Wilson, Twania Hayes, Shauna Trower, Victoria Christopher Murray, Dan Navarro and Travis Hunter.

FANNIN'
THE
FLAMES

1

"Ohhhhhhh, oh my God! Uhhhhh!"

Nicolle paused to wipe sweat from her eyes. "Come on, gurl, come on!" she encouraged herself aloud. "You can do this. Eighty-six. Eighty-seven. Eighty-eight. Ohhhh, dang! Eighty-nine. Ninety!"

Nicolle collapsed onto the floor mat as sweat oozed from every pore in her five-foot-six-inch, two-hundred-thirty-five-pound body. With ninety sit-ups, she had reached an all-time high in her morning exercise routine, but she had a feeling it wouldn't matter. She laughed out loud. Lordy, she thought, I know if I step on that scale I'll see that I haven't lost an ounce!

It's all right to say I love you out loud, and it's all good so you don't keep it inside—Luther Vandross's voice filled the room as the upbeat tempo of "Say It Now" gave Nicolle the momentum to move to the StairMaster for the final phase of her workout in the bedroom she had converted into an at-home gym.

The clock on the twenty-inch television perched in the corner near the ceiling read 7:08 A.M. Listening to music while watching the previous night's bad news with the closed-captioned display was how Nicolle Devereaux-Winters spent every morning that her loving husband of eighteen years was on duty at Fire Station 27 of the County of Los Angeles Fire Department.

Slumber was always elusive on the nights she spent alone. Even though she went to sleep late and rose early, the hours still seemed to drag far past the twenty-four Jerome worked on C Shift. So far they'd been lucky Jerome's only injury in the fifteen years he'd been with the fire department was a broken hand, and that had happened off-duty during an annual boxing tournament.

This morning, KTLA Channel 5's wacky morning news team seemed more sedate than usual. Giselle Fernandez's lips formed silent words as the white letters flowed upward over the black box at the bottom of the screen. A small picture of a firefighter hovered in the upper right-hand corner above the early morning television icon's head. Exercise regimen forgotten, Nicolle hit the Mute button on the remote control to hear the report.

"Three firefighters were injured in the early morning hours, battling a three-alarm apartment house fire, when the floor collapsed. Two were taken to the Alisa Ann Rush Burn Unit while the third, with less severe injuries, was taken to Harbor-UCLA Medical Center. The cause of the explosion and subsequent blaze is not known, but it is suspected that a drug-manufacturing lab is to blame. The names of the three injured firefighters are being withheld pending notification of family."

Nicolle wasn't sure what the newscaster had said after revealing that three firefighters had been injured. The Hispanic woman's words seemed to all run together. With trembling hands, Nicolle reached for the cordless phone. She speed-dialed Jerome's cell phone number, and the voice mail picked up before the first ring. His phone was off. Her fingers were numb as she shivered from the coldness brought on by her fear. She then dialed Jerome's pager number and managed to key in their home number, followed by 9-1-1, a code that meant "No matter what you're doing, you betta call me now!"

Nicolle made the ten steps to the office across the hall and picked up the handset on the fax machine to call Nellie, her best friend and the wife of Lloyd Frederickson, one of Jerome's colleagues and godfather to their second son.

Nellie picked up on the first ring. "I'm already watching the news."

"How did you know it was me?" Nicolle spoke quickly, her words tripping like a five-year-old with loose shoelaces. "I called you from the fax phone because I didn't want to take a chance on Jerome calling when I called you."

"It's always you when there's a news report about a firefighter being hurt or killed." Nellie's cool tone unnerved Nicolle.

"Have you heard from Lloyd?"

"I've paged him, but nothing yet," Nellie said. "It's only been two minutes, Nicky."

"How have you been able to do this for thirty years? This makes me so nuts. I want Jerome to take an administrative job so badly, but of course he has to be 'in the thick of things,' as he calls it."

"Gurl, I do a lot of praying." There was something in Nellie's voice Nicolle couldn't quite discern, but she was so caught up in her own panic that she didn't give it much consideration. "Of course, there isn't anyone answering at the station, either. I've hated this job since day one—but they're fine. The chief would call if either one of them was hurt."

"What if the chief is one of those that's been hurt?" Nicolle felt like she was bordering on hysteria. "The news report said it happened in the middle of the night. They had the news footage. Why don't they call?"

"Making yourself crazy isn't going to help anyone, especially the boys." Nicolle heard Nellie exhale cigarette smoke. "We just have to stay calm until we hear something one way or the other. Trust me, they're fine. Bad news travels on the wings of an eagle. Believe that."

"I'm so glad the kids are off school today and sleeping in. Otherwise, they'd be up, looking for breakfast and watching me freak out. I do so loathe this about myself. I have no control over my fear where Jerome's job is concerned."

"You'll survive. We always do," Nellie continued without emotion. "I'll call you as soon as I hear from Lloyd, and you do the same when you hear from Jerome."

"Okay. And Nellie?" Nicolle said softly.

"Yes?"

"I just really love and worry about my husband—don't be mad at me for that."

"I don't know what you're talking about," Nellie said. "Why would I be mad at you?"

"I'm just saying."

"I'll talk to you soon. And stop worrying."

Nicolle stood in the center of the room that functioned as her home office. The smallest of their five bedrooms, it was equipped with all the latest and greatest equipment: computer, fax machine, copier, color laser printer, scanner. You name it—she had it. Whatever her job hadn't provided, Jerome had acquired for her. The walls proudly boasted of her many accomplishments in her personal and professional life, and family pictures featuring her boys in varying stages of growth filled the wall opposite her desk. Her degrees, diplomas and certificates from every academic institution she'd ever attended were on the wall behind where she sat. A statistical analyst for an insurance company, she was able to work from home ninety percent of the time. For the past eight years she'd been a working, stay-at-home mom. Jerome and her boys loved it, but not half as much as she did.

The early morning sunlight streamed into the room through the beveled windowpane, casting a rainbow onto the hardwood floor. The squeaking sound of Nicolle's tennis shoes on the freshly treated surface frayed her last good nerve. Halfway to the door, she bent to untie and remove her walking shoes. She had nothing left from which to draw to work out. She would do what she was worst at— wait.

Nicolle and Jerome had a picture-perfect marriage and family life, complete with three sons, a home with a picket fence and a Rottweiler named Brutus.

She had been lucky that her parents had moved into the new housing development for middle-class working black families, just two doors down from the Winters. Thanks to that bit of good fortune, there had always been a Jerome and Nicolle. They had been stroller buddies, played in the sand at preschool together, shared graham crackers in kindergarten, graduated from Miss Davis's sixth-grade class, and then, on that magical night at the spring formal, they fell in love.

Older than Jerome by only six weeks, Nicolle had loved Jerome since the fourth grade. They had begun dating in the eighth grade and had been inseparable since that dance so many years ago. Nicolle's and Jerome's families had lived on the same street since before both of them were born, and the Devereaux and Winters families had attended the same church for more than forty years. Jerome had proposed to Nicolle on the night of their senior prom, hoping she'd finally give in to his constant request for an expression of the love she'd proclaimed since before puberty. Although she had flatly refused to give in to anything that night, she'd accepted his proposal, and they were married the Saturday following graduation—both still virgins.

Jerome had attended California Polytechnic Institute at Pomona while Nicolle worked for the County of Los Angeles Fire Department as a secretary. When he'd graduated with honors with a degree in engineering, he'd hoped to work for an auto manufacturer. Nicolle's mother had become seriously ill during his senior year in college, but he hadn't had the heart to ask her to move to Detroit, where he'd planned to secure a job.

Because the department was in need of what the powers-that-be termed more "intellectual" blacks on the firefighting force, his wife's boss, the fire commissioner, had suggested Jerome take the test to become a firefighter. Although Nicolle had taken offense at the implication that there was a shortage of qualified blacks available, she mentioned the opportunity to Jerome without the additional commentary.

Jerome placed first on the entrance exam and had ranked in the top three on every test he'd taken since that day. With his consistent high scoring, she still couldn't understand why he hadn't made captain, but Jerome discouraged her from discussing it. As much as she respected her husband's work, she still hated worrying about him every time he worked a shift.

Walking back into the gym, Nicolle stepped onto the black-and-white-checked flooring, her socks sliding and causing her to lose her footing. Landing on her rear end, she began laughing uncontrollably until tears streamed from her eyes like spring rain. The joyous sounds of laughter quickly turned to moans of anguish. Jerome always chastised her about walking on the tile floor with only socks on her feet. "You're going to fall—or worse, your legs are going to spread apart and you'll pull your groin muscle. Then a brotha won't be able to hit that bootie." She'd do anything to tell him he'd been right again.

As she reached to turn off the television, she heard the hum of the garage door opening. Jerome was home. Forgetting his warning about socks on tile, she sprinted toward the staircase. Taking the steps without caution, she jumped onto the Spanish marble foyer, feeling the cool through her white crew socks. Slipping slightly, she regained her balance without missing a beat. She flew past the living, formal dining and family rooms into the kitchen. Throwing open the door that led to the garage, Nicolle startled Jerome at the back of their flame-red Durango, where he was gathering his bag.

"What's wrong?" he asked, looking concerned as she rushed toward him.

"I was so worried!" Nicolle stepped back to take in the full view of the man she loved more than the air she breathed. He reeked of smoke, exhaustion had drawn deep lines around his bloodshot, dark brown eyes and soot had darkened his cinnamon-brown complexion by at least two shades, but he'd never looked so good to her. "Why didn't you return my call or page?"

"Oh, baby, I'm sorry. My cell and pager are both on the table in the family room. I forgot them yesterday. I was going to call you when I thought you were up, to tell you we weren't on the fire call that made the news—we were already on a rescue run when that call came in—but at three thirty we got our own fire, and we just finished up about an hour ago. I know I should have called. I didn't even bother to take a shower—I just got in the truck and headed home to you, Babe-ski." He pulled Nicolle close and buried his face into her very ample bosom and moaned seductively. "Girl, you sho' nuff smell good. The boys still sleeping?"

"Don't Babe-ski me!" Nicolle teased, pressing herself into his body; she could feel his arousal. "You should've called me before you went on that last run. You know I don't really sleep when you're not here. And how can you want to have sex now?" she pretended to protest. "You're so exhausted. I can see it all over you."

"Look at you. How can I *not* want to make love to the woman who is sexy enough to make me look at Halle Berry like she's a man?"

"Now, see, if you'd said Queen Latifah, you know I might even believe you. Come on, I'll make you some breakfast while you take a shower."

"I have a better idea. You come take a shower with me, and I'll have you for breakfast."

"Hmmmm. I'll race you!"

2

Nellie lit a fresh cigarette off the smoldering butt she held in her left hand as she hit the Off button on the cordless handset. She really loved Nicolle, but the woman's constant fear for Jerome's safety aggravated her to no end.

Or maybe she just envied the love Nicolle and Jerome shared. Despite being married three days past forever, the Winters always acted like newlyweds. Even a little child could see the sparkle in their eyes when they looked at each other. At the mere mention of Jerome's name, a smile would sweep across Nicolle's face like sand on a windy day in the desert.

Although Nellie knew in her heart Lloyd was safe, him being hurt—or worse—would make her decision so much easier. She couldn't remember when she'd stopped loving him; she just woke up one morning and knew love had taken up residence elsewhere. They'd been married when she was twenty-one, and as she looked forward to her fifty-first birthday, she knew she couldn't live the lie any longer. She hated how she felt. Her husband of thirty years had done nothing different or wrong by most people's standards, yet she was constantly angry, bitter and resentful toward him. Guilt now filled the space where love should live. Lloyd's incessant planning for their thirtieth-anniversary celebration had sent her into a depression so deep that she'd had to seek counseling, and as usual, he was so wrapped up in his own world he hadn't even noticed.

The phone rang again. She watched the caller ID box as Nicolle's number stared back at her. She'd let the voice mail pick it up. Nellie just wasn't in the mood for her friend's blissful news that Jerome had made it home safely. She pulled the smoke deep into her lungs, closing her eyes as the toxicants from the fiery tranquilizer soothed her.

She'd loved Lloyd for many years after she married him. Back then she was young and idealistic. Maybe in some abstract way she still loved him—after all, he'd worked overtime to help pay for her doctorate degree in social work. That alone was the reason she hadn't left him before now. How do you repay someone for sacrificing so much of his soul's blood for your dream? When was the debt paid?

Her eyes remained closed as she wondered why she'd fallen out of love with the man who should by anyone's definition be her ideal life partner. He was the same caring, meticulous, detail-oriented man he'd always been. He tinkered with the old 1958 Chevy Cameo pickup he'd been restoring for at least five years, which still looked exactly the same as it did the day he towed that piece of junk into *her* garage. He could account for every penny he'd ever spent and had educated her and their two daughters without ever borrowing a single cent. Lloyd was in top physical condition and consistently outperformed his younger counterparts. His chiseled body would turn any woman's head, and yet he'd never cheated on her. He was an awesome lover. She never had to ask him to take out the garbage or wash her car. So what was the problem? What was her problem?

Hell if she knew. All she knew was that she'd had all she could take. She wanted out. When was the right time to tell him? She had to do it before he sent out the invitations to the anniversary party. She took another long drag from her Virginia Slims Menthol.

Nellie heard Lloyd's zinc-yellow Mustang GT convertible pull into the driveway, making her want to run and hide. She was supposed to show concern for the man who risked his life every day saving other people and their property, but today she just couldn't muster a cheerful concerned-wife greeting.

"Hey, baby. I'm home," Lloyd called from the back stairs, which led from the kitchen to the second level of the spacious, four-thousand-square-foot house they'd purchased for their twenty-fifth wedding anniversary.

After what seemed like several minutes, Nellie finally answered.

"I'm up here." She debated whether to pretend she was still sleeping, but the smell of burning tobacco would have been a telltale sign she was definitely awake.

"I'll be right up," Lloyd called. "How's my best girl this morning?"

Lloyd's cheer made Nellie want to cringe. "Doing just peachy."

Not noticing the ice in Nellie's voice, Lloyd cheerfully said, "That's what I like to hear."

Ll oyd moved about the kitchen, humming as he arranged a yellow floral bouquet in the lead crystal vase and placed it in the window box overlooking the expansive yard and swimming pool. "You'll love these, my Georgia peach!" he murmured under his breath.

Checking the kitchen one last time to make sure he'd left nothing out of place, he took the stairs two at a time. His shift had been a rough one, with a fire and countless rescue runs. He hated full moons. Many people thought it was an old wives' tale that people reacted strangely at the completion of the lunar cycle. After almost thirty years, he knew for himself there was more than a little validity to the rumor. But he'd left all of that in the garage as he walked into the haven he called home.

He didn't understand the empty-nest syndrome everyone told him he'd experience when his daughters had left home. Loving his girls was like breathing. Portia, the oldest of the two by eleven months, was a third-year surgical resident in Seattle. An overachiever who had to be at the top of her game in all she did, Portia rarely had time to call, let alone come home for a visit, but he could do nothing less than respect her. With her wanderlust spirit, Victoria was more like her mother. After playing basketball for three years in Italy, she still showed no interest in returning to the States. The Italians were fascinated with the six-foot-three-inch, two-hundred-twenty-five-pound sistah from Los Angeles who was lightning-fast on the basketball court. He'd wanted her to try out for the WNBA, but she'd insisted she needed more court time to prove to the league she was worth the money she'd be asking. He wasn't mad at her. Even though he loved his two girls more than anything, he understood and respected their need for independence.

He reached the top of the stairs, strolled into their master suite and smiled at his wife. Man, he loved that woman.

"Hey, baby! You look stunning this blessed morning."

Lloyd's voice grated on Nellie's nerves. "Morning," she said. "Heard the news about some firefighters getting hurt." Nellie turned her back as Lloyd climbed on the king-size, four-poster oak bed. "Nicky called, frantic as usual. Did you know them?"

"Yeah, two of them belong to the Stentorians. They're hurt pretty bad. Not sure if the woman is going to make it. She hit her head when they fell through the floor." Lloyd leaned over to kiss her shoulder. "But your sugar bear is here and just fine."

"You smell like smoke," Nellie said, wrinkling her nose. "You're getting it all over the covers. You really need to shower and change before you come home." She pulled away from his amorous touch. Despite Nellie's lovelorn feelings, the sex between them was still steamy, to say the least, but this morning even she, in her menopausal peaking mode, wasn't in the mood.

"You know, you could show a little concern for a brotha who could just as easily be lying in a burn unit this morning as here on this bed with you," Lloyd said, sounding disappointed. "Sometimes I wonder if you still love me. You're always so blasé lately. Have I done something wrong?" Hurt quickly turned to anger as Lloyd pushed himself off the bed.

"Why are you always talking about me loving you?" Nellie's voice started to rise. "I've been married to you for thirty years. If that ain't love, please tell me what is!" Nellie didn't mean to strike at him, but he just wouldn't leave well enough alone.

"Here we go." Lloyd's voice raised a few tones of its own. "You've been pissy with me since I started planning the anniversary party. Would you rather have a vacation? What is it you want? I don't seem to know anymore!"

"You shouldn't ask questions better left unanswered." Nellie suppressed her desire to scream at him that she wanted a divorce. "Be careful what you ask for."

"I'm beginning to wonder if you're still happy here with me. I give you everything you could possibly want—this should be the best time in our lives, the kids gone and out of our pockets. I want to take you to exotic lands and do erotic things to you, but you seem more excited about getting your teeth cleaned than having a date with me." Lloyd paced, trying to suppress the anger he felt welling up inside him.

"You need to get some rest," Nellie said, suddenly tired from arguing. "I have an appointment in an hour. I'll shower in one of the other bedrooms." Nellie slid from under the beige down comforter, slipping her feet into the fuzzy slippers Lloyd had given her when he returned from one of his precious firefighter conferences.

"I think we need to discuss this some more," Lloyd said. "Why do you always run away when I ask you what's going on with us?"

Nellie turned sharply and stared at him, her gaze cold. "Lloyd Frederickson, let it be!"

"I'm going to let it go for now, but we *will* talk about this." Lloyd moved around the bed, tripping over the purple-suede-covered bench at its foot, until he was standing in front of his wife. "You're the center of my universe. I'm not going to just sit around and watch something cancerous eat away everything good and healthy between us."

"Then we better sign up for chemotherapy treatments," Nellie muttered, leaving Lloyd with a view of her back as she walked away.

3

"Honey, you know I worry about you," Antoinette St. Vincent said to her son as he maneuvered through the streets of Culver City, no doubt at lawbreaking speeds, driving the convertible sports car she and her husband had given him as a graduation present when he'd finished the firefighter academy.

"Mom, I'm fine," Andrew St. Vincent responded, speaking into the headset attached to his wireless phone. "We didn't make that call. I wish we had, though. I was on the pumper truck yesterday. I'm so ready to knock down a big one. They treat me like some kind of second-class citizen. Hell, they're forgetting who my daddy is—Jules St. Vincent is a battalion chief with thirty-three years of service!"

"Watch your mouth, young man! I can't believe I'm going through this worrying for a second generation." Antoinette sighed deeply. "I was so glad when your father finally became a chief and stopped going on every call. And you know one thing, young man? Your daddy being a chief doesn't have a thing to do with your ability to put out a smoldering trash can. Why do you think you rank some kind of special privilege?"

"'Cause I'm Antoinette St. Vincent's baby boy!"

Andrew must have guessed his quip would draw a genuine smile from his mother, and if he were there, he wouldn't have been disappointed.

"So what're you doing now?" she said. "You need to get some rest. Why don't you just drive your pompous self on over here, and I'll make you breakfast with all the trimmings." She pulled her bathrobe tighter around her to keep out the early morning chill.

"Sorry, Mommy. No can do. I've got a date for breakfast, this honey I met when I did a rescue run. Her father had a heart attack,

I gave him CPR and she gave me her number. She took one look into these baby blues and melted."

"Boy, show some respect. You need to be ashamed calling women honeys. And what are you doing going on a breakfast date? Like I said, you need to take your butt home and get some rest. I tell you, these honeys, as you call them, are going to be the death of you!"

"I can rest then, I promise you! Gotta go. Love you, Mom." Andrew closed the sleek flip-style phone and placed it on the black leather seat next to him and turned up the volume of his favorite Maxwell CD, *Now*. He felt a warmth roll through his heart as he thought of his mother's love.

"Love you, too." Antoinette hung up the phone and poured herself another cup of decaf. She had been livid when Andrew changed his major from pre-law political science to fire science. She'd been overprotective of her only child since the moment she'd known she was pregnant, a little more than twenty-four years before. Because of a tilted uterus, the doctors had told her she'd never have any children. After three years of being rejected by adoption agencies—she and Jules were an interracial couple—she'd finally missed two periods and spent every morning for three weeks feeling nauseous. Because her son had been so hard-won, she'd always been more cautious than perhaps she should have been.

Antoinette had married Jules in a time when being seen with a white man could have gotten you killed. They'd met on a beach on Martha's Vineyard during the summer between her junior and senior year at Rutgers, when she was working as a waitress, while Jules vacationed with his family. He'd been taken with her from the first moment their eyes met and had spent much of the week trying to convince her to talk to him. Antoinette had never had any interest in white boys—or they in her—so she rebuffed his advances, even though she thought he was funny, interesting and cute in a different sort of way. But Jules hadn't given up. Her deep-chocolate skin had been flawless, and her perfectly aligned pearly whites had made her smile irresistible to him. On his last day at the resort, he'd finally been able to convince Antoinette to reveal her address so he could write her.

When she'd shared the story of the weeklong pursuit with her sister and mother, the two of them had agreed that the white boy from the good family in St. Louis only wanted her for one thing, and since she hadn't given it to him, she'd never hear from him again. Antoinette felt they were wrong but didn't dare to say so.

Several months had passed, well into the fall semester, when a small package arrived, containing a journal and Christmas card. In the card Jules had explained how he'd written an entry every day since they'd parted because he'd thought of her constantly. As she'd begun reading the entries in the small book, she'd seen that Jules had dreamed and fantasized about her, genuinely longing to be near her. She'd been stunned by what she'd read. On the last page, dated three days prior, he'd written these words:

I don't know what spell this woman of such exquisite style, grace and beauty has cast upon me. I've told others of my obsession, only to be ridiculed. I only know that I must go to her and share my feelings. This woman is to be my wife. I don't know if my family will accept or reject her. I don't care what they think of me. I will move from this place with these people of very narrow minds. Antoinette must say she will marry me.

She, too, had thought of him often. She hadn't dared to share her feelings with her mother and sister—because she hadn't heard from him since he'd left Martha's Vineyard, she'd begun to believe their dismissive words about Jules. As she read the words on the last page of the journal over and over again, she began to weep. How could she even think of marrying a white man after all her people had suffered at the hands of the Europeans? At the same time, how could she deny what she felt for him at that moment?

She responded with a seven-page letter explaining why she didn't think things would work between them. She tried to justify all of her reasons for a negative response to his proposal. Jules responded with a five-page letter of his own explaining why they *must* be married. When she didn't respond in what he considered reasonable time, he began phoning the dormitory. They would talk for hours, with the conversation always ending the same—Jules's begging Antoinette to marry him and her refusal. Despite the longing in her heart she still refused to entertain the notion she could become Mrs. Jules St. Vincent.

On the last day of classes before the spring break, the dormitory mother announced Antoinette had a visitor. As she bounced down the stairs expecting to see her mother and sister, she stopped so quickly she almost tripped when she saw Jules staring up at her with a huge bouquet of flowers in his hand. There was something in his eyes that moved Antoinette to tears. He fell to one knee and asked for the last time, "Will you marry me?" And here she sat, thirty-seven years later, content beyond measure. Notwithstanding the outside pressures, they'd had a happy, wonder-filled marriage. Although the dozen years of their marriage had been rough, the St. Vincent family had finally accepted her after she'd given birth to Andrew. While she still didn't have the best relationship with her in-laws, they were more cordial than her family, who had never forgiven her for marrying a white man.

Antoinette moved aimlessly about the spacious den as she tried to stifle the pain in her chest. Whenever she thought about her separation from her mother and sister, which had started the day she'd married Jules, she felt sadness so deep that it became a physical pain. Shaking it off, she looked at the handsome picture of her two favorite guys that was resting on the mantel above the marble fireplace. Her two men had made bearable the years of pain she'd suffered from her family's inability to accept Jules as her husband.

The plush, black sectional sofa invited her to sit with a mug full of Jamaican Blue Mountain coffee and meditate on God's goodness. Because Jules's job provided such a wonderful life for them, she hadn't had to work outside of their home, instead volunteering at the local hospice, which consistently reminded her just how blessed she was to have a healthy family. Jules no longer worked overnight, and she was very glad to have him in her bed every night.

She stared at the picture on the chrome-and-smoked-glass end table, where she set her coffee mug on a crystal coaster. In the picture, a grinning Andrew held up his high school diploma. He'd been a child of privilege, for which she made no apologies. The one thing she'd learned from her white neighbors was that they spoiled their children. Andrew had received his first car, a ten-year-old blue Honda Civic, on his sixteenth birthday, and then a new silver Toyota Corolla at his high school graduation and, finally, the fully loaded absolutely red sports car, a real babe magnet, as he called it, when he completed the fire academy.

Despite their overindulgence, Andrew had turned out to be a good son. He'd graduated at the top of his class in high school and made the dean's list the last three years at St. Louis University, where his grandparents had kept a very watchful eye. Yes, she was a very proud Mommy, as he always called her when he wanted his way.

Antoinette worried that Andrew's naïveté with regard to the social issues that blacks faced in the workplace, especially at the fire department, was going to cause him grief, serious grief. He'd seen his grandfather retire with full honors from his position as the assistant chief of the St. Louis City Fire Department, with hundreds of people in attendance, including the mayor, at the gala retirement party. His father had likewise moved through the ranks quickly and easily, recently reaching the battalion chief position.

In the depths of her soul, Antoinette knew it would be different for her only son. Someday, perhaps even someday soon, his sheltered existence would come crashing down like a house of cards, and there was nothing she could do to prevent it.

4

Though he had been asleep for only thirty minutes, Jerome awoke instantly, fully alert, at the first chime of the fire bell. With smooth and well-rehearsed movements, he pulled his uniform over his sports shorts and undershirt and headed for the engine truck within forty-five seconds. He stepped into his waiting boots by the driver's door and climbed into the truck. The dispatcher's voice echoed their destination for the second time: "Engine Company 27, report to Manchester and Avalon. TC-overturned vehicle. Victims reportedly trapped. Squad 39 en route."

Precious seconds ticked by as the other members of C Shift scurried to their assigned positions. Jerome pushed the starter button—nothing.

"Let's go!" Lloyd Frederickson barked into the microphone from the right front seat reserved for the captain.

Five seconds passed, and Jerome pushed the starter button again, not hearing even a faint whine from the sixteen-ton, three-hundred-horsepower mobile fire extinguisher.

As though reading Jerome's thoughts, Andrew, the hydrant man, leapt from the seat directly behind the captain and opened the door to the battery compartment. Immediately, Andrew realized the problem. The negative battery cable had been removed from one of the three batteries.

"What the f—?" Andrew exclaimed while replacing the cable.

In less than a minute, Andrew replaced the cable, checked all the others and secured the compartment door. Jerome looked questioningly at Andrew as he climbed back into the truck, pointing to the headphones to indicate that he wanted to talk. The truck rumbled to life with the first push of the starter button, and Engine 27 barreled out of the firehouse with lights flashing and sirens blaring. Five minutes had been lost.

Nodding up at Jerome, Andrew placed the noise-canceling headphones over his ears and adjusted the microphone. "Someone removed the cable from the battery," he spat.

Jerome slammed his fist onto the steering wheel as he turned the corner as fast as he dared. Over the past three weeks, little incidents had occurred on C Shift—called the "Colored Shift" by the white firefighters on the A and B Shifts—that had him worried there might be a saboteur among them. C Shift was predominantly firefighters of color—black, brown and red.

Since the early eighties, Los Angeles City and County Fire Departments had adopted a hiring policy that stated the makeup of the fire department would be representative of the population in the community it served. Even with this policy in place less than twenty percent of new hires were of color or female. It was sad to say, but even at the beginning of a new millennium there were those who would rather judge a man, or woman, by the color of his or her skin, rather than by competence on the job. What was even sadder was that men of all hues judged women by their curves instead of their courage. Though frustrated with the politics of the job, Jerome was determined to be the best firefighter/paramedic he could be and to lead by example.

Subtle things had begun to happen the fall of the previous year. Watermelon would mysteriously appear in the refrigerator, and no one would take credit for buying it. A lawn jockey was found in the showers one morning. Though aggravating, these pranks were deemed harmless and chalked up to ignorance of the few. Within the last three weeks, however, the pranks had turned dangerous. This last incident had cost them more than three minutes, minutes that could mean the difference between life, death or brain damage.

"We've got to put a stop to this madness." Jerome spoke into the microphone through clinched teeth, never taking his eyes off the road as he maneuvered through the streets of South Central Los Angeles. "This fool is going too far. Who do you think it is?"

"I don't know," Andrew replied. "But the brass had better do something about this before someone gets hurt. I'm afraid of this guy. This is not just stupid pranks anymore. It's a life-death thing."

"I'll talk to the chief as soon as we get back. Maybe now he won't think I'm just being paranoid," Lloyd assured the others.

Across the street from Station 27, the man watched the engine and paramedic wagon roll onto the street. It amazed him how quickly they had been able to detect the source of the problem and correct it. Perhaps he had underestimated their intelligence.

He checked his Tag Heuer timepiece and made note in his journal of the precise lapsed time from the receipt of the initial call and the engine rolling. Four minutes and thirty-nine seconds. Not bad.

He turned the key, and the 1983 El Camino roared to life. He merged into traffic and drove seventeen blocks to his five-hundred-square-foot, one-bedroom apartment. He parked in the carport, disconnected the shortwave radio and slipped from behind the wheel.

He set the radio on the ground and meticulously covered the vehicle with a tan car cover. After picking up the radio again, he looked over his shoulder. He was sure that his comings and goings were of no concern to anyone who happened to be watching, but nonetheless, he wanted to be sure not to arouse any suspicions.

After climbing the steps to his apartment, he carefully locked the dead bolt before sitting down at the computer. He double-clicked on the icon that opened his web-mail account and began typing:

Our mission has been accomplished. I am dealing with those people. They will know their place when I am finished with them.

—One of Your Boys

Jerome raced through the dark, deserted streets, moving closer to an intersection.

Eight minutes had passed since the dispatch call, and he should have been approaching the traffic accident, but instead he was still a full minute away.

Jerome knew he was breaking the rules as he removed his safety ear guards, but anger was making his ears sweat. "Hang on, peo-

ple," he said aloud to himself. "The red knights are coming." He
gave the engine just a little more gas.

Engine Company 27 should have been the first rescue unit on
the scene. Instead, they pulled into the intersection behind Truck
Company 12. Police officers scampered pointlessly as the cries of
those trapped inside the overturned white Ford Explorer filled the
night air. Steam escaped from the punctured radiator of the tan
Nissan Quest with a caved-in front. The rear driver-side fender was
crunched, making it apparent the vehicle had been hit more than
once. The driver, looking lost and disoriented, sat inside, gauze on
his forehead and a deployed air bag in his lap. A twenty-year-old
rusted-out Cadillac sat ten feet from the other vehicles, bearing
only minimal damage. The driver stood near her vehicle with her
finger to her nose. You didn't have to be a criminal scene investigator to figure out who'd caused this mess.

Lloyd looked over the accident scene, sized up the situation
within seconds and began barking orders: "Let's move! Winters,
Nelson, St. Vincent, take the van. I'll take the Explorer." The police
officers lit flares and began rerouting the sparse flow of early morning traffic. Captain Merrick of Truck 12 ordered his crew to assist
with the van.

Jerome climbed onto the van to assess the situation. He could see
there were three passengers, plus the driver. Fortunately, they were
each secured by a seat belt. The driver struggled to get loose.
"We're going to get you out of here just as soon as we possibly can,"
Jerome said in his most reassuring voice. "Is everyone conscious?"

"Please get us outta here." The driver's voice was extremely
weak. "I think my arm is broken. That crazy woman driving the
Caddy ran the light and hit both of us."

"I need to hear everyone else speak to me," Jerome said, craning
his neck to look inside at the other passengers. "What about you,
miss? Do you think you have any broken bones?" He heard multiple sirens fast approaching. "Miss, can you hear me?"

"Yes," a young voice answered. "My head really hurts."

"We're going to get you out in just a few minutes." Andrew joined
Jerome on top of the van's driver-side door. "What about you fellas
back here? You okay? Anyone having any trouble breathing?"

"Just get us out of here. I think I'm going to throw up." The young man with dreads seemed on the verge of tears. "This seat belt is really cutting into me."

"We're going to need some more help over here. Captain radioed for Bubba Junior's squads." Andrew leaned into Jerome and whispered, "It's leaking gas."

"Man, don't call Joe that," Jerome chastised, mildly annoyed. "You know he's a good man. Just because he's not a brotha, there's no need to disrespect him. You'd be fighting mad if he called you Leroy, now, wouldn't you?"

Andrew let his eyes shift down as he acknowledged Jerome's counsel.

"Hang tight for just a few more minutes." Jerome spoke in a soothing tone, carefully keeping the concern out of his voice. Gasoline leaks were bad news. "We're going to remove the windshield and come inside to get you out one at a time. Be sure you don't try to undo your seat belts. They'll keep you stable while we're working to get you out of there. We'll talk you through everything we're doing."

Ambulance and rescue workers pulled to the scene, leaping into action immediately. The back doors of the units flew open as emergency medical technicians pulled stretchers, trauma kits, oxygen units and backboards onto the ground. While the scene appeared chaotic, in actuality it was a symphony of skill and training. Without a word of instruction, the additional squad members moved into place and began removing the shattered windshield. With a few pries and pulls the glass was removed and Joe Smith, a good ole boy from Texas, his skin flushed red with adrenaline, stood next to Jerome and smiled.

"You ready, Winters? You let 'em know we'll have 'em out quicker than an amateur guitar picker breaks his first string."

"Joe, you know you're the best," Jerome replied.

"Stand by with the foam," Andrew barked. From the look on his face, Jerome thought Andrew might be feeling embarrassed by his earlier comment.

"Just doing with these here hands what the good Lord intended."

The strong smell of gasoline made Jerome nauseated; he wasn't sure if it was the odor or raw fear. One small spark could send them all up in flames.

Additional members of Joe's team positioned themselves proportionately around the van. "Please help us!" a male voice screamed. "We don't want to die."

"Mommy! Mommy! Mommy!" a young female voice moaned in rapid succession.

"Don't worry," Jerome said reassuringly, "you're going to be fine. Just a couple more minutes."

"Okay, we're going to come inside and make sure you're okay before we try to get you out of there." Andrew spoke gently. "We don't want you to get hurt any worse than you already are." Andrew climbed into the van first, contorting his body to move into the backseat.

Jerome lay on the ground to make eye contact with the young woman and spoke to her through the space that had once held the windshield. "Don't be scared. Just keep your eyes focused on me. I'm going to come in there with you and put this backboard on you and check you for broken bones."

The group of six men and two women worked in a synchronized rhythm as tight as the best ballet company. Within thirty minutes, the victims were freed and the crew began working frantically.

The pumper truck pulled into place and began spraying foam on the gasoline.

"What's your name?" Jerome asked, not breaking eye contact with the young victim.

"Melody," she responded faintly.

"What a beautiful name for a beautiful lady. Songs come to mind immediately." Jerome smiled. "Okay, Miss Melody, I need you to help me if you can. Does your neck hurt?"

"My neck doesn't hurt, but my head does."

"Where does it hurt? Do you remember if you hit it or not?" Jerome spoke as softly and soothingly as he could.

"No, I don't remember."

"I'm going to put this collar on your neck and then check your eyes with this light."

Jerome slid the C-collar around her neck efficiently, and it didn't appear that Melody's neck was moved in the slightest. He then moved the penlight from side to side in front of Melody's eyes. "You're very lucky you were wearing a seat belt. Now I want you to follow my fingers with your eyes. Don't move your head, okay?"

Melody tried to nod, but the collar restricted her movements. She obeyed with the innocence of a five-year-old child as he shone the light in her eyes. Her eyes reacted to the light, and she seemed to be okay despite the headache.

"Now I want you to squeeze my fingers together as hard as you can." Jerome placed Melody's hands, palms up, on her torso, putting his index and middle fingers in them. "Do you understand what I want you to do?"

"I think so," she said softly.

Despite the blue-and-purple lump on the side of her head that was crusting with blood, Jerome could tell Melody was a very pretty woman. Her crystal-clear eyes also told him she was not under the influence of drugs or alcohol.

"Squeeze them as tight as you can," he said.

"Like this?" She squeezed his fingers tightly.

"That's perfect. As soon as I get this IV started we're going to try to get you to the hospital so they can check you out a little more. Are you ready? You'll feel a tiny prick."

"I think so. Is Marcus okay?"

"Who's Marcus?" Jerome gingerly pulled Melody's arm toward him.

"He's my brother." Melody squeezed her eyes shut as Jerome hit her vein on the first try. "Today's his twenty-first birthday. We went to dinner and then to a club. He had such a great day from the time he got up this morning. That car ran the light. He never saw it coming."

"Was Marcus drinking?"

"No! None of us drank anything tonight."

"My partner is working on Marcus. Who are the others? Are they family, too?" Jerome looked in the direction where Lloyd and a female paramedic worked on a victim Jerome thought might be Marcus. He lay motionless on the backboard ten feet away.

"How is he?" she asked again.

"My buddy is a captain and the best at what he does. He's in charge of those working on Marcus right now. He'll let me know how your brother is in a few minutes, and you'll be the first person I tell."

Opening the case that held the tools of his trade, he removed the stethoscope and blood pressure machine. He laid the stethoscope around his neck, freeing the Velcro grip of the blood pressure cup to fit it onto Melody's left arm. He spoke gently as he began pumping the black round rubber ball. "This is going to get a little tight. I just need to check your blood pressure. Are you dizzy at all?"

"A little bit. I feel like I have to barf."

"If you feel it coming up, let me know, and I'll roll you over. We don't want you to choke." He released the pump, keeping his eyes on the readout dial. "Your blood pressure is a little high, but that's no surprise."

"You need any help here, Winters?" Sean, a blond paramedic with eyes the clear blue of Caribbean water, approached, the paramedic patch stretched tightly over his bulging muscles, making his shirt appear too small.

"Hey, Sean," Jerome said. "Melody here seems to be shaken up with a nice bump on her head. But she's going to be as pretty as ever in no time at all. How are the others?"

"The driver is the worst off. He's just lost consciousness. The others are rattled pretty well, but they, too, are going to be okay. Transport is ready whenever you are."

"Marcus was driving!" Melody tried to raise herself from the backboard. "Is he going to be okay? Nothing can happen to him. Today is my baby brother's birthday!"

"I need you to stay still." Jerome applied slight pressure to her shoulders for emphasis as he made eye contact with Sean. "They're working on Marcus, and they'll do everything they can before they take him to the hospital."

"I want to see him!" she screamed.

"You can't get up, Melody. Come on, let me take care of you. We're going to transport you to the hospital where we can get some pictures of your head."

"I'm not going anywhere until I know Marcus is okay!" The once-quiet, demure young woman was becoming increasingly belligerent.

Jerome became alarmed at the sudden change in Melody's attitude. She could be suffering from hypoxia. He pulled the oxygen unit from the trauma kit and placed the mask over her face.

"I'll check on him," Sean said, kneeling beside Melody and holding her hand. "But only if you promise me you'll calm down."

Lifting the oxygen mask to speak, Melody said in a calmer tone, "Please hurry! I promise to calm down. Just make sure Marcus is going to be okay." Her eyes implored him to tell her good news.

Sean patted her arm and rose without a word. Jerome watched as Sean's long legs moved him the ten feet to where Marcus lay in a fraction of a second. The paramedic looked up only momentarily as Sean asked, "How's the kid? I promised his sister he was going to be fine. Don't make a liar out of me."

"We've got him stable. But he's in and out. His pupils are reactive to light. We're going to airlift him to a trauma center. The others seemed to be okay. And of course the drunk driver doesn't have a scratch!" The paramedic focused on Marcus as he spoke.

"Now, you know that is 'alleged drunk driver,' " the female paramedic added playfully.

"Well, allegedly when she hit these kids, her bottle of Skyy vodka broke, and she cut her hand trying to pick it up. They're taking her in," Sean added.

The steady click of the helicopter blades grew louder as they spoke. Sean walked back over to where Jerome and Melody lay waiting.

"How's Marcus?" Melody asked.

"To be honest, we're not sure. We're going to take him by helicopter to a trauma center, where they'll do everything humanly possible to make him as good as new. He's been slipping in and out of consciousness, and he has what appears to be a bad head injury. Now, I've kept my promise, so it's time for you to keep yours." Sean returned to the kneeling position, looking kindly into Melody's face. "Firefighter Winters here is going to make sure you get to the hospital and all fixed up."

Melody looked at the heavens as Jerome strapped her head to the backboard. Tears streamed from her eyes, but she remained silent.

"You ready for us to lift you onto the stretcher so we can slide you into the ambulance?" Jerome asked as he beckoned the medical technicians standing near the back of the ambulance.

Still saying nothing, Melody tried to shake her head in affirmation, but her movements were constricted by the neck brace and head restraints.

The ambulance attendants quickly moved to place Melody onto the stretcher, just as the helicopter sat down at an intersection one block away from the hub of the activity, causing a great wind to stir. The doctor leapt from the helicopter before it came to a complete stop. A middle-aged woman in surgical scrubs began running toward the accident scene, moving like she was in a track and field meet. It could only be one doctor, Donna Vandross.

"Well, Miss Melody, your brother has got the best of the best coming to see about him." Andrew joked, "The only bigger miracle worker than Dr. Vandross is Jesus Christ, Himself!"

"We ready to transport?" Vandross ran up to where Marcus lay, sounding only slightly winded. "You did a great job. I like how you work, Captain Frederickson. I've got it from here, though. If he has a shred of a chance, he'll have it thanks to you and your crew." The good doctor smiled.

"Doc, you know we do the best we can out here." Lloyd smiled proudly. "But thanks for recognizing it."

Donna Vandross had been a second-year resident when she and Lloyd had met more than twenty years before. Since then, they'd been on more airlifts together than either dared venture a guess. The years had been kind to her—Dr. Vandross now headed the emergency department at one of the best shock-trauma centers in the country, a facility that boasted an impressive success rate.

Within sixty seconds, Marcus had been moved to the stretcher and into the back of the waiting ambulance, ready for the one-block ride to the waiting medevac helicopter.

"Who was that masked woman, Kemosabe?" Jerome bent down to help the captain gather his equipment.

"How's your kid?" Lloyd asked absentmindedly.

"She's banged up a little, but she'll be fine. She was more concerned about her brother. You think he'll make it?"

"Hard to tell. He'll be one I say a prayer for today. If he survives, he may have some brain damage. This is the part of the job I hate the most, these TCs with drunk drivers walking away with barely a scratch, and poor kids like this killed or worse. I'll never get used to this. Guess 'cause I've got kids of my own."

"I surely understand what you say. My boys will be driving soon. I know my wife will never sleep then. We'll clean up and head on back." Jerome slapped Lloyd on the back.

"You do aiight out here, son." Lloyd never looked up from his trauma kit.

"I had the best teacher."

As Jerome turned to walk away, he smiled to himself as he thought of his fifteen years working with Lloyd Frederickson. The older man's steps had slowed only slightly, but what he lacked in agility he more than made up for in wisdom.

"You about finished here?" Jerome asked as he approached Andrew.

"Man, what a mess. I can't believe the destruction caused by one fool. Look at her. She still doesn't even know what she's done. She talking some crazy yang about having to get home by curfew." Andrew finished sweeping up the last of the dirt used to absorb the gasoline and glass fragments.

"I'd say, 'You'll get used to it,' but I never do. Someone said she's seventeen." Jerome began packing his equipment in the back of the tanker.

"Yeah, that's what I heard, too. I can't even imagine having to face Antoinette St. Vincent if I had caused some mess like this."

"I know what you mean. I'll see you back at the station. As soon as we get back, we've got a meeting to discuss what happened with the battery cable."

"That's some really crazy stuff. You think it has anything to do with the other weirdness going on?" Andrew grabbed on to the side of the truck to pull himself into position.

"I don't know. But if it is, they're messing with people's lives. We have to get to the bottom of this madness. Don't mention this to anyone outside of our shift, including your father."

"Why not my dad? He can do something about this."

"Just trust me on this one." Jerome failed to mention the racially based hate mail they'd been receiving for the past six weeks. Jules St. Vincent was one of the good ole boys, and no one was quite sure where his loyalties rested. Until they knew for sure, neither Lloyd nor Jerome wanted to involve the white man.

5

Lloyd sat at the dining table, mindlessly stroking Casper's thick, white coat. A permanent fixture in the fire station for more than five years, the Siberian Husky had been rescued from an abandoned storefront that had collapsed under the weight of the roof after a heavy rain. She had a broken leg and a few bruises, but the firefighters of C Shift had nursed her back to health. Now she spent twenty-two hours a day sleeping, while the other two were reserved for eating.

"Pass me a cup from the top shelf, please." Mychel stood a little closer to Jerome than he was comfortable with. Freshly showered, her hair still damp, she smelled like springtime.

As Jerome attempted to give Mychel the cup, his elbow grazed her breast. "Oh, sorry, Hernandez," he said, embarrassed. "Maybe you should back up a little."

"Do I look like I mind?" She smiled suggestively.

Mychel made Jerome nervous, and he'd considered reporting her behavior to Lloyd, but Jerome thought his boss would ridicule him. What man would mind being flirted with by this petite package with the Hispanic fire that made her almost irresistible? Jerome Neville Winters, that's what man!

Mychel moved toward the kitchen counter. "I'm thinking we should report this to HQ. This is some scary stuff. What're they going to do next?" She removed the plastic lid from the large coffee can as she spoke.

"Somehow this would get turned around on us, and it would be our fault," Lloyd said. "They'll say we didn't check the equipment after maintenance or didn't get it maintained at all. I know these people."

"Aaaaaaaaaaawwwwwwwwww! Oh my God!" Mychel screamed, and coffee grounds and the red three-pound coffee can flew through the air.

"What?" Jerome leapt to his feet and moved to Mychel's side. A dead rat had flown out of the coffee can, landing on the floor next to Mychel's feet. "Oh, now, that is so foul." Casper left her usual resting place and slowly approached the dead animal, sniffing.

"You all right?" Jerome looked at Mychel, who was panting with fear, her five-foot-one-inch body trembling.

Leaning into Jerome a little farther than he thought necessary, Mychel managed to say, "Yeah, I'm fine. How did that disgusting thing get in the can? I made coffee earlier, and I know there was nothing in there." Mychel waved her small, delicate-looking fingers at the rat on the gray linoleum floor.

Andrew entered the kitchen, took in the situation and laughed. "So the little giant is afraid of something?"

"If you did this, I'll kick your pompous a—" Mychel lunged in his direction.

Andrew raised his hands in a surrender motion. "Whoa, sistah. I think it's real funny Ms. Bad Booty is scared of a dead rat, but I didn't have anything to do with this. Besides, I drink coffee. How many pots of coffee have been made out of that can?"

"You're just jealous because I'm stronger and had more nozzle hours than you. You're spoiled—"

"That's enough!" Lloyd took command. "Are you okay, Mychel? Andrew, get the broom."

"Why do I have to get the broom? She's the one who spilled it. You told me we oughta clean up behind ourselves because our mamas don't work here. Well, I ain't her daddy!"

"You're going to get the broom because I told you to do it! As your captain, if I tell you to lick it up, you'll do just that. I'm not through with you for thinking this incident was so funny. Believe that." The veins in Lloyd's forehead pulsed.

Reluctantly, Andrew walked to the corner closet and grabbed the broom. Using the light that had filtered in from the kitchen, he bent down to pick up the dustpan. He immediately jumped back, losing his balance. "Whoa!" he shouted as he landed on his butt and scurried back in the same movement.

"What's wrong with you?" Jerome turned his attention to the corner.

"Something touched my hand!" Andrew's face flushed red as he tried to gain his composure.

"I thought you were the man." Lloyd tried to cover a smile as he moved to the corner to investigate.

The hairs on the back of his neck stood at attention as he peered at another dead rodent. "Well, I guess we found Mighty Mouse's first cousin."

"What in the hell is going on here?" Mychel hugged herself. "It could be a fluke that that disgusting thing is in the corner, but a rat in the coffee can is no accident. Who would do such a revolting thing?"

"Well, as scared as pretty boy here was, we can rule him out." Jerome picked up the broom and dustpan to scoop up the hairy corpse.

"Cap, what are you going to do about this?" Andrew moved to the far side of the large, white dining table that occupied the center of the room. "All kinds of strange things have been going on here lately. At first I thought it was coincidence, but I think all of us would agree this is a bit much. Who knows what else they've done?"

"As much as I hate to agree with St. Vincent, we need to report this to someone." Jerome's long strides moved him quickly across the kitchen as he began sweeping up the mess on the floor. "This only happens on our shift, and I'm starting to take it a little personally."

"I'll call the chief," Lloyd said grimly. "This is reminiscent of the old days. We've caught hell since the late 1800s, and here we are, in 2004, still being harassed. Gone through a whole century, and we still proving we're as good. Good men like Winters can't get promoted. Trying to find a reason to get rid of me before I'm ready to retire. Well, I'm not going for it." Anger framed his handsome, well-aged face.

"Oh, here we go, talking about 'back in the day.' You need to stop living in the past, old man." Recovering quickly from his rat scare, Andrew had resumed his normal cocky attitude.

"Uh-oh. St. Vincent, you need a lesson in common sense, my man." Jerome patted Andrew on the back, shaking his head. "You have stepped in it this time."

"See, boy, that's your problem," Lloyd said. "You think you got here all by yourself. You think you're so special because your daddy and granddaddy worked in the fire service. Well, you are on C Shift! Do you know what they nicknamed us?"

"Wha—?" Andrew tried to respond.

"The 'Colored Shift,' boy! Do you know how much disrespect it takes to call a black man 'colored'? Then, to add some indignation, they call Mychel a 'girl.' What she gotta do to be a woman? She can outperform most of you, and she's fearless, but she's still a 'girl' or a 'gal.' See, in case no one ever told you, you can't know where you're going if you've forgotten where you've been. Your blue eyes may impress the women, but you still a nig—" Lloyd stopped himself as he felt bile rising in his throat.

"I am so tired of you—" As Andrew moved to confront Lloyd, the fire alarm interrupted him.

"Engine Company 27 and Squad 39, chest pains and shortness of breath, fifty-seven-year-old female. At 161½ Lawrence Way, cross street Broadway." The familiar female voice squawked over speakers that were strategically placed throughout the firehouse.

"I guess your bacon has been spared some frying until we get back," Jerome teased as he ran for the pole that led to the truck. "Lloyd is gonna cut you a new one later, my brotha!"

"Whatever!" Andrew took the steps two at a time and arrived at the paramedic vehicle only seconds after Jerome reached his truck, parked side by side.

Within four minutes, the engine and paramedic wagon pulled in front of a small cottage residence in desperate need of repair, with three even smaller units clustered behind it. The yard was littered with auto parts, beer and wine bottles, dirty diapers and garbage. Jerome, Mychel and Andrew looked from one to the other. Their unspoken words screamed volumes. They each silently wondered what horrors awaited them on the other side of the dilapidated chain-link fence.

"First rats, and now this," Mychel mumbled as she pulled the drug box, O_2 and defibrillator from the back of the paramedic squad. "Sometimes I wonder if they pay me enough to do this."

"You can always become a nurse," Andrew teased. "Just leave all this to us menfolk. Be at home at night with your man, making pretty babies. Oh, my bad, you don't have a man."

"Yeah, but I bet you do!" Mychel ran the twenty-five feet up the badly broken driveway that led to the cottage numbers 161¼, 161½ and 161¾. She stopped short before the half-unit's door, which was actually plywood leaned against the frame. She gingerly mounted the two steps of rotting wood that led to the tiny porch. Jerome wondered if her petite frame would break through the weak-looking boards.

She turned to Andrew and Jerome before pressing the doorbell. Of course, it didn't ring. "You fellas need to be careful on the steps and porch—the wood is fragile. It's creaking under my weight."

"Yeah, it looks real weak." Andrew was all business. "You think we should get a backboard to walk on? I don't think it will hold all of us."

"That might not be a bad idea." Jerome returned to the truck as Andrew evaluated the strength of the steps and porch.

Mychel began knocking. "Fire department. Please open up."

As the wood was moved to one side, the smell of urine, feces, vomit and dirty animals rushed to assault Mychel's nose. She turned to struggle for fresh air, but the foul stench permeated the air around her. She stepped inside, her face a mask of disgust.

"Oh, man!" Andrew grabbed his nose and mouth.

"Whew. This is going to be interesting. Let's go." Jerome laid the backboard across the porch. "You go, and then I'll follow."

"Ma'am, did you call the paramedics?" Mychel, holding her breath, spoke to the woman standing before her who was wearing a faded and filthy housedress.

"Yeah, I been having chest pains for a couple days, and now I can't seem to catch my breath." The woman looked to be eighty-seven, not fifty-seven.

"May we come in?" Jerome asked, eyeing four dogs and more cats than he could count, all milling around the woman's feet.

"Why would I call you if you couldn't come in?" The woman slowly turned and began walking deeper into the den of filth.

Andrew climbed the stairs cautiously and crossed the makeshift plank to the doorway. *Please don't let me hurl,* he thought to himself as he stepped into the living room following close on the heels of his partners.

Jerome had thought the stench was overwhelming until he actually stepped into the house. As his eyes began to adjust to the dimly lit room, he saw there was no place to walk without stepping in animal feces, newspapers, magazines or carryout food containers, which filled every centimeter of the room. As he looked beyond the living room into the tiny kitchen, he saw the sink, table and stove were overrun with dirty dishes, and the roaches were in full command. His flesh crawled.

As the woman sat on the couch, she forced yet another odor into the cloud of foul air so heavy it appeared visible.

"Ma'am, what's your name?" Mychel managed through short breaths.

"Corinna."

"Corinna, how old are you? I'm going to put a blood pressure cup on you so I can take your pressure. Is that okay with you?"

"I'm fifty-seven next Tuesday. Yeah, do what you need to do."

Mychel raised the sleeve on the woman's garment, which was made for a woman at least one hundred pounds heavier and hadn't seen the benefit of detergent in many lunar eclipses. Dirt had darkened her butterscotch skin to a milk-chocolate brown.

"Let me have some gauze, saline and Betadine," Mychel barked at Andrew, who had turned the color of guacamole.

"What are you going to do? She doesn't have any wounds that I can see."

Jerome shot Andrew a questioning glance.

"We're going to clean the area before we apply the blood pressure cup. It's standard procedure." Mychel made eye contact with Andrew. ·

"I've never heard of such a procedure," Andrew said, looking confused.

Jerome sighed to himself. Andrew could be absolutely clueless.

"Sonny, she's trying to spare my feelings," Corinna said weakly. "I know I'm not so clean. I don't know when I stopped cleaning up the house—or myself for that matter. When Alvin, my only boy, got shot by some bangers, I just didn't want to live no mo'." Tears stood in Corinna's eyes.

"We're really sorry to hear that. Miss Corinna, when was your son killed?" Mychel asked as she applied Betadine and saline to her right arm.

"In eighty-nine."

"You haven't had a bath since 1989? Oh my God!"

Andrew could be as heartless as he was dense. Jerome sighed again.

"Oh, I didn't start this way. At first it was just a few days here and there. I couldn't get out of bed. Then days turned to weeks, and then months, and now I don't even know how many years it's been."

"Well, we're going to get you to a hospital, and they'll get you cleaned up," Mychel said, her voice sounding compassionate. "I'm sorry, but we're going to have to call Animal Control and Social Services."

"Please don't take my family." Corinna looked stricken. "These animals are all I got. My sisters don't come see about me. They don't call since Mama died ten years ago. If you take my babies, I'll have no reason at all to live."

"I'm so sorry, but we're bound by the law." Jerome's heart went out to the woman, who could have been his mother.

Mychel frowned. "B.P. 199 over 123. Pulse 100. Let's hook up the EKG before we call it in. Miss Corinna, do you have high blood pressure?"

"Not that I know of, but I haven't been to a doctor in a long, long time."

"St. Vincent, do you think you can make yourself useful and get the EKG hooked up to her? We're going to have to clean her chest area before we hook it up. Do you think you can handle that?" Jerome asked sarcastically.

"Yeah." Andrew looked like he wasn't sure if he could hold the contents of his stomach in place much longer. With Mychel's help, Andrew cleaned her chest, breasts and torso and attached the electrodes. Immediately, it was apparent Miss Corinna was experiencing premature ventricular contractions. The irregular firing of her heart was for sure the source of her discomfort.

"Is the transport unit rolling?" Jerome asked as he encircled her left forearm with a tourniquet. "Miss Corinna, we're going to get you to the emergency room. Looks like your heart is protesting just a little. I know you said you don't have any family, but is there a friend we can call for you?"

Corinna shook her head. The empty look in her eyes answered Jerome's question.

"Let's get the Betadine and saline and clean up this arm so I can start an I.V." Jerome directed his command to Andrew.

Andrew seemed to be moving in slow motion. Jerome barked, "Now!"

"Sorry. Here you go." Andrew attempted to pass the gauze to Jerome.

Jerome's stern eyes looked right through Andrew. Without words, he communicated his message.

"I'll clean the area." Andrew wouldn't make eye contact with Jerome or Corinna.

The two worked in silence while Mychel held the woman's hand and asked her questions. "Tell me what the pain in your chest feels like."

"It's a lot of pressure. I feel like I have a fat man sitting on my chest." She managed a smile at her own attempt at humor.

"On a scale of one to ten, ten being unbearable, where would you say your pain would rank?"

"Oh, I guess it's about a five or six."

"Okay, we're going to call this information in to the doctors at the hospital and find out what they want us to do for you while we wait for the ambulance." Mychel pressed the button on the handheld radio to begin communication with the emergency room. "Base, this is Squad 27, we have a fifty-seven-year-old female, B.P. is 199 over 125, pulse 100 and thready. Stand by for EKG transmission. Transport is en route. ETA is ten minutes."

"Start an I.V. with thirty cc's of epinephrine. Transport as soon as possible. Maintain radio contact and EKG transmission," the voice across the radio commanded.

"Affirmative," Mychel responded.

"We're going to give you some medicine that'll relieve some of the pressure in your chest," Jerome said compassionately.

A knock on the door frame announced the arrival of the Los Angeles Sheriff's Department. A squad car was routinely dispatched with each paramedic call. The deputy would call Animal Control and Social Services, and Corinna's world, as she knew it, would cease to exist. Jerome wondered if this was best for the lonely woman who'd suffered more than a decade and a half of depression, but there was nothing he could do about it. He sighed a third time, hearing a siren approaching quickly.

"Look, St. Vincent, I don't know what your problems are, but as long as you work on my shift, you don't ever act like you did tonight." Jerome was in Andrew's face, so close his breath made Andrew's curly hair move. "We make more paramedic runs in a month than we'll do fire runs in five years. Now, I admit that most of them are not as bad as this woman's place, but you are going to go into a lot of places where you're going to feel like you need a shower when you leave. But we treat everyone the same. Do I make myself clear?"

"I'm sorry." Andrew hung his head sheepishly. "I just didn't know how to react. I know there are parts of the job that aren't great, but that place was so filthy and smelled so bad that I thought I was going to throw up. Tell me it didn't get next to you!"

"Of course, it got next to me, but my concern was for the health and feelings of that woman. We don't know what these people have gone through that has gotten them to these low points in their lives, but believe me! Except for the grace of God, there go you and I!

"If you're lucky," Jerome continued, "you'll be able to lie down and not dream about that place tonight, but chances are it'll haunt you for days to come. This is the job, St. Vincent, and you knew the job was hard when you took it."

"You don't need to worry about me," Andrew said, looking defensive. "I got this! Now if it's okay with your high-and-mighty, Captain-wannabe self, I'm going to take a shower and see if I can get fifteen minutes of sleep before the bell rings again." Andrew turned on his heels and disappeared through the door that led to their dormitory.

"We haven't had one quite as arrogant as him in a while, but he'll learn." Mychel smiled as she looked up at Jerome. "I need to wash Miss Corinna's house off me, too. Want to join me?"

"What?" Jerome did a double take. He wasn't sure he'd heard her correctly.

"I mean take a shower. Want to wash Lawrence Way off that wonderful body? Not with me, of course." She winked.

Jerome backed away slightly. "I'll pass. Maybe later."

"Well, Andrew has the right idea. Some sleep would be most welcomed. Give him a chance. Remember how frustrated you were with me when I first came? Now look at me." She made a pirouette, hands gesturing to her own trim body.

"Yeah, look atcha! You know, Mychel, if I wasn't a happily married man, I'd be flattered. But as it stands, *this* testosterone seeks only one woman's estrogen. *Capiche?*" Jerome said sternly.

"I have no idea what you're talking about," Mychel said, her face blank. "I've had a rough night, and I know you have, too. I was just suggesting we clean up and get some rest. But if you think I'm being a little too concerned, I'll just take care of myself. *Comprende?*"

"What's a brotha got to do to get a job around here?" Mychel and Jerome turned to see Austin Fitzgerald, Mychel's longtime paramedic partner, approaching.

"Hey, man!" Jerome gave Austin a brotherly embrace.

Hugging Mychel next, Austin said, "Hey, firecracker, did you miss your partner?"

With a warm and sincere gesture, Mychel hugged him back. "Like you wouldn't even believe. Since you're in uniform, does this mean you're back?"

"It does! I wasn't supposed to report until seven, but I couldn't sleep. Besides, who in the hell comes to work for an hour?"

"You feeling okay, man?" Jerome had missed the fifth member of their team. The firefighters had pulled double duty on the rescue calls while Austin recovered from knee surgery.

"Never better. Looks like you're just getting in? Where's the captain?"

"The lights are on in the office. If he's not there, he's probably trying to catch some winks. Good to have you back." Jerome slapped his back.

Austin smiled and started to walk away. Mychel caught up to him and slipped her arm through his, looking over her shoulder at

Jerome. Joking about how much Austin had missed her, they laughed as they disappeared into the captain's office.

Jerome needed to wash Miss Corinna's place off him as well, but he decided to clean the paramedic truck instead. He wanted time to think about everything that was happening around the station— most particularly on C Shift.

Why in heaven's name would anyone want to sabotage them? The dead rats had certainly given him the creeps. What made his blood run cold through his veins, though, was that the saboteur had to be someone within the department. No stranger had access to the firehouse.

Wiping off the equipment allowed Jerome to meditate about everything that was happening. As he put away the polishing rag, he decided that he would find out who was behind these destructive acts against the "Colored Shift" and put a stop to them for good.

"I bet you think I forgot about your comment, didn't you, son?" Lloyd poured coffee as he spoke, not looking at Andrew. It was a few hours after their visit to Miss Corinna's house, and Lloyd, Andrew, Jerome, Austin and Mychel were enjoying a cup of coffee before the end of their shift, all of them hoping they wouldn't get another call before A Shift arrived.

"Uh-oh," Jerome said, rising from the table. "I think I'm going to watch a little television—it's about to get really deep in here! I've heard this speech more times than Oprah has lost weight. Good luck, St. Vincent. You're going to need it." Jerome held his hands up as he surrendered.

"I don't know why this is such a big deal," Andrew said, sounding petulant. "I *do* live in America, and I *can* have an opinion about things. I think we're overreacting. I don't think the pranks have anything to do with race—but they do have everything to do with crazy."

Mychel picked up a copy of *Body & Soul* magazine from the table, rolled it and used it as a pointer. "You're right about the crazy part, but what is crazier than hating people because they look different than you? You know what? You're no better than they are because you think the only purpose a woman serves is to please you. You don't even see us as equals. So, of course, you'd be hard-pressed to see the injustices if our problems are race related. You better come on off that high horse, St. Vincent. Your daddy may be white, but newsflash, my brotha, you ain't. And you know the rule in America: One drop of black blood, and tag, you're it!"

"Why is Jules St. Vincent always the subject of discussion here?"

Andrew asked. "I got here on my own. I worked my ass off. I was in the top of my class all the way through college and at the Tower."

"But, you see, you *didn't* get here on your own, son." Lloyd spoke slowly and deliberately. "Thousands of black men endured less than humane treatment just so that you could even apply for this job. Have you taken even a minute to learn the history of the black fire-fighter?"

"I know all about fire service history. I grew up listening to all those stories."

"No, what you heard were the stories of the white firefighters, the men who only had to know someone to get hired. This is one of the original good ole boy clubs. Do you think some of these guys could have even passed the first-level test to get into the department? Some of them can barely read. Now, I'm not saying they aren't good at the job, but they learned it all here.

"When you first started, I gave you a brochure from the International Association of Black Professional Fire Fighters. Have you even looked at it?"

"I don't want to be painted as a militant black man." Andrew was fidgeting.

"Why would joining a professional organization paint you as a militant?"

Andrew only stared.

"Let me tell you a little history, son. You may want to get one of those energy drinks you're always having. This may take a while."

Lord, where was the fire alarm when you needed it? Andrew thought to himself, but said, "Captain, do I really have to listen to all of this?"

"As your captain, I'm going to answer with an affirmative."

Andrew sighed, pulled a Red Bull from the refrigerator and returned to the table, where Lloyd sat, poised to enlighten him.

"Back in the late 1800s, right here in Los Angeles, this place you claim is so forward-thinking, black firefighters had to sleep and eat with the horses, which were kept out near the kitchen. They had their own utensils, cookware and plates, because the white fire-fighters didn't want the germs that Negroes carried.

"When HQ forced them to allow us to sleep in the dormitory

with everyone else, they put the beds for blacks by the bathroom, so that every time someone used the latrine, the door would hit their beds.

"They would give the black firefighter duty that kept him up all night. When he was finally able to come to bed, he would find a little gift waiting for him: Someone had crapped on his pillow, and because they wouldn't allow him to turn on the light, he'd lay in it."

"But, Captain, that was in the 1800s!" Andrew protested. "This is two centuries later."

"Then let us fast-forward to right here in 1977, when we were doing hydrant checks. We had to jog behind the truck."

The color drained from Andrew's face. "I don't believe that happened in the seventies. My father was a captain back then . . . he wouldn't have let that happen." Andrew stared at the floor. "I don't know what else to say."

"I don't want you to say anything," Lloyd said gently. "I just want you to sit there and listen. That's part of your problem—you love the sound of your own voice."

"Whatever, man!" Andrew sighed and stared at the alarm bell, willing it to ring.

"Something is going to come along and knock that chip off your shoulder, son. I just hope it doesn't take your head with it."

"This little history lesson is over." Andrew rose to leave.

Lloyd grabbed his wrist. "Sit down!

"You want to hear about something happening 'two centuries later,' as you put it? In Houston, a captain told one of his crew his Confederate flag was offensive. Internal Affairs conducted an investigation, and even the mayor got involved. The captain was all but fired. He received hate mail, and it's still not over. In some of the mail he received, it said that they needed to stay on the other side of town, that they were incompetent and were unable to compete. The 'they' they referred to look like you and me.

"But there is strength in numbers!" Lloyd said. "In the IABPFF, we have legal counsel to fight for us, just for what's rightfully ours. But the Stentorians started long before the international organization. We started in 1954, and in case you can't do the math, that makes us fifty years old this year. Now, do you honestly believe it'd still be around, if the organization wasn't needed?" Lloyd finally took a breath.

"What does the word 'Stentorian' mean?" Andrew's attitude had changed.

"It's from the Greek word *Stentor,* a Greek herald described in *The Iliad* as having the voice of fifty men, extremely loud and powerful with a very forceful sound. In other words, a Stentor can be heard when you and I can't."

"I'm not saying I agree with everything you're saying," Andrew conceded, "but I did learn something here tonight. I still think we're just dealing with a nutcase, though, nothing more, nothing less."

"Oh, there is no doubt this guy is crazy, but what motivates a crazy person is what's scary. Do I need to give you another brochure for the Stentorians? You going to reconsider joining?"

"Pops, I'm not joining anything. If this job is all bad, then why have you been doing it for so long? Why did those men back at the turn of the century stick around?"

"For the same reason Dr. King and Malcolm did what they did: So your little arrogant black ass can sit here and argue with me, your black captain. If you asked any one of them if they would do it over, I'd bet every one of them would say yes.

"I love this job. It's one of the few jobs where a black man with a GED can make sixty or seventy thousand dollars a year." Trying to lighten the mood Lloyd added, "And in what other job do you think a brotha can have Mrs. Gonzales bring them breakfast burritos?"

Both men began to laugh, just as the fire alarm sounded. "Saved by the bell, Captain!"

"Station 27, fully involved car fire in the alley behind 400 block of East Bennett Street, structures threatened."

Andrew and Lloyd leapt to their feet simultaneously, their enthusiasm increasing a thousandfold at the mention of the word "fire." Jerome was in full gear and waiting in the truck. With a push of the starter button, he brought the red beast to life. Austin and Mychel hit the squad unit as Lloyd and Andrew stepped into their waiting boots and pants. Within seconds, both men were in the truck. Andrew slipped his arms into the jacket as the truck rolled into the street.

Reruns of *Emergency!* played in the background as the man sat with his ear attuned to the rebuilt shortwave radio. Station 27 was rolling on a real fire.

He spent his time off monitoring the dispatch calls for all of Los Angeles City and County Fire Departments. He knew when every fire engine and paramedic truck pushed their starter buttons.

His adrenaline and testosterone level increased, causing his heart to race at the thought of flames licking the early morning sky.

He grabbed his coat from the back of the faded dinette chair and headed for the door.

"Nicolas, Jordan and Christian, you are working my patience." Nicolle crossed her arms, exasperated with her offspring. "You know I have to get you to practice, but you're sitting here playing this video game. I swear it's easier on days when we all have structure—it seems like we just ate breakfast, and here it is four o'clock!"

"Mom, we're ready. It's you that's being slow." Jordan never took his eyes off the sixty-inch flat-screen television.

"So, you've got your little brother ready, too?" She raised an eyebrow. "And what about you, Nicolas, are you ready?"

"Dang, Mom," Jordan whined. "Why do I have to get Christian ready?"

"Boy, don't you play with me. Put his jacket on and grab the diaper bag off the rocking chair in his room." She turned and went into her bathroom for a last-minute makeup application.

"Yes, ma'am," Jordan said with reluctance, but he stood up, putting the game control aside. By now, he knew he'd better do what his mother asked. "And what are you laughing at?" Jordan punched his brother in the arm.

"Mom, Jordan's hitting me!" Nicolas screamed.

"If I come in there, you're both going to be sorry." Nicolle brushed her cheeks with her favorite blush.

Lord, how am I ever going to be raising children for thirty-one years? she thought. *Life was going so good, and then comes along super-sperm and finds an egg that wasn't even supposed to be there. And the next thing I know, it's my little man, Christian. I'm going to be able to handle it all one of these days, but not today.*

Nicolle laughed aloud as she remembered the afternoon the doctor told her she was pregnant again. Of course there had to be a mistake—she had been on the pill for the last fifteen years of their marriage, except when she had planned to get pregnant with Jordan and Nicolas. "You'd better see what other Nicolle Winters you have in your records, because it's not me," she had protested. Needless to say, the doctor's ten-pound, two-ounce surprise, Christian Donnel Winters, had burst forth, kicking and screaming, thirty-one weeks later. She loved all of her boys with more than her heart, but on days like today, she just needed a little break.

"I'm finally ready. Now where are my keys? Dang it!" Nicolle was going to be late for Nicolas's soccer practice if she didn't leave three minutes ago.

"Daddy's home! He can take us!" Nicolas leapt to his feet and ran toward the garage.

Like the cavalry, her beloved Jerome had once again come to her rescue. He'd returned from a meeting with the officers at the Stentorians just in time to take at least one of the boys to his practice.

Her husband was the epitome of good black manhood, a strong Christian man who knew that if he let God lead him, he wouldn't go astray. Intelligent, funny and sporting the body of an African warrior, Jerome spent hours every week working the muscles in his six-foot-five-inch, two-hundred-forty-pound body. His large hands seemed to be able to press coal into diamonds, and yet his soft brown eyes let the most fragile of creatures know he would protect them with his life.

"Hey, guys. I thought you had practice this afternoon." Jerome picked up Christian as the toddler ran to welcome his daddy.

"Oh, honey, you're just in time. I'll take Nicolas if you take Jordan." She greeted him with a short, yet warm kiss.

"I tell you what—I'll make you a deal. I'll take them both if you promise me you'll take this"—he handed her a black bag—"and go sit out on the patio with a glass of wine and enjoy a little peace and quiet for a couple of hours."

Nicolle couldn't imagine what the black bag held. She snatched it from him like a little girl at Christmas. By the heft, she knew it was books. "Oh, baby! How thoughtful. And they ask me how I put up with you."

"Girl, you know you not going to find another lover man who brings you autographed, first-edition, African-American literature."

"Signed? How? When?" Nicolle's face felt flushed with pleasure.

"Slow down! There was a book expo thing at the hotel where we had the planning meeting for the international conference. There must have been twenty black authors signing their books. I had a hard time remembering what you already had, so I picked three of the new, self-published authors. You can tell me later if I made the right choices. I'm going to take Christian, too, so you enjoy your free time, Babe-ski. I'll take them to dinner when we're done. See you around sevenish. Let's go, boys."

With that, all four of the men in her life were out the door. It had all happened so quickly that she stood in the family room for a few minutes, not knowing what to do with all the quiet. She looked down at the three books and smiled from the inside out.

As long as she could remember, Jerome had always thought of her first. When she insisted she remained a virgin until their wedding night, he never threatened to leave her, the way other boyfriends had pressured girls she knew. When she was content to work as the fire commissioner's assistant forever, he told her she needed to have her own assistant and had nudged her into a decision to go back to school. Flowers, candy and diamonds were the norm, and she never wanted for anything. She had never even kissed another man, nor had she ever once wanted to. This strong black man was all she would ever need.

She kicked off her sandals, and as she bent to pick them up, a song struck her heart. She began to sing, *"I will cross the ocean for you. I promise you, for you I will."* Jerome loved her voice and encouraged her to sing to him. She tossed the shoes up the stairs and went to the refrigerator in the garage to retrieve a bottle of white zinfandel. When she opened the door, a dozen roses lay before her.

8

The shrill sound of the whistle indicated Nellie was not pleased at the last play her star center, Symoni, had just missed. "Time out!" she screamed, forming a T with her hands. She gestured the girl over, reminding herself to be gentle.

"Is there something wrong, Moni? You seem sort of out of it today."

"No, I'm just tired," the young girl said. "I've been preparing to take the PSATs next week. I have to get into Tennessee." The star player began to cry. "I just have to."

"Stephanie, you go in for Symoni," Nellie yelled. "Moni, you come sit and talk to me." She led the girl over to a bench. "Why are you crying? You know, with your grades and talent on the court, you're going to have to fight off the schools. So tell me what's *really* going on." Nellie put her arm around the girl's shoulder.

"It's my aunt," Symoni confessed. "She says I won't get into any good schools. She says that I'm not that good at anything. I don't know if I can try any harder, Mrs. F.!"

"Look at me!" Nellie grabbed her shoulders and turned Symoni McGehee to face her. "I want you to give your aunt my card and tell her to call me. She and I need to have a little woman-to-woman chat. In the meantime, I want you to get back in this game one hundred percent. You'll do superbly on the test, and even if you don't, your GPA is 3.97—and you're varsity in your sophomore year! Now, if your aunt isn't impressed, I'm your coach, and I sure as hell am!"

Nellie just couldn't understand the mentality of some of the parents of the girls she coached at the youth center in Watts. While most were supportive of their daughters' efforts, some were just looking for a ticket out of the ghetto—or worse, they were content to stay and wanted to keep as much company with them as possible.

Nellie had become involved with girls' basketball many years before, with Victoria, her youngest daughter, who had showed enormous potential as a young girl. When she was nine, she was hanging tough with the boys' league because there were no girls' teams in their neighborhood. Most of her friends were in dance class or scouts, but Victoria, five inches taller than everyone else her age, wanted nothing to do with the frilly or the feminine. Over the years, they'd spent more than a few afternoons in emergency rooms, getting one injury or another checked, as her tomboy daughter protested she was fine and was no "punk."

Too busy working or lobbying for this change or that at the fire department, Lloyd had never spent any time with the girls when they were growing up. Everything had been left to her. She hadn't noticed during the time, but like everything else in her marriage these days, his absence was now irksome, and she resented him for it. While she was busy at the Department of Children and Family Services and going to school, she'd still always had time for her children—and she worked twenty-two days a month, not ten. When the girls had graduated from college, Lloyd was so proud that you would have thought he'd been at every game, parent-teacher conference and doctor's appointment since their birth. He always thought writing checks was enough, not unlike her own father.

A movement on the court brought her attention back to the game. "Are you blind, ref? Murphy was fouled! Here, you want my glasses?" Nellie moved in the direction of the referee as she yelled in response to the bad call. She waved her glasses in the face of the woman, who was at least six inches shorter and fifty pounds lighter than her, flirting with a technical foul.

9

"Do you have any idea what you're saying, Frederickson?" Chief Marlborough asked in disbelief. "This is 2004, and we're in California, not the backwoods of Mississippi in 1967!"

Lloyd took a deep breath and tried to remain calm. "Chief, I realize what I'm saying, but we have not been imagining this stuff. On the last shift, we lost precious time because someone jacked with the battery. Do you think I would come to you if I wasn't sure?" Lloyd was furious. How dare Chief Marlborough question his integrity!

"You're a good man and an outstanding firefighter, Fredrickson. I know there must be something to what you're saying, but it's just so hard for me to believe. I'll take a day or two to mull it over and get back to you. In the meantime, make sure your people double-check everything. We don't want to have any more equipment failures."

Lloyd stared in disbelief. Was this man accusing his company of negligence? He shook his head. He had said it would be like this. Why was he surprised? "I'll look to hear from you by Monday, since a couple days will be on a Saturday?"

The chief's face flushed red, and Lloyd realized the chief hadn't planned to do anything about the allegations. His heart fell even further as he realized he was on his own.

"Yes," the chief said, fiddling with some papers on his desk. "You'll hear from me by Monday."

Getting up to leave, Lloyd turned and said softly, "My crew puts their lives on the line every minute of every shift. We shouldn't have to fight more than fires, Chief."

When Lloyd arrived at the elevator, he stabbed the button repeatedly. Realizing he couldn't wait, he headed for the stairs to walk down the five flights to the street. All of a sudden he couldn't breathe. Why couldn't a black man get any respect? His record was exemplary within the department. Yet he was known as a troublemaker because he'd always pushed for what was fair. He got politicians involved, wrote letters, hired lawyers just to get what rightfully belonged to his people. Why were there color lines when they were all supposed to be on the same side? Why couldn't everything just be blue?

The crisp Los Angeles day was a rare treat in late September. An unseasonably early rainstorm had cleared all the smog and deposited snow on the uppermost tips of the San Bernardino Mountains, which painted a portrait against the perfect shade of blue sky demonstrating God is the ultimate artist. As Lloyd walked swiftly to the waiting red department-issued Chevrolet Suburban, he wondered how he would tell C Shift the chief would take a couple days to think about what they alleged happened.

The soulful sounds of George Benson's guitar filled the car as soon as he turned the key in the ignition. Good music always improved his mood and attitude. As he eased into traffic, Lloyd concluded that if the chief didn't open an investigation, he would contact the Stentorians' lawyer. She'd know what they should do next. When Glynda Naylor-Sanders had taken their first discrimination case, she'd been wet behind the ears, a still crawling, recent-bar-passing rookie. In just a few short years, she had become one of the most respected civil rights lawyers in the city.

He took in a deep breath as he lowered the driver-side window to enjoy the autumn morning. Just the thought of Glynda on the case helped him relax. He put the ordeal out of his mind momentarily, cranked up George a couple of notches, placed his arm out the window and began to hum along.

When he reached the firehouse, Jerome and Casper met Lloyd at the car.

"So what happened?" Jerome asked before Lloyd could gather his briefcase from the front passenger seat.

"The chief will get back to me by Monday." Lloyd bent to rub

Casper's head, more out of habit than anything else—his mind was already back on their saboteur. George Benson's calming effect had been wiped away when he turned off the ignition.

"Is he going to get an investigation started?"

"He'll get back to me on Monday," Lloyd repeated.

"Ain't this about a b—" Jerome caught himself and took a deep breath. "Why am I thinking it would be otherwise? Well, I made up my mind that I'm going to start my own investigation. We need to set some traps to catch this guy. What do you think about setting up some cameras out here with the equipment?" Jerome kept pace easily with Lloyd, who seemed to be trying to outrun the younger man's probing questions.

He slowed down. "Cameras cost money. You know there is no way HQ will approve them without the backing of the chief."

"Hell, we could chip in and pay for them ourselves."

Lloyd turned quickly to see if Jerome was serious. "Boy, I'm not spending a dime on equipment for this here department. I was thinking of calling Glynda. You know she's done some real good work for us in other cases. Maybe she can tell us what we should do next. And you know the Stentorians have a fund set up for just this kind of thing."

"Airport security doesn't have a thing on your wallet." Jerome laughed. "Well, you're the captain, and you've done this for a minute or two longer than I have. I'll defer to you for the time being."

"Jerome, son, you see, my money ain't never funny, nor my change ever strange. So yes, you could feel safe in your deferral." Lloyd smiled for the first time since he'd met with the chief.

"I guess you're right, Grandpa." Jerome winked. "Hey, I've been monitoring on the radio. Nice and quiet this morning. I sure hope that doesn't mean we're going to have a wild night."

"Shhh! Let's just enjoy the quiet while it lasts."

"Good morning, Cap." Andrew joined the others. "Hernandez said you were at the chief's office this morning. Let me guess, he said you were nuts, right?"

"Son, you may take all of this as a joke, but there's someone that wants to discredit C Shift and someone may get hurt in the process." Lloyd's tone was stern.

"Cap, you need to come out of the dark ages of the civil rights movement. Haven't you heard black folks have been to the mountaintop? We have the same rights as everyone else. Look around you; our whole shift is minority. This is California. This is where black folks came when it was bad everywhere else."

Jerome snorted. "Andrew, you are so naïve. But you'll see. You think you're so different from the rest of us?" Jerome tried to hide his frustration. "Time will tell. In the meantime we need to come up with a plan to protect ourselves."

"Now, I agree we have a problem," Andrew said. "I just don't think it's racially motivated. I think we're just dealing with a fool. Some firefighter groupie gone bad. You know the type, Winters, a wannabe—or maybe, a woman scorned."

"I don't think we're dealing with a woman. That whole rat thing would rule out any woman I know." Jerome chuckled.

"Well, my point is," Lloyd broke in, "whoever is behind all this needs to be stopped—with or without the help of the brass. We're just going to have to be on our toes, checking and rechecking everything. Did you fools leave an old man some breakfast? I'm starving."

As the three men headed for the stairs, Jerome said, "Mrs. Gonzales brought breakfast burritos that are off the chain. You know, I do love this job."

Andrew laughed. "I know, brotha. Everybody loves a firefighter. The children wave and women blow kisses. When I'm in a club, all I have to say is that I'm a firefighter, and panties start flying in my direction."

"See, that's your trouble, son," Lloyd said, shaking his head. "That's all you think about—panties."

"And when you were my age, you thought about what?"

"Money!" Jerome and Lloyd sang in unison.

The men laughed as they entered the large entertainment room that led to the dining area. The big-screen television broadcast *SportsCenter* to an empty room. Ten red recliners ringed the TV, inviting a body to partake of their comfort.

Hernandez sat alone at the long conference-style table, *LA Times* in hand. "Let me guess, the chief is going to look into it and get back to you?" Mychel looked up from the metro article she was reading.

"Seems like you were there with me." Lloyd made his way into the well-equipped kitchen.

"I just know how it all works." Mychel went back to the newspaper.

"Captain, those burritos are going to make you propose marriage to Mrs. Gonzales." Jerome tried to lighten the mood.

The alarm sounded. "Engine 27 and Squad 39, multiple GSW, two victims, both juvenile male, Hoover and 88th. Area has been secured." The familiar voice spoke between the high-pitched alarms.

"Don't you just hate gunfire before breakfast?" Lloyd said as he rushed toward the pole.

Jerome was on his heels. "I'm just tired of our children killing each other."

10

loyd made good on his word to call the lawyer.

"Good afternoon. Isaac, Townsend and Parker," said the cheerful voice at the other end of the line.

"Good afternoon. May I please speak with Glynda Naylor-Sanders?" Lloyd inquired.

"I'm sorry, Ms. Sanders is in Washington, D.C., this week. May I connect you to her voice mail, or can someone else help you? She will be checking messages daily."

"Yes, I'll take her voice mail. Thank you." Lloyd listened patiently as the pleasant, professional voice of the young woman whose legal abilities he'd come to love and respect informed him of her absence and impending return on the following Monday. *How ironic,* he thought, *so much is riding on Monday.*

"Hello, Ms. Glynda, this is your ole buddy Lloyd Frederickson with the Los Angeles County Fire Department. I have some questions for you. We've had some strange things happening, and I need your advice on how to proceed. I look forward to hearing from you on your return. Please call me on my cell phone." After leaving his phone number, he hung up.

The next number he dialed was his home. He had to figure out what was bothering Nellie. He'd loved that woman since the first moment he'd seen her, at his cousin's wedding more than thirty-five years before. When he'd seen her glide down the aisle in her hideous, pink taffeta bridesmaid's dress, he'd never seen a more beautiful creature. She was so very tall, and with her hair swept up on top of her head, she looked even taller. He was so mesmerized that he didn't even remember any of the wedding festivities. He could only concentrate on Nellie. He'd asked her to dance, but she'd refused. When he'd tried to get her phone number, she'd looked down at him and laughed. "Do you really think I'd date someone whose head I can see the top of?" They had laughed many times at how pathetic he'd been that day.

Following the wedding, he'd badgered his cousin until she finally agreed to have a party inviting all of her friends, and he'd be the bartender. He was so nervous that he had cut his nose shaving, bumped his forehead on the open medicine cabinet and worn a black shoe with a brown one. The party had been a raving success, and he'd been the jovial bartender who had everyone buzzing. As the minutes ticked by like years, Lloyd had finally concluded that Nellie was not going to show. Then, as though on cue, as The Temptations crooned "My Girl," he'd seen her.

She'd floated into the crowded room on the wings of timeless beauty. Her hair was down, falling well below her shoulders. Her full lips were glossy and inviting, her eyes sparkled even in the blue light, and the navy blue pantsuit wore her six-foot, perfect body with style.

One of the partygoers had broken the spell: "Say, brotha, you gonna give me that beer, or you gonna hold it all night?"

"Oh, man, sorry, here ya go," Lloyd had said as he moved from behind the bar.

"Hey, I want a drink!"

"I'll be right back." Lloyd had called over his shoulder as he made his way to the center of the room, where she stood, taking in the scene.

"M-m-may I have this dance?" Lloyd had stammered.

"Where do I know you from?" Nellie had asked with a confused smile. "I've met you before."

"Charlotte and Jeffrey's wedding, a couple months ago."

"Oh, that's right. What's your name again?"

"Lloyd Frederickson. I asked you for your number, but you refused, so I had my cousin throw this little gathering just so I could get a second chance."

"Oh, really now?" She'd arched her brow. "Well, I guess the least I could do is dance with a man who has gone to so much trouble."

Lloyd didn't really remember too much of what happened after that, but he had left with her phone number, and he'd pursued her for the next four years, until she'd finally agreed to become Mrs. Frederickson. He'd worked so hard to make her happy for all those years, and he refused to let something foul slip between them now.

As he listened to the phone ring, he wondered again what was wrong with his wife. She seemed so unhappy. Nellie picked up the phone on the fourth ring. "Hello?"

"Hey, honey bun. I was thinking we could go to Palm Springs or Las Vegas this weekend, so we could have a chance to talk uninterrupted. Maybe do a day at the spa. What do you think?"

Nellie was silent for a moment and then said, "I think we can talk right here. We can start when you get off work tomorrow morning. There are a few things I need to say, and I don't want to be someplace else when I say them."

"What is that supposed to mean?" Lloyd's pulse increased slightly. "Why does it matter where we talk?"

"If it doesn't matter, then 44 Malcolm Lane should do just fine. I have to go now. I have an appointment."

"Nellie—"

The dispatcher interrupted Lloyd. "Engine 27 and Squad 39, we've got a possible hit-and-run, auto versus pedestrian, at Florence and Normandie. Young female down."

Without saying good-bye to Nellie, and before the dispatcher could repeat the call, Lloyd, Andrew and Jerome were in the truck. Mychel and Austin fell into the paramedic vehicle. The large, double, roll-up doors began to rise slowly as both vehicles inched toward the opening. The doors cleared the tops of the vehicles, and they rolled into the street. Jerome simultaneously hit the switches for the lights and siren.

Pulling into traffic, Lloyd announced, "All clear on the right."

Looking to his left, Jerome proceeded with caution through the intersection, blowing the horn. Rush-hour traffic precluded a clear path; looking ahead three blocks, he saw that he stood a better chance taking the opposite side of the street. He had more than a block open.

At the next intersection, Jerome maneuvered to the left and proceeded into oncoming traffic. To his dismay, several cars refused to yield. Without a doubt, the drivers' music was so loud that they couldn't hear the deafening siren. He began blowing the horn in rapid succession. Braking slightly, he reduced his speed to fifty miles per hour. Within three minutes and forty seconds, they arrived at the scene.

"Where's the victim?" Lloyd asked as he reached for the door.

"I don't see anyone; let's check with the people gathered here on the corner." Jerome put on latex gloves as he left the truck.

"We had a call there was a hit-and-run on this corner," Lloyd shouted. "Do any of you know anything about that?"

One of the bystanders spoke up. "We don't know nothing about no hit-and-run. But you know, if you need to put out a fire, I got one for ya, pretty boy." The thin woman, wearing too much makeup and not enough teeth, smiled at Andrew.

"I just bet you do," Andrew said slyly. "But I'm going to pass this time. I'm just a rookie, but my boy Jerome here is a veteran, perhaps he can help you out."

"Hmm. Can I slide down your pole, Fireman Jerome?" The other woman, wearing an ill-fitting blond wig, asked suggestively.

"Afraid not, miss."

"What about you, ole-timer?" She leered at Lloyd. "I bet you won't need no Viagra with me!"

"I'll call it in." Lloyd ignored the woman in need of a bath. "We're done here."

The three men returned to the truck, one teasing the other. Before they could call in an all clear, a second call came through.

"Female with her arm stuck in a waterbed. Neighbor reports victim is not in distress. Arm is swelling. 8810 Wall Street."

"Engine 27 and Squad 39 responding. We're all clear on the Florence and Normandie. No victim, apparent false alarm." Lloyd released the button on the two-way radio. "Arm stuck in a waterbed? Well, I must say that's a first in thirty years."

"This should be interesting," Andrew said wryly. "You think she's dressed? I do hope she's fine!"

"Bring it up a level, St. Vincent!" Lloyd snapped at Andrew.

"Now, Cap, don't tell me you weren't thinking the same thing. You're not that old, and, Winters, you ain't that good. If we can rescue a damsel in distress and get our peep on at the same time, you gonna be mad?"

Lloyd sighed. "Andrew, son, she is probably one hundred with a cruel stroke of luck from the gods of gravity."

"Ewwww—why you painting a graphic like that for a brotha?" They all laughed.

Engine 27 pulled onto Wall Street to be greeted by graffiti tagging, old abandoned cars and apparent gang members loitering about. As they pulled in front of 8810—a medium-size, well-maintained residence that looked out of place—the front door opened, and a large woman wearing a floral muumuu ran toward them, shouting, "She's in here. She was trying to get her watch that fell behind the bed and got her arm stuck. It's swelling pretty badly, and she's starting to panic." The woman smelled freshly bathed and exuded high energy. The firemen looked from one to the other.

The three men moved quickly up the walkway as Mychel and Austin pulled in behind their rig, jumping out of the paramedic truck, their equipment box in hand, by the time the others had reached the door.

Beautifully tended flowers lined the front of the freshly painted porch. The pleasant woman led them through a very stylish front door with stained-glass panels on each side. As they stepped inside, they stopped, awestruck. The huge living room looked like it had been taken from the pages of *Architectural Digest*. Their feet sunk deeply into the rich blue carpet; the couch, love seat and tables were pure white, and the blue accents throughout the room matched the carpet. Pillars separated the dining and living rooms. The dining room furniture matched. Candles burned. The room smelled heavenly.

"This is a beautiful room, ma'am." Mychel managed to speak first.

"Oh, my friend has great decorating taste. You'd never expect to see something like this in this neighborhood. She's upstairs. Follow me."

The large woman took the hardwood steps with ease, resting her hand on the oak banister as she climbed the stairs. In the center of the steps lay a blue runner that matched the carpet, gold-looking rods holding it in place. At the top of the stairs was a loft with a pool table and big-screen television, part of an expensive-looking home-theater system. The blue carpet covered the second level, and to the right of the loft were slightly opened French doors.

"Right this way," the woman said, gesturing. "By the way, my name is Blanche."

"Well, Blanche, your friend has a really nice home," Jerome responded. "Now, let's see if we can get her free from that waterbed."

"I surely have to agree with my partner," Lloyd said. "This is one of the nicest homes we've ever been in."

As they stepped into the bedroom, they saw an exquisitely decorated, extremely large space. The decorations in the room gave the feeling of the tropics: Ferns and palms graced every corner, and the smell of gardenias permeated the air. The beautiful canopy bed, with a post twelve inches in diameter, was draped in white netting. The mattress was at least four feet above the floor. Mychel would definitely need a stool to get into this bed.

The crew of five moved through the room, across the plush, white-carpeted floor. "Hi there," Jerome said as he approached the bed and the woman laying facedown. "Looks like you got yourself stuck in here pretty good."

"I'm so embarrassed," came the muffled voice from the bed. "I dropped my watch. I could see it, and I thought I could just stick my arm in here and grab it. But as you can see, it wasn't quite that easy."

"What's your name?" Mychel asked as she slipped her hands into latex gloves.

"Allyson Nixon. I really feel silly. Thank God I was dressed! I would have been mortified otherwise."

"Well, Allyson, we're going to do whatever we can as neatly as possible." Andrew actually said something appropriate for a change. "Your home is quite nice."

"How is the hutch attached to the base of the bed, Mrs. Nixon?" Lloyd asked.

"Please, call me Allyson. I'm not sure—my former husband set up this whole thing, and that was quite a while ago."

Lloyd was in charge. "Jerome, take the other side. Let's see what we're working with here."

In the six-inch clearance between the wall and the bed, Jerome could see that the fasteners that were supposed to attach the hutch to the base of the bed were not connected. He and Lloyd looked up at each other simultaneously, smiling.

"Allyson, I think we'll be able to have you free in just a second,"

Lloyd said. "On the count of three, I want you to try to pull your arm free."

"It's really swollen from me tugging on it. Is this going to hurt?"

Lloyd tried to suppress his laughter. "Oh, I don't think so."

Jerome began. "One."

"Two." This time it was Lloyd.

"Three." Everyone said it in unison. Lloyd and Jerome tilted the mirrored, bookcase-style hutch back less than two inches. Allyson was immediately able to free her arm.

"Oh my God, please tell me that wasn't all I had to do. Now I'm so ashamed." She turned her body so she could roll over on her back and then sat on the side of the waterbed. Jerome extended his hand so that she would take it, and he helped her to her feet.

As she stood to face them, the beauty of her home paled in comparison to that of her person. Her perfect, Afrocentric features needed no makeup. She, like her friend, was a large woman, approximately five foot eight, with a full bosom, large round hips and buttocks, an almost flat stomach and a very small waist for a woman of her size. Jerome, who had eyes only for Nicolle, was struck speechless along with all of his male coworkers.

Mychel stepped in to save them any further embarrassment. "Allyson, we're glad we were able to free you without any damage to your lovely furniture. We'll just write our report and be gone."

"Oh, please don't tell me you have to report this."

Lloyd managed to find his tongue. "Yes, Allyson, we have to report all calls, but I assure you, you're not the first person to have to be rescued in their own home. At least your toe wasn't stuck in the faucet in your bathtub." He grinned.

Of course, Andrew couldn't resist chiming in, "Allyson, anytime you need to be freed from *anything*, you just give Fire Station 27 a call."

"We'll be going now." Mychel looked at Andrew in amusement.

"May I offer you some homemade coconut cake and coffee? It's the least I can do for being so silly." Allyson looked genuinely embarrassed, a flush creeping up her chocolate skin.

"No, but thank you," Lloyd said.

"I'll be sure to bake a pineapple upside-down cake and bring it by the station to show my gratitude." She smiled.

"Well, just be sure you say it's for C Shift!" Mychel said as they turned to leave.

They filed down the stairs in silence. As they reached the truck, they moved out of the view of Allyson and Blanche, who stood on the front porch, waving. The men all said at the same time, "Wow!"

Lloyd spoke first. "God gave that woman some pieces."

"And He sho' nuff knew where to place them!" Austin high-fived Jerome.

"Oh, for goodness' sake, get in the truck," Mychel grumbled. "Y'all act like you've never seen a beautiful woman before. And Jerome, you and Lloyd are married. Get a grip!"

"Married, not blind," Lloyd said. The others laughed.

"I'll see you back at the station." Mychel tugged on Austin's arm, and he followed obediently.

"Boy, I would pay some good money to bury my face in those big, beautiful . . ." Andrew began, but knew he would draw severe chastisement from both of his partners if he finished that sentiment.

"Andrew, if you've never had the pleasure, I highly suggest five servings daily as recommended by your nutritionist." Jerome surprised himself with his hasty words.

"Both of you need to quit, and, Winters, I'm surprised at you," Lloyd said.

"Now, Cap, you must admit she's a beautiful woman with enough to keep any brotha at the florist." Jerome looked deliberately at his boss and best friend.

"Just drive," Lloyd said grimly.

They were silent on the ride back to the firehouse, each man lost in his own thoughts. Allyson Nixon had shaken each of them a little differently it seemed.

Mychel stood outside the firehouse, awaiting the arrival of her partners, a disturbing look on her face. Her eyes were cloudy and her brow contorted. They had left her only moments before—what could possibly have happened?

Jerome backed the truck into the driveway. As he opened the door, Mychel yelled, "Captain, I can't work under these conditions. You have to do something about this."

"Calm down, Hernandez," Lloyd said. "What happened?"

"Calm down? Calm down?" Mychel shrieked. "You come see this and tell me if I should calm down. How dare someone do this to Casper?"

The three men followed her into the station. Austin stood in the middle of the floor, dumbfounded. Casper, the station dog, was hanging from a beam in the ceiling.

Every one of the firefighters, on every shift, loved the old dog who was good for nothing but eating, sleeping and pooping. They took care of her, gave her medicine, took her for walks. Casper was family. What kind of monster could do something like this?

"I'm calling the police!" Austin spoke through clinched teeth.

"Wait!" Lloyd commanded.

"Wait for what? Even if you don't think this has gone too far, the rest of us do. If HQ won't handle it, the sheriff will. Maybe next time it will be one of us."

In the background, Dr. Phil played on the thirteen-inch television/VCR as the man sat down on the egg crate with a cushion he used as a computer chair.

After opening his web-mail account, he browsed the list of mail in his in-box. There was nothing that interested him.

He opened one message that simply said, "We need to talk," and much to his disappointment, a blond woman with very large breasts greeted him.

Delete.

He clicked the icon to create new e-mail.

Maybe they will take us seriously now. Next time it will be a man down. They think they are so much better than everyone else because they wear the blue. I'm so tired of watching them come and go in their fancy cars. Who do they think they are? They should all be buying one-way tickets to Africa!

Keep the faith because I am on the case.

—One of Your Boys

ntoinette stood at the opening of her closet, which was larger than their first living room had been, and tried desperately to decide what to wear to the monthly Sistah-Friends meeting.

The third Friday of the month was her time. The thirty women in her group, ranging from age twenty-five to seventy-one, were students, hairstylists, doctors, secretaries, lawyers, entrepreneurs, stay-at-home moms and, yes, housewives. The one thing they all had in common—they were all of African decent. With her Sistah-Friends, she could be who she really was.

She had been asked to join the club by the owner of the African-American bookstore where she purchased all of her titles, Miriam Rodgers, who had been a member for more than eight years. The group had started as four women getting together to play bid whist once a month, and twelve years later they were seventeen chapters strong. Whenever a group reached thirty members, one of the members was elected to start a new chapter. The chapters came together once a year for a joint meeting held over a weekend that was filled to the brim with fun and fellowship in some exotic location decided by the democratic process.

Chapter Six's meeting was being held at the home of her sponsor and dear friend, Miriam. Each hostess decided what the entertainment would be. Though they had started as a games-only club, they had evolved into a ladies' entertainment organization. The agenda had included widely diverse events, from a prayer meeting during the war to a stripper/massage party for their oldest member's seventieth birthday.

Tonight Miriam was having a book discussion. She had arranged to have one of her favorite authors join them to discuss her latest release. A fan since the author had self-published, Antoinette loved the way the woman wove a tale *and* told about God, all while not sounding preachy.

But what was she going to wear? She stepped to the right side of the closet and chose three pantsuits: a red one, a white one and her favorite black one. She didn't want to appear overdressed, but she felt the need to look sophisticated.

Antoinette was one of those women who never lost or gained any weight. She was the same one hundred thirty-five pounds she'd been on her wedding day. She'd gained fifteen pounds when she'd been pregnant with Andrew but had lost it all by the time she was discharged from the hospital. Her friends hated her. Most of her wardrobe she'd had for many, many years.

Antoinette smiled at her reflection in the full-length mirror. *I'll decide after my bath,* she thought. The feeling of marble under her bare feet refreshed her as she stepped into the spacious bathroom adjoining her closet. The faux-marble tub with gold fixtures dominated the center of the room. Though the bathtub was built for two, she had never shared it with Jules. "Real men don't take bubble baths," he always said when she invited him to join her. She measured her movements as she bent to turn the water to just the right temperature. Her back had ached since she'd worked in the vegetable garden that ran along the side of the house more than a week before. She loved the fresh tomatoes, lettuce and cucumbers so she really didn't want to have to give them up, but the lumbar pain was more frequent, and gardening didn't help any.

She opened the beveled-mirror cabinet doors above the tub to choose just the right bath salts for her mood, adding a little Epsom salts for medicinal purposes. She sat on the side of the tub and thought back to her humble beginnings in North Carolina, a place and time that seemed a million miles and a millennium away. Her mother had raised her and her sister on what she'd earned as a grocery store clerk, until she'd made the decision to move north to New Jersey. There, she could make real money for the education of her daughters. She'd been determined they wouldn't work for nickels a day. She'd begun working in the kitchen of Rutgers College, taking classes at night until she'd managed to get a bachelor's degree. She then became secretary to the assistant chancellor, a job she'd worked until she'd retired at age seventy-two.

The sacrifices her mother had made had given Antoinette and her sister, Margaret, golden opportunities, so her mother was furious when Antoinette had dropped out of college to marry Jules. "What will happen to you when the white man grows tired of his colored wife?" her mother had said. She'd predicted Antoinette would be alone, uneducated and colored, the perfect combination for failure. Margaret went on to graduate school and still taught at her alma mater, where she was currently up for the position of dean. Margaret had no idea that Antoinette was keeping tabs on her.

Though Antoinette had disappointed her mother at first, Jules had insisted she return to school when they moved to California. After being married for less than six months, the pressures from both families had become overbearing. Jules applied to the fire department in Los Angeles and was hired before the ink dried on the application, and Antoinette graduated with honors in English from the University of California at Los Angeles a year and a half later. She taught for the Los Angeles Unified School District until she'd discovered she was pregnant with Andrew.

Antoinette absentmindedly stirred the water with her fingertips. She often thought about her mother, wondering if she would approve if she could only see how well Jules had provided for her daughter. Somehow Antoinette doubted it. White men had lynched her great-uncle because they claimed he had smiled at a white woman. The last words her mother had ever spoken to Antoinette were painful and filled with anger: "You will burn in hell for your disrespect of our ancestors."

Almost forty years later, those words still caused a chill to creep over Antoinette's body. She blinked several times and looked around at the expansive room and the beveled mirrors, granite and marble stonework with brass fixtures and Egyptian cotton towels that cost more than what her mother had earned in a week when she'd worked at the grocery store. Antoinette hadn't sold out. She'd married the man she loved, a man who loved her in return and missed no opportunity to show her. If her sister still hated her, she was the one who was missing out. Antoinette only wished she'd been able to reconcile with her mother before she'd passed . . .

Enough of those thoughts! Tonight I will be with my Sistah-Friends, and I'm going to meet Ms. Murray! Antoinette slipped her robe off, returned it to its hook and stepped into the water, which was the perfect temperature, and turned on the Jacuzzi jets. She'd been tired most of the day, and a long, soothing bath was just what she needed to feel better.

After soaking for an hour and rewarming the water three times, Antoinette decided it was time to get dressed. Her back felt better as she toweled with the luxurious fawn-colored bath sheet. She went to her dressing table, wrapping herself tightly in the towel, and sat to moisturize her body. It was funny—she'd read somewhere that you knew you were becoming marvelously mature when it took longer to rest than it did to get tired.

The invigorating aromatherapy was beginning to work its magic. She quickly applied a little makeup and pulled matching bra and panties from the drawers positioned in the middle of her closet. She'd decided the black pantsuit would do quite nicely; she felt sexy in the low-cut jacket. Hopefully Jules would be awake when she returned.

Within twenty minutes of stepping from the tub, Antoinette was dressed and picking up her keys and heading for the garage. She hit the garage door button and slipped behind the wheel of the new forest-green Jaguar that still possessed that new-car smell. Opening the sunroof so she could feel the wind in her closely cropped, almost fully gray natural hairstyle, she carefully backed into the cul-de-sac and waved to her neighbor.

Despite her family's inability to forgive her, Antoinette knew she'd made the right choice.

12

Lloyd began dialing the chief's phone number from memory, applying very deliberate pressure to each of the eleven digits. Voice mail. He pressed the pound sign to skip the annoying voice of his leader.

"Chief, this is Frederickson. In case there was any doubt in your mind that we were imagining all of this, I just wanted you to know that when we returned from a call just now, we found Casper, our firehouse dog, with a noose around her neck, hanging from the pipes. As clever as she was, I don't believe she committed suicide. I need to hear from you today. Monday is too long to wait to start the investigation." He hung up, frustration and worry roiling in his stomach. His cell phone rang.

"Hello." Lloyd answered on the first ring without looking at the caller ID.

"May I speak with Mr. Frederickson, please?" the pleasant and familiar voice asked.

"Mrs. Sanders, is this you?" A sense of relief washed over him.

"How are you, Mr. Frederickson? And, please, call me Glynda," she said, a smile in her voice. "It's been a while. You sounded a little distressed, so I didn't want to wait until Monday."

"Well, Glynda, you'll have to call me Lloyd, and then everything will be just fine. I understand you're back working in D.C. Will you get to visit your family while you're there?"

"I've been really busy, but my sister Dawn has come over three times this week to have dinner with me. I'm trying to convince her to move out to L.A. But enough about me. I'm sure you didn't call me just to chitchat."

"As much as I'd like to say that I did, we're having a bad time over here at 27. Someone is doing some really foul stuff." He quickly filled her in on all the strange happenings around the firehouse, including his suspicions that the actions were racially motivated. "And then today," he continued, "when we returned from a call, we found Casper hanging from the ceiling beam. All the other stuff was bad enough, but losing Casper really hurt."

"Whoa!" Glynda's voice took on a sharp note. "They killed the dog? Did you contact the police?"

"Yes, they left a short while ago." Lloyd shook his head. "You know, I reported all this to the chief just this morning, but he doesn't seem to be taking us seriously. I need to know what we should do—that's where you come in." Lloyd sighed.

"Lloyd, I'm really sorry about Casper. I know how much you all loved her." Glynda's voice sounded sad and strained. "When will the chief get back to you?"

"He said Monday." Lloyd could hear the lack of conviction in his own voice.

"I'll be back in the office on Monday as well. Have you talked to the Stentorians about any of this?"

"Not yet. I plan to meet with the president early next week."

"Great, then we can come up with a strategy on Monday. Do you work this weekend?"

"No."

"Good. And, Lloyd, please be careful. You remind me a lot of my daddy. I couldn't stand it if something happened to you, too."

"I promise to sleep with one eye open. We'll touch base on Monday. Travel safe."

As Glynda hung up, her spirit felt heavy. She had come to love all the firefighters she'd worked with on one civil rights matter or another, but Lloyd Frederickson seemed so much like her father that just talking to him made her feel warm inside. Shortly after she passed the bar, her father had died suddenly and upset her entire world. As if that alone weren't enough, she and her sisters had discovered they had a sister that none of them knew had existed.

Though Glynda had been a pillar of strength the whole time she was in Baltimore after her father's untimely death, when she returned to California, her world crumbled. With the urging of her best friend, Rico, a physician, she took a six-week, mental-health leave of absence. After a few grief-counseling sessions and a short honeymoon, Glynda returned to work with a new outlook on life, a new husband and, unbeknownst to her, a new job. She had been assigned to the firm's civil rights division.

While she thought the partners might have felt she'd be mad enough to quit, the new job was a dream. In her new position, she was able to fulfill the goals she had set when she'd chosen a career in law: to make her father, Edward Zachary Naylor, proud of her and to enable the legal system to really work for her people.

She had done so well over the past two and half years that the firm allowed—actually encouraged—her to do work for the Stentorians at a tremendously reduced rate, if not pro bono. She hadn't seen her old buddy Lloyd Frederickson in almost a year, and she looked forward to seeing him on Monday. She checked her watch and realized she needed to change before her baby sister arrived for a late dinner.

Her father's death had caused what threatened to be a permanent rift between the four sisters. With the introduction of a fifth sibling the day before her father's funeral, the lines had been clearly drawn dead center. The assumed-to-be-oldest, Renee, and her partner in crime, number-two daughter, Collette, had refused to accept Eddie's love child, Nina.

The scandalous scene at the funeral was forever burned into her retina. When Collette showed up in a tight orange suit complete with miniskirt, Glynda had lost it. She started a fight in the middle of the church. She didn't think she would ever be able to show her face at First United Church again. They had managed to return to some semblance of civility, and even seemed to have reconciled. The week following the funeral the five sisters spent hours going through the only house four of them had known to be home until adulthood. The time was filled with laughter, tears, happiness and anger. They parted with promises they would each work hard to help one another heal. That lasted about as long as Glynda's flight back to Los Angeles.

She and Dawn remained as close as they had ever been. They had found there was enough love to share with their newly discovered sister and made a conscious effort to make Nina feel like family.

Trading Anne Klein for Levi Strauss, Glynda slipped on her "Nothing Like a Black Man" sweatshirt, grabbed her purse and room key and was off to an evening with Dawn.

13

"I spoke with the lawyer," Lloyd announced as he entered the recreation room. "She expressed her condolences for losing Casper. She'll be back on Monday, and I plan to meet her in the afternoon."

"Why didn't you want to talk to the police, Cap?" Mychel stood, blocking his path.

"I knew you all would handle it." Lloyd didn't make eye contact. "I just needed to think. I left another message for the chief. I really hope he can feel the urgency of this now."

"What if he doesn't? Then what?" Jerome paced to relieve his tension. "We need our own plan. We need to hire a private investigator instead of a lawyer."

"I agree. An investigator will catch whoever is doing this in the act." Austin's normally quiet demeanor seemed shattered.

"And how do you propose we pay for a private investigator?" Lloyd toyed with the saltshaker.

"Hell, we'll chip in and pay for it, just so we can show HQ we weren't making this all up." Mychel took a deep drink of her soda. "I sure could use a little something in this Coke."

"This person is slick." Lloyd slammed his fist into the table. "They have access to the firehouse. They know our routine. As much as I hate to say it, it's one of us."

Andrew leaned against the wall, a distant look in his eyes. "I know what you mean. This has me more than a little spooked." He stood up. "Let's get some dinner. Maybe food will make us think clearer. Winters, count me in for that private investigator. If everyone else is down, then so am I."

"I'm not paying one red cent," Lloyd snapped.

"Of course, you're not." Austin got up from the table. "But that isn't going to stop us. I agree with St. Vincent. Let's get something to eat. I'm starving."

As if the universe knew the emotional state of the 27 crew, not one more call came in before the C Shift turned it over to the A Shift. The A Shift captain, John Fontana, handled the shift change with his normal sarcasm. "So you boys have a slow night? Nothing out of the ordinary to report? By the way, where's ole Casper?"

"Why do you think something unusual happened?" Mychel spat.

"Hold on to your bloomers, girlie." Captain Fontana flushed red. "I'm just asking. Y'all just seem a little preoccupied." Fontana was one of the original good ole boys. He'd been on the department since his daddy got him the job when he was nineteen. He became eligible for retirement more than a year before but refused to even entertain the idea. The out-of-shape leader, who always looked like he had a hangover, had as much respect for the female members of the department as he did blacks.

"My name is Mychel Hernandez. You can call me Firefighter Hernandez or Paramedic Hernandez or Mychel or Hernandez or Ms. Hernandez, but if you call me girlie again, you may find *this* girlie's foot up your arrogant ass with her toes wiggling around." She turned to Lloyd. "I'm outta here. See you on Monday." She snatched her jacket and headed for the dormitory to change.

"I guess we're done here." Lloyd closed his notebook and headed for the stairs. He turned slowly and made contact with his contemporary's empty eyes. "Someone killed Casper last night. Hanged her, you know, lynch style. At this moment in time, we don't know who did this terrible thing, but believe me, we're going to find out, and I promise you this on my mother-in-law's grave—somebody is going to pay."

As Lloyd stepped onto the landing, Jerome stared him in the eyes and began laughing. "That was pretty good, considering your mother-in-law is alive and quite healthy."

"He doesn't know that," Lloyd said. "That redneck made me mad. I'm so fed up with this mess. Plus things are kinda rocky at home. I don't know what's up with Nellie, but I'm getting to the bottom of it today."

"Oh, man, I had no idea. You guys'll work it out. You've got a thirty-year investment. Communication is the key. Talk it through." Jerome patted him on the back.

With a rare expression of emotion Lloyd smiled. "*I'm* supposed to counsel *you*, not the other way around. But you and Nicolle have a great relationship . . . you're a lucky man, my brotha."

"I know that every day, and I thank the Heavenly Father accordingly. Believe that. Obviously, nothing's perfect, but I think Nicolle and I are as close as it's going to come on this here earth."

Lloyd smiled, looking a little sad. "I'll see you Monday."

"If you need to get a beer or something, call me. It's going to work out, man."

The men parted without another word, the understanding passing between them. As Jerome backed the SUV out of its parking space, he tried to imagine his life without Nicolle. Her laughter intoxicated him. Her smell mesmerized him. Her touch stimulated him. Her love captivated him. As he pulled onto the boulevard, he pressed the gas just a little harder. He wanted to get to his wife as soon as possible.

14

Nellie sat at the breakfast table, a steaming mug of coffee and a Virginia Slims Menthol between her fingers, as Lloyd opened the kitchen door.

"Good morning." He spoke with an even tone.

Taking a long drag off the cigarette, Nellie mumbled, "Morning."

"I really wish you'd try to quit smoking, honey," Lloyd said, concern in his voice. "You're killing yourself. I wish you could see some of the rescues we do for people with smoking-related diseases." Lloyd bent to kiss her, and she pulled away. He sighed. "I guess there is no time like the present to get to the bottom of all of this. So what *is* the problem?"

They sat, staring at each other, neither wanting to be the first to blink.

Lloyd finally spoke. "Out with it."

Stubbing out the cigarette, Nellie shifted her weight in the chair. Staring the only man she'd ever loved in the face, she wasn't so angry now. She was disappointed and tired. "Are you sure you're ready to hear this?" Her voice reflected her weariness.

"I'm ready," Lloyd said firmly. "Once we get it out in the open, we can handle it. But we must talk about it, or the problem will only fester like a cancer and destroy us."

"I think it already has." Despite her strong resolve, tears began to gather in Nellie's eyes. "I haven't been happy for a long time. I want a divorce, Lloyd."

Standing so abruptly that he turned over the dinette chair, Lloyd shouted, "You what?"

"Please don't yell," Nellie said, trying to soothe him. "We *can* discuss this calmly."

"Calmly? You just told me you want to leave me after all these years, and you want me to be calm?" Lloyd looked shaken. "You've obviously had time to think this through!"

She took a deep breath and began again, feeling irritated at his obtuseness. "Lloyd, it's so like you to not even notice that there's been something wrong between us since Victoria went off to Europe. You bury your head in the sand and think everything is just hunky-dory. You haven't even cared enough to ask me if anything was bothering me until the other day."

"What do you mean I haven't cared enough? Look around you." He waved his arm in a half circle. "You're living in the nicest house on the block. You have a Ph.D. behind your name. You drive a fifty-thousand-dollar car. You can shop when and wherever you choose. I make all of this happen, Nellie. I bust my ass—I sweat blood to make sure you want for nothing."

Nellie slammed her hand on the table, frustrated. "Lloyd, it's not about writing checks. Yes, you provide everything material, but what about you? When are *you* available? When the kids were growing up, how many of their games did you attend? Did you once see Portia's science fair entries? Did you ever go to Disneyland with us? Did you ever even read to the kids?"

As he paced back and forth, Lloyd's face was flushed with anger. "Do you think it was easy to manage all the finances for this family? I always thought you had the kids under control. I worked and provided, and you nurtured. I thought that was our unspoken agreement. Why in the hell didn't you say anything before now?"

"I did!" Nellie said, feeling her blood pressure rise. "You just would never hear me. You'd shrug it off saying, 'Oh, you can handle it.' I've resented you for being able to do everything you've always wanted to do without even once considering that there was something else I wanted to do besides taking care of everyone else." She dropped her head into her hands and stared at the tabletop. "I'm tired," she whispered.

"But you always handled things! Now, when there is nothing to handle, you want to leave me? Things should be perfect between us now! This makes no sense!" Lloyd slid the kitchen chair near him under the table, and then pulled it out as though he was going to sit. He remained standing, looking confused. "Nellie, you're a social worker for goodness' sake. You *know* people have to talk. You made me think everything was fine between us. Now, after thirty years, I find out it was all wrong. What the hell do you want me to do now to make this right?"

Tears welled in Nellie's eyes but refused to fall. "You can just leave," Nellie said, her words barely above a whisper.

"You what?"

"I want you to move out," she repeated, feeling a little stronger. "I'm just tired, Lloyd. Please don't make this any harder than it already is." The tears finally found their way to her cheeks and dripped onto her peach terry cloth bathrobe.

"Woman, you are straight up trippin'." Lloyd moved in front of her, just inches from her nose. "You tell me we have problems, and your first request is that I move out? Move out of the house that I'm paying for? Do you have another man?"

Nellie shot out of the chair, forcing Lloyd to back away. "Why does it always have to be another man? Why can't it be about you and your thirty years of emotional neglect?"

"I'm not accepting that! There's no way I've emotionally neglected you for thirty years. Maybe I did leave all of the activities with the girls to you, but I never thought of it as neglect. I just always thought we each were working our talents. If I was so terrible at all of this and you said nothing, then guess whose fault it is it never got any better?"

"Don't even try to turn this around on me! How could you possibly think you weren't supposed to participate in raising our children?" Nellie reached for a cigarette.

"You want to talk about working my nerves for thirty years?" Lloyd began pacing and rubbing his freshly shaved face. "That damned smoking. This whole house reeks! I've asked you to quit a thousand times, and you promise you will, but you never even try."

"Now who's trippin'? I tell you I want a divorce because I'm tired of coming second—hell, I would have been happy with second . . . let's try fourth or fifth in your life—and you start talking about annoying habits? Negro, puh-leeze!"

"Again, I have to ask you why you haven't said anything in all these years," Lloyd said, his voice cracking slightly.

Expelling a long, overexaggerated breath, Nellie returned to her chair. "Lloyd Frederickson, I did say something, but you just wouldn't take heed. You refused to listen to anything you didn't want to hear! After a while, I just stopped trying. I don't want to do this anymore. I just want to start over. We've grown apart."

"Woman, what are you talking about? I have you climbing walls and swinging from the ceiling fan!" Lloyd finally felt he had a defense for her allegations.

"Now, see, that's a major part of the problem. You think that sex, albeit good sex, is the answer to any problem. You also seem to think that if you mess up big, like forgetting a birthday, then a really big present will make up for it. Some things flowers or even diamonds just can't fix, Lloyd."

"I never saw you turning anything down either." Lloyd faked a laugh.

She sighed again. "Sex between us is the one thing that made me hold on. But even that's not enough anymore. I just want a fresh start," she repeated, stressing each word.

Lloyd opened the kitchen cabinet and removed a crystal water glass. Setting it on the counter, he turned to the woman he knew carried his rib and softly said, "Then start over with me."

"What?"

His thirst seemingly forgotten, Lloyd moved quickly across the expansive room, falling to his knees in front of Nellie. "Let's start over. I'll go to counseling; we'll start dating again. I can't get back all those years, but I can change. I won't lose you, Nell. Right or wrong, let's wipe the slate clean. You have to take some responsibility in all of this. You know as well as I do that silence grants consent. If what you say is true, if I wasn't listening, then you should have screamed until I heard."

Nellie moved her head, trying to shift her gaze from his pleading eyes. Lloyd gently placed his fingers on her chin and turned her head back toward him. For a long moment, she looked at him, silent, and then said, "You're so accustomed to getting what you want with so little effort that you'll never change. You're fifty-three years old. You know what they say about old dogs?"

"That we're stupid? Or that we have old fleas?"

Despite what she felt inside, Nellie laughed. "Don't make me laugh when I'm so mad at you. When I woke up this morning, I knew that by the time I went to bed again, I'd be living alone."

"Nell, you know good and hell well I wasn't going anywhere without a Tyson-Holyfield battle." He smiled. "I'm sorry that I didn't take heed, as you say, but I can't lose you. I'll make every effort to change. But you have to make me the same promise. Find a counselor, and we'll go."

"Why do I have to find a counselor?" she asked. "You can do it just as easily as I can."

"No, I can't. See, this is a good beginning. Let's talk about what we're good at. This is your field of expertise. You work with therapists and counselors all day, every day. So why should I start from the bottom, working my way up slowly, when you're already at the top? It would be like me telling you to find a mechanic to get the brakes fixed on the car. Sure you could do it, but it would take you so much longer, and it would be inefficiency at its best."

Nellie hated it when he convinced her that he was right. Maybe she should give the old fart another opportunity. At least with him, she knew what she was working with. Yet as he extended his arms she resisted.

"Come on, my Georgia peach," he pleaded. "I'm going to give this thing all I've got. Please don't throw away thirty years without trying."

Sighing heavily and pushing him away, Nellie began slowly, "And just how long am I supposed to wait on this change? I can guarantee you it won't be another thirty years—or thirty weeks for that matter. I want things to change today, but I know that's not realistic."

"I can change today!" Lloyd hesitated for a moment. "Okay, well maybe that is a little too optimistic. Do you know how I've created such a comfortable financial life for us?"

"You hold on to a dollar until George's eyes water?"

Laughing, Lloyd stepped to Nellie and took her hands in his. "That, too, I guess. But I set small attainable goals. So I think we should do the same thing. We should write everything down and then prioritize. The ultimate goal of course is to improve our relationship, and we can start by listing the steps we need to take and assign a date to get each of them done. For example, the first goal is to set up a counseling session. That'll be our most important responsibility, and we want that done, say, on Monday. Do you see where I'm going with this?"

"Yes, and I'm not so sure I like it. It feels real familiar," Nellie said, wishing she could believe her husband. "You're leaving everything up to me to fix."

"Nell, I swear I'm not," he insisted. "Let's see, the first thing I need to do is get someone to take on some of the responsibility I have with the Stentorians. That way, I can concentrate more on our problems. I want to plan a romantic getaway for us. I'm gonna rock your world, girl!"

Taking a deep breath, Nellie said, "Lloyd, I think we shouldn't have sex for a while. You making love to me always clouds my judgment. It's like being on drugs."

A slow grin spread across his face. "That's how I do it, baby! You've always seemed to like it like that. I'm your vitamin D." Lloyd struck a sexy "who's your big daddy" pose.

She shook her head, her eyes troubled. "But that's just the point, Lloyd. I want to work on these issues without getting caught up in some mind-altering, forgive-you-no-matter-what-stupid-stuff-you-do sex."

"I don't get your point, but okay." He sighed, looking unhappy. "How long do you propose we wait?"

"At least a month." Nellie held her breath. Other than when she had the girls, she couldn't remember being without Lloyd's magical touch for more than a week. No matter how mad, disappointed or disgusted she was, come nightfall, it was on.

"Oh, hell, naw!" Throwing his hands in the air Lloyd began walking in circles. "A month? Are you insane?"

"Okay, maybe a month is too long. But let's see what our therapist has to say, and we'll go from there."

"So now someone else is going to tell me when I can get some p—"

Nellie interrupted him. "I thought you were willing to work on this. In case you didn't know, work ain't easy!"

"Okay. Okay. Okay," he said, calming her with his hands. "I'll cooperate. But just remember, if I ain't gettin' it, neither are you. And last time I checked, you were all up on a brotha, real regular, like," Lloyd teased.

"You are just so full of yourself aren't you?" Nellie pretended to be angry, but in reality, for the first time in longer than she could remember, she felt a sense of hope.

"Can a black man at least get a hug?"

Nellie slowly stood and walked into Lloyd's waiting arms. She'd almost forgotten how good it felt just to be held, with no other motive but to exchange love. She laughed inside as she began to feel her womanhood stir.

Maybe a month was a tad too long.

15

"Babe-ski, have you seen the rebate receipt for the new battery I bought at Costco?" Jerome yelled from the loft that doubled as his office and the game room.

"You know, my uterus really doesn't contain a tracking device," Nicolle joked as she dropped the basket of dirty clothes in the laundry room. "Why do I always have to keep up with my stuff *and* yours?"

"Because you're so good at it?"

Nicolle ran her hand along the smooth surface of the pool table as she passed it on her way to Jerome's desk. Stacks of receipts and bills cluttered the built-in computer center and workspace. "Whatever! You're just trying to flatter a sistah so she can find your stuff."

"Baby, would I do that?"

"Absolutely." Nicolle lifted the desk calendar, pulled a long register receipt from under it and handed it to Jerome.

"How do you do that?"

"The last thing you said to me was, 'Babe-ski, I'm going to put this under here so I know where it is.' No magic, just memory." Nicolle kissed him playfully on the chin.

"Girl, that's why you on my Christmas list." Jerome pulled her soft body into his. It always felt so good to be close to the only woman he'd ever touched. "You know the boys are going for that backyard camping thing tonight. How about you and I go on a date?"

"What about Christian? You want me to call a sitter?"

Rubbing her ample behind as he looked down into her eyes, he kissed her on the forehead. "We could do that, or we could have a date right here. I'll do all the prep. We haven't done that in a long time."

"Well, we can tire little man out and he'll be asleep by seven thirty. You know, I like the sound of this. Whatever shall I wear?" Nicolle laughed.

"You know, *nothing* works for a brotha like me."

"Why, Mr. Winters, whatevah do you mean?" Nicolle faked her best Scarlett O'Hara voice.

"Now, see, you know how that Southern belle stuff turns a brotha on. You must be tryin' to get—"

"Mommy, I'm hungry." Christian interrupted them.

Nicolle jumped involuntarily as though Christian had caught them doing something inappropriate. "Good morning, baby boy. How's my little man? What do you want to eat?"

Christian ran to her open arms and leapt up as her hands went around him. "Cheerios," he sang.

"How about Daddy's world-famous French toast?" Nicolle turned and winked at Jerome.

"Okay, now, who's trying to flatter who?" Jerome took Christian from her and gave his spitting image a kiss. "You going to help me, little man?"

Christian nodded his head and hugged his dad's neck. Nicolle bubbled over inside at the sight of Jerome with their son. Moments between Jerome and the boys were frequent, but she never grew tired of seeing their exchanges.

"Should we get Mommy to help, too?"

Christian nodded his head again.

"I tell you what—I'll start the laundry and pull the sheets off the bed and then meet you two downstairs in fifteen minutes. That should be just enough time for you to have destroyed the kitchen." She kissed them both and disappeared down the hall to their bedroom suite.

Jerome pushed the receipt deep into the pocket of his sweatpants and headed for the stairs. He had an afterthought and solicited Christian's help. "Go wake up your brothers."

With pleasure, Christian ran down the hall, first to Nicolas's and then to Jordan's room, screaming "Get up!" the entire time. Saturday mornings were Jerome's favorite time. He was able to be with his family and feel all that life was about. His picture-perfect world was no illusion. God had blessed him beyond measure, and everything in his universe was perfectly aligned.

"Mommy, get Christian!" Jordan yelled from behind the door that was slightly ajar.

"It's time to get up, boys," Jerome heard Nicolle yell from their bedroom. "Daddy's making French toast, and if you're good, he'll probably take you to Costco."

"Can we get hot dogs?" Nicolas stood in the doorway to his room, rubbing his eyes.

"I'm making French toast, remember?" Jerome smiled.

"Yeah, but we're going, like, after breakfast, right?" Nicolas inquired.

"Boy, all of my overtime goes just to feed you. Hurry and brush your teeth, and then come on down and help me with breakfast." Jerome turned and descended the stairs. His heart was light with fatherhood.

Nicolle hummed the Betty Wright tune "Tonight Is the Night" as she pulled the linen from the closet. Her heart skipped like a schoolgirl playing double Dutch at the thought of a romantic evening with Jerome. Life had gotten in the way of their quiet time, and they were long overdue. As she pulled the three-hundred-fifty-thread-count burgundy sheets from the closet, she remembered the red satin ones she hadn't used in at least three years.

Pulling the sheets from the neat, yet overstuffed linen closet, she decided that since tonight *was* the night, she'd do something special. The satin sheets were tucked way in the back of the closet. Though they had been put away clean, they hadn't been used since before Christian was born, but a little Gain detergent and Downy would fix them right up.

After tossing them into the washer, she returned to the bedroom and began pulling the dirty sheets from the bed. As she removed Jerome's pillowcase, his scent tickled her nose. Smiling to herself, she buried her face in the fabric and inhaled deeply, her eyes closed. The thought of Jerome's touch stirred something deep within her. She knew she'd be watching the clock all day. After removing the heavily quilted mattress cover she sprinkled the dusting powder that went with Jerome's favorite scent of hers, White Diamonds, onto the extra-thick, pillow-top mattress. She then replaced the feather bed and sprinkled it with more powder before replacing the mattress cover.

As she tossed the dirty sheets into the washer with the satin ones, she remembered she had White Diamonds–scented candles somewhere. While checking the top shelf in the hall closet, she found a champagne bucket and lead crystal flutes but no candles. She made a mental note to chill two bottles of Chandon.

She checked under the bathroom sink. Because the housekeeper had thoroughly cleaned everything the week prior, Nicolle noted that she needed only set the mood in the bathroom. No cleaning would be necessary. She didn't find any scented candles, but she did find a one-hundred-count bag of tea light candles, which she began placing around the edge of the double Jacuzzi tub. Giving up on the White Diamonds candles, she arranged the partially burned jasmine-scented pillars into a wax bouquet on the vanity. She'd pick up fresh flowers when she went to the market.

After checking the supply of bath salts, she gave the room a last once-over and smiled with satisfaction. If she didn't find the White Diamond–scented candles, who would ever know? She was ready for a date with her husband.

It was no secret that Nicolle and Jerome were hopefully and happily living well within the realm of wedded bliss, but reality got in the way of even their romance. Not tonight, though. Tonight belonged to these best friends and lovers. She would have Christian so tired by dinnertime that he'd have trouble staying awake to eat.

Nicolle spent a few more minutes gathering laundry from the boys' bathrooms, waiting for the sheets to finish the wash cycle. After moving the sheets to the dryer and reloading the washer, she headed to the kitchen.

"But, Dad, if we tell her we'll be really, really careful, you still think she'd say no?" Nicolle overheard Nicolas asked desperately.

Nicolle slowed her cadence to listen.

"Nick, you know your mother. If she thinks you have the slightest chance of getting hurt, the first response is always 'No way.' But let me talk to her. You really want this, don't you?"

"Yes! I'm better than all the others. I know I can win the championship. I've been doing it for a real long time, and I've never been hurt!"

Unable to restrain herself any longer, Nicolle rushed into the kitchen. "You've been doing what?"

Startled, the four turned suddenly. Nicolas's horror-filled face touched his mother's heart. "Mom, I—I—"

"Baby, we didn't hear you come in." Jerome tried to give Nicolas a moment to gather his thoughts. "We were just talking about upcoming activities. Nick wants to do some skateboard competitions."

Nicolas looked from his parents to Jordan for the right answer. "Mom, please listen to me before you get mad."

"Why would I get mad?" Nicolle said angrily. "Just because you're out there risking your life, and I had no clue you were even doing it."

"Mooooommmmmmm. Please, just listen to me. I always wear my pads and helmet. I don't do stupid stuff. I board really hard, and I'm good."

"And how long have you been doing this kind of skateboarding?"

Looking at the floor Nicolas mumbled, "Since I got the board."

"Three and half years ago?" Nicolle screamed, grabbing her chest for emphasis, pretending to have a heart attack.

"Calm down, baby. That proves our point. If he's been doing stuntlike riding all this time, and he's not been hurt, he must be really good. Let him be a boy!" Jerome tried to mask his frustration.

"I spend all this time worrying about you, and now you want me to worry about him, too?"

"You volunteer for the worry part." Jerome flipped French toast on the stovetop griddle. "He's a man-child. We're different than you womenfolk. A little blood or a broken bone—that's all a part of the package."

"Well, it probably doesn't matter what I say. He's going to sneak off and do it anyway." Nicolle's body language relaxed slightly as she extended her arms.

"Thanks, Mom!" Nicolas ran into her waiting arms.

"If you end up with your elbow coming out of your shoulder, call your father. You man-children can take care of one another. I want no part of it."

"Arg, arg, arg." Jerome made the grunting sound from the television show *Home Improvement.*

Looking around the kitchen, Nicolle was pleasantly surprised at the effort Jerome had made to keep the mess manageable. She began replacing the spices in the cabinet, remaining quiet, mainly to make them think she was still mad. In reality, she knew she had to let her little men grow up. She'd been praying to God to help her worry less and trust Him more, and this must be how He was answering her prayer.

"You fellas excited about your sleepover tonight?" Jerome asked, placing the French toast on yellow floral plates.

"Oh, yeah. We're sleeping outside! They have a tree house and a really cool shed." Jordan looked happy finally to have input in the conversation. "Devin has really cool snakes and stuff, too."

"Snakes?"

Jerome eyed Nicolle, no doubt to get her to nix the overprotective mother-hen thing before she responded to the snakes remark.

"Oh, that sounds like fun," Nicolle lied.

"Can I have a snake, Daddy?" Jordan asked.

"Absolutely not!" Nicolle answered for her husband.

"Beside, Brutus would probably eat it." Jerome winked at Nicolle. "Dogs don't like snakes very much."

Nicolle pulled Christian's high chair in close as the rest of them gathered around the breakfast table. Jerome had prepared a small feast, including honey-baked ham slices, scrambled eggs, fresh orange juice, milk and coffee. The five held hands as the head of the Winters household gave God thanks for their many blessings.

Nicolle quietly closed the door to Christian's room and breathed a sigh of relief. Between shopping, gardening and playing on the jungle gym in the backyard, Nicolle didn't know who was more worn out. But right on schedule, Christian had fallen asleep. Now the night belonged to Mr. and Mrs. Jerome Neville Winters.

Whistling a tune Nicolle didn't recognize, Jerome climbed the stairs, holding a tray of chocolate-covered strawberries and a bottle of champagne. "Hey, baby. He asleep?" He nodded his head toward Christian's room.

"Oh, yeah. I made sure of it. I don't want him needing anything tonight. I've got a date with this foine brotha." She stepped close and ran her fingers down his chest. "I heard this man has sexy on lockdown . . . tall, not so dark and gorgeously bald!"

"Girl, see, you keep talking like that, and this romantic planning will go to waste." He leaned down and gently licked her lips.

"Hmmmm." Nicolle wanted to put her arms around him and kiss him long and deep, but the tray usurped her efforts. "Whatcha got there? They look wonderful. Where in the world did you find those huge strawberries?"

"I'd tell you, but then I'd have to kill you."

She reached for the biggest, reddest one, only to have Jerome playfully raise the tray out of reach. "Dang," she said playfully. "I don't want to know that bad!"

"Come with me."

"And where are you taking me?"

Nicolle slipped her arm through Jerome's offered arm, and they headed toward the closed double doors that led to their private paradise.

Jerome's strong arms made Nicolle feel indomitable. Nothing or no one could touch her with her black man to protect her. As they stood before the doors, Nicolle looked up at Jerome with wide-eyed anticipation. "Well?"

"Open the door."

All the ten hours of anticipation in no way prepared her for what she saw when she opened the door. The room was filled with flowers and white Christmas lights. Rose petals were tossed about the room. The covers had been turned down, and a bed tray filled with cheese, crackers and grapes sat in the middle of the bed. The soft lights in the bedroom were warm and inviting.

Nicolle turned to Jerome with moist eyes. "Jerome, if I weren't speechless, I'd say something really witty. Honey, this room looks so wonderful. You set such a mood—without lighting one candle!"

"Your face says it all, but you know Fire Marshall Bill isn't going to leave candles unattended. I'm glad you like it."

"Like it?" she said, incredulous. "Like it? I love it! You've done some really special things in the past, but I'd have to say that considering there aren't any carats involved, this has to be in the top three."

"You're so silly." Extending his arm again, Jerome smiled. "Come, my sweet."

As Nicolle drew closer to the bed, she saw a beautiful satin nightgown, a card sitting on top of it. She turned to Jerome, who looked surprised. "I wonder how that got there?"

She kissed him again and ran to retrieve the envelope. Ripping into it like a three-year-old at Christmas, she read:

My Dearest Nicolle,
You bring me . . .
. . . Spring in winter
. . . Christmas in July
. . . A cool breeze on a sweltering day
You refresh my soul and fill me up when life has drained me. For this and all things wonder-filled you bring me, I say thank you.
Love,
Your Honey Bunny

As Nicolle raised her tear-filled eyes, she opened her mouth to speak, only to find she was tongue-tied. She slowly walked toward him, taking the tray and champagne and placing them on the bed. Then she very slowly and deliberately pulled him into her. As he bent to kiss her, she felt lost, swept away to another land. As his lips met hers, an electrical current surged through her body.

Their kiss was long and deep. His tongue searched her mouth with the urgency of a shopaholic at a clearance sale. She folded into him, as his arms seemed to encircle her twice. They both moaned softly. Like a man sitting at the Thanksgiving dinner table who hadn't eaten for two weeks, Jerome tried to consume all of her.

"Oh, baby."

"Shhhhh." Jerome sat her on the edge of the leather-covered chaise lounge, kissing her lips, ears and neck. He bent to untie her walking shoes. He slowly removed each shoe, then her socks. He gently massaged the arch of her foot with his fist. As he worked toward the ball of her foot he felt her relax. He gently massaged each toe, kissing them lightly.

"Promise me something," Nicolle managed weakly.

"What's that?"

"You'll never stop."

Jerome laughed. "How about if I stop to do this?" Pushing her back onto the chaise, he raised her sweatshirt and kissed her stomach with tiny kisses, working his way from her left hip to the right one in a triangular motion.

As he worked his magic with his lips he slowly removed her clothes. Small whimpers managed to escape periodically from her. As he undressed her he covered every centimeter of her with kisses. Jerome replaced his lips with his hands as he softly and methodically touched his wife's beautiful body.

Nicolle opened her eyes to find Jerome standing over her, also naked. She opened her mouth to speak, but he covered it with his own. He devoured her as he laid his body on top of hers.

In her head she wanted to protest that she wanted to shower first, but she couldn't form the words. Lost in his own passion, Jerome slipped his long arms around her waist to bring her closer to him. Time stood still as the very walls seemed to scream in ecstasy. Melodies filled the air around them. The room fixtures broke into a sweat as they looked on. As eternity and a split second collided in Nicolle's mind, a rapturous explosion began at her equator and slowly spread in the four directions of the wind. Colored lights flickered in Nicolle's head as she tried to hold on to reality. She lost her battle as she slipped into a wave of euphoric semiconsciousness.

Jerome removed the bottle of champagne from the ice bucket that sat on the floor next to the tub. "More champagne?"

"Absolutely." Nicolle passed Jerome her flute.

While pouring, Jerome began, "You know, I don't think I've ever seen you look this beautiful. The candles make you glow."

"That ain't hardly the candles—that's you! Folks in church are going to need sunglasses tomorrow."

"Say that!" Jerome passed her the full champagne flute. "You know, this is not how it was supposed to happen. The plan was to wine you, romance you, dance you and then . . ."

"Well, you know, we can pretend it never happened and start over."

"I love the way you think."

Nicolle gazed into Jerome's expressive eyes. She loved so much about this man. "Oh, yeah? Why don't you tell me something good?" She smiled as she tried to remember when they started the tell-me-something-good game. They normally played just before drifting off into dreamland. It was a very pleasant way to remind each other just how special they were.

"Why don't you turn around and come lay in a brotha's arms."

Jerome repositioned himself as Nicolle turned to sit next to him. "Now let me think. Tell you something good, hmm. I guess you don't want to know how good your stuff is, huh?"

Nicolle playfully splashed water on him. "I already know that! Got a brotha babbling like a brook."

"Oh, listen atcha! Think ya all that!"

"Because I am!"

"That you are, Babe-ski! The good thing for today is I love the way you love our boys. You show them what a good woman is supposed to be and a girl is going to have to come so correct to win their love. They have the perfect example of good black womanhood in you. You're making my job so easy when I sit down to have *that* talk with them." Jerome kissed her forehead. "Now your turn."

"Wow. I never thought about taking care of our sons as preparing them to pick a woman in the future. But I know you're right, because my daddy was certainly the benchmark for all other men. But I guess you never even gave anyone else a shadow of a chance. You've loved me my whole life. First you were my buddy and then you became my friend. And you're my friend first. Always encouraging me to take it just one step further. Not just in my professional aspiration, but also in everything I do. You love me the way I am, in spite of overreactions and my overprotective nature."

Nicolle passed Jerome her champagne glass and turned to kiss him at the same time. He placed both glasses on the floor and pulled her on top of him. There was going to be lots of water to mop up.

16

"Good morning, Chief. This is Frederickson. I need to know what you plan to do about our situation. I'm sure you've heard my message by now that someone killed Casper."

"Yes, I heard your message on Friday." Chief Marlborough paused. "Lloyd, I need you to remain calm. I think this is a prankster who is getting a little carried away. I honestly don't believe anyone within the department is responsible for this."

"A little carried away?" Lloyd yelled into the phone. "If this is someone outside the department, how do you explain the access?"

"That's a bit of a conundrum, but I just can't see one of our people being responsible for such senseless acts." Chief Marlborough spoke slowly as if trying to placate Lloyd. "I'm going to talk to Internal Affairs and see where they want to go with this. I just don't want you doing anything rash before we've had a chance to sort all this out. Do you understand what I'm saying to you?"

Lloyd began gritting his teeth, feeling constriction in his chest. He understood perfectly that he was about to tip the wagon upon which the good ole boys rode. "Please define 'rash.' " His words were well measured.

"Frederickson, don't go getting that black organization you belong to involved. Let us handle this. I can almost guarantee you that this isn't racially motivated. If you get your people involved, then that NAACP organization will be breathing down our necks. The important thing is we'll wind up spending all our resources dealing with PR, instead of dealing with the troublemakers directly to get to the bottom of this thing."

"Chief, why do I get the feeling you're trying to sweep this out the back door?" Lloyd struggled to rein in his rage.

"No such thing. I just need more time for our people to investigate these little incidents. I need your assurance that you'll let my office handle this, and I don't feel like I have that."

"That's because you don't. I can't promise you that I won't get my people involved. You see, my primary concern is the safety of my crew. After these last few 'little incidents,' I just won't take any chances. You should know that I've contacted the Stentorians' lawyer. I plan to retain her services, and I'll be speaking with her today."

"You're jumping the gun, Lloyd. Come back to my office, and we'll come up with a plan. You don't need to get a lawyer involved. Besides, the D.A.'s office would handle this once we catch whoever is responsible."

"I'm not so sure the D.A. will pick up this case, but our Ms. Sanders is a civil rights attorney." Even over the phone, Lloyd could feel the chief flush as he sucked in twice the air his lungs could hold.

After a long pause the chief finally said slowly, "I'd really advise against that. There's no need. I promise you—my people will handle it. You're wasting money."

If this weren't such a serious matter, Lloyd would have thought it was humorous. Shouldn't it be "our" people? After all, they worked for the same fire department, on the same team. "Chief, I think that if we both work toward a common goal, then we'll meet somewhere in the middle." Suddenly a wave of satisfaction washed over him.

"Very well. I need to see you in my office this afternoon. I want to give you an update on my plan to resolve this unfortunate matter. I also want to tell you how sorry I am about Casper. I know you all loved him." Humility didn't become the chief.

"Thank you, Chief. *She* will be missed. What time this afternoon? I'd like to meet with Ms. Sanders first." Lloyd dug his heels in. "I think it'll be important to share our strategy with you as well."

Clearly exasperated, Chief Marlborough sighed. "Three o'clock."

"See you then." It was difficult to shroud his fleeting pleasure.

Jerome stood in the doorway of Lloyd's office, listening to the entire conversation. As Lloyd hung up the phone, Jerome began to applaud slowly. "At least you stood your ground. We'll see what Glynda has to say about all this. I surely hope she has some ideas."

"Me, too. Do you have a minute?" Lloyd motioned for Jerome to close the door.

"Until the bell rings. Why? What's up?"

Lloyd looked down at his hands and wondered if he should lighten his burden by sharing with his friend. Though he encouraged others to lean on him, he found it more than a little difficult to reciprocate.

"So, what's up, Cap? I know you're not letting the brass get to you?" Jerome took a seat as he searched his best friend's face for a clue. "Somehow I feel this is a little more important to you."

"Believe it or not, there are a few things more important than this job." He smiled wryly. "Although Nellie doesn't seem to think so."

"Uh-oh. What you do? I know that look. I've worn it a time or two myself." Jerome tried to break the tension with levity. He'd never seen his friend so serious.

Without looking up Lloyd slowly said, "She wants a divorce."

"What?"

"You heard me. She asked me for a divorce. Told me I have never been there for her and the kids and all I ever did was write checks. Can you imagine?"

Pondering the correct response, Jerome was slow to speak. "Man, by all counts you seem like a good husband and father. You work your ass off, that's for sure. You have a beautiful home, nice cars, and college-educated children. I don't know what to say."

"How do you think I felt?" Lloyd shook his head as he stared at his hands. "All of a sudden, a curveball is thrown at my crystal palace, and all is shattered."

"What did you say?" Jerome watched his friend closely. "Are you going to give her a divorce?"

"Hell, no! I'm not going to let thirty years of my life just pack its bags and waltz out the front door."

"Well, I don't want to be the one to break it down for you like this, but if she wants to leave, you really can't stop her." Jerome muttered. "Man, I can't believe this. The Fredericksons? I'd believe almost any other couple, but not y'all."

"We haven't broken up yet. We talked a lot over the weekend, and we agreed to get some counseling. She was talking about stuff I did—or I guess I should say *didn't* do—twenty years ago." He looked up, his face a mixture of sorrow and confusion. "That's what I don't get. Why wouldn't she say anything before now? Here I am, going along thinking all is right with the world. How's a brotha supposed to play a game if he doesn't know the rules?" Their eyes met, and both men laughed. Sobering quickly, Lloyd looked back at his hands. "I don't feel like laughing. This is so not funny."

"It's funny when you talk about knowing the rules when it comes to dealing with women. You know, as soon as you think you know the rules, they have some big conference or Oprah, the high priestess of Queendom, speaks, and all the laws change for us humble servants."

"I'm just mad," Lloyd said. "I feel like nothing is within my control anymore. We got this madness going on here, and then I go home to invite my wife on a romantic weekend, and instead of packing a bag, she offers to send *me* packing!"

"Are you going to move out?" Jerome asked, surprised.

"Man, what do you think? With all the blood, sweat and money I've put into that place? If she wants out, she can move. I'm not going anywhere." Lloyd was quiet for a moment and then said, "I sure hate to bring this to you, Jerome. I mean, I'm the one *you* come to with problems."

"Now, don't you think it's time I paid you back?"

"Paying it forward works a whole lot better for me!"

"Just know I'm here for you, no matter what it is you need."

Jerome couldn't shake his sense of helplessness in the face of his friend's vulnerability. Both men fell silent, not knowing what to say next.

A knock interrupted their thoughts. "Enter," Lloyd said, his voice sounding aggravated.

It was Hernandez. "Sorry to intrude, but Glynda Naylor-Sanders is on line three. I kinda figured you wanted to talk to her," Mychel said with a spitfire attitude. "Should I take a message or what?"

"No, no. I'll take it."

Not closing the door behind her, Mychel mumbled something in Spanish, and Jerome and Lloyd exchanged a glance. The woman was a force to be reckoned with.

Lloyd stood up. "I'm going to take this call. We'll talk more later?" As Jerome rose to leave Lloyd added, "This is between us. Okay?"

"Man, you know I'm not going to breathe a word." Jerome was almost offended his old buddy'd had to ask.

"Including Nicolle." Lloyd gave him a level stare.

Feeling stunned, Jerome managed, "Oh." How was he going to be able to keep this from his wife? They had no secrets from each other. What was he going to tell her when and if the news became public? She wasn't going to be a happy camper, and when she was unhappy, the campgrounds were not a place you wanted to be.

"Let me just work through some of this," Lloyd said. "I know you and your wife have an open policy of communication, but do me— and yourself—a favor, and ask her point-blank if she's happy. Don't assume you are ringing her chimes when all the time the bell tower is crumbling." The look on his face was downright sorrowful.

Jerome chuckled. "If you knew the weekend we had, you wouldn't even have to ask! It was like we were newlyweds again. She's happy, trust me!"

"I thought that, too." Lloyd lifted his chin at Jerome, a gesture the younger man took to mean that he should look further into his own house. "I shouldn't keep Glynda waiting any longer. I'll catch up with you later."

As Jerome left the office, he collided with Mychel, who stood just beyond view outside of Lloyd's office. "Oh, sorry," he said. "What are you doing here? Are you eavesdropping?"

"Why? Is there something I shouldn't know?" Mychel was good at avoiding an answer.

"You know, it's rude to listen in on private conversations. But whatever you heard needs to stay between us. Is that clear?"

"I only heard that you and the Mrs. are blissfully happy." Mychel tilted his chin with the tip of her index finger. "Let me know if you ever want to add a little salsa to that burrito."

Stupefied, Jerome stared after Mychel, watching her shapely behind challenge the seams in her standard-issue uniform pants. Why wouldn't she let it rest? Everyone, especially Mychel Hernandez, knew that Jerome Winters was a one-woman man—he was actually stymied by any man who could handle more than one woman at a time. Nicolle was a full-time job—with mandatory overtime.

17

"Wow, you look wonderful!" Lloyd rose as Glynda approached. "Life is really treating you well!" They were at the Stentorians building, where they had agreed to meet when they'd spoken on the phone earlier that day.

"Oh, aren't you sweet, Mr. Frederickson." Glynda hugged him warmly.

"Will we be hearing the pitter-patter of little feet soon?"

"Oh, not you, too! Everyone keeps badgering us. They actually thought I was pregnant when Daddy died, especially when we got married so quickly. They were all so disappointed, but we're just taking our time. Maybe in a couple of years." She shrugged her shoulders, smiling.

"Why don't we have a seat in here?" Lloyd opened the door to a small room dominated by an eight-foot conference table. The Stentorians building had been converted from an old firehouse, the modest structure rich in the history of the struggle of the African-American firefighter in Los Angeles. You could almost feel the reverence upon entering the building.

Lloyd pulled the plush chair out, offering Glynda a seat. As she sank into the comfortable chair, she looked into Lloyd's eyes. "How are you doing? You look wonderful, too. Mrs. F. had better watch out—you're just so foine!" she teased.

Glynda's words were kind, but they stung like an angry wasp as he wished Nellie felt the same. Recovering slowly, Lloyd sat opposite her, managing to say, "I'm doing okay. All this madness at the station has everyone on edge." He took a deep breath. "I'm going to cut to the chase. What can we do? We have no proof. But as sure as

I'm George and Sally's second oldest, this is some Confederate-flag-flying, Adolph-Hitler-worshippin', Dr.-Martin-Luther-King,-Jr.-hatin', wannabe cross-burnin' individual—or group."

"Well, Mr. Frederickson—I mean, Lloyd—you shouldn't hold back like that. Let me know how you really feel." She winked.

Glynda managed to draw a laugh from him. He felt more relaxed already.

"So, Lloyd, tell me exactly what happened when you met with the chief."

"He was patronizing, at best. He tried to tell me he would 'handle it,' said he's putting 'his people' on it to investigate." Lloyd's tone was harsh as his voice rose. "In other words, he said nothing more than what he'd already told me on the phone. I would have been less frustrated had I not gone."

Glynda gave him a sympathetic smile.

Lloyd sat back in his chair, trying to calm himself. "I'm sorry, but I just get so riled up about this. We've covered all the incidents here in these reports." Lloyd passed Glynda a stack of papers more than an inch thick. "There's been nothing since we buried old Casper, but it hasn't been that long, either. I just don't know if it'll end or get worse. And to add a little alcohol to the gaping wound, headquarters wants to keep it quiet. They advised me against meeting with you, told me not to waste my resources. Chief said they'd handle it. So far, I haven't seen them handle anything. They've managed to alienate my shift—they don't trust HQ, and I'm beginning to wonder if they even trust me."

Glynda reached across the table, touching Lloyd's hand reassuringly. "I can almost guarantee you have the same respect and trust you've always had. I'll read these over." She patted the papers. "But I don't need to tell you that in order to make a case, we need evidence. We need to show cause that someone's civil rights have been violated. Although we have proof these things have occurred, we need to show the actions were meant to harm you because you're black." Her tone was straightforward, and she stared at him levelly as she spoke.

"Why doesn't anything happen on A or B Shift?" Lloyd's voice rose as he became upset once more. "I can tell you why—because they're white. You know, someone from one of those shifts might even be responsible for all this! It may be a team of them conspiring against us. But why?"

"I wish I had an answer for you," Glynda said, sounding as though she really meant it. "But I don't. I do know, however, that it's my job to seek justice, and I do that with everything within me!"

Calming slightly, Lloyd sat back in the mid-back chair. "What can you do to help us?"

"The first thing I'll do is read these reports and see if there are any patterns. I'll also start to interview the folks on C Shift. I'm going to contact Chief Marlborough to see where he stands, what he plans to do, and then you and I will sit down and plan a strategy, blueprint the steps to file our formal complaint."

A wave of relief washed over him. He finally felt as though he had some hope. "Glynda, thank you. I've felt so alone, with several sets of eyes looking to me for answers. I had none and still don't, but I know you'll help me get to the bottom of this."

"Has the D.A. gotten involved at all?"

"No. Though we reported Casper's death. It went no further than a police report. Chief wants to handle it with Internal Affairs. I think it's a major cover-up. Instead of FUBU—For Us, By Us— we're dealing with TYBY—Teach You by Beating You."

Glynda burst out laughing. "Now, that's funny! Together, we're going to seek justice, I can promise you that. It's what I'm building my reputation on."

"Eddie Naylor would have been so proud." Lloyd squeezed her hand. He knew how important the memory of her father was to Glynda.

Lloyd's words seized something deep inside Glynda and held it captive for what seemed like hours. "I think he would be proud, too, Lloyd." Although her eyes shone with unshed tears, she smiled.

"You know, you should visit the Black Firefighter Museum down on Central. That way you can see firsthand the struggle."

"You've told me about that before. I'd love to go! Will you be my tour guide?"

"It would be my honor," Lloyd said. "I have to warn you, though—you're going to be touched by what you see. Those who went before me suffered greatly to serve this community."

"Did they only go on calls to black neighborhoods?"

"Not hardly!" Lloyd scoffed. "You know they have no problem taking from us—it's giving to us that presents the challenge. But we don't have to go very far back in time to see people who refused rescue service from black paramedics."

Glynda shook her head, looking troubled. "People having a heart attack will refuse treatment because the rescuer is black?"

"Those who are truly sick never refuse treatment. You could be Osama bin Laden, and they would welcome you with open arms. But those who have options sometimes opt to be helped by those who look like them." Lloyd sighed.

"What an insult. Do people ever get mad at you because you weren't able to save their loved ones? You know, blame you?"

"Oh, heck yeah! All the time. But that's more an 'I've gotta blame somebody' issue than a black one.

"My fore-brothers and -sisters have suffered greatly so that I can sit here with these bars on my shoulders," Lloyd continued. "I don't ever want to take their sacrifices for granted."

"But, Lloyd," Glynda said, "you only ever talk about what is so wrong with your job. You've been doing this almost as long as I've been living—there has to be an upside."

"Oh, Miss Glynda, the first time you hold a baby in your arms that is less than a minute old, with ten fingers and ten toes, whose cries make a fire engine sound like a ringing phone, that's heaven. Or the young woman who might end up paralyzed had you not gotten her out of the mangled ruins of her sports car in time. That's all the reward I need. Sometimes just a 'thank you' from a mother whose baby was choking reminds me that there's no better job on earth." Lloyd smiled, feeling a surge of warmth as he began to believe in his own words again.

"But I guess all this B.S. gets in the way of what's really important, huh?"

"Exactly!"

"Do you have any suspicions about who's behind all of this?"

Dropping his head, Lloyd quietly said, "No."

"Llooooyd?" Glynda searched for his eyes. "Are you not telling me something? I can't help you if you keep things from me."

"No, Glynda, I swear to you I've told you all that I know, which is zilch. Nada. Nothing. I'm so ashamed that this is happening under my watch."

"This is not your fault!" Glynda said. "You can't control the actions of another person. You should know that better than anyone. Do you think this is aimed at you personally?"

"I honest to God don't know. Sometimes I wonder. This is all so senseless."

"In the mind of a crazy person, all is rational." Glynda tried to ease his guilt. "This is the work of a sick mind, one that gets off on the suffering—mental or physical—of others."

She sat back, her voice taking on a brisk, take-charge note. "So, let's not waste any energy on self-pity. You have nothing to be ashamed of—actually, quite the opposite. Instead of sitting by, waiting for the powers that be to handle this, you've made the decision to get to the bottom of the matter on your own."

Lloyd's eyes locked on to Glynda's, and he smiled slightly. "Let's kick some ass!"

"Now that's what I'm talkin' 'bout!"

18

"Oh, I'm sorry. I didn't mean to get so close," Mychel said coyly after her breast grazed Jerome's back.

Jerome didn't like where this was going, yet once again he let the advance go unchecked. "No problem."

Jerome and Mychel had been assigned to clean the equipment bay. All things being equal, it was Mychel's turn to mop.

"I like days like this, when we get a chance to just kick back and hang out together." Mychel ran water in the industrial-size bucket.

"This ain't hardly hanging out," Jerome said, feeling slightly surprised. "You slinging a mop, and me emptying trash cans?"

"Yeah, but I get to spend time one-on-one with you. It's great working with everyone—well, maybe with the possible exception of St. Vincent—but you're different. You're kinda special. Know what I mean?"

There was no denying it this time. Mychel was getting her flirt on.

Jerome thought carefully before speaking. "I hope you're not suggesting anything besides a professional relationship, Hernandez. I have the utmost respect for you professionally, and you're a spirited woman, which I like about you. But make no mistake about it—I'm married. Been married half my life, and sho' nuff happy about it. I love Nicolle and would wrestle a polar bear in a snowstorm for her, so even the thought of hurting her doesn't enter my mind."

"I've seen you look at me, especially when I work out. You know you like this tight body," Mychel responded suggestively.

"Woman, you're trippin'." He couldn't believe she didn't get it, even when he spelled it out for her.

"Am I?"

"I'm committed, not confined," Jerome said. "You're beautiful, and yes, your body is kickin'. Some man would be very fortunate to have you—but not me. Don't do this, Mychel. I like working with you. If you try to change the dynamics of our relationship, everything will get uncomfortable. Don't get me wrong—I'm flattered—but I ain't the one."

She snorted. "You know what? You're not all that good. No man is. There's never been a man I wanted that I couldn't get. I even had a priest! So don't underestimate me."

Jerome's amusement began to turn to anger. "There's nothing to estimate, Mychel. I've known for a while that you've been flirting with me, but I chose to ignore it. Please don't make this a difficult situation. What you're doing is sexual harassment."

Mychel threw her head back, laughing. "Puh-leeze. Who in the hell would believe you? You'd be the laughingstock of 27. No, let's make that of the whole department. I know I'm hot, and so do you. I want you, and I always get what I want. I have nothing but time, Jerome. We'll see who gives in first."

Staring at Mychel in disbelief, Jerome shook his head. "You're deluding yourself. This is where we work. Why would you want to bring this kind of pressure here? We have to live together ten days a month. I don't want to have to start avoiding you. Please, Hernandez, rethink this."

"I want you, Jerome. Case closed."

The fire bell rang.

19

"Gurl, you need to come out for a visit. All you do is work, work, work." Glynda sat on the expansive patio of her Quartz Hill home, which was nestled snugly in the Antelope Valley, enjoying her weekly phone conversation with her sister Dawn. "You haven't even seen our new home. You'll love this kitchen."

Glynda adored the new house she and Anthony had purchased a year after they'd been married. They discussed, rather heatedly at times, that she needed to move back to Los Angeles, but Glynda had grown to love the desert life. Though she worked in Los Angeles, she was able to take the train to work, and the firm provided a car for off-site meetings. Shortly after they were married, Anthony had begun working for Edwards Air Force Base, and everything had just fallen into place for the newlyweds.

Since her father's sudden death she had tried, but failed miserably, to mend the broken fences with her two older siblings. Her phone conversations with Dawn seemed to be the only ties that bound her to the life she'd once known. A full reconciliation didn't appear to be possible, so Glynda wanted to persuade her youngest sister to come west.

"I don't know. I haven't been on a plane since nine-eleven." Dawn lay in bed with the twenty-five-inch television on mute in her cozy home in Baltimore.

"Gurl, you sound so old-fashioned. Remember what Aunt Ida Mae always says, 'God ain't gotta getcha in no airplane to take you home.' But funny how she never flies, huh?"

"I know, that's correct. We had to delay Daddy's funeral for a day until she could get there on the Greyhound." Dawn stifled her laughter. "I do need a vacation. Maybe we could all come out to visit you."

"See, you're so far to the left you can't even see right. You know good and well if Renee and Collette came to California, we'd have to have a restraining order placed on me within seventy-two hours. I've tried to get along with them I swear . . ."

"I know. But they're even wearing *me* a little thin these days. All Collette talks about is how she's turned the two hundred fifty grand Daddy left her into over a million in less than three years." Dawn sipped from her glass of white zinfandel and propped herself up on two more pillows.

"Renee isn't quite so bad, but she just takes everything that Collette aka Evileen says as gospel. They still don't talk to Nina—she called me last week." Glynda enjoyed a cold glass of lemonade as she watched the sunset and dished the dirt to Dawn on the latest installment of drama in her new, but oldest, half sister's life. "She's having trouble with Edwina acting out in school. She just needed to talk, so of course I focused on her every word like I hadn't heard it all before. I wanted to tell her she needed to put some heat to her child's behind. You can tell Daddy didn't have much to do with her growing up."

"Gurl, you know that's right. Eddie Naylor did not play! What's going on with her in school?"

"Apparently, she's been cutting class and running with this man. Nina is fit to be tied. Victor has threatened to go to the police, but they don't have proof they've actually had sex. I felt sorry for her. She's going to be in L.A. in three weeks, and she's going to spend the weekend before and after the conference with us."

"She invited Devin and me out to St. Louis for a visit. I really am considering going. I like her a lot." Dawn paused. "What do you think about Daddy keeping her a secret all those years? I mean, honestly. This is just you and me talking now."

"At first I was hurt," Glynda said. "How could he have another daughter? It was hard enough sharing him with you all. But as time went on, and I got to know her a little better, I became angry. I feel cheated out of a lifetime with her. She has more of Daddy's personality than any of us." Glynda sighed deeply. "What about you?"

"I guess I feel the same. I've grown to love her and that wonderful husband very much. She's been here to Baltimore three times in the last year. Each time we got to know each other just a little better. The last time she was here we went to the cemetery together. The hardest part is dealing with Renee and Collette's reaction when I tell them she'll be in town. They act even worse than when they know you're here."

"Daddy would be so disappointed in us. The thing he worked hardest to preserve was buried with him. What does Uncle Thomas say about all of this?" Glynda smiled as she refilled her glass thinking of her father's only brother.

"You know Uncle Thomas. He just goes with the flow. Oh, but did I forget to tell you that he has been in touch with Thomas Junior? Seems like their mother is real sick and wants to make things right before she passes on. He's going to Anchorage in a few weeks. He's so nervous about the whole thing, but I assured him it would be all right."

"Talk about some lost years. How long has it been since he's seen them?"

"I don't even know, but at least twenty. I can't imagine denying Devin's triflin' daddy visitation if he wanted it. A boy needs his daddy. Victor calls to talks to him all the time, which I think is so sweet."

"Oh, that *is* great. I think Nina, Renee and I have found our own little piece of Edward Naylor. Our husbands are the best of the best." Glynda immediately regretted her statement. Her youngest, most sincere and loving sister was as lucky at love as Elizabeth Taylor. She'd hit at, but mostly missed Mr. Right all her adult life. Without meaning to do so she had just cut her sister very deep.

With a mark of sadness in her voice Dawn responded, "The three of you hit the jackpot for sure. I guess Collette and I are destined to be alone. But at least I like myself and know that I'm good company. Collette can't even stand to be in the same room with herself."

"Ain't that the truth." Like a bolt of lightning an idea struck Glynda. "You know, I've been doing some work with the firefighters here. Got a real interesting case going on. They have a lot of social events—you should come out, and I'll take you to one of them. There're some real good single brothas working for the Los Angeles City and County Fire Departments!"

"Gurl, I don't know. I'd have to get on a plane to get there, and what about Devin?"

"Stop making excuses and start making reservations. Bring him with you. My neighbors have boys his age. Let me get a schedule of event dates and we'll start making plans. I'll even take a few days off. What do you say?"

"You know you're right. I have almost six weeks vacation, and as much as I love my job I could use some time to take care of Dawn for a change. And you know what?"

"What's that, my baby sis?"

"I'm going to leave Devin here with Renee. She is always telling me to do just that. How does nine days sound?"

"Ahhhhhh suki, suki now! Oh, I'm too excited. You'll have the time of your life."

"I love talking to you, Glynda. Why are two of us rational and two of us totally outrageous?"

"Which ones are we?"

Dawn laughed. "Lord, please say the rational ones."

"Beats me. But we're going to work with what we have. I'm going to get a move on. Anthony should be home any minute. I'll call you from the office tomorrow. Love you. Good night."

"I love you, too. And Glynda?"

"Yes?"

"Thanks."

"What on earth for?"

"Just being you."

"Now you're being outrageous. I'll check with you tomorrow. I'll have dates and will have our travel department check on fares."

The sisters broke the connection, both smiling. Glynda's mind raced while cataloging blind date possibilities for her sister. She'd solicit Anthony's help. He had lots of single successful friends. The excitement almost made her giddy.

Pouring another glass of lemonade, she decided to enjoy the rest of the high-desert evening while she waited for Anthony to arrive by reading through the incident reports she'd received from Lloyd.

The patio ran along the entire backside of the fifty-five-hundred-square-foot dwelling. Faux and real French doors created the illusion that the young couple lived in a glass house. She walked the twenty feet to the office doors and entered. She loved the view from this space and had known the moment she'd stepped into the model that she'd make this room her office. She and Anthony had plans to install a pool and Jacuzzi, but for now she enjoyed looking at the lush grass and beautiful plants along the perimeter of their half-acre lot.

She sighed. As beautiful as the view from her office was, it didn't compare to sitting on the patio with the warm desert breeze kissing her cheeks. She gathered the documents and returned to her outdoor sanctum.

She didn't realize she'd been reading for more than an hour until the hum of the garage door announced Anthony's arrival. She put her work aside and ran through the kitchen to the garage to greet him.

Her husband's smile broadened at the sight of his beautiful wife waiting for him with outstretched arms. "Hey, baby! Come here and give your lover man some sugar."

With three short steps, Glynda was in his arms, and they exchanged a warm and passionate kiss. "How are you? You look tired."

"You've renewed my strength." Anthony kissed her again.

"I miss you when I'm in this big ole house alone."

"Girl, you don't have to tell me. You were gone all last week, remember?"

"I guess you do know a little something about that. I've got a glass chilling for a beer. Want one? Dinner is all set. Just let me know when you're ready."

"Yes on the beer. Give me a minute to get as comfortable as you, and we can have dinner on the patio." Anthony kissed her cheek firmly.

"What a great idea. I'll set the table while you change." Glynda spanked him on the behind on her way to the kitchen.

"You betta watch out," Anthony called after her. "Dinner's going to have to wait if you keep that up."

"Like I would be mad!" Glynda smiled slyly.

"Back in a few."

Glynda's heart sang the Chanté Moore and Kenny Lattimore

tune: *I love you from your head to your toes because I was made to love you.* She thought back to the day of her daddy's funeral, when she'd felt so alone and lost. Out of the corner of her eye, she'd seen Anthony, dressed in combat fatigues, running up the aisle toward her. Despite the military rules that had prohibited him from attending the services, he'd found a way. She'd known at that moment that she should be Mrs. Anthony Sanders.

As she moved the place settings from the kitchen table to the patio, Anthony approached her from behind and slipped his arms around her waist, kissing her on the back of her neck—one of her many erogenous zones. "Need some help?"

"Grab the salad, and we'll be all set. I'm starving."

On his way to the kitchen he said, "Me, too, but let's eat first."

"You're so bad!"

He came back out with the salad. "Thank you very much!" They both laughed as they sat at the round, glass-topped patio table. The citronella candles cast a glow on Anthony's beautiful face as he bowed his head to say grace. He took Glynda's hand and began, "Bless, oh Lord, this food for our use and us to Thy service for Christ's sake."

They both said, "Amen."

Anthony kissed her hand before letting go. "Anything exciting happening in your camp today?"

Between bites, Glynda managed to say, "Just getting back into the swing of things after being out of the office all week. I met with LAFD Captain Lloyd Frederickson today, and I was just reading the incident reports he gave me before you got home. Speaking of the fire department, I've asked Dawn to come for a visit."

"That would be really nice. She's my favorite sister-in-law."

"What do you mean—it's not Collette?" Glynda laughed so heartily that she began choking, thinking of her second-oldest sister's cantankerous disposition.

"See, God don't like ugly." Anthony patted her on the back.

Still laughing and coughing, Glynda said, "I'm sorry, but I couldn't resist. Anyway, I want you to help me to fix Dawn up with someone while she's here."

"No can do."

Glynda stared at her husband in disbelief. "What?"

"You heard me. I'm not going to be the one who introduced her to Tyrone, and it don't work out, and then I'll be in the doghouse with not one but two Naylor women. Oh, hell no!" He shook his head for emphasis.

"You didn't even think about it," Glynda protested. "No one will blame you if things don't work. What about your brother? You know she has a thing for him."

"There is nothing to consider," Anthony said. "John is just playing the field. He hasn't been in a serious relationship in, like, three years. My brother is a good guy, but he's not ready to be *fixed* up. And I know women—a good date or two, and you're picking out wedding colors. For the last time, woman, no!"

"Now, that's not fair," Glynda said, pretending to pout. "You asked me to marry you twice, and I said no. Every woman is not looking to march down the aisle. Dawn just wants to have a good time. She needs to let her hair down."

"I agree, but I won't be an accomplice to your little scheme. I bet Dawn doesn't even know you're doing this, does she?"

Blinking her eyes rapidly, Glynda knew she had been called out. "I just told her I'd show her a good time, but she knows I'm going to try to hook her up."

He slapped his thigh. "I was right! She has no clue what you're cooking up. Well, you're on your own. You have lots of male friends and associates. Hook her up with one of your lawyer friends."

Glynda sighed, then brightened up. "I know, I'll get Mr. Frederickson to introduce her to some of the single firefighters. That's it! That'll work, and I don't need your ole stinky help."

Filling his mouth with chicken breast, Anthony smiled and said, "Remember, you heard it here first. If love is blind, then blind dates will make your vision twenty-twenty."

She playfully hit him with her napkin and smiled. "We'll just see about that!"

20

As the C Shift left Station 27, the crew was in good spirits. For the first time in a very long time, they'd had a light shift, with only three rescues in twenty-four hours. Considering all that had transpired over the past several weeks, C Shift was long overdue for an easy night.

Most of the shift had gathered in the parking lot to leave, when Mychel passed Jerome from behind, sliding her hand across his tight-as-an-NBA-basketball butt. Jerome jumped involuntarily.

"What's wrong, son?" Lloyd asked.

Searching for a good lie, Jerome paused and then said, "I had a little muscle spasm, I guess. I wasn't quite sure what it was."

From behind Lloyd, Mychel winked. Quickly averting his eyes, Jerome looked at the ground.

Lloyd noticed the suspicious behavior and turned to look at Mychel. "Is there something going on here I should know about?" He looked back and forth between them, his brow furrowed. "Y'all were going at it pretty strong last night. In all the years we've worked together, I don't think I've ever heard the two of you argue like you did last night, and over what? None of us could even figure that one out."

"Everything is cool between us." Jerome quickly changed the subject. "We're going to meet the Stentorians president for breakfast, right? Where?"

"Roscoe's in Long Beach. Brian knows he loves some chicken and waffles." Lloyd laughed.

"I'll meet you there." Jerome headed for his vehicle without looking in Mychel's direction.

Mychel slid behind the wheel of the late-model white Mercedes CLK320 with a smile. He was weakening. She was making him uncomfortable because he was feeling something he shouldn't. She was one step closer.

Gripping the wheel tightly, Jerome headed south on the Harbor Freeway toward the Vincent Thomas Bridge. Why did Mychel make him so uneasy? Women made passes at him all the time. While it was flattering, he always laughed it off. Mychel made him nervous perhaps because he had to work, live, eat and sleep near her ten days a month. He shook his head and tried to concentrate on the matter at hand—the C Shift Menace.

Lloyd pulled into the parking lot of the world-famous restaurant thirty seconds after Jerome did. As the two walked to the restaurant, they were quiet. After being seated, as they waited for Brian Smithworth, Lloyd pried a little. "I've known you a lot of years, Winters. I love you like a son. What I'm about to say is probably none of my business, but as your friend I have to say it. Don't get caught up in Mychel's game. I'm about to tell you something that I shouldn't—it qualifies as confidential information—but she was almost transferred out of 27 for sexual misconduct. They moved her to C Shift instead. She has a thing for married men—likes to break up homes. What's worse is that she's real good at it."

"How did you know?" Jerome was stunned. He'd been so careful to downplay Mychel's advances.

Lloyd chuckled. "I'm an old man, and some say with age comes wisdom. I've seen so much on this job. I like having women in the department, but when you start mixing estrogen and testosterone, there is sure to be an explosion somewhere."

Jerome shook his head. "I've done nothing to encourage her. In fact, I've warned her that if she didn't stop, I'd file a formal complaint. She laughed in my face. She said that all the men would laugh me right out of the department."

"Women like her don't need encouragement. Just be careful. Don't find yourself alone with her if you can help it. I won't put you on house detail together anymore."

"I appreciate that," Jerome said, feeling a little better. "How are things with you and Nellie? You're smiling a little more today."

"How do they say it? One day at a time," Lloyd said. "We've got a lot of work to do, but we both believe we can work things out. We start counseling next week."

"That's good," Jerome said neutrally. He wanted to be supportive, but he didn't want to give Lloyd the idea that he was taking sides. After all, Nellie and Nicolle were good friends. It would be best to keep things simple.

"We plan to talk some more this evening," Lloyd continued. "We're going to be fine. I canceled the anniversary party, so that pressure is off us. Once we work through our problems, we'll take a second honeymoon, maybe renew our vows. It's a bit premature, but if we do, I'd be honored to have you as my best man."

Grinning from ear to ear, Jerome slapped his back. "No, the honor would be all mine, brotha. We pray for the two of you every night, Nicolle and me. I know it's going to all work out, just because you're willing to do whatever it takes to make it happen."

Just as Lloyd was opening his mouth to respond, Brian approached the table. "Sorry I'm late. I was delayed leaving the station. How are you two this morning?"

"Good to see you, Smithworth. Doing just fine." Lloyd rose to give him a brotherly hug.

Jerome stood and extended his hand. "Doing quite well, myself. Just want to get to the bottom of this mess on C Shift."

"That's why we're here, to come up with a solid plan of action," Brian said. "I understand you met with Glynda yesterday. I haven't had a chance to speak with her, but I know you've got it under control."

"I gave her the overview and a copy of all the incident reports," Lloyd said. "She said she'd get back to us in a couple of days. She was real candid, said that in order for this to be a civil rights case, we have to find some evidence that all this is happening because our shift is all minority."

"So I guess all us black folks knowing without a shadow of a doubt isn't good enough?" Jerome toyed with the small tray holding pink, blue and white packets.

"Have you all ordered?" Brian opened his menu.

"No," Lloyd said. "We decided to wait for you." Lloyd waved to a young woman wearing skintight black jeans and a T-shirt with the

Roscoe's logo. Suddenly, the Ohio Players song "Skin Tight" rang out in his head.

"Hi. May I take your orders, please?" It didn't sound like the young woman's heart was into her work.

"I'll have a number nine with coffee." Jerome ordered first.

"Make that two," Lloyd added.

"I'll have number nine with an extra order of wings, orange juice and decaf." Brian stared at his two friends, who stared at him, and asked, "What? I'm a big man! I need fuel."

They all burst into laughter and handed the young woman their menus.

"I guess we should get down to business before the food gets here, while we still have Brian's full attention." Lloyd chuckled. "Now that we have Glynda on board, what we need to get is some hard evidence that these acts are directed at our shift because we're black."

"How do you propose we go about getting that kind of evidence?" Jerome asked. "That it hasn't happened on any other shift is not proof enough?"

The busboy brought over their beverages. "The decaf and orange juice go there," Lloyd said, pointing to Brian, and then turned his attention back to Jerome. "That was my same question, but unfortunately the answer is no. The only way to say that these incidents are racially motivated is if we were called names or something similar.

"She's very anxious to help us, but of course there's nothing she can do yet. She's reading the incident reports, hoping to find something in there that I've forgotten, but it doesn't look good for filing a civil rights violation case."

"We see this every day in our work, innocent victims having to prove they were wronged." Brian gulped the orange juice. "Justice seems so one-sided."

"There's nothing stopping us, the Stentorians, from requesting a formal investigation from headquarters." Lloyd blew on the hot coffee. "When we ask in writing for the chief to do a formal inquiry, he has no choice. If he ignores us, his lack of action will come under some heavy fire."

"I agree. I assumed that's why we're having this meeting this morning, to get the Stentorians fully involved." Brian added several packets of sugar to his coffee.

"We've got to come up with some way to draw these fools out," Jerome argued. "They're going to make a mistake, and when they do, I want to be right there to catch them in the act. I suggested hidden cameras, but Lloyd isn't interested in spending any money. I feel so helpless."

Lloyd gave him a sympathetic look.

"I wish I had some answers," Brian said. "But you know the Stentorians are behind you in whatever you decide to do. When you make the request to the chief, I want you to be sure to include the letter I'm going to write to you." He chuckled. "You know how they hate to deal with the Stentorians."

"Yeah," Lloyd said, nodding. "He told me straight up when I last met with him that it wasn't necessary to get you or Glynda involved—which of course made me know all the more that I needed to do just the opposite."

Their waitress arrived heavy-laden with a tray full of chicken and waffles. As she placed the food in front of the men, conversation ceased though their minds raced. All other business would have to wait.

21

Dashing up the eight steps on his parents' front porch, Andrew felt warmth move through him in sweet anticipation of an evening with his parents. He smiled as he thought of his mother's cooking. Antoinette always made his favorites, and he knew tonight would be no exception. As he slipped his key in the door, it opened.

"It's about time!" Antoinette stood in the doorway with her hands on her hips. "I thought I was going to have to feed your father without you. You know how he hates to wait for dinner. Why're you so late?"

"Hi, Mom. I'm doing quite well this evening, and yourself?" Andrew hugged her as he mocked her anger.

"Don't you 'hi, Mom' me," Antoinette said, hands still on her hips, refusing his embrace. "You're more than an hour late." Giving up, she hugged him warmly even as she fussed.

"I'm sorry, Mom. I didn't get to bed until late this morning, and I overslept," Andrew lied. "I should have called when I woke up." He didn't make eye contact with her as he thought back to the young woman he'd dropped off on his way to the family dinner. Though he had been in bed, he had hardly been sleeping.

"Don't just stand there. Come on in. The pot roast is turning to beef jerky," Antoinette teased.

Andrew asked hopefully, "Garlic mashed potatoes?"

"Of course, dear." Antoinette led the way to the dining room.

Jules St. Vincent entered from the kitchen, carrying a bottle of red wine. His father's steps had slowed in recent months, and Andrew wanted to ask if he was feeling well, but decided against it.

"Men don't have emotions, son" had been said to him for as long as he could remember.

"Hi, Dad. Whatcha got there?" Andrew moved around the table and shook his hand. "Sorry I'm late. Mom told me you were going to start dinner without me."

"We weren't sure if you could fit us into your social calendar," his father said archly. "This is just an inexpensive merlot I thought would complement your mother's pot roast. I've got some of the good stuff, if you want, in the wine pantry." Jules sat the bottle in the center of the twelve-foot maple table.

Without checking the label Andrew said, "This is fine, Dad. Mom, can I help you bring the food in?"

"No, just wash up so we can sit down to dinner. I have everything prepared." Antoinette disappeared into the kitchen.

"How've you been, Dad?" Andrew dug his hands into his pockets. "I didn't see you the last couple of times I was here. Mom tells me you've been politicking for the new mayoral candidate." He felt slightly on edge, which was the norm when he talked to his father.

"I've been just fine," Jules said, sounding no more comfortable than Andrew felt. "Yes, the police chief wants to throw his hat into the ring. I think he'd be good for Los Angeles. We need someone who has served this city and knows its people."

"How do you like the politics thing?"

Before Jules could answer, Antoinette entered, carrying a silver tray filled with serving dishes.

"Let me take that." Andrew rushed to help her.

"Aren't you sweet?" Antoinette released the heavy tray to Andrew, who set it on the table. "We can be seated."

"Let me wash up. I'll be right back." Andrew darted off to the small guest bathroom with the gold fixtures and cloth napkins for hand drying.

Before him was a succulent rump roast, a mound of garlic mashed potatoes, fresh green beans with onion and homemade rolls. Their crystal goblets were filled with ice tea and, as his father uncorked the wine, the three of them sat at the end of the formal dining table that was closest to the kitchen. The table had been dressed with a fine, off-white linen tablecloth and sported matching napkins, and the crystal and china gleamed in the soft lighting shining down from the chandelier overhead. The table was fit for royalty.

"As usual, Mom, you've outdone yourself. Everything looks wonderful. I'm starving!" Andrew piled food onto his plate in great measure. "What are y'all going to eat?"

Antoinette looked on admiringly. "There's plenty—please eat up. Your father hardly eats anything these days. I think he should see a doctor. He has almost no appetite."

"Don't start this again, Antoinette," Jules said as he sliced the roast. "I told you I'm fine. I've just cut back. I'm pretty hungry tonight, though, since we had to wait for more than an hour."

His father never lost an opportunity to shoot him down. Trying to remain cheerful, Andrew decided to ignore the barb. "You should be due for your annual soon, right?" He began shoveling potatoes into his mouth.

Jules shot him a chastising glance. "Yes, it should be coming up in the next few months."

Sensing the mounting tension, Antoinette struggled to defuse the situation. "So," she said brightly, "how is one of L.A. County's newest and most promising firefighters doing?"

"Everything is great," Andrew said as he cut the roast with only his fork. "I'm still waiting to knock down a big one. The rescue runs are okay, but I live for the heat, the orange beast. They treat me like a rookie, but I love this job."

With amusement in his voice, Jules interjected, "I've got a newsflash for you, son. You are a rookie! Give it some time. You'll be the front man before you know it."

Antoinette cleared her voice. "Well, it works for me. I worry about you enough, running around town in that sports car. Now that you're active, I hardly sleep at all when C Shift is working." Antoinette spooned a small portion of potatoes onto her white, gold-trimmed bone china plate.

"He's a man." Jules rested his fork on the side of the plate. Looking at his wife, he continued. "Let him be one. Cut those apron strings! He knows what the job entails, and he has chosen to meet the challenge." He took a sip of wine and patted the corners of his mouth with his linen napkin.

"Dad's right. I love this job more than I ever thought I could. It gets my blood pumping. I leap out of bed in the morning on my shift days . . . I can't explain it. But I don't want you to worry. I take great care of your baby boy." He patted his belly, which was beginning to get full.

"It's in my genes to worry," Antoinette said with a sigh. "I worried about your father, and now I'm in for another tour." Her voice brightened as if she had decided the meal was becoming too maudlin. "So, how is everything else going with you? Are you seeing anyone special?"

Jules sighed. "Let the boy be. He's too young to be serious about any one woman."

Antoinette shot her husband a reproving look. "I'd like to have some grandchildren before I die, Jules. At the rate he's going, with these women coming and going like they're in a revolving door at Bloomingdale's, that isn't going to happen."

"Whoa, you two," Andrew said, holding up his hands. "I'm not seeing anyone special, and since you're both going to live a very long time, you'll be around to see my children graduate from college. I'm just having a really good time, and I'm not ready to give that up right now. Can we please change the subject?"

Reaching for another buttered roll Jules asked, "How's everything down at the 27?"

With a slight hesitation, Andrew began, "Since you asked, we have been having a little problem. Maybe you can help."

"You know I'll do whatever I can." Their identical blue eyes locked. "What's going on?"

"There's been some strange stuff happening lately, stuff that's only happening on C Shift. First it was just annoying things, and then someone messed with our equipment, but last week someone killed the firehouse dog. Everyone thinks it's racially motivated because our shift is one hundred percent minority."

Jules gazed at his son with level eyes. "And what do you think?"

Andrew considered the question, then said, "I think it's just some nut job. At first I thought it was a woman scorned. You know I have a little experience in that department." He chuckled.

"That's where I'd put my money." Jules began waving his fork.

"This is the new millennium; our racial woes are behind us. It was a dark time in our history, but it's just that—history."

"Under what rock are you living?" Antoinette spoke up angrily. "Need I remind you about Jasper, Texas, New York City or right here, in our own backyard, in Riverside, California? Bigotry is alive and well, Jules. Of course, you don't experience it, but I do. Andrew does. And the only reason Andrew doesn't get pulled over three times a week for driving while black is because he has a firefighter emblem on that cop magnet he calls a car."

"Why are you attacking me?" Jules looked genuinely surprised.

"Because you speak foolishness," Antoinette said. "We've sheltered Andrew from the ugliness in the world, and now, in reality, he hides his head in the sand just like you."

"Mom, Dad, please. I didn't mean to make you argue. Actually, the captain didn't want me to say anything at all about this, but I thought you could help. Apparently, this wasn't good dinner conversation." Andrew refilled his wineglass and took a sip before continuing. "I do have a question for you, Dad. I learned that back in the late seventies, black firefighters had to run behind the trucks when they did hydrant checks. Do you know anything about that?"

Antoinette looked at her husband, stunned.

Jules fidgeted nervously.

"Well?" Antoinette tossed her napkin on the table.

"Back then, there were some bad things happening within the department." Jules spoke slowly and carefully. "Many of the old-timers were angry because of the Affirmative Action laws. The department was recruiting more blacks and women than any of us. So, yes, it was difficult for minorities back in those days—but that is long behind us. The department is different now."

"And you did nothing about it?" Antoinette said, her voice a mixture of rage and incredulity. "Or were you content because it wasn't happening to *us*, as you put it?"

"You don't know the crap I went through because I was married to you," Jules said angrily. "I had to watch my own back. I wasn't about to make any waves. I just did my job and kept my mouth shut."

"Dad, I can't believe what I'm hearing." Andrew stood so quickly that his wineglass tipped over, the rich burgundy liquid bleeding across the table. "So you just stood by and let this happen to these men and did nothing?" He turned to look at his mother. "Mom, did you know about this?"

Blotting the wine stain with her napkin, Antoinette spat "Absolutely not" as she turned to make eye contact with her husband of nearly four decades. "I knew there were some unpleasant circumstances because of our marriage, but this comes as a complete shock. Why was I never told?"

"To what end, Antoinette? We'd had enough problems with your family, my family, our neighbors . . . why should I have brought even more complications into our home?" Jules looked and sounded tired.

"So do you think it's impossible that what's happening on Andrew's shift is racially motivated?" Antoinette began pacing. "These are some of the same people—or their sons and nephews—working in the department that did those horrible things back in the sixties and seventies. Don't you understand bigotry is generational? Children aren't born knowing hate!" Antoinette paused near her husband, her fists clenched next to her thighs.

"Of course I don't think it's impossible," Jules said. "I just think it improbable. Please, Antoinette, let's not argue about this. It isn't our battle."

"If it's our son's battle, then it's our battle."

Andrew tried to placate them both. "I didn't mean to make you fight about any of this. I just was hoping Dad could talk to the chief. He's dragging his feet about opening an investigation."

"Chief Marlborough?" Jules stammered. "What do you think I can do if he doesn't want to launch an investigation? In case you don't know, he's my boss, too."

Andrew felt like he had when he was seven years old and had been stung by a bee. He'd seen the insect lodged in his hand, but the pain hadn't come. He'd opened his mouth to scream but had lost his voice. It had been horrible, and hearing his father retreating in cowardice at the thought of challenging the chief on his own son's behalf brought back the same feeling of helplessness. "Dad, are you saying you're not willing to go to the chief and ask him to open an official investigation, even though I, your son, have just asked you?"

Jules sighed and took another drink from his wineglass. "It's not that simple, son. If I go in there saying these acts are racially motivated, he's going to look at me cross-eyed. We've all worked long and hard to eradicate racism from the department. No one wants to stir up that same old trouble."

Andrew's feelings of helplessness became chest pains. "I think I'd better go," he said tightly. "I may say something I'll later regret. Mom, I'll call you later."

Grabbing his jacket, he left his parents' home in a state of fury. He'd not once dealt with his father on this level, and he didn't like what had just happened. Why hadn't he ever noticed his father's passive-aggressive nature before? His mouth filled with a bitter taste that felt like disgust.

The man's excitement about his upcoming adventure made it impossible to sleep. He'd awakened every thirty minutes until he finally got up at two thirty. Clicking on the television, he watched as the *World News Now* logo filled the screen.

He needed to be in place early this morning.

He dressed quickly, never bothering with soap, water or toothpaste, and turned on the shortwave radio to monitor the activity at Station 27. He trusted that some junky or wino would need the services of B Shift in the wee hours of the morning, and he wanted to be ready.

Just before he pulled the worn jacket from the back of the tattered chair, he opened the small refrigerator. The plastic twelve-inch-wide door was left ajar by the frost crusted on the tiny frozen compartment.

He reached inside and retrieved a double Ziploc freezer bag.

Inside were the last remnants of Casper.

It was true of both dogs and people that when they were hanged, they let go of "everything."

22

Something was twitching in the back of Jerome's neck as he drove to the station.

He'd had a wonderful four days off with his family. The romantic evening the week before had sparked something magical in Nicolle, and they'd been like newlyweds, kissing and touching and . . . He was going to surprise her with a very special trip soon. He'd implore his coworkers for help to make the trip one that neither of them would soon forget. Maybe this was just what Mychel needed to see—his full commitment to his marriage vows. He'd be damned if his marriage would wind up like Lloyd's.

Despite his light mood, he felt a dark cloud looming. He touched the number four button on the CD changer, and BeBe Winans's voice filled the car. There was nothing like a little prayer and good gospel to get him back on the right track.

As he pulled into the parking lot, he noticed the B Shift captain and Lloyd having an intense conversation, members from both B and C Shifts gathered around them. Jerome quickly parked and moved toward the crowd.

"Maybe *this* will get Chief Marlborough's attention!" Lloyd shouted. "I know that all of you thought we were crazy and imagining things, but now you've witnessed it firsthand. I want to get pictures of this for the report." Though Lloyd spat the words at Captain McDonald, it was clear his anger was directed elsewhere.

"What the hell happened now?" Jerome asked as he walked up.

McInerney from B Shift answered, a trace of a smile on his face. "There's a message for you boys written on the floor of the equipment bay. We found it when we came back from a fire run around five forty-five."

Something in McInerney's voice seemed to catch Captain Mc-Donald's attention. "You think this is funny?" He left his position with Lloyd and strode over to the now-cowering paramedic, his anger written on his face for all to see.

"No, sir," McInerney answered with a swift change in attitude.

"Since you find so much humor in this disgusting act, I think it would be fun if you got a mop and bucket and helped them clean up this mess." Captain McDonald was just inches from McInerney's nose.

"But—"

"Now!"

"What happened here?" Jerome asked for a second time.

Burch, the engineer from B Shift, answered, "Someone wrote, 'Welcome C Shift,' in feces on the floor of the equipment bay while we were out on a run. It stinks to high heaven in there. That's why we're all standing out here."

Jerome left the rest of the crew and followed McInerney into the bay. The smell made him stop short. Burch hadn't adequately prepared him. "Whoa."

"It's pretty bad," McInerney agreed. "And it's getting worse. I really don't think it's funny, Winters." He sounded apologetic. "It was stupid of me to laugh. We've been hearing about what's been happening to you all, but to be perfectly honest, until someone killed Casper, none of us took it seriously." McInerney walked toward the utility closet. "I need to apologize for any jokes we made. I just want you to know right here and now that I don't condone this type of thing."

"I appreciate your forthrightness. Come on, I'll help you." Jerome held his breath as he went to open the forward-bay door. Hopefully, a cross breeze would help. "I do need to ask you a question, if you don't mind."

"Sure, go ahead. What is it?"

"Do you have any idea who's doing this?" Jerome tried to keep his voice neutral.

McInerney was quick to respond. "I swear, man, I don't know. I can tell you this, though—whoever is involved knows when we come and go, and he has access to the firehouse. We locked this place up tight when we left, but he got in anyway, with no signs of forced entry. This dude is no stranger to Station 27."

With a hint of trust Jerome dropped his head and said, "Cap wants us to take pictures before we clean up."

"I'll get the Polaroid." McInerney left momentarily to retrieve the camera. When he returned with Jerome's direction he took several shots from various angles of the disgusting sight.

The foul message covered an area about the size of a compact car. Satisfied they had captured the incident to the captain's satisfaction, Jerome and McInerney undertook the miserable clean-up job. McInerney filled the industrial-size bucket with hot water and disinfectant while Jerome retrieved the large mop and poured pine cleaner onto the floor.

While Jerome and McInerney cleaned up the mess inside, the two captains discussed what they would do about the "C Shift Menace," as everyone was now calling the saboteur.

"If you need me to go to the chief with you, then consider it done," McDonald said. "It takes a sick mind to perpetrate these types of acts against your shift, especially the most recent, but what makes me real sick is that I agree with you now—it's one of our own. To be able to pull off these stunts and not be caught, time and again, takes some inside knowledge." McDonald's face mirrored the disgust he said he felt.

Lloyd Frederickson felt the same way. "It would surely help us, Bob. With you cosigning, at least he'll know it's not all in my head. We need to get some proof that this is a hate crime."

"You mean, you think this is happening because your shift is all minority?" McDonald looked shocked and confused.

Lloyd stared at the other captain in disbelief. "You think it's not?"

"I swear, I never once considered this was anything more than some lunatic. At first, I thought it was some pissed-off woman. You know how our fellas can share the love . . . but then I began to have second thoughts." McDonald pointed toward the equipment bay. "These are just not things a woman would do. She'd slash a tire, key a car, but this . . ." He shook his head.

"I agree with you," Lloyd said, the first stirrings of faith in the other captain blooming inside his chest. "Now that you're on our team, do you have any ideas?"

"Not a one."

23

The only thing fouler than the air was everyone's mood. By eight thirty that morning, the bay had been cleaned and disinfected, and B Shift had departed, but the day's tone was set.

Lloyd sat in his office, his head in his hands. He had to do something to boost morale, but he couldn't think of what. Having the B Shift captain on his team was certainly a step in the right direction, but he needed to do something more. His crew couldn't work a full shift in their present mood.

"Cap, you got a minute?" Andrew entered after knocking on the door frame.

"Come on in, St. Vincent. Just having a pity party—and that is never any fun alone."

Andrew shuffled his feet and looked at the floor. "I don't know how to say this, so I'm going to just come out with it. I think I've been wrong about this whole thing. I now believe this is happening because we're black."

Lloyd sat back, placing his hands behind his head. "We? I don't think I ever remember you calling yourself black, St. Vincent. Why the change of heart?"

"I don't know that I've ever really considered myself black, until the other night."

"Do tell." Lloyd pointed to the chair next to his desk.

Taking the seat, Andrew spoke softly. "I was raised in an all-white neighborhood, went to all-white schools, dated white women and saw these blue eyes in the mirror every morning." He pointed to his face. "Somehow, I never knew the true suffering of black people—*my* people." He looked away, a flush spreading across his face. His voice became hard and angry. "I'm the spitting image of a man who looked me in the face the other night and told me that in this new millennium, prejudice didn't exist in the workplace—especially not the fire department."

Lloyd stared at the young man, wondering where this was going.

Andrew continued, "I listened to the stories you've been telling, and, believe it or not, I've now taken them to heart."

When he spoke, Lloyd's voice remained neutral. "What brought on this epiphany?"

"Listening to my mother and father argue about bigotry," Andrew said. "He either has no clue or refuses to believe, and I don't know which is worse."

"What do you want from me?"

"Nothing, Cap. I just want you to know that I'll do whatever I can to help catch this fool. I want to be on the investigation team."

"I'm glad to hear that," Lloyd said. "Do you have any ideas to help catch this guy?"

"I thought one thing we could do is always leave someone behind here at the station."

"Not practical. To get the job done, we need every warm body we have."

Andrew frowned. "Then we need to hire an investigator, like Winters said, someone who can be our eyes and ears."

"That costs money, son." Lloyd's voice was gentle. He was glad the young man had finally come to his senses, even if he wasn't able to come up with any new ideas.

"Well, I'm sure we can come up with something," Andrew said, sounding as frustrated as Lloyd felt, "if we all work together."

"I agree—" Lloyd was interrupted by the dispatch alarm.

"Station 27, car fire on the 110 northbound at the Manchester exit. Victims are standing clear. CHP en route."

"They're playing our song," Lloyd said grimly. "Let's go."

"Do you think we'll have time even to eat dinner?" Mychel fell back into the red recliner. "We've been on one call after another since the car fire."

Andrew retrieved a Red Bull from the refrigerator. "Today sure is making up for the other day, when we had nothing to do."

"Is there even any food in here?" Austin asked, sounding weary.

Jerome looked through the C Shift pantry. "There's some of this chunky chicken in a can. We can have chicken salad."

"That sounds great. I'll help you make it," Mychel volunteered.

Jerome stared helplessly at Lloyd, whose eyes gave little hope. "Sure," Jerome said flatly, reaching for the can opener.

Mychel smiled wickedly as she passed him—closer than necessary, of course—on her way to wash her hands.

"I need some help from you fellas. Well, not you, St. Vincent," Jerome joked.

Raising his hands in the air, Andrew questioned, "What I do?"

"You didn't do anything, but this is for the menfolk who've been in a relationship for more than three and a half minutes." Jerome reached for a bowl and dumped the chicken into it, using a fork to dig out the last of the meat from the can. "I want to plan an extraordinary weekend getaway for Nicolle."

"You may have underestimated Andrew," Austin said. "He probably has more tips for romancing than the rest of us combined."

"You could have a point there, Austin. Lover boy has plenty experience with the ladies." Lloyd began to make a fresh pot of coffee. "Why don't we ask Mychel, our resident lady, what she'd consider an extraordinary romantic weekend?"

"A beer in a glass instead of out of a can!" Andrew offered.

"Forget you, St. Vincent," Mychel said, sneering at Andrew. "What's the budget, Winters? That'll determine just how romantic you can get."

"I want to make it real special without dipping into the boys' college fund."

"Local or out of town?" Austin asked, getting out a cutting board and knife to chop celery and onions for the chicken salad.

"It can be out of town," Jerome said. "But I don't want it to take a long time to get there."

Andrew spoke up. "Santa Barbara, Goleta Beach, Pismo . . . those are all wonderful resort towns. There's a slammin' hotel in Pismo with really nice rooms, fireplaces and a hot tub on the balcony. You'd be right on the ocean."

The captain had other ideas. "What about staying right here in town and getting a place in Newport Beach? Talk about not taking much time to get there . . ."

"A suite at the Four Seasons in Santa Monica would be the bomb!" Mychel volunteered, wiping her hands on a paper towel and throwing it in the nearby trash can.

Jerome snorted. "That would be about twenty-five Benjamins a night."

"I thought nothing was too good for the little woman," she retorted with sarcasm. "I asked you for a budget . . . There's nothing less romantic than a penny-pincher."

Jerome shook his head. "It's not the money, although I don't want to spend too much. The main thing is that I want something that screams 'you're special,' without being overly commercial."

Andrew tossed his empty can into the trash. "Too bad you don't have a lot of time. There's this unbelievable Hilton on Bali. When I get married, that's where we'll honeymoon."

"I think the big question is *if* you get married, wouldn't you say?" Lloyd laughed.

"I plan to settle down one day," Andrew said. "But right now, it's so many women, so little St. Vincent."

"I just bet it is 'so little'!" Mychel taunted.

"You're just mad because you ain't getting any of this," Andrew shot back, running his hands down his torso. "You're so confused— you want to have a man and to be one at the same time. Surprise, Hernandez, it doesn't work like that."

"Who the hell said I want to be a man?" Mychel stepped up to him, putting her face just inches from his.

"Okay, I need help here, people." Jerome began mixing the ingredients for the chicken salad. "Can we focus?"

Hernandez and St. Vincent returned to their separate corners, eyeing each other warily.

Austin spoke. "How about a first-class plane ride to Monterey, and then a bed-and-breakfast on the ocean? Wake her up to croissants and orange juice." Austin seemed pleased with himself.

"That's not bad," Jerome mused. "I like the Newport Beach idea, too. Mychel, should I send flowers?" Jerome intentionally drew her into the conversation, hoping to break the tension between her and St. Vincent.

"If you like." She seemed a little hostile.

"Your wife is so special." Lloyd made eye contact with Mychel, seeming to give her a signal. "She'll appreciate anything you do. You keep the lines of communication open—you're asking us, when maybe you should be asking her."

"Where's the surprise in that?" Andrew asked.

"Not 'Oh, baby, where can I take you for a romantic weekend?' Gently prod her for information," Lloyd clarified. "Find out what she's been thinking about. I can guarantee you that if you listen, you'll get your answers." There was a faraway look in Lloyd's eyes. Jerome wondered if the older man was wishing he'd listened more in his own marriage.

"Mychel, what are some of the things you like to do on a romantic getaway?" Jerome was still looking for ideas, but he also wanted to be sure she understood his commitment to his wife.

"Her and Bertha walking hand in hand on a moonlit beach," Andrew said, ducking as Mychel threw the Lawry's Seasoned Salt at his head.

Turning to Jerome, Mychel seemed to look through him, as if mesmerized. Jerome wondered if she was getting the point or getting even more hostile. Did she really think he'd ever take her up on her offer? She stuck to her guns, he'd give her that. Still, it wasn't going to change his mind. He loved his wife.

The men grew quiet as her silence became louder and louder. Finally, Mychel snapped out of her trance when she seemed to realize all eyes in the room were on her. "I don't really have an opinion on this subject," she said tautly. "You should know what your woman likes. As you say, you've been with her your whole life. Why should you need to ask someone else what would please her?"

Jerome felt his dander rise. "Believe me, I know what my wife likes, and I try to provide it every minute of every day. This is different. I want to do something that'll take her breath away. I want to surprise her."

Austin piped up. "How about dinner and theater in the city?"

"What city? L.A.?"

"Not hardly. There is only one city—New York!"

"Oh, man! Now that's an idea. We could fly in and stay at a five-star hotel. Have dinner, go to a show . . ." Jerome was genuinely excited.

"No, no, no," Austin said, seeming sure of his knowledge. "You have drinks and light hors d'oeuvres before and go to dinner after. There's nothing like having a midnight dinner in the city that never sleeps. Then take her to the Village at two in the morning for a poetry reading, and bring the sun up by reminding her why she calls you Big Daddy." He winked, pleased with his suggestion.

Lloyd laughed. "You a man of few words, but when you speak . . . I gotta say, if you can afford it, Winters, that sounds like a weekend to remember. Have her favorite flowers and champagne waiting for your arrival. It would take a little while to get there, but make that part of the adventure. You been saving your frequent-flyer miles?"

"Actually, I have. We have almost one hundred thousand."

"Then upgrade your tickets to first class," Lloyd said. "The getting there and back will be a part of the whole weekend."

Austin grinned. "I know the concierge at the Hilton in Times Square. If you stay there, my girl, Annabelle, will hook you up!"

"You know," Jerome said. "This is sounding better and better. I'm starting to feel this. I haven't taken a bite of the Big Apple in a long time."

"Well, now, if you're dining in the Apple you must, must, *must* partake of the very fine cuisine at Maroons." Lloyd looked like he was beginning to get excited for Jerome and Nicolle. "It's at 244 West 16th Street. When you pull up in front, the owner will probably come out to greet you, and the food . . . Lord, Lord, Lord." He shook his head, eyes closed.

"She will love it. Throw in a little shopping, and she'll think she's died and gone to heaven." Jerome tasted the chicken salad. "If we get a break after dinner, I'll get on the Net and start making plans."

Mychel mumbled something to herself that sounded like "whatever."

The crew was able to finish dinner undisturbed. Afterward,

Austin pulled a deck of cards from the kitchen drawer and began to shuffle. "Losers do the dishes. Of course, you can always buy your way out . . . best three out of five."

"I'm feeling real lucky tonight." Andrew pulled a crumpled pile of money from his pocket. "I'm in. Deal 'em."

The others gathered around the table to play five-card draw, agreeing that the two with the lowest hands three times out of five would draw kitchen detail. Much to everyone's chagrin, Andrew was right: It was his lucky night. He raked in the cash with a full house, three of a kind, a straight and a pair of kings. Jerome and Mychel lost the most, so they were stuck with K.P.

"I give up," Jerome protested good-naturedly. "I could have hired someone to come in here and clean the kitchen for less than I've lost tonight. I just don't think it's fair that the cook has to do the dishes."

"Since when does mixing in the ingredients that everyone else chopped up qualify as cooking?" Austin questioned while laughing. "We *all* cooked, my brotha."

"Miss Lady," Andrew goaded, "not only have you given up the most *dinero,* but those little hands of yours will receive a therapeutic treatment courtesy of Dawn dish detergent—fresh spring scent, of course."

Ignoring Andrew, Mychel willingly began to gather the dishes. "You coming?" she asked Jerome.

With a deep sigh and much regret, he moved toward the kitchen. The remaining three repositioned and began playing spades. Mychel cranked the stereo, and Keri Tombazian's sexy voice filled the kitchen and dining area.

The Wave After Dark program provided the perfect mood music Mychel sought. Secure in that she couldn't be heard over the music she said, "You know, if you really want to have a special time, you could get a room at the Four Seasons, and I'll provide the rest."

"Why don't you just let it go?" Jerome didn't try to hide his annoyance. "I wouldn't go to Super 8 with you if you paid, Mychel. You're really starting to irk me. I want a professional relationship with you. Nothing more. You're one of the best here at 27. Let's not complicate what I think of as a great working relationship with this nonsense. It'll never go anywhere or serve any purpose other than to frustrate both of us."

But Mychel seemed undaunted. "You know, they told me I wouldn't get a high school diploma, and then they told me I could never get this job. As you can see, telling me I can't have something makes me work that much harder. So you just keep thinking what you will, Jerome, but I know what I know. Once you've gotten a taste of this salsa, you'll be real mad for fighting so hard." She chuckled, a low throaty sound that got on Jerome's last nerve.

Staring at Mychel, Jerome opened his mouth, closed it and opened it again. "Just back off, Hernandez," he said with such authority that Mychel stepped back.

"You don't have to get hostile." She laughed. "I'm just having a little fun with you."

Getting close to Mychel, not caring if the others saw him, Jerome spoke in slow, deliberate words. "Fun means we're both laughing and feeling good about what's happening. You're a very attractive woman and could have any available man you want, but I'm not available. Don't make me report you."

Rolling her eyes, Mychel put her hands up in a surrender motion. "Have it your way. I can take a hint."

Jerome thought, *Somehow I doubt it,* but he said, "Thank you." He finished loading the dishwasher while Mychel washed the mixing bowls and wiped down the counters in silence. He was disturbed by the direction his relationship with Mychel had taken. There was no doubt she was attractive, sexy even, and for a single man she would be a great catch—though he was beginning to wonder about her emotional stability.

Women came on to him almost daily when he was working. For many of them, he represented their knight in shining armor, a hero even. Some had brought him gifts, from food to jewelry, but no one had ever gotten next to him—until now. Mychel unsettled him. He feared her. He feared the way she made him feel.

Life with Nicolle had been unbelievable. Everything about their life together had been effortless. Singles and couples alike had coveted their relationship for nearly two decades. When Nicolle turned onto their street, Jerome could feel her presence. When their eyes met in the produce section of the supermarket, electrical current surged through his body. When she whispered his name to wake him gently after he'd fallen asleep on the couch, warmth washed over him. There was a purity and beauty about their love that was unparalleled.

Why in the world would Mychel Hernandez even think she could shake that?

24

"We started counseling last week," Lloyd said, tossing peanuts into his mouth. "It's real hard for me to tell a stranger how I feel. I still don't understand it—how in the world do you stay married to someone for all these years and not know or understand them? Nellie is bringing up stuff from thirty-one years ago." He shook his head, focusing on the sports bar's TV, which was showing the Los Angeles Lakers versus the Phoenix Suns basketball game.

"You've only been married for thirty years." Jerome took a sip from his Heineken. "Where do you get thirty-one years?"

Lloyd managed to laugh. "Exactly!"

Jerome glanced at the big-screen television to check the score. "Do you think she's really willing to give this a go? Or is she just going through the motions because you refused to leave without trying?"

Lloyd shook his head. "I only know what I want to believe. I'm just not sure what she really wants."

"I haven't repeated anything you've told me, but Nicolle has been talking to Nellie. I don't know if it'll do any good, but it can't hurt."

"What does Nellie say?" Lloyd sounded like he was trying to remain indifferent, but Jerome suspected he was fishing pretty hard for information. He wondered how beneficial the counseling sessions had really been.

Unfortunately, he was unable to help his friend. "Nicolle never tells me any details. You know that female 'code of silence' thing."

Shaking his head, Lloyd said with a smile, "When I get to heaven,

I'm going to ask God to explain women, His greatest gift to man. Because I could live to be as old as Noah, and I'll never get it."

"They defy explanation, but I do know they are His greatest gift, and I thank Him but that does *not* mean I come close to understanding Nicolle." Jerome tipped the green bottle until it was empty. "I can't wait for the shift to end on Thursday morning. We leave at noon for New York. I haven't told her where we're going— I just told her to pack a bag. The suspense alone has her so excited. It's going to be like a second honeymoon."

"Boy, y'all been on like fifteen honeymoons since I've known you." Lloyd chuckled. "But that's a good thing. I hate to bring this up, but has Hernandez been pitching her panties at you anymore?"

"Not lately," Jerome said, relieved. "I think she's finally got it. I don't understand why she felt it necessary to throw herself at me— or any married man for that matter. She's got it going on, and like I told her, if I wasn't married, I would've been flattered."

"Just watch your back," Lloyd cautioned. "I've seen women like her all my life, and she is lying in wait. Don't let your guard down for a second."

Feeling puzzled, Jerome asked, "You think she hasn't given up?"

"She may have, but it's been my experience that women who set their sights on a goal—whether it's a pair of pumps, a house or a man to pay for both—don't usually just give up."

"Maybe she figured out that work isn't the place," Jerome said.

"Yeah, maybe." Lloyd didn't sound convinced.

The two old friends turned their attention to the final two minutes of the basketball game, seeing the Lakers were having a comfortable, twelve-point lead. Suddenly, Keon Clark stole the ball from Rick Fox and shot a three-pointer, reducing the lead to nine. Within the next thirty-seven seconds, the twelve-point lead had turned to a one-point deficit.

Jerome felt a stabbing pain in his gut and thought, *You never can be caught lunchin'.*

25

The man sat in his El Camino, Station 27 in plain view.

He watched as they moved about, as though everything was normal.

They had no idea the suffering he planned to deposit at their feet.

He had lots more plans for C Shift, but he'd had to lie low for just a little while. The morning he'd left the little message courtesy of Casper, three weeks before, he'd almost been caught by B Shift.

But he was making lemonade from the lemons he'd picked from the justice tree. Since nothing had happened for six shifts, he knew they thought it was all over. It was always so easy to get them to trust anyone, except each other.

They were just that naïve.

Yes, indeed, this little hiatus was going to work quite well in his favor.

"Oh, I'm sorry. I wasn't paying attention." Mychel started to enter Jerome's dorm room, wearing a loosely wrapped towel that exposed her abundant breasts and full, muscular thighs. Her freshly shampooed hair filled the air with a clean, flowery spring smell.

"What the hell are you doing in here?" Jerome barked.

"I said I was sorry," she purred. "I wasn't paying attention to where I was walking and just wandered in here by mistake. Don't get your BVDs in a bunch. For someone who's not interested, you sure are nervous about seeing me like this." She loosened her grip even more on the towel.

Jerome averted his eyes. "Just get out of here, and you'd better get dressed. Why are you taking a shower in the middle of the shift, anyway?"

"I had a good workout and just needed to get the sweat off me. Gotta keep all of this in shape." She turned and left the room, giving him a flirtatious glance over her shoulder as she walked away.

Jerome slammed the door behind her and swore to himself, his pulse racing. He fell back onto the twin bed with both hands over his face.

Lloyd had been right. She hadn't given up.

This was the last straw. He'd have to report her. He just wouldn't tolerate her behavior any longer. He wasn't going to put himself in a position for her to falsely accuse him of misconduct.

His palms began sweating. How dare she disrespect him, not to mention herself in such a manner? What had happened to her? She was like a person obsessed.

Jerome didn't know how long he'd lain on the bed when the piercing sound of the alarm bell reverberated throughout the station. "Station 27, three-car, high-speed, head-on TA with injuries at Manchester and San Pedro. Police on scene."

Leaping to his feet, he hoped Mychel had come to her senses and was dressed. This was a call that would take all their skill—plus some reserves. There was no way to know what to expect with a head-on. He met Mychel in the hallway, neither acknowledging the other. They both rushed in the direction of their equipment. At this moment, nothing mattered except getting to the scene.

The engine and paramedic unit rolled out within one minute and twenty-one seconds of the initial call. Jerome maneuvered easily through the light, midday traffic, Austin only a few feet behind him. The accident scene was less than a minute away.

As they pulled up to the scene, Andrew and Lloyd grabbed latex gloves from the box as Lloyd called orders. "I'll take the passenger side of the Lexus. Winters, you take the driver. Hernandez and Austin will take the Honda. St. Vincent, you take the Camry. Your victim is out of the vehicle. I'm going to have dispatch roll another squad."

There was something familiar about the pearlescent-white Lexus. Retrieving the equipment from the truck, Jerome rushed to the driver's side of the vehicle. With the crowbar, he quickly pried the door open. As he rolled the victim toward him, he realized why the car had looked familiar—it belonged to one of Nicolle's girlfriends, Daphne Daniels, who had been friends with Nicolle since she'd worked for the insurance company. They were shopping buddies and frequently enjoyed spa days together. Daphne was bleeding and unconscious. How was he going to break the news to Nicolle?

W h i l e Jerome approached the driver, Lloyd ran around to the passenger side and opened the door. To his horror, there before him was Nicolle Devereaux-Winters. Blood gushed from the gaping head wound like a raging river. For an eternity, he stood, helpless. Then, in a split second, he looked over at Jerome as he cut the seatbelt from his victim. Thoughts collided in his head at the speed of light, and he snapped out of his daze, barking orders to his crew. "Hernandez, I need some help over here!" Lloyd applied pressure to the wound.

Jerome looked up and for the first time seemed to realize that Daphne was not the only person he knew in this mangled mess that had once been a fine automobile. He froze.

As Mychel rushed to aid Lloyd, the captain yelled, "Take over for Winters." Without hesitation, she ran the distance around the car. Jerome stood, transfixed.

"What's wrong with you? Let me in here!" Mychel demanded, nudging him slightly.

Without warning, Jerome began screaming, "Nicolle, Nicolle, Nicolle!" as he rushed to the passenger side of the car. He pushed Lloyd so hard the older man fell backward, falling butt-first to the ground.

Jerome removed the blood-soaked gauze to check her wound. The deep, six-inch gash left little doubt that her skull was fractured.

Lloyd sprang to his feet. "Get out of the way and let me take care of her. You can't do this." He struggled with Jerome. "Duncan," Lloyd yelled to the police officer. "Get Winters out of here."

The burly officer rushed over to see the source of the commotion between two firefighters he'd known for years to be friends.

"Get Winters out of the way!" Lloyd repeated.

"What?" Duncan seemed immobilized by confusion.

"This is his wife!" Lloyd shouted.

"Oh my God!" Duncan tried to pull Jerome away from the car, but he pushed the police officer aside, trying desperately to get to Nicolle.

Within a microsecond, four police officers had descended on Jerome to restrain him. Pure chaos broke out. None of the other officers understood what had set Jerome off. One officer drew his weapon, but Duncan yelled for him to put it away.

The second rescue unit arrived on the scene and began working frantically. Before they could give the information to the second unit, Austin and Andrew told Rescue Unit 117 to take over, and the two men rushed over to see what was going on.

"What the hell?" Andrew approached the police officers still restraining Jerome.

"Let me go!" Jerome struggled. "I have to save Nicolle!"

Andrew and Austin looked first at each other, and then to where Lloyd worked on the accident victim. It took a moment for the information to compute, but then they collectively yelled, "Oh my God!" and began running in the direction of the Lexus.

In a very soothing voice, Duncan spoke softly to Jerome. "Winters, I need you stay out of the way so they can do their job. You know they're going to do their best work for one of their own. The ambulance is en route. We're going to get her to shock trauma, and she'll be fine. I don't want to cuff you and put you in the unit, but I will. You have to stay out of their way."

"That's my Nicky," Jerome moaned. "My wife. She gave me three beautiful sons." Jerome broke. His mind was numb, but every fiber in his body felt pain. He collapsed against the four officers restraining him and began sobbing.

Duncan signaled for the officers to let Winters go. The man no longer posed a threat to the rescue team. He spoke to Jerome reassuringly. "Man, I wish I knew what to say. I can't even guess what you must be feeling right now. I just know that we have to let your friends do what they do. I'm going to help you up. You promise me you're going to stay here with us?"

Jerome stared blankly at Officer Duncan. His words made no sense. Why would he want to stay with them? They were cops. He was a firefighter. He saved people. They protected them. They worked together, but separately. So why would he want to stay with him?

The tears in his eyes were replaced with bewilderment. What was happening? Suddenly, he couldn't breathe. He began pulling at his collar. There was no air. He thought he said, "I can't breathe," but no one was reacting.

Duncan stared at him. There was something wrong—very wrong. "Winters, are you all right? Winters?"

Jerome struggled to get air. Fear was literally choking him.

"Over here! Winters has gone into shock!" Duncan yelled.

Andrew was assisting Lloyd, and Austin worked with Mychel. Both victims had been removed from the vehicle and laid on the ground. The ambulance was in the distance, its sirens growing rapidly louder.

Daphne had regained consciousness. Mychel placed a tourniquet on her right arm. "I'm going to start an I.V.," she said, speaking clearly. "Your blood pressure is a little high, but that is not so strange, considering what has happened to you."

"Do you remember what happened?" Austin spoke softly.

The woman looked confused as she spoke, her voice soft with pain. "No, the last thing I remember is getting off the freeway. Nicolle and I were bringing a picnic lunch to her husband. She wanted to surprise Jerome. They leave tomorrow for this trip he's planned for her. She is so excited." The woman tried to rise. "Nicolle? Where's Nicolle?"

Mychel made a soothing sound and gently held the woman down. "My partner is taking care of her. I just need you to relax. You'll feel a little prick."

"Is she hurt?"

"I'm not sure," Mychel lied as she searched for a good vein.

Nicolle's peach blouse had been dyed red by her own blood. Despite their efforts, the bleeding couldn't be contained. Lloyd worried as he applied pressure to the wound. Andrew slid the needle into Nicolle's vein, starting the solution that would replace the fluids rapidly leaving her body.

"We've got to get her to shock trauma," Lloyd said more to himself than to Andrew. "She's going to bleed out."

Lloyd heard Duncan yell again, "I need some help over here. Winters's in trouble!"

"You go," Mychel demanded of Austin. "I've got this under control. See what's going on with Jerome."

Austin grabbed the blood pressure cup. Laying his stethoscope over his neck, he trotted to the crowd that encircled the downed firefighter.

Jerome's lips had turned blue, and his hands were ice-cold. He was in shock and hyperventilating.

"I need a paper bag." Austin removed Jerome's jacket and laid him on the ground. "Come on, man. Snap out of it. Nicolle and the boys need you."

"What can we do?" Duncan asked helplessly.

"Grab a paper bag from the box. We'll sit him up and have him breathe into it. The shock's been too much for him."

Duncan returned quickly, and within a few minutes Jerome's breathing had returned to normal. "I'm sorry," Jerome said. "I'm taking you away from what you should be doing. How's Nicolle?" His eyes pleaded for good news.

Austin couldn't give it to him. "I've got to be honest with you, man. She's bleeding a lot, and we can't get it under control. But you know we're working with everything we have. Medevac is on the way."

"I want Dr. Vandross. She's the best. If she has a chance—" Jerome cut himself off, dropping his head into his hands. He began sobbing again.

Austin and Duncan stood watching, powerless to help him.

"What in the hell is she doing over here in the first place?" Jerome demanded of the air around him. "I need to see her!" He tried to stand up.

Duncan tried to reassure him. "You'll just get in the way. Let them do their jobs. You'll be able to ride with her to the hospital."

"I promise, I won't get in the way. I have to see my wife," Jerome pleaded.

"The chopper's approaching," Andrew said, standing.

Austin and Duncan helped Jerome to his feet. He felt light-headed and weak. They attempted to help him walk, but he refused. "I can do this!" he said, shaking them off.

He walked in the direction of his beloved Nicolle, where she lay on the ground, bleeding her life out onto the pavement. He felt nauseous.

Suddenly, there was no sound. Everything was moving in slow motion. He saw Lloyd and Andrew working frantically, and the transport company medical technicians stood by, ready to move her to the helicopter when it arrived. She looked fragile and lifeless.

Jerome slipped back to the first time he'd kissed her. They were eleven, and though he hadn't known what he was doing, it'd felt as natural as breathing. She had been afraid and was trembling. He assured her that kissing her would not get her pregnant.

There on the tarmac, Jerome began laughing. Everyone turned to him, but he couldn't stop. He laughed until he fell to his knees, and then his laughter turned to anguish. Then he felt a rush of wind from the approaching helicopter's blades, and his hearing returned.

Austin went to assist Lloyd and Andrew. "Let's get her moved to the stretcher." He held the I.V. bag while Lloyd compressed the wound. The bleeding hadn't diminished—the valve was wide open on the I.V., running freely into her body, but it was entering at a much slower pace than the blood was leaving.

The helicopter touched down a block away, and it was time to lift Nicolle into the ambulance. "Let's get her into the unit," Austin said, shouting to be heard over the helicopter's chop-chop. "I'll ride to the helicopter with her. Have Duncan bring Jerome in the squad car."

The medical technician took the I.V. bag from Austin. Lloyd held the bandage to Nicolle's head as Andrew and one of the technicians lifted the backboard moving her to the stretcher. Lifting the stretcher, they quickly moved the twelve feet to the waiting vehicle.

Lloyd climbed into the back of the ambulance as they locked the stretcher into place.

"Hang on, Nicolle," Austin said to the unconscious woman. "We're going to get you to the hospital, where they'll be able to fix you right up." Austin patted her foot just before he closed the double doors on the back of the ambulance.

Andrew went to where Jerome knelt on the ground, staring at the ambulance. Speaking to Duncan, he quietly said, "Captain wants you to take him to the helicopter in the squad car. We'll meet you down there. He can fly with her."

"Who's the doctor on the medevac?" Jerome managed weakly.

"Man, I don't know. But if it was Doc Vandross, she would have been on the ground, running toward us before the 'copter set down."

Please, God, let her be on duty today, Jerome prayed.

Standing again, he moved to the squad car without word. Duncan opened the back door, and Jerome slid in, his zombielike movements causing him pain. His muscles were as tight as an overstretched rubber band.

Two minutes later, Jerome was stepping up into the helicopter behind Nicolle's stretcher. The paramedic and doctor immediately went to work. He'd promised he wouldn't interfere, but it was very difficult to sit back and just watch.

The flight to the hospital took only twelve minutes. During that time, Jerome's entire life with Nicolle ran through his mind like a feature film.

Her infectious laughter was what he loved most about her. She'd said time and again that they laughed at what most couples fought about. She never took herself too seriously. They talked for hours and hours about politics, religion, cars, mysteries, diet and exercise—you name it, they talked about it. She was witty, funny and, at times, downright sassy. She wasn't afraid of having an opinion. She loved who she was, and he loved what she brought to his life. Her sensuality brought him to a place that could only be rivaled by heaven. He'd told her parents that while they thought they'd given her life for themselves, the truth was that her life was for him.

For the first time, the realization hit him that he had to call her parents. He had to call her job. Worst of all he had to tell his sons. How could he tell them that a man talking on a cell phone had crossed the double yellow line and hit the car their mother was riding in? How could he tell them that she might sleep forever?

Tears began to form again. He began to call her name, softly and rapidly. He wanted so much to hear her speak. Suddenly, he couldn't remember what her voice sounded like. Looking at her swollen and quickly bruising face, he couldn't remember what she looked like. He felt reality slowly slipping through his fingers.

The helicopter touched down gently on the roof of the hospital. The trauma unit crew rushed to the helicopter, and the team of two turned to six. The doctor, who hadn't taken the time to introduce himself, finally spoke to Jerome as Nicolle was whisked away.

"Mr. Winters, I'm Dr. Fulton. I'm the new assistant chief of emergency medicine. Your wife has sustained a serious head injury. She's lost a lot of blood. The field paramedics did an excellent job stabilizing her, but we've got our work cut out for us. I'll be working with our chief, Dr. Vandross. I'm sure you know she's top-notch."

"I mean no disrespect to you," Jerome said, his voice sounding weak in his own ears, "but I've known Donna for a very long time, and I've seen her perform one miracle after another. I feel so much better knowing she's here."

"Absolutely none taken," the doctor said. "This is your wife. You need to feel as confident as possible. You'll be a very big part of her recovery."

Jerome sighed. "This is all so hard to believe. When I left her this morning, we were so happy. She was packing for our trip tomorrow. She kissed me and said, 'The next time I see you, we'll be heading for our great adventure.' I still don't understand why she was near the station." He remembered his wife's friend. "Do you know how Daphne is doing?"

"I'm not sure who Daphne is, Mr. Winters."

"She's my wife's friend, who was driving."

"I'm not sure, but she'll be taken to the hospital closest to the scene. Her injuries weren't as severe.

"I know you have many more questions, and I promise that as soon as I know more, I'll be back with you. We've set up a special room for trauma victims who've been brought in by helicopter. We're on the top floor now. There's also a waiting room just outside. This way, you'll be away from the other family members of patients less critical.

"I need to join the rest of my team," the doctor continued. "I'll be your point of contact for now. Donna has another patient, but as soon as she's free, she'll be here. Before I leave, do you have any questions?"

"What's her prognosis?" Jerome held his breath.

"It's too soon to tell, but I'll be straight with you. I think you should call your family and, if you're a praying man, get in touch with your God. I'll be back as soon as we get the CAT scan results."

Dr. Fulton trotted off in the direction of the hospital. Jerome wanted to run behind him, but he didn't have the strength.

26

Jerome walked slowly toward the building and began to talk to God.

Father, please don't take my Nicolle from me. Touch her, stop the bleeding, bring her back. Let there be no brain damage. Please give me strength to tell the boys. Give me strength to do whatever it is I need to do to help us all make it through this. I don't understand why this is happening, but I promise not to question You. In Your precious son, Jesus', name, Amen.

The prayer renewed his strength, and his gait became more pronounced. He made his way to the waiting room. In the small room were three sofas, a coffeepot, a twenty-seven-inch television, a computer with Internet access and two telephones. On the wall above the desk was a sign prohibiting the use of mobile phones. He pulled the sleek, silver device from his waistband and pressed the End button until the phone powered down.

A middle-aged Hispanic man and teenage girl huddled in the corner of one of the sofas. The girl lay sleeping on the man, whom Jerome presumed to be her father. The man stroked her hair.

Just as he sat on the blue sofa closest to the door, his pager buzzed. He recognized the number. It was the station. He slowly rose, moved to the table, picked up the receiver and dialed the number. He hoped it was Lloyd, but he didn't know what he would say to his friend.

"Hey, Lloyd," Jerome said with relief when his best friend picked up on the first ring.

Lloyd got right to the point. "I'm waiting for a relief captain, then I'll be right there. Where are the boys? Have you called her folks yet?"

Jerome signed deeply. "The boys are in school. I'll call Mom and Dad and ask them to go pick up the boys and bring them here—at least Nicolas and Jordan. Christian would work everybody's last good nerve, and he's too young to know what's going on anyway. Then I'll call Nicolle's parents." Sighing again after a long pause, he continued, "Man, how do I tell them their child is lying at death's door? How do I tell our children? How do I convince myself she's going to be okay?" Jerome's body shook with fatigue.

"I don't have any answers for you, man. Everyone wants you to know they are praying and holding good positive thoughts. It's like all of L.A. City and County knows what happened. My relief should be here within the hour. We're on bypass for the next two hours. Everyone is pretty shaken up."

"Thanks, man."

Lloyd asked tentatively, "Have they been able to tell you anything yet?"

"Just what I already knew. She's lost a lot of blood and has a severe head injury. Do you know where they took Daphne?"

"Yeah, she's at King. She regained consciousness at the scene. I know her arm is broken and possibly her ankle, but she'll recover one hundred percent if she follows the doctor's orders."

"What about the man who hit them?"

"He's hurt pretty bad, too. He's at King. He was dialing his cell phone while doing more than fifty miles an hour."

"I heard," Jerome said, unable to let himself feel anger for the stranger who had caused so much pain. "I really need to call our folks, Lloyd. Just get here as soon as you can. Oh, and do you think Nellie will be able to take care of Christian tonight?"

"You know you don't even have to ask. Do you want her to pick him up from school or come by the hospital to get him? Better yet, let her pick up all the boys. They're all right there together."

"If she could come by here, it will give me a chance to talk to them. I don't know how much they'll understand, but I need to be the one to tell them. I need to let them know that I'm not going anywhere . . ." Jerome couldn't bring himself to complete the sentence: . . . *even if their mother never wakes up.*

"I understand," Lloyd said. "I'll call Nellie now. I'll see you as soon as I can get away."

"Thanks, man."

"You know none is necessary. Bye."

"Bye." Jerome hung up the phone and let his hand linger for a long moment, trying to decide which set of parents he should call first. After much inner battle, he finally settled on calling his parents first. His mother picked up on the first ring.

"Hello?"

"Hi, Mom."

"What's wrong?" Mrs. Winters knew instinctively something had happened.

"There's been an accident, and Nicolle's been hurt pretty badly. I think you should come to the hospital right away." Jerome braced himself for her barrage of questions.

"Oh my God, son. What happened? Where are you?"

"She was not far from the station, and someone on a cell phone crossed the double yellow. We're at the shock-trauma unit. She was airlifted here."

"I'll call your dad, and we'll be right there." Mrs. Winters's voice cracked. "What about the boys? Do you need me to pick them up from school?"

"No, Nellie Frederickson is going to get them, and then she'll take Christian home with her after I've told them what's happened. The other boys can decide to go or stay."

"That's very kind of her. Maybe your father can come straight from work, and I can leave from here now, rather than wait. I'll call the church to get the prayer team started. What're her injuries?"

"She lost a lot of blood, and she has a real bad head injury." His own voice cracked.

"Oh, sweet Jesus. What are the doctors saying?"

"They haven't said anything yet. I'm just waiting. They promise to come out as soon as they get the results from the CAT scan."

"Are you there alone?"

"For the time being. Lloyd's waiting for a relief captain. I'm sure Nellie is on her way, too."

"Okay, I'm going to get off the phone so that I can get there, too. Have you called the Devereaux family yet? Maybe I should ride with them . . ."

"That's my next call. Mom?"

"Yes, son?"

"Please hurry," Jerome whispered. "I can't face this alone."

"You won't have to, honey. Just pray, and I'm on my way."

"Thanks, Mom."

Jerome felt a minute sense of peace that his mother was on her way. The next phone call was the one he'd dreaded most. How would he break the news? He didn't know if he should beat around the bush or get right to the point. Should he speak with her mother or father?

As he picked up the receiver, Dr. Vandross entered the room with a somber face.

Jerome's heart stopped.

27

Jules St. Vincent waited impatiently for his meeting with Chief Marlborough. As he thumbed through a newsmagazine, he wondered if he'd made the right decision. Antoinette had pressured him to set up the meeting, against his own better judgment. It was possible the events at Station 27 were racially motivated, but not likely. They'd come too far to experience such a setback now, in the year 2004.

For many years, he'd looked the other way when minorities were on the receiving end of cruel jokes. He'd never been one to participate, but he'd also never done anything about it. Did that make him an accomplice? No way. However, if what Andrew said was true, his own son could be a victim. Somehow, now, racial cruelty didn't seem so harmless or distant.

"Chief Marlborough will see you now," said Heather, the chief's young, beautiful secretary.

The office walls leading into William Marlborough's office were lined with pictures of the fire department chiefs since the early 1900s. One thing was evident—they all looked to be white Anglo-Saxon men.

Chief Marlborough rose to greet Jules. "How've you been, Jules? It's good to see you again. We should get in a little practice on the golf course before the next chiefs' conference. Los Angeles could use a trophy." He gestured to the chair opposite his desk.

"That sounds like a plan," Jules said, sitting. "I could surely use the practice."

"What can I do for you?" He sat back down. "My secretary told me you said it was rather urgent."

Jules shifted in the burgundy leather armchair. He was having serious second thoughts about his decision to come, but he was here, so he'd better start talking. "I'll get right to the point. I'm here about the situation over at 27, C Shift."

"Jules, 27 isn't one of your stations." Marlborough eyed him suspiciously. "Why does this concern you?"

"It was brought to my attention, and I was asked to speak to you."

Visibly angered, Marlborough leaned across his massive desk. "Did that troublemaker Frederickson come to you after I told him I'd handle it here?"

Jules tried to remain steady and just barely succeeded. "No, Captain Frederickson didn't come to me. I'm sure he would have dealt with his own battalion chief." He paused, then said, "My son asked me to look into what HQ is doing about the situation. He's on C Shift, as you know." He looked steadily at the chief.

Marlborough blanched. "Your son is on C Shift at 27? I was under the impression that everyone on that shift was black or Hispanic. I guess I've been misinformed."

"Does my son being on C Shift change the way you investigate this matter?" Jules tried to control his pounding heart. He knew his anger would show on his face immediately if he didn't keep his emotions under control.

"Well, you know we have to take care of our own," Marlborough said, backpedaling. "I had no idea that your son was even in the department. I guess that since I haven't been with this department very long, I have much to learn about the makeup of the various shifts." The chief now looked downright nervous.

"I still don't quite understand what any of this has to do with your investigation of the incidents at Station 27."

"Well, of course it doesn't have anything to do with the investigation." Sweat began to form on the chief's brow.

Jules felt his advantage and pressed on. "Have you or have you not opened an investigation into the incidents on C Shift at the 27?"

"I put out some feelers, told some people that this thing was getting out of hand," Marlborough said sheepishly.

Jules was startled by this slight admission of guilt. "What the hell are you talking about? Are you telling me that you are aware that someone in the department is behind these events?"

Marlborough raised his hands. "Now, now . . . You know the boys get a little rambunctious from time to time. I promise you things will stop."

Jules's eyes narrowed. "You mean you know who's doing this?"

"I don't know specifically, but it's probably the boys."

"What boys?"

"You act like you don't know what I'm talking about."

"It's because I have no clue what you're talking about. Is this some sort of group or club?"

The chief seemed to fumble for a believable explanation. "No, no. Umm, there are just some kids who make trouble around the city."

Jules didn't buy his flimsy elucidation. "So why haven't you brought the police in on it? The things they've done are hardly harmless."

"Actually, it was the police that I spoke with when I told them to get the message to the group."

"I see."

"Was there anything else?" Marlborough rose.

Looking up at the massive man, Jules thought how little he knew about this person who'd been chief for less than two years. He needed to do a little research. "No, I guess we're done."

Jules left without a good-bye, his head filled with conflicting thoughts. Could Andrew be right? Was there a group working within the department perpetuating hate?

28

Later that day, Chief Marlborough asked his secretary to get him the personnel jackets on St. Vincent the older and younger. He brought his thoughts back to Jules St. Vincent. How could the veteran chief not know about the undercover group in operation for more than a century?

As Heather sat across his desk from him, taking notes, a square gray rectangle announcing the arrival of new e-mail caught his attention. *New mail has arrived. Would you like to read it now?* glared back at him. Unthinkingly, he clicked on Yes.

Shaken by the words on the screen, Marlborough flushed and told Heather he was done for now. When he was sure Heather had returned to her office, he turned back to the computer. He clicked a button, and the e-mail appeared instantly:

The target is in my sights.
I'm moving in for the kill.
It won't be much longer before justice is served.
—One of Your Boys

The chief rose from his chair and went to lock the door. He didn't want to chance anyone hearing him as he made this call. He pulled his untraceable prepaid cell phone from the drawer and dialed.

On the second ring, a deep voice answered. "Yeah?"

"What the hell are you up to?"

"I know Frederickson has hired that niggra lawyer woman. We need to stop them. If they win a civil rights case against the department, it will be like they won against you. We're not going to stand for these people making you look bad. Your boys have got this under control."

"But you can't do anything stupid. This is why I had to get you out of Texas. You would've ended up in jail. I really don't want you doing anything. Let me handle this," the chief insisted.

"Like you handled that colored boy in Texas? It's *my* job to look out for *you*."

"I can handle this. I've told you I'm a big boy. Just back off."

The connection was broken. William held down the End key until the display went dark.

29

"Jerome, what are you doing here?" Donna Vandross approached, extending her hand.

Standing, Jerome took her hand in both of his. "Hi, Doc. It's Nicolle. You didn't know?"

"No, I'm sorry, I didn't. Please give me just a moment to speak with Mr. Peña."

Jerome exhaled deeply as Donna Vandross slowly walked toward the now-alert father and daughter in the far corner of the room. She sat opposite the pair, speaking in Spanish. She'd only said a few words when the man began weeping. Jerome had seen tears of joy before—these were not them. The young girl buried her face into the chest of the man and began crying loudly.

Donna and the gentleman stood and shook hands as the doctor continued to speak. Turning to leave, the father and daughter followed her. She turned and whispered to Jerome, "I'll be right back."

Jerome could only imagine that the chief of emergency medicine brought the worst of all news to Mr. Peña, the type of news from which you never recover, the kind of bad news that forever alters the course of your life and the lives of all of those around you.

Realizing he hadn't called Nicolle's parents, he returned to the chair at the desk and picked up the receiver again. This time he dialed quickly, and Mr. Devereaux answered on the third ring.

"Hi, Dad, this is Jerome calling."

"Well, hey there, son. To what do I owe this pleasure?" Unlike his mother, Mr. Devereaux had no inkling there was something terribly wrong.

"Dad, there's been an accident."

"What kind of accident? One of the boys been hurt? You know that's the way it is with a man-child. Always breaking or bruising something."

"No, sir. It's Nicolle." Jerome waited a beat to let the news sink in. "She was in a car accident, and she's in the hospital. I think you and Mom should get down here as soon as you can."

Mr. Devereaux's voice changed instantly. "Oh, sweet Jesus. What's happened to my baby girl?"

Jerome could hear Mrs. Devereaux, his father-in-law's wife of forty-three years, saying something in the background. After telling him about the accident, Jerome added, "It's not so good, Dad."

Slow to speak, Nicolle's father managed, "Were the boys with her? Where was she?"

"She was near the firehouse, and her friend Daphne was driving. The boys were in school."

There was a rustling sound over the phone. The next voice he heard was that of Nicolle's mother. "Jerome, what is Dave talking about? He's not making any sense. He's saying that Nicolle's been hurt?"

"She's been in an accident, Mom. You and Dad need to get here as soon as you can. She's having a CAT scan now, but she's unconscious." Jerome wondered how many times he'd have to repeat this same story over and over.

"What hospital?"

"USC Medical Center. Big General."

"We're leaving now. It will take us about an hour."

"My mother's getting dressed, and she thought you could come together," Jerome said. "Who's driving? I don't want y'all to drive yourself."

"Desmond just went to the store. He should be back within ten minutes, and I'll get him to bring us. You know, Dave can't see so well anymore." Maxella Devereaux sounded amazingly calm, and Jerome wondered if she was in shock.

"Mom, I just want you to be prepared when you get here. She's in the shock-trauma unit. She's in the best hands in the country, but it's still not certain what will happen."

"I need to go take care of Dave. He's not doing so well." Maxella hung up the phone without saying good-bye.

Jerome was relieved Nicolle's younger, if irresponsible, brother, Desmond, was with Jerome's in-laws. Although at thirty-five Desmond hadn't held a job for more than three months in his entire life, he would at least be a good chauffeur if he was sober.

Suddenly, the large room seemed so empty, and yet at the same time, it was closing in on him. How long had it been since Dr. Fulton left? It felt like hours, but it could have been only a few minutes. How long would it take for his parents to arrive? Where was Lloyd? He had to leave this confined space.

He opened the sliding-glass door that led to the solarium and stepped out into the midday sun. Nicolle loathed the direct sunlight. She said her rich brown skin was the perfect shade, a brown that had been kissed by the angels themselves. He walked to the edge of the area and peered out over the city. Life seemed so normal from where he stood. How could his beloved be struggling for her life less than one hundred yards away? He wanted so desperately to change places with her. He was stronger. He could fight harder.

He didn't hear Dr. Vandross approaching. "Jerome?" She touched him on his back.

Seeing the grim look on her face, Jerome sank to his knees. "No, Donna, nooooooo!"

With pure satisfaction, the man smiled as he heard the news of Jerome Winters's wife's accident. This was better than anything he could have planned on his own.

He massaged orange hand cleanser into his hands methodically as he imagined how distressed Station 27 must be at this very moment.

One of their own, once removed, had fallen.

It was God's will that he rid the fire department of these inferior people.

He was doing God's work.

30

"In all of my years, this has to be the worst day on the job." Lloyd spoke in a defeated tone as he waited for a replacement to arrive. "I've imagined the worst-case scenarios, and this has never even come into play."

Andrew tried to console his leader. "Cap, I don't know what to say. When you get to the hospital, please tell Winters that I'm pulling for him." They'd done all they knew how to lift the dark cloud that had descended upon Station 27, and now there was nothing to do but wait.

Mychel made coffee while Austin opened a package of assorted giant cookies. Lost in her own thoughts, she didn't seem to hear the conversation around her.

Nellie Frederickson's voice broke the silence that had descended on the room. "Hey, everybody. How're you all doing?"

"Hey, Mrs. Frederickson. Nice to see you again." Austin extended his large hand. "Just wish it wasn't because of all this." He shook his head sorrowfully.

"Austin, it's good to see you, too. You look very well. I haven't seen you since you've been back to work." Nellie walked to where Lloyd sat and laid her hands gently on his shoulders. "How're you holding on? I was in the neighborhood and decided to roll through here to see if you were okay."

Laying his hand on top of hers, Lloyd felt tears welling up in his soul. He felt like this had happened to one of his children. "Just waiting for someone to get here to relieve me. If they don't show up soon, I'm just going to leave. I need to get to Jerome. He needs me. What are you going to tell the boys when you pick them up?"

"Nothing works like the truth. I don't know just how I'm going to tell them, however. They're too old not to see through a lie." Nellie sat across from Lloyd now, holding his hand. "She called me this morning, you know."

"Who, Nicolle?" Lloyd sat more erect.

"Yeah. She was so happy. She said she was bringing lunch here for you guys." She waved her hands, fighting back tears. "She wanted to surprise Jerome, since he'd planned their special get-away. She was like a schoolgirl. She couldn't imagine where he was taking her. She insisted that I knew and that our friendship was in jeopardy if I didn't tell her immediately." Nellie laughed shakily. "She was really over-the-top, and we were laughing so hard. I had no idea that just a few hours later . . ." Nellie withdrew her hand from Lloyd's, placing it up to her face and trying to hide her tears.

Lloyd quickly moved around the table to where his wife sat and placed his arms around her. "It's going to be okay. It just has to be. All we can do is pray and trust God. You're in no shape to drive. I'll take you to get the boys."

"Captain, why don't y'all just go?" Austin said. "We're on bypass for the next hour or so, and if we need to extend it, we will. You're not doing anybody any good by staying here."

"That's a good idea, Cap. I promise not to mess things up before they send someone else to watch over us." Andrew tried to make a joke.

"I guess y'all are right. Let's go. It'll be at least an hour before we get to the hospital as it is." Lloyd helped Nellie up, and the two left without further words.

As they descended the stairs, Nellie thought how far removed her problems seemed at this moment. Why was she so mad at Lloyd in the first place? For thirty years, he had loved, honored and provided for her. He was never taken away from her, suddenly leaving her to fend for herself. What in the world was Jerome going to do? If Nicolle even survived, her recovery would be long and painful. If she didn't survive—Nellie shook her head to clear away the negative thoughts.

Moving through the equipment bay and out into the parking lot, they decided to leave Lloyd's car and travel in her County of Los Angeles–issue Taurus. As they pulled onto the street, she realized they didn't have a car seat for Christian. "We need to stop at Target or Kmart to get a car seat," she said.

"You're right! That's going to take even more time. I should have left immediately. What was I thinking about, waiting around for someone to replace me? My man needs me now!" Lloyd swore under his breath as he maneuvered the car through traffic with the skill of a man who'd driven a fire truck for more than half his life.

The two quickly purchased a car seat and other supplies for Christian. They were out of the store in fifteen minutes to pick up the boys.

"You know, I have a bad feeling about this, Nellie," Lloyd said grimly. "Nicolle is struggling for her life."

"What happened?"

"Some bozo on a cell phone crossed the double yellow and hit them head-on." Visibly angry, Lloyd gritted his teeth. "I'm so tired of peeling people out of cars because somebody just couldn't wait to take or make a call. We need to outlaw the damned things in cars that are moving. People sit in restaurants talking loud. I've even heard a phone ring in church . . ."

"I know how you feel about cell phones, honey, and I guess if I sat in your seat, I'd feel the same way."

The traffic gods of Los Angeles were kind to them, and they pulled into the parking lot of the Good Shepherd Christian Academy twenty minutes after they'd left Target. Nellie entered the office and explained why she was there.

The young woman behind the counter looked as though she had been crying. "Hi, Mrs. Frederickson. We've been expecting you. If I can see some identification, the boys are waiting in the vice principal's office."

Removing her license as she spoke, Nellie asked, "How much do they know?"

"We only told them that you were picking them up early to take them to their dad. We're so very sorry to hear about Mrs. Winters. We all love her so much around here. The faculty is having a special prayer service after school."

Feeling a lump in her throat, Nellie simply said, "We really appreciate all your prayers."

"If you'll come this way, I'll take you to Jordan and Nicolas. Christian is across the quad at the preschool."

Nellie followed the woman in silence, rehearsing in her head what she would say to the sons of a woman who might never see them again. No words seemed right. As they entered the vice principal's office, the boys ran up, hugging her.

"Hi, Auntie Nellie. Are we in trouble?" Nicolas asked anxiously.

"Absolutely not." Nellie hesitated, then plunged forward. "Your mother was in an accident today, and I came to take you to the hospital. Your dad is with her."

"Is she dead?" Jordan's words assaulted her.

"Oh, no, Jordan. She is hurt bad, but she's alive, and we're all praying she gets better real soon." This was not how she had planned to break the news.

"Let's go get Christian so we can go see her." Nicolas led the way.

Nellie received the same warm welcome at the preschool, and in short order she and the three boys were on their way to the waiting car. Lloyd had used the time to unpack and install the car seat. With Jordan's help, Nellie strapped Christian in, and each of the boys sat on either side of him.

One hour and thirty-five minutes after Lloyd and Nellie left the station, they pulled into the hospital parking lot. Trepidation engulfed Nellie. She didn't know what awaited them in the shock-trauma unit.

Lloyd had the same thoughts.

31

"D r. Vandross, please say something. Is she gone?" Jerome stood, took her shoulders and shook her. "Talk to me!"

"Jerome, I need you to stay calm. We've been able to stop the bleeding, but she has lost a lot of blood. Nicolle is back from the CAT scan. She has a fractured skull, and there's swelling in the brain. We're going to take her to surgery to relieve some of the pressure.

"One of the nation's best neurosurgeons is on her way from Orange County. We've known each other a very long time.

"Jerome, I've known you since you were a snot-nosed rookie, and I only know how to be one way—straight. Nicolle has a battle. The loss of blood has weakened her, and the surgery is a tough one."

"What are you saying, Doc?" Jerome's voice sounded calm, but his eyes betrayed him.

"I'm saying that I don't know what will happen over the next few critical hours, but I do know that we've called in the top people in Southern California, and Nicolle could have no better team." She hesitated. "Is anyone coming to be with you? I don't think you should be alone."

Struggling to keep his composure, Jerome answered slowly, "Our parents are on the way, and the Fredericksons are picking up the boys and bringing them here."

"Good. Family is very important to her recovery and to your sanity. Don't try to carry this burden alone. It's way too big. You're going to have to draw strength from all of those who love you. I've called the counselors to come speak with you."

With much commotion, Mr. and Mrs. Devereaux entered the solarium. Maxella ran to Jerome with outstretched arms. "They won't let us see her! They won't tell us a thing. What do they mean they can't give me any information? I gave birth to her!"

"I know, Mom," Jerome said, holding her. "They're busy trying to stabilize her before they take her to surgery." Jerome had never noticed how much Nicolle favored her mother until this very moment. He held her tightly, trying to feel a tangible connection to Nicolle.

"Surgery? They didn't say anything to us about surgery." Mr. Devereaux moved closer to his wife and son-in-law.

Extending her hand, Donna introduced herself. "Hi, I'm Dr. Vandross. I'm not in charge of your daughter's case, but I work very closely with Dr. Fulton. By law, we can only speak with the patient or the next of kin. In this case it's your son-in-law."

"What kind of stupid law is that?" Mr. Devereaux demanded. "Our child is lying in there, struggling to survive. I don't understand how you can stand here and tell me we don't have a right to know what is going on with her care!"

"Dad, please," Jerome said. "Dr. Vandross is doing her job. I'll give them permission to speak with you and tell you whatever they can. Nicolle has some swelling in her brain, and they have to go in and relieve the pressure."

"Oh, Lord, Lord, Lord. No! Not my baby!" Jerome caught Maxella Devereaux before she fell to the floor. "My baby can't die!"

David Devereaux knelt next to the chair where Jerome sat his mother-in-law. David took her hands and spoke softly. "God promised not to take us where His grace couldn't keep us. My child is not going to die, and I need you to believe the same thing. Where is your faith, woman?"

Sobbing, Maxella fell into her husband's arms. "I'm sorry, Dave. I'm so sorry. You're right. She's going to make it through this. She'll be all right!"

Jerome felt he needed to do something for her, but he craved comfort himself. That was always Nicolle's job. She would know the right thing to say and do to make him feel better. Who was going to do that for him now?

"I need to get back to the trauma unit to see if I can assist Dr. Fulton," Dr. Vandross said. "I'll come out and tell you the minute anything changes. I know it's not easy, but keep the faith. There's a counselor on the way, and she'll be able to help you with all of these feelings you're having." Looking at Nicolle's parents, the doctor said gently, "There's no better trauma team gathered anywhere in Southern California than those working on your daughter. With God's help, we'll have her as good as new in no time."

"Thank—" Tears broke into David's words. "Thank you, Doctor."

The three of them watched as the good doctor disappeared through the automatic sliding-glass doors. Maxella turned to Jerome with tearstained cheeks, puffy eyes and trembling lips and asked, "What are we going to do now?"

"All we can do is wait." Jerome thought of something. "Where's my mom? I thought she was coming with you and Desmond?"

Maxella rubbed Jerome's arm. "Your father was close to home when he got the call, and she decided to wait for him. We saw him a block from the house when we were leaving, so they should be here any minute. Desmond hadn't returned from the store and I just could wait no longer."

"Lloyd and Nellie are picking up the boys," Jerome said. "All the people who love Nicolle will soon be here, and we can be strength for one another."

Just then the Winters boys arrived, with Lloyd and Nellie following behind them. Seeing their grandparents, they sang in unison, "Grandma, Grandpa!"

"What did you bring me?" Christian asked innocently.

Maxella laughed and picked Christian up into her arms, hugging him tightly. "Grandma didn't have time to stop. I promise next time!"

Jerome's eyes met Lloyd's, and a special moment passed between them. Jerome seemed to draw strength from his longtime friend. The adults hugged without words. Before the greetings had dissipated, the Winterses arrived, and the hugs started up again. Jerome brought everyone up to date.

"What do we do now?" Montgomery Winters asked, looking at his son.

"The only two things we can do at this point, Dad: pray and wait."

32

The station was morbidly quiet.

SportsCenter was on the big-screen television, but the sound had been muted. Austin and Andrew had gone to the gym to lift weights, trying to relieve some of the tension. Headquarters had put Station 27 on a four-hour bypass—out of respect, they'd said, but if the truth be known, it was because they were having trouble getting a stand-in captain.

Mychel had returned to the dormitory. Removing her uniform, she stood, admiring her firm, well-contoured, naked body in the full-length mirror. "Mirror, mirror on the wall, who's the luckiest girl of us all?"

A smile spread across her full lips as she thought of Nicolle's funeral. She'd be so supportive of Jerome during his time of grief. She would be there to supply his every need. She'd become indispensable. Then, one morning, Jerome Winters would wake up and see that he was in love with her.

Her bone-chilling laughter seemed to rattle the very rafters of the dormitory.

33

Minutes ticked away like hours as Nicolle's family filled the waiting room and solarium. Pastor Blake and members of the New Missionary Baptist Church had come, gone and come again. Jerome yearned to be alone, all the while wondering why more people hadn't come by the hospital. Christian was growing restless, and Jerome's nerves felt as frayed as an overworked pulley rope.

"Daddy?"

Nicolas's voice and touch startled Jerome from his exhausted reverie. "Yes?" Jerome didn't mean for his voice to sound so sharp. Catching himself, he smiled gently at his son.

Jordan joined his brother. "We were just wondering . . ."

Finishing his brother's sentence, Nicolas said, "Is Mommy going to die?"

Jerome realized that in all of the comings and goings, he hadn't taken the time to talk to his sons. He'd been so caught up in what he was feeling that he didn't stop to think what Nicolle's sons, both of them mama's boys, must be going through. Jerome took them by the hand and led them to the far end of the solarium. He pulled out two chairs and sat in the third. "Sit here for a moment."

Obediently, they followed their father's orders.

The right words were elusive, and the knot in Jerome's throat altered his voice. "Do either of you know what it means to die?"

With Nicolle's warm eyes, Jordan looked at his father in bewilderment. "Yeah. It means you go away and don't come back. Ever."

"They put you in a casket and put you in the ground," Nicolas responded with sadness.

"So you know what you're asking me about your mom? You want to know if she is going to go away and never come back?"

They both nodded.

Drawing a very deep breath Jerome began, "I wish I knew what to tell you. I wish I could tell you that when the doctors finish what they're doing in the operating room, your mom will come out and wake up and in a little time she'll be running you around town like she always has. But I can't, because I don't know. She may go to sleep for a very long time and wake up and be fine. She may wake up and still be very sick, not able to take care of herself, or she may just sleep her way right into heaven."

"But I don't want Mommy to go to heaven." Nicolas hopped from his seat and ran to his father, almost knocking him over with the force of his fear.

"I don't think you mean it quite like that, Nick, but I do understand. I don't want Mommy to go to heaven *right now,* either."

"Who'll take care of us?" Jordan looked very somber.

"I will," Jerome said, trying to sound strong.

"But who will take care of *you*?" Nicolas asked very seriously.

Jerome laughed and gathered both boys into his arms. It was the first time he'd laughed in what seemed like a decade. "You know, that's a really good question, Nick. I guess you and your brother are going to have to take care of me. We'll take care of each other."

Jerome let the boys slip from his arms as he saw Dr. Fulton—and someone he guessed was the neurosurgeon—approaching. He couldn't read their expressions, and his heart raced.

His family and friends trailed behind the green-clad duo.

What were they coming to tell him?

34

"Hi, I'm Glynda Naylor-Sanders. Is Captain Frederickson in?" Glynda extended her hand to Andrew. "I took a chance he'd be here. I don't have an appointment."

"Miss Lady, you don't *ever* need an appointment to stop by Station 27 on C Shift." Andrew broke his body down into his best player pose.

Ignoring Andrew's very poor attempt at flirting, Glynda looked around the station. "Is Lloyd here?"

"Please ignore the station mascot." Austin pushed Andrew aside and extended his hand. "Can I help you? Captain isn't here. We've had a bit of a tragedy."

"Tragedy?" Glynda began rapid firing. "What's happened now? Did the Menace strike again? Has Lloyd been hurt?"

"Slow down, my fine brown cup of sugar." Andrew licked his lips. "Who did you say you were again? How do you know about what's been going on around here?"

"St. Vincent, please!" Austin chastised.

Turning back to Glynda, Austin looked at the floor before speaking. "I know you're the civil rights lawyer Cap has been talking to. No, he isn't hurt. One of our guys' wife was in a bad accident, and Cap is over at the hospital."

"How bad?" Glynda looked concerned.

Andrew dropped his Mack-Daddy manner. "Real bad—so bad we've been on bypass for almost four hours. We have a relief captain on the way, so we'll be back up and running soon. I personally ain't mad about doing nothing and getting paid."

"Why am I not surprised?" Glynda rolled her eyes and turned her attention back to Austin.

Andrew chuckled. "Feisty! I like that in a woman."

"Please forgive this fool, Ms. Sanders," Austin apologized.

Glynda eyed Andrew. "My money says your only requirement in a woman is breath and breast."

Placing his fist to his mouth, Austin had a belly roll of a laugh. "Oh, brotha, she told you." Turning back to the lawyer, he asked, "May I get you some coffee?"

"No, I'm not going to stay. I just wanted to run something by Lloyd. But in light of what's happened, I'll wait until he contacts me. You all have my prayers. Please tell Lloyd to call me."

"Let a young brotha walk you out?" Andrew offered his arm.

Austin eyed him suspiciously.

"I know my way out. Thank you though."

As Glynda walked from the equipment bay to the parking lot, she could feel their eyes boring a hole into her round behind. She tried not to sway her hips, but of course they did their own thinking.

"That is a fine sistah right there!" Andrew high-fived Austin. "She could make a brother like me settle down."

"Man, please. There is no one woman that can make you settle down, but I agree with you. That is one classy sistah. But by the two last names and the Rock of Gibraltar on her hand, I'd say that 'fine brown sugar,' as you call her, sweetens someone else's coffee."

"Yeah, but I sure could—" Glynda's return interrupted Andrew. "Well, well, well, you couldn't stay away?"

"Excuse me, but all my tires have been flattened." Glynda trembled slightly. "There's an ice pick sticking out of one of them. We need to call the police."

"What the f—?" Austin maneuvered around the paramedic wagon and sprinted to the parking lot.

"Do you want me to call the auto club?" Andrew was fishing for the right thing to say. He didn't want to come off as a smart-ass at the moment.

"Not yet. We need to wait for the police. They can only tow me. This is such a pisser. Who'd do such a thing?" Glynda flipped open her cell phone and put in her call to the police. "I'm going to have to get back downtown in order to catch the train home," she complained as she closed the phone.

"I bet it was whoever's been doing all of the other stuff, but they messed up this time. How much do your tires cost?"

"They're those high-performance ones. I'm not sure how much they cost—the car belongs to the law firm."

"I bet they are in excess of three hundred dollars each, which makes this a felony. Now the police have to do something, and the silly rabbit left the weapon. Let's hope we can get some prints." Andrew actually made sense.

"You know, you have a good point," Glynda mused. "This is a criminal act. But we'll only get lucky with the prints if this is a repeat offender."

"Or in the fire service."

Frowning, Glynda stared at him.

"We're all fingerprinted for our background checks."

"Could this person be so stupid not to know that?" Glynda said. "Or do you think they're just messing with us? Maybe they had someone else do it to throw us off . . . but they've messed with the wrong sistah."

"I just bet they have. You *are* feisty! I was just messing with you earlier. I knew you wouldn't fall for the play."

Glynda tried to relax. "Then why do you even bother? You have to know I'm married."

"Can I be straight with you?"

"Of course."

"You made me nervous."

"How could I have made you nervous? I hadn't even said anything to you."

"You stepped in here like you owned the place. Knew what you wanted and weren't going to let anyone stop you from getting it. Women like you never even glance over their shoulder at me."

"Maybe because you're being so offensive. You're so much more appealing just like this. Just be natural. I bet you can be really funny. Do you know there is nothing better than when a man makes a woman laugh?"

"Laugh?"

"Not laughing at you, laughing with you."

Genuinely interested, Andrew invited her to sit on the back

bumper of the fire truck to wait for the police. "Do you mind sitting here or would you rather wait inside the office?"

"No, here is fine." Glynda sat her briefcase on the ground next to her.

"Glynda—is it okay if I call you Glynda?"

"Of course."

"The honeys at the club are all over a brother and eat up the game I'm running. I have a one hundred percent record. I never miss." He smiled wickedly.

"But what're you catching . . ." She rolled her eyes. "Have you ever tried to approach a woman you thought could hold a good conversation? You know, Andrew, getting a woman into bed doesn't take a lot of work. Getting into her head and heart . . . that's another story. You just need to chill out and look for a woman who likes herself, one who'll challenge you."

"Oh, hell naw. I don't want one of those women who's constantly on you about where you going, been, thinking about going. I'm single, and I like it that way."

"Not that kind of challenge. A woman who'll challenge your mind, one who'll encourage you to be all the man you can be for you. One who is smart and isn't afraid for you to be smarter. She'll be able to watch CNN with you and understand what she's seen."

A slightly overweight Los Angeles police officer, with Austin on his heels, interrupted their conversation. "I'm Officer Hartford. You reported a vandalism?"

Immediately turning her attention to the officer, Glynda stood and greeted him. "Yes, my car—actually, it's my law firm's vehicle. I'm sure you saw the LX-470 down on all fours."

"What's your name, ma'am?"

"Glynda Naylor-Sanders."

"Ms. Sanders, how long was the car parked before you noticed the tires flattened?" The officer removed a pad and pen from his breast pocket.

"I wasn't in here more than ten minutes."

"No more than fifteen," Austin interjected.

"Sounds like someone must have followed you. Is there someone who you've made angry? Old boyfriend, estranged ex-husband? Someone's wife?"

"None of the above. There's been a rash of incidents against the C Shift here at 27, and I think it's just another incident."

"What kind of incidents?"

"Everything from rodents in our coffee to somebody jacking with the equipment. Someone even killed our dog," Andrew answered.

"Have you notified the police before now?"

"The captain is dealing with headquarters. We reported the dog's death but nothing was done. Not really a crime," Austin responded. "We're not exactly sure what HQ has done—I just know it's not a whole hell of a lot."

"Where can I find your captain?" Officer Hartford asked while making notes.

"He had to leave because of an emergency." Andrew spoke up this time.

"What kind of emergency?" The officer looked concerned. "How can a fire station function without a captain?"

"We're on bypass until a replacement arrives. One of our crewmembers' wife was in an accident this morning—the head-on collision on Manchester?" Austin fished to see if the officer was informed about what happened in his territory.

Looking up from his notes, the officer asked, "The one where the guy was on the cell phone?"

"That's the one," Andrew said with a tad of sarcasm.

"I'm really sorry. The word on the street is it was pretty bad." Eyeing Glynda suspiciously, the officer asked, "What brought you to the station?"

"I'm an attorney, and I came here to meet with the shift captain. Why are my actions coming into question?"

"Just trying to get all the facts, ma'am."

Exasperated, Glynda walked to the end of the equipment bay. "Look, this has been a bad day here. Can we just write the report so I can call triple-A and get towed into the tire place?"

Trying to relieve some tension, Andrew interjected, "Officer, this is a felony. Those tires cost more than three hundred bucks. Each."

"Nice." Officer Hartford was suddenly cordial.

"The ice pick should be dusted for prints."

"You watch *CSI*, huh?" The officer smirked.

Now Glynda was mad. "Look, Officer. You need to contact Chief Marlborough and tell him what has happened here. If this were a lone incident, I wouldn't be making such a big deal, but this could be critical. If we can lift prints from the ice pick, it may just solve this mystery."

The officer looked to Andrew and Austin, as if Glynda's explanation needed confirmation. They nodded.

"What's the chief's number? Maybe with a word from him we can get the dicks involved."

"Are you taking any of this seriously, Officer Hartford?" Glynda didn't try to hide her annoyance.

"Little lady, I take every call seriously." Officer Hartford's face flushed red. "But I'll give this one a little special attention myself. If we think this is directed at the boys in blue, it becomes personal.

"We appreciate any help you can give us, but I think the ice pick will prove to be a very valuable piece of evidence. I'll get an evidence bag from the patrol car. Also, let me get a phone number for each of you."

Each of them gave the officer their contact information, and they walked with him as he went to gather the evidence. His attitude had turned the corner, and he was warm and cooperative by the time he left.

"Do you think he's really going to do anything about this or was he just trying to humor us?" Austin asked as the trio returned to the equipment bay.

"Who knows? But if he does, then maybe this will light a fire under the chief. Cap is so frustrated with this whole situation and HQ's lack of action," Andrew added.

"Well, gentlemen, I need to call the auto club and get going."

"You mentioned you needed to get back downtown. Would you like for me to drive you?" Andrew asked with sincerity.

"I think you need to stay around, be here when the replacement captain arrives, but I appreciate your offer. When I spoke to the office manager they told me to have the car towed back to the garage and they would handle getting the tires replaced, so I'll just ride with the tow truck driver."

"Anytime. And thanks, Ms. Sanders. I hope we meet again." Andrew winked.

Austin stared from Andrew to Glynda and back again. What in the world had he missed?

35

Jerome held his breath as he waited to hear if his wife had survived the surgery.

"Mr. Winters, this is Dr. Hale. She headed the surgical team that worked on your wife." The petite, fair-skinned woman extended her hand.

Unable to control his trembling, Jerome took her hand in both of his. "How's Nicolle?"

"There was some bleeding in the brain, but we were able to stop it." The doctor spoke very slowly. "There was a fair amount of swelling."

Wanting to drag the words out of her, Jerome asked, "Is she going to be all right?"

The entire family had gathered behind Jerome, clinging to the silence that hung around them. Maxella Devereaux began to cry. "Please, Dr. Hale, say something."

"At this point, we honestly don't know. We've done all that we know how to do medically. The next forty-eight hours will determine her prognosis."

"What are her chances?" Mr. Devereaux insisted. "Be straight with me, Doctor."

Jordan grabbed his father's hand.

"At this moment? I can't give her better than a twenty percent chance of a full recovery. I'm sorry."

"Oh, sweet Jesus, noooooooo!" Maxella collapsed into her husband's arms.

Nicolle's father assisted his wife to a nearby chair. One of the church members went to offer assistance.

"What are her chances of survival?" Jerome's words were barely audible.

"The next forty-eight hours will determine that." There was no emotion in this woman. Didn't she realize what her words were doing to this family?

"Mr. Winters," Dr. Fulton broke in. "What Dr. Hale is saying is that if your wife survives her injuries, there is a possibility of brain damage because of the massive blood loss. We just don't know. Again, we have to wait and see what the next few hours bring. I'm very glad to see that you have your family here with you. Praying surely couldn't hurt our cause one bit." Dr. Fulton's people skills far exceeded those of his colleague.

"Can we give blood?" First Lady Blake asked.

"That would be wonderful," Dr. Fulton replied. "I can show you to the blood bank."

"Do you have any more questions?" Dr. Hale asked very matter-of-factly.

"What happens now, besides the waiting?" Jerome's father, Montgomery, asked.

"Mrs. Winters will be in recovery for the next ten to twelve hours. We'll monitor her very closely. If we don't have to take her back to surgery in that time, her chances of a full recovery improve greatly. If she progresses during that time, we'll move her to SICU, where she'll remain for several days. I must warn you that if she survives the next forty-eight hours, she may be in a spontaneous coma for several days. Even if she regains consciousness, we may induce a coma with medication to give the brain swelling time to reduce."

Jerome opened his mouth and moved his lips, but he couldn't hear any words. His mother moved to his side.

"I will be with your wife until we see a change. You may call on Dr. Fulton at any time if you have questions. I really need to get back to the recovery room." Dr. Hale turned and walked away without another word.

The group was numb both from the doctor's lack of compassion and from the news she'd delivered. They stared from one to the other until Reverend Blake said, "Let us pray."

36

Pastor Blake's prayer brought a sense of peace to the group gathered in the solarium awaiting news of a change in Nicolle's condition. Jerome teetered on the thin tightrope of reality and disbelief as he reflected on how his life had changed in such a short time.

As night fell, the crowd began to thin. More than one hundred people had come and gone in the eight hours since Station 27 had rolled onto the scene of the head-on collision.

"Jerome?" Nellie softly touched his back as he stared blankly at the city lights.

"Hey, Nell. Did the boys eat good?"

"Christian and Jordan did. Nicolas just picked at his. I think I should take all three of them home. They can get a good night's sleep and we'll decide in the morning if they should go to school or not."

"Let me talk to them first."

Jerome moved to where his sons sat stoically. "Hey, fellas. Nellie told me you had dinner. Are you tired?"

Jordan nodded his head as Christian rubbed his eyes. Nicolas slowly said, "I don't want to go to sleep. If I go to sleep, Mommy might die."

Jerome could imagine the burden his boys carried. His load seemed unbearable, and he understood everything that was happening. In his young mind Nicolas thought he could control his mother's fate. "Son, I wish I could tell you that if you went to sleep your mother will be alive when you wake up. But I can't do that. Pastor Blake has prayed, and we believe God has healed her and she'll wake up. But whether you go to sleep or not, what happens to Mommy won't change."

"Are you going to go to sleep?" Jordan asked.

"Yes, but not right now. My body won't stay awake forever, and when your mommy wakes up I need to be strong and rested so I can help take care of her."

Nicolas stared at Jerome. "What do you want us to do, Dad?"

After some hesitation, Jerome finally said, "I think you should go home with Aunt Nellie and Uncle Lloyd. Sleep in one of those big comfortable beds, and I promise to be over in the morning to talk to you about your mother and to see if you feel up to going to school."

Jerome hugged Jordan and Nicolas tight and they walked back to where the Fredericksons were standing with Christian near his and Nicolle's parents.

"Jerome, remember you don't have a car here. I can take Nellie and the boys home and then come back and stay with you," Lloyd offered.

Nellie stared at him. Didn't he think she might need some help with the boys? She hadn't been with little children in a lot of years. This was so like her husband. But he insisted he could change.

As though Jerome had read her thoughts he said, "Lloyd, man, I think I should just hang out here alone. I think Mr. and Mrs. Devereaux are going to stay, maybe Mom and Dad, too. But you go home and help Nell with the boys. Read them a story or something. You can go by the house and get them some clean clothes, diapers, toothbrushes and such. Jordan and Nick can show you where everything is."

Reluctantly Lloyd agreed. "Okay. I'll come back in the morning to pick you up."

"That sounds like a plan. I can't tell you guys how much I appreciate what you're doing. The boys should go to school unless . . ." Jerome's words trailed off.

"We're not even going to think that way," Nellie consoled.

"I'm really trying. Really, really trying," Jerome said. "I just know she has to be okay. I can't survive without her. I just can't."

Pastor Blake, along with a few other members from the church, remained and gathered around the family. There were hugs and kisses all around from the grandparents as the boys prepared to leave.

"Daddy, are you sure you're going to be okay?" Jordan seemed so much more mature to his father at that moment.

"I promise" was all Jerome could manage.

37

"I don't know what to say. It's just really scary to be out of control. I was in the firehouse for only ten minutes, and when I came out someone had flattened all my tires." Glynda chatted on her cell phone with Dawn while she waited for the commuter train.

"What do you think Anthony is going to do?" Dawn asked, concerned for her sister's safety.

"I'm not sure I'm going to tell him. He's so paranoid about everything anyway. Now that he's on the national security task force at the base, he is so cautious. He doesn't like me working in a downtown high-rise either. But you know what Eddie Naylor always says?"

"What God has intended, no man can interrupt," both sisters sang in unison.

Laughing, the sisters felt their love reach across the miles. "I had dinner with Estelle tonight." Dawn quickly changed the subject.

"Oh, how is she? I surely do miss her. Ever since Daddy died she just doesn't come around anymore. She has never recovered from losing Daddy."

"Can you blame her? The way your sisters acted toward her, I wouldn't come around either."

"My sisters?" Glynda quipped. "Don't I know it! If Collette stopped talking about how she doesn't need a man and tried to find herself a good one that she didn't scare, maybe she wouldn't be so hard to get along with."

"She is such a hypocrite because she is running around with a flashlight, match and candle at high noon looking for a man. She is always trying to get someone to fix her up. And besides, what's Renee's excuse? Are you saying that me not having a man gives me an excuse to be a witch?"

"Point very well taken. I stand corrected." Glynda chuckled. "So what's new and exciting with Estelle?"

"She's going to retire in December and wants you to come to the party. She's selling her house and buying a condo on the Potomac, gurl."

"Wow! I would love to come! You know we were pretty silly to begrudge Daddy a life with her. They were so good for each other. I just wish he hadn't died just weeks before they were to get married. At least have a few happy years together."

"What's this 'we' stuff? I never thought anything but happy thoughts for them. It was the rest of you selfish heffas that didn't want Daddy to have anybody. She looks really great though. Jamaica is coming home for the retirement party and staying until the first of the year."

"I heard from my sistahgurlfriend about a month ago, and he seems to be doing fabulous. His Parisian production was extended again. There's another production company that's courting him here in the States." Glynda moved to a less crowded area of the metro station.

"He's one fantastic talent. I'm sure if he were here, he'd be up for a Tony." Dawn paused thoughtfully. "I asked Estelle if she was dating anyone."

"What did she say?"

"She got real melancholy, stared off into space and said, 'Two years ago a part of my soul died. That's not something you can ever get back. Why would I put a man through the constant test of trying to measure up? I've been to the summit—anything else is strictly downhill.' "

"That's deep, but I do understand. Is she happy though?"

"She seems really at peace. Renee and Collette haven't spoken to her since shortly after the funeral. All Collette talks about is the two hundred and fifty thousand dollars Estelle received. I'm so glad you were the executor of the estate. I couldn't have handled it, and if Collette had been appointed, I think we'd all be in jail by now."

"It was a really hard job, but Daddy knew what he was doing. The emotional turmoil of going through everything he owned was just too much at times. I had one of the law clerks handle most of it. I'm so glad it's done and over with. Collette seemed happy with what we got for the house."

"Gurl, Collette is never happy. But the rest of us are set for quite a while if we manage our money right. I think Uncle Thomas washes that Lincoln every day."

"I bet he does. Speaking of Uncle Thomas, when does he go to Alaska?"

"He left on Saturday. He called me this morning. He sounded a little full. He was at Thomas Junior's, and he saw his grandsons for the first time. Michael is coming over this weekend with his three," Dawn reported happily.

"Michael has all boys, too?"

"No, he has two girls and a boy. Uncle Thomas is beside himself. He said he had a long talk with T.J., that's what Thomas Junior calls himself, and explained what happened when they were young. He said T.J. understood because he had to take his oldest son's mother to court for just that reason."

"Sounds like it's come full circle, huh? How's their mother?"

"She passed away a week ago."

"Too bad she didn't have a chance to make peace with Uncle Thomas, too."

"The most important thing is he gets a second chance with T.J. and Michael. Better the chance be late than gone forever."

"Amen to that. My train will be here in about three minutes. I wanted to ask you one more time if you have reconsidered coming out for a visit. I've given you dates of several events. Given you a contact in travel and you still haven't made up your mind."

"You know what, my sister, I'm going to do just that. Let me check at work tomorrow and see what's available vacationwise and get back to you tomorrow night. For sure this time. Before you go, I think you should tell Anthony what happened to you. He's in the protection business. Maybe he can help."

"I'll think about it. I just don't want to worry him unnecessarily. I love you, Dawn. Gotta go. My train is coming."

As Glynda boarded the train she never noticed the tall stranger with the dark hair and gray eyes who followed her onto the train.

38

"Mr. Winters?" Dr. Fulton gently shook Jerome.

"What happened?" Jerome was on his feet instantly and fully alert. "Did something happen to Nicolle?"

"I just wanted to give you a status report. We've taken another CAT scan and the swelling is decreasing. She is by no means out of the woods, but the reduction is significant and that's a positive sign. If you want to go see her for five minutes, we can allow that."

A sigh of relief escaped Jerome. He didn't know what to say to the doctor—he wanted to hug him, kiss him even. But he settled on shaking his hand. "Thank you, Dr. Fulton." Jerome pumped his hand. "Thank you. I just want to wash my face first."

"Just let me know whenever you're ready. I want to prepare you. I know you're a firefighter, but this is your wife. She has severe bruising and swelling on her face. We shaved her head, though you can't see that because of the bandages. There are tubes and I.V.s. I'd like to tell you it looks worse than it is, but in this case it is pretty representative of her condition."

"Can I touch her?"

"Absolutely. We also want you to talk to her. We don't know why it works when loved ones talk to comatose patients—we just know it does."

"I'll be right back." Jerome darted off in the direction of the men's room and disappeared through the door. Once inside he rushed to the stall and emptied the contents of his stomach. He had to get ahold of himself. He felt weak and helpless. This was no way for a man to act, a man who made his living being a hero.

On the counter were deodorant, lotions, disposable toothbrushes and mouthwash. This was a bathroom devoted to the families of trauma patients—those who stayed at the hospital for days waiting for news on those who clung to life. He quickly brushed his teeth and washed his face. He couldn't believe he'd fallen asleep. He remembered walking both sets of parents to the parking lot at four forty-five and the elevator ride back to the seventeenth floor. The next thing he knew, Dr. Fulton was shaking him and the sun was shining bright through the glass of the solarium. He checked his watch for the first time and noted he'd slept for one hour and fifteen minutes.

Rejoining the doctor, Jerome had no words. He realized none were needed. The two men solemnly walked toward the SICU. Jerome's feet felt like they weighed one hundred pounds each. Dr. Fulton stopped, and Jerome knew they had arrived at their destination. "Are you sure you're ready, Mr. Winters?"

"As ready as I'll ever be."

With the press of a few buttons the double doors swung outward, and a world filled with the sounds of life-sustaining machines rushed out to greet them. The doors opened onto a corridor lined with glass-walled rooms. At first glance Jerome assumed there were a dozen entryways. As they walked deeper into the unit the noises grew louder until Jerome couldn't hear the thoughts in his head. They passed space after space occupied by patients with tubes and machines connected to what looked like every part of their bodies. Jerome was no stranger to this environment, but he felt another wave of nausea coming on.

Dr. Fulton stopped at the fourth entry on the left. "Remember you only have five minutes. I wish I could grant you more."

"I understand." In actuality Jerome didn't. If he sat quietly and promised not to get in anybody's way, why couldn't he stay with her? He just wanted to watch her, to touch her hand.

Dr. Fulton stepped aside, and Jerome's heart broke as he gazed upon his beloved. Her beautiful face had been distorted by the swelling. Her milk-chocolate skin was purple beneath the bandages. She lay so still, while only her chest moved up and down by means of the respirator.

"I'll be back in five minutes." Jerome never saw the doctor leave.

Slowly he approached Nicolle's bedside. As he drew closer, the distortion of her face became more vivid. His heart ached. He knew he would never forget the sight of her at this moment. How could this have happened to the woman he cherished so much? Grief filled his heart while anguish overtook his soul.

Gently taking her hand to avoid the I.V., he fell to his knees. "Dear God, please . . ." No other words came, only sobs. The beeps of the heart monitor and hum of the respirator grew louder, stealing his words as he tried to speak to his Father. "Help her, Lord. Touch her broken body. Make her whole again. All praise and honor are Yours."

Raising his head with tear-filled eyes, Jerome gazed upon Nicolle. What a wonder-filled life they'd had. He realized without intent he'd taken for granted that she would always be around to take care of him. She consistently knew where he put things when he had forgotten. She finished his sentences and verbalized his thoughts. They were one soul that occupied two bodies. She could not leave him. He wouldn't let that happen.

Talk to her. Dr. Fulton's word echoed in his head. "Hey, Babeski," he began softly. "It's your lover man. You gave us a bit of a scare. But you're going to be just fine. The boys are with Lloyd and Nellie. I promised to take them to school this morning so when I leave here I'll do that. They are quite the young men, very brave. They want me to tell you they love you and can't wait for you to fry some chicken. Actually, you know that was Nicolas who was concerned about food. Christian isn't real sure what's going on. You know him—just kinda goes with the flow and hopes his brothers don't torture him.

"Pastor Blake and half the congregation were here yesterday. We filled the solarium to overflow. You know how pastor loves a big crowd. Your mom and dad will be back this morning. I hope they let them in to see you."

"Mr. Winters, I'm sorry, your time is up." A middle-aged woman with a short haircut and a bright smile touched Jerome on his back.

"That's impossible. It can't be five minutes already," Jerome said, louder than he'd planned.

"You can come back in a couple of hours, but right now we need to conduct some tests. I think you should go home and get some rest. When she wakes up she's going to need you to be here and not exhausted."

When she wakes up. A ray of hope warmed Jerome like the sun on an island beach. Looking up from where he knelt, Jerome whispered, "You think she's going to make it?"

"Mr. Winters, I believe until I see differently. I've seen people with much worse injuries get up and walk out of here, while others with marginal injuries not make it. It's all in the believing, son."

Standing, Jerome looked at the woman's badge and then into her eyes. He took her hands and smiled. "Thank you, Kathleen."

Looking a little perplexed, she asked, "For what?"

"Making a brotha remember from whence cometh his help."

"I'll give you one more minute, but then you'll have to go for now."

Turning his attention back to Nicolle, Jerome said, "I promise I will."

Kathleen left as quietly as she had entered.

"Well, Babe-ski, they're making me leave. But you know I won't be far. I can't wait to look into those beautiful eyes of yours again." Jerome bent to kiss her swollen cheek gently. "I love you, Nicolle Devereaux-Winters."

Jerome stopped at the nursing station. "Will you let Kathleen know that I've left?"

"Kathleen who?" A young woman with a badge that read R. PERKINS, R.N. asked.

"I don't know her last name. She came into my wife's room when I was there and told me it was time to leave because you needed to do more tests."

"You're Mr. Winters, correct?" Ms. Perkins inquired.

"Yes."

"Well, I'm your wife's nurse, and we don't have anyone on this floor by the name of Kathleen. Besides, our badges don't have first names. Are you sure you aren't mistaken? What did she look like?"

"Mid to late fifties, short, natural salt-and-pepper hair, about five foot seven, one hundred seventy-five pounds. She was wearing a uniform similar to yours."

"I'm sorry, but I have no idea who you're talking about. This is a secure area, and only those who are authorized can even get in."

The hair on the back of Jerome's neck stood up. He knew he wasn't imagining his conversation with Kathleen.

Had he been touched by an angel?

39

"Mornin'." Lloyd approached Jerome while he sat at the computer in the waiting room. "How's Nicolle? Any changes?"

"Hey, Lloyd. You startled me." Jerome stood to greet him. "I was just sending an e-mail to Pastor Blake to tell him what happened to me this morning. Nicolle's about the same. They did let me see her, though."

"Well, that's real good. Are you ready to go get the boys? You know we can handle this. Nellie can take them to school."

"They need to see me. I want them to understand I'm not going anywhere. I need to shower and change anyhow. They're going to be running some tests this morning that will be a couple of hours, or maybe . . ."

"Maybe what?"

"Something very interesting happened to me this morning when I was in Nicolle's room. I was kneeling and praying, and a woman, who I thought was a nurse, came into the room and touched me. Told me that it was all in the believing. I thanked her, turned my attention back to Nicolle and then she was gone. I didn't think anything of it until I went out to the desk to let her know I had abided by her one-minute-more rule. When I spoke to the other nurse, she said no one by the name of Kathleen worked here, and when I looked at the badge, the names were displayed differently."

"Did you report it to security?"

"Ms. Perkins, the nurse I was talking to, said it's a secure area. No one can get in or out of there without the appropriate codes. I'm just perplexed."

"Maybe you imagined it," Lloyd suggested. "You know, stress does strange things to you."

"She was real. I know it like I know you're standing here." Jerome regretted his strong stand on the matter. Lloyd would think he had lost his grip on reality. But had he? He knew in his heart of hearts he'd been visited by an angel. "Well, no matter who it was, she left me with a message that will sustain me through this."

"And that's all that really matters," Lloyd said.

Changing the subject, Jerome asked, "Anything else happening with the Menace of C Shift?"

"You need to focus all of your energy on Nicolle and the boys— speaking of which, we need to get going." Lloyd walked toward the door.

"Something did happen, didn't it?"

Letting out a great sigh, Lloyd turned to face Jerome once more. "Someone punctured Ms. Sanders's tires when she came to visit me yesterday."

"You are kidding me!" Jerome couldn't believe the Menace had struck again, at such a bad time for everyone.

"But this is not for you to be concerned with and especially to do anything about it. I'll put you in for as much leave as you think you'll need to get you through this."

"Leave?" Jerome looked surprised. "I have four days off starting today. I know Nicolle will wake up before then and be just fine. What can I do to help. I'll be able to come back to work because she is going to be fine."

"Are you sure about this? You should think this through. How are you going to be able to handle all that has been put on you and work? At least take a couple weeks off. I tell you those boys are a handful."

"We'll see. I just have to keep busy. This sitting around here will drive me nuts. They won't let me see her more than five minutes at a time."

"How often?"

"They haven't said yet. I guess it depends on what they have going on with her. And some of those five minutes will have to be shared with our parents. I don't think the boys should see her. Her face is pretty messed up. I know I will never forget what I saw when I entered that room."

Walking toward the elevator together, the two friends fell silent. Jerome was lost in thought as he pondered what Lloyd had suggested. Would he be disrespectful to Nicolle's condition if he went to work while she was still in a coma? But what could he do sitting in the waiting room? As he walked through the hospital lobby, the bustle seemed a stark contrast to the seventeenth floor where there was almost no foot traffic. The area was alive with people hurrying about.

Lloyd took Jerome first to the station to pick up his vehicle. As they entered the parking lot, A Shift members were straggling in. Jerome's intuition told him he should just leave, but habit forced him inside.

Lloyd gave Jerome a confused look. "Where you goin'?"

"I just want to say something to the crew. Let them know how everything is. You know, we're like family."

"Yeah, everyone is real shaken up about this. We do have a little time. The boys won't be up until seven thirty."

The men took the stairs to the recreation and kitchen area two at a time until they were at the top.

Austin was the first to see him. "Winters, how's your wife, man?"

"She's about the same. They have her on medication that will keep her in a coma until the swelling goes down in her brain."

"We're all pulling for her. We don't even know what to say. It's just such a shame," Andrew offered.

James Parker, an A Shift crew member added, "Hey, man, we just heard. We're real sorry. If we can do anything, just let us know. We can start doubling up to cover your shifts as long as need be."

"I appreciate that, Parker, but let's just see how things go over the next few days."

"Jerome, I'm so sorry!" Running in his direction, Mychel approached him with outstretched arms. When she reached him, she threw her arms around him and held on tight. "If there is anything

I can do, please don't hesitate. I can help with the boys, come over to cook, clean, you just name it."

Breaking free from Mychel's embrace, trying not to seem ungrateful, Jerome smiled as he looked into her tear-filled eyes. "Thank you, Mychel, but between our parents and close friends I think we've got it all covered."

With no shame, Mychel hugged him again and said, "Just know that I'm here for you twenty-four, seven, three sixty-five." She ran her hand down the length of his arm and took his hand in hers.

Their colleague's outpouring of affection stunned the others who stood watching the exchange. Sensing Jerome's seeming helplessness, Lloyd suggested, "We'd better get going. The boys will be waking up soon."

Relieved, Jerome smiled and said, "Thank you, everyone, for your positive thoughts and prayers. Our family has experienced a tremendous blow, but we believe God's going to bring us through this, and we'll be back to normal in no time. I really appreciate your offers and believe I'll be calling on you whenever the need arises."

Andrew patted him on the back, while Parker shook his hand. Austin gave him a fraternal hug and reminded him to call on him anytime. Mychel took his hand in both of hers and stared up into his eyes. "I'm here for you, my friend."

Avoiding her eyes, Jerome said, "Thanks again to all of you for your support. We'd better get going."

Jerome and Lloyd descended the stairs, encountering more of the A shift crew. They, too, expressed their commiseration. As they exited the station the too bright sun collided with Jerome's cloudy cold mood and gave him a thunderous headache.

Squinting against the sun, Lloyd looked him square in the face. "What in the hell is up with Hernandez?"

"Man, I wish I knew. She's been acting weird for a while now. I never told you, but she came into my room wearing a towel and accidentally let it fall. In all my years on the department, I've never had this problem with a colleague."

"It happens, but we've been lucky around here, I guess. She's making it look bad for all the women. She's so capable, but she's falling into the good ole boys' stereotyping. They want women to do this kind of thing so they can say, 'We told you this would happen.' She's one of the most talented members of our crew—top-notch paramedic, one of the best firefighters I've got—but I'll transfer her out faster than ice melts in the desert in July."

"I can handle her. I just don't appreciate her doing this. If she thinks I'm going to have her in my house, she's out of her mind."

"Well, we know she's got issues."

"Seems more like a subscription to me. All these single brothas with the department, and she comes after me."

Laughing, Lloyd said, " 'Cause you da man! I'll see you back at the house."

The friends parted, each getting into his own car. Jerome was consumed with thoughts of Mychel. What was she trying to prove? She pressed her body hard against his when she hugged him, and for a split second did he like what he felt? For as long as he could remember, another woman's advances had never shaken him. When in college, on the job, in social settings, there were always times when panties were pitched, but he never once even thought of putting on his catcher mitt, and coming up to bat was definitely out of the question.

Once again Jerome wondered why Mychel sat next to him.What was so different about her than all the women who'd set their sights on him in the past? Guilt eased its way from his toes up through his loin and settled smack-dab in the middle of his chest. The weight of his confusion made it difficult to breathe.

The drive to the upscale Los Angeles neighborhood in the hills high above the famed Crenshaw district was short and uneventful. His mind shifted quickly from Mychel to Nicolle and the long recovery period ahead of her. He had prayed and asked God to spare her and bring her back to him. He knew in his heart that his request had already been granted.

As he pulled onto the Fredericksons' street, anxiety overtook him. Jordan had been accurate in asking who would take care of them. Nicolle made it look so easy. Yet she had her days when she was overwhelmed. He knew how to go to work, boy scouts and soccer practice. He thought he knew how to turn on the washer and dryer, but he wasn't certain since they had purchased the new one a year before. He knew his way around the kitchen, but how many meals of French toast could he serve his sons in a week?

Surely their parents would be of help. But this was his responsibility. Somewhere along the way he had taken for granted all that Nicolle faced daily.

Jerome pulled into the driveway and parked behind Lloyd's Mustang. Hesitating for a few moments, he pulled deep from inside and put a smile on for the boys. He didn't want to let on how scared and inadequate he felt at this moment. He hadn't been such a hodge-podge of emotions before in his life. The closest he had ever come was at the birth of his sons. But grief and guilt were now added to the card deck.

Nellie opened the door as he and Lloyd approached. "Good morning, sweetie." She stepped onto the porch to greet him. "How are you feeling?"

"Good morning, Nell." Jerome hugged her back. "I'm not sure how I feel, to be honest. I guess numb best describes it."

"I understand. Come on in. The boys are in the kitchen having breakfast. Can I get you something?"

"Just some coffee."

"When's the last time you ate?"

Jerome stopped to think. "I guess it would have to be breakfast yesterday."

"Then you'll be having some grits, eggs, bacon and biscuits. There's no need for discussion. The last thing we need is for you to just faint away."

"I'm really not hungry," Jerome protested.

"Leave the man be, Nellie. He knows if he wants to eat or not," Lloyd said as they entered the house.

"Nonsense. Since when did a man know what was really good for him? If he doesn't eat, he'll become weak and won't be any good to himself or anyone else."

"Okay. I'm in the room. I get it. I'll eat a little."

Jordan and Nicolas ran to embrace him as he entered the kitchen. "Hi, Daddy!" they said together.

"Did Mommy wake up?" Jordan asked, looking up at his father.

"Not yet—but I did get to see her this morning."

"Can we see her?" Nicolas asked excitedly.

"Not just yet. I could only see her for five minutes, and they made me leave. There is so much equipment and stuff in the ICU they don't allow children in there. But as soon as they move her to a regular room you can go for a visit."

Jerome exchanged glances with Lloyd and Nellie. He prayed to himself he was not lying to his sons.

He walked over to Christian, who was busy stuffing scrambled eggs into his mouth, and picked him up. He hugged him close, and Christian put his greasy hands around his father's neck. In the past, Jerome would have been disturbed by the possibility of staining his uniform shirt. At this moment he never gave it a second thought. Funny how in a split second all of life's priorities changed.

"Do we have to go to school today?" Nicolas asked as he returned to the generous portions of eggs and grits on his plate.

"Yes, sir, you do. There's no reason for you to stay home. We'll be at the hospital all day."

"Ahhhhh, Dad!" Jordan pouted.

"Don't 'ahhhhh, Dad' me. I've spoken and you're going. Let's get a move on so you won't be late." Jerome pretended to be stern.

"Yes, sir." Jordan looked at the floor.

In general terms, Jerome shared with Nellie what he knew about Nicolle's condition as she prepared a plate for him. Did women do men a disservice by meeting all of their needs? He had come to expect this kind of treatment, and life was going to be a lot harder without it.

"You know we can take care of the boys, at least for the next few days. That way you don't even have to worry about them. I'll just go get them some clothes. We'll be just fine. Won't we, fellas?"

"Yes, Auntie Nellie. Can we stay, Dad, please?"

Jerome looked from Nellie to Lloyd and back again. "Are you sure?"

"Of course, we're sure. We wouldn't have it any other way," Lloyd answered quickly. "You just concentrate on Nicolle. She's the one who needs your attention."

"I don't know what to say." Jerome spoke just above a whisper, fighting the lump in his throat.

"Just say, 'Thank you, Lloyd and Nellie,' " Nellie teased.

"Thank you, Lloyd and Nellie." Jerome stood and hugged her. He drew strength from her as she held him for a long moment. Feeling another well of emotion springing up inside, he returned to the delicious breakfast.

40

"**G**ood morning. This is Glynda Naylor-Sanders."

"Well, top of the morning to you, missy." Lloyd struggled to put cheer into his voice.

"Hi, Lloyd. I didn't expect to hear from you today. I thought you would be with Jerome."

"I just dropped his boys off at school and he's gone home to change. They won't let anyone see her except Jerome and her parents, so there isn't much need for me just to sit around at the hospital. I want to go ahead with our meeting. I want to present the chief with our recommendations."

"I have everything ready. Are we going to just drop in, or do you already have an appointment?"

"I think the element of surprise would do quite nicely. Were you able to find out anything about the department he came from?"

"Not a whole lot. His record is clean. Been in fire service for thirty-seven years, with heavy political connections in Texas. He was a battalion chief and the deputy chief there before he came here. I think those are all things you already knew. I do have an investigator assigned to do some digging down in Houston. But it's a little too soon to know anything."

"Yeah, those are all the things I already know. But as sure as my hair is thinning and my waist is thickening, there's something that ain't right about that man."

"If you're right, hopefully we can dig some stuff up on him. What time do you want to meet?"

"Do you want me to pick you up?"

"I think I'm actually going to walk. It's such a gorgeous day. I want to feel the wind on my face, and the walk will do me good."

"Did you get your car back yet?"

"Oh, it was a company car. I'm sure it's all taken care of. But if not, I would just get another one from the pool."

"Those are some pretty fancy wheels for a company vehicle." Lloyd laughed.

"You should see what some of the partners drive!"

"That'll be you soon enough."

Laughing heartily, Glynda said, "Civil rights attorneys don't make partner here. But I love what I do so much it doesn't even matter to me."

"And that's all that matters. How about we meet right after lunch? Say one thirty?"

"That works great for me. I'll meet you in the lobby of the head-quarters building."

"Until then." Lloyd hung up first.

Glynda pulled the file from the stack at the edge of her desk. There was something tickling at the back of her neck, but she just couldn't put her finger on the pulse of it at the moment. She made a note to give it more thought later. Her gut instincts were rarely ever wrong.

She opened the folder and read the list of the formal complaints. The demands were simple and the minimum C Shift at Station 27 should expect. After reading the complaint document, Glynda moved to the investigative report on Fire Department Chief William Thomas Marlborough.

The report included pictures with both renowned and infamous political leaders. His tenure as the assistant fire chief had spanned more than a decade before coming to Los Angeles. As the assistant, most of the department's administrative duties would have fallen under his control, Human Resources included. The statistic for the makeup of the department might prove useful in their investigation. She made a note to have the research department gather the data for her.

41

The prayer service was a beautiful thing. More than half the congregation was there. We lit candles and called on God. And I know He heard our prayers. She is going to pull through this. I just know it." Pastor Blake sat down next to Jerome on the couch in the waiting room.

With his head hung low, feeling not even the slightest hint of hope, Jerome asked, "Do you really think she will? It's been ten days, and nothing has changed."

"I've never known you to doubt God about anything."

"I guess I've never been put to this kind of test before, Pastor. I know I'm failing. I feel so hopeless and helpless. When I saw her this afternoon she looked even worse than she did this morning."

"Brother Winters, you could use a nap. Are you sleeping at all?"

"A couple of hours last night. Every time I close my eyes, I see Nicolle at the scene, bruised and bleeding. I just can't get the images out of my head."

"I understand, son, but if you don't get some rest, you're not going to be any good for Nicolle, the boys or yourself. I know you want to be here when she wakes up, but we don't know how long that will take. I believe she'll wake up soon, but you need to get some routine back in your life for you and the boys."

Stunned, Jerome retorted, "How can I get routine in my life without Nicolle? She *is* my routine. Without her, I don't even know where to begin."

Ignoring Jerome's flare-up, the pastor answered, as any good man of God would do, "Have you eaten anything today?"

"I had breakfast with the boys this morning."

Pastor Blake glanced at his watch. "Jerome, that was several hours ago. Let me take you to get some lunch."

Jerome started to protest, but decided he *was* hungry. "You're right."

"How are your parents holding up?"

"Nicolle's parents were here earlier, but Mr. Devereaux was so shaken up after he saw her this time that they had to leave. He's so upset his baby girl is not improving. My parents wanted to come down, but I didn't think there would be much point since they can't see her."

"Have you thought that they might just want to see you? See how *their* child is doing? Don't think you're so strong that you don't need to lean on others. That's what we're here for."

"I'm a man, Pastor Blake! People lean on me, not the other way around." Jerome couldn't control his anger. "I shouldn't have to explain that to you."

Ignoring Jerome's tirade, Pastor Blake replied in a soothing voice, "No one will think less of you as a man if you bend. The important thing is that you lean toward those who love you and Nicolle so you won't break."

Feeling the exhaustion and frustration cave in on him, Jerome stopped pressing his back against the wall. Pastor Blake went to him and took his hand. "Son, we can do this. With God's help, we will make it through."

Convulsing sobs escaped from Jerome as he tried to speak. "I feel so ill-equipped. I just don't know if I can handle this. I don't know if I can take care of my sons. What about if and when Nicolle wakes up, what then? How do I take care of the woman who has always taken care of me?"

"Look at me. You can and you will do this because there's no alternative. How will you do it? One moment at a time, with the help of all of us and with faith in God is how. This is what your religious fortitude is all about. Anybody can be strong when things are good. I know you have faith and, brother, it is all in the believing."

Startled by the words, like a child he cut off the tears. "What did you just say?"

Stymied for a moment, Pastor Blake hesitated. "That your faith in God will sustain you?"

"No, the last thing you said."

"It's all in the believing?"

"That's what she said. She used those exact words."

"Who're you talking about? Nicolle?"

"This woman, I thought she was a nurse, but now I'm convinced she was an angel."

"Tell me more about this woman," the Pastor said soothingly.

Jerome proceeded to relay the story as they boarded the elevator to make the visit to the cafeteria. At the end of the account of what happened, Pastor Blake only smiled. "You see, that's what I've been trying to tell you all along. Now let's go have us a man-size burger and fries."

As the shepherd and one of his wounded sheep enjoyed their meal, something miraculous was happening in the surgical intensive care unit, bed seven. The index finger on Nicolle's left hand twitched.

Nurse Perkins was sitting at the desk busy making notes on charts and did not notice the slight movement of Nicolle's left hand.

Tears welled up in the man's eyes as he stared at the small television screen, where a news story relayed an unbelievable story: A wannabe firefighter had set several fires and then showed up to help fight them. He had been found out and arrested, and he would go to jail for a very long time.

He wiped his tears as he pulled his schedule from the drawer to see when he could get to New York to visit his comrade. He knew he could only be a comfort to him, but he would do all that he could.

He had to balance the trip with his schedule of events planned for Station 27.

With careful planning, he could swing it.

42

The afternoon sun kissed Glynda's face as she briskly walked toward the fire department headquarters. She loved fresh air, and today was perfect. After dining alfresco on a Greek salad and a chicken sandwich, she felt invigorated. As she rounded the corner, the hair on the back of her neck stood up. She felt someone's eyes on her.

She stopped abruptly, and an Asian woman walked into her. Apologizing, the woman moved on quickly. As Glynda stared into the afternoon crowd of pedestrians, she saw nothing out of the ordinary. Everyone seemed to be scurrying about their business. She felt silly and continued her trek, unaware that her brief encounter with the Asian lady had given the stranger with dark hair and gray eyes a chance to duck into a coffee shop.

Glynda continued the four-block walk and arrived right on time. She had glanced over her shoulder a few times on the journey and one last time as she entered the lobby where Lloyd waited patiently. "I hope I didn't keep you waiting."

He rose as she approached. "Not at all. I've only been here a minute or two myself. Are you ready?"

"You'd better believe it. I'm anxious to hear what the good chief has to say about his unwillingness to get at the bottom of what's happening on C Shift."

The two walked into the elevator, just as the dark-haired stranger entered the lobby.

As they stepped into the corner office on the fifth floor of the headquarters building, Lloyd sported a newfound confidence with Glynda at his side. Everyone took you more seriously when your lawyer did the talking.

"Good morning, Heather. Please let Chief Marlborough know that I'm here to see him." Lloyd smiled smugly.

A little taken aback, Heather searched the computer screen all the while clicking the futuristic-looking mouse. "I don't have you in the appointment calendar for today, Captain Frederickson."

"That's because I don't have one, Heather. But if you tell him I'm here with Ms. Sanders, my lawyer, I think he'll squeeze us in."

Flipping her blond hair over her right ear, Heather dialed four digits. "Chief Marlborough, Captain Frederickson and his lawyer—what's your name again?"

"Glynda Naylor-Sanders."

"Captain Frederickson and Ms. Sanders are here to see you." She listened for a moment. "No, sir, they don't have an appointment. I'll tell them." Turning her attention back to Glynda and Lloyd, Heather flashed a pert smile and said, "He's tied up and would like for you to schedule an appointment."

"Well, little lady, you can just pick up that phone and tell him we'll wait until he has time to see us." Lloyd reared back on his heels. "It's my day off."

Flustered, Heather rose from her chair and disappeared behind the double doors leading to the chief's private sanctum. In her haste she failed to close the door completely. Lloyd and Glynda moved a little closer.

"What is it now, Heather?" The chief was a little shorter-tempered than normal.

"They won't go away. Captain Frederickson said he'll wait as long as it takes."

"How dare he just show up here? Who does that nig—Who does Captain Frederickson think he is?"

Lloyd shot a glance at Glynda, who only shook her head thinking, *Oh, I know he wasn't about to use the N word!*

After a long pause, Heather said sheepishly, "Sir, what would you like for me to tell them?"

"Make them wait ten minutes and then show them in." Marlborough swore under his breath as Heather quickly left the office.

Looking like she'd had too much sun on a Hawaiian beach, Heather began speaking to Lloyd without making eye contact. "The chief has some business he needs to conclude and will be with you in about ten minutes. May I get you some coffee?"

"No. Thank you, though." Turning to Glynda, Lloyd offered, "Maybe Ms. Sanders would like something?"

"No, nothing for me either. We'll just wait over here."

The two walked to the area nicely appointed with two sofas and two straight-back chairs upholstered in rich forest-green leather. Lloyd pointed to the couch facing away from Heather.

"Did you see her face when she came out of that office?" Glynda laid her briefcase on the cushion next to her. "I wonder if she knows we heard their conversation?"

"Beats me, but she looked like a lobster pulled from a pot of boiling water. You could tell in his tone he was angry, but I can't imagine he would take it out on her that we dropped by unannounced."

"You've never worked in the corporate world, have you?" Glynda asked, only half joking. "That's just the way it is sometimes. He's mad and she's available—the perfect equation."

"He probably thinks I'll just go away. But he's the new kid on the block. Lloyd Frederickson never says die."

"But why wouldn't he want to see this thing resolved? Someone is terrorizing his people."

"His people?"

"Firefighters. No matter what your differences are politically, there is one thing you all share—the common goal to save people and property."

"Very nicely put. I wish everyone in the department felt the same way."

While the two recessed into quiet reflection, Chief Marlborough sat behind his massive cherrywood desk, speaking forcefully into the telephone receiver. "Look, I've tried to discourage him, but he just won't quit. But you need to back off. Let this blow over and then maybe in six months or so—No, I can't look the other way. It'll look more than a little suspicious if I don't do something."

"We've got a plan in place, and I just don't know if we can stop it. So much has already been done. We want to teach them a lesson once and for all," the man on the other end of the line whispered. "Don't you see what's happening? They are hiring them two to one. My boy couldn't get on the department. They rigged the test so he couldn't pass."

"Why didn't you tell me that one of my battalion chiefs is married to a black woman?" Marlborough tried to put him on the defensive.

"Now you see what I'm talking about. They've tainted our bloodline. Got pickaninnies running around all over the place." The man's voice began to rise.

"So you knew that St. Vincent's father was a white man, a battalion chief?"

"Of course I knew. And you didn't? But you say you don't need us. Don't tell me you've come out here to La-La Land and gotten soft on me."

Chief Marlborough sighed. "Look, I know you're frustrated, but you need to lie low. I think you've gotten out of hand. I just wanted you to shake 'em up a little."

"I know that niggra woman and Frederickson are up there with you. Those people are just too arrogant here. They don't know their place. You get that black man under control, or we'll stop him for you." The man's tone sent a chill up the chief's spine.

"What do you mean, you'll stop him? What are you talking about?" The chief shifted nervously in his chair.

"You handle your business, and we'll handle ours. I just hope you understand this is a runaway train."

"Look—" The harsh sound of silence as the stranger ended the call cut Marlborough off. His first instinct was to press redial but returned the handset to the cradle instead. Chief William Marlborough sat back hard in the Corinthian leather high-back chair. Letting his hands fall to his side, for the first time he realized he had a problem. His lifelong friend and his associates had been the sponsors of much chaos within the fire department, and Marlborough had thought it best to get him out of Texas before he hurt someone seriously.

Though Marlborough had never personally participated in the antics, he'd known about them for years. If the truth be known, the secret organization kept some balances and helped to keep the coloreds and women in their place. He was finding Los Angeles to be a different kind of place, however. He was worried that his friend may be in over his head this time. For sure Lloyd Frederickson would not just lie down. He'd have to be careful now that the captain had that woman lawyer on his side.

He needed to calm his nerves. Opening his top right-hand drawer, he removed a brown plastic bottle with a white top. He swallowed the little yellow pill without water. He'd give Frederickson and his lady lawyer a few minutes more to squirm, giving the pill a chance to work its way into his central nervous system.

As he closed the drawer the e-mail notification flashed on the computer screen. He quickly clicked on Yes.

> Time has proven to be our enemy. I may have to leave for a few
> days to visit a friend in need. But fear not. I will resume the task
> at hand upon my return.
> —One of Your Boys

Why in the hell did he send him an e-mail when he'd just hung up the phone talking to him? He feared his friend may be losing his grasp on reality.

"You know he's just making us wait out of spite, don't you?" Lloyd said, tossing the *US News & World Report* onto the marble-top coffee table.

"Well, he could really be busy. It was your idea to just show up here unannounced. So is this what they call a pissing contest?"

Throwing his head back laughing, Lloyd said, "Yeah, I guess it is."

Heather approached without making eye contact and said, "Chief Marlborough will see you now."

Rising, Glynda said, "Thank you."

"Right this way."

Glynda watched as Heather led the way and wondered how she walked in four-inch heels and a skintight skirt. With the slightest wrong move she would fall flat on her face.

As Glynda and Lloyd entered the office suite, the chief rose and extended his hand. "Captain Frederickson, sorry to keep you waiting. I had some loose ends to tie up. And who is this lovely young lady?" Lloyd cautiously took his hand.

"Glynda Naylor-Sanders, Chief William Marlborough." Lloyd introduced them.

The chief pointed to the two conference chairs in front of his desk. "Please have a seat. How can I help you two today?"

Eyeing the chief suspiciously, Lloyd wondered what had caused his demeanor to change so drastically. "We're here to present the plan of action we feel your office should take to get to the source of our problem."

"I want to assure you that this office has every intention of getting to the bottom of the mischief that has been wrought on the C Shift of Station 27. I am filing a report with Internal Affairs this afternoon, and I'm sure they will get the D.A.s involved."

Glynda and Lloyd stole a quick glance before Glynda spoke. "Chief, with all due respect, why haven't you gotten them involved before now?"

"Little lady—"

"You may call me Glynda or Ms. Sanders." Glynda was very curt.

"Sorry, Ms. Sanders. As I was trying to explain, I wanted to make sure these weren't some childish pranks. When an Internal Affairs investigation is opened, it is a very serious thing."

"I'm very cognizant of how serious it is. But wouldn't you say what's been happening at 27 is a serious matter? The crew on this shift has been subjected to demeaning and even dangerous acts. Two police reports have been filed and yet the D.A. *isn't* involved? How do you explain that, Chief Marlborough?"

"Now, li'l—I mean, Ms. Sanders, you hold on just one cotton-pickin' minute. Not one member has ever been in danger that I have been made aware of." His cordial behavior had given way to frustration and anger.

Lloyd moved to the edge of his seat and banged his fist on the massive desk. "What do you call it when someone tampers with equipment and flattens tires?"

Taken aback for a moment, Marlborough sat quiet. "We haven't determined whether someone tampered with the truck or your maintenance checks were inadequate."

"Look, Chief, I'm not going to sit here much longer and let you call me a liar. I told you before that all of the maintenance checks were done and someone intentionally removed those battery cables." Lloyd rose, leaning over the desk into the chief's face.

"Boy, you'd betta sit down before you get yourself in a whole heap of trouble."

Glynda felt the wrath welling up in her client and thought quickly about what she could do to defuse the situation. The chief had let his true colors show this time. When was the last time she had heard a white man call a black man "boy" and walk away unscathed?

Touching Lloyd's arm, Glynda said in a small voice, "Please, Lloyd, let's discuss this calmly."

Snatching his arm away from Glynda, Lloyd walked to the door, then turned around and said, "Let me explain this to you so you get it. If I have to go to the press, or the mayor's office, or the White House, I will do just that. This office *is* going to investigate what has been going on with our shift with some alacrity."

"Sit down, Frederickson! I'll write you up on insubordination before you get to the elevator. I've told you what I plan to do. These things take time."

"Don't you see we may not have time, Chief? This person is a lunatic. There's no telling what he'll do next. I'm truly scared someone is going to get hurt." Lloyd calmed a little as he tried to appeal to the chief's common sense. "As the captain of C Shift, I have one responsibility only—to bring them home safely."

Pointing at the chair where Lloyd had been previously seated, Marlborough said, "Look, I understand your frustration, but together we can solve this thing. Just let me do my job. You've never filed a formal complaint, gone through the ranks, but I give you my word. I will get this ball rolling."

"Chief Marlborough, if I may interject—we have a formal complaint here. Because we don't know at what level these incidents are being perpetrated, we are bringing it directly to the top. Though we have no evidence to support our suspicions, we believe—as is outlined in our filing—that these acts are racially motivated and thereby a violation of the civil rights of all who work on C Shift."

"As you say, there is no evidence to support this. Therefore we will treat this like any other incident. I believe it is some kids getting their kicks at our expense. But I'll keep an open mind."

Passing the chief a folder and rising at the same time, Glynda extended her hand. "Chief, I believe you'll do everything within your power to bring this unfortunate chain of events to a satisfactory resolution."

Folding his brow, the chief looked down at the folder and back up at Glynda. "I don't know that we're done here, Ms. Sanders."

"Oh, but I think that we are. Besides, you need to contact I.A., and the hour grows late. You ready, Captain Frederickson?"

43

A s Lloyd and Glynda stepped into the afternoon sun, it took all of their reserve not to scream.

Instead, Glynda looked at her favorite client and offered advice. "The next time you're going to threaten your boss's boss's boss, will you let me know in advance? I swear I thought you were going to clock him. What were you thinking?"

"I thought I'd had enough. But thank you for the intervention. That could have ended with my black ass being fired, and what good would that have done any of us? Do you think he's going to act?"

"He has no choice at this point. I stipulated in the complaint that the protocol laid out for filing grievances wasn't followed because it isn't known at this time at which level these acts are being initiated. So you're in the clear there. I just really hope this stops now that we've got some outside attention on it. I don't want anyone to get hurt. It has been my experience that these things only get worse."

"I would strongly agree. When they killed ole Casper, it took some big hairy ones. Everyone loved her—all three shifts—so I can't even imagine it being someone who is at 27."

"I promise you, we're going to get to the bottom of this."

"Thanks so much, Glynda. I'll be in touch. Would you like for me to drop you off?"

Thinking for a moment that if she walked back, she would save herself some treadmill time when she got home, she nevertheless decided to take Lloyd up on his offer. "You know what? I'd love to have a ride. I can get back to the office and finalize some things be-fore it's time to catch my train."

The two returned to the building and took the elevator to the garage.

Neither noticed they were being followed.

44

"erome?" A small, familiar voice called his name as he sat with his head in his hands.

"Oh, hi, Mom." He rose to hug and kiss his mother-in-law. "Where's Dad?"

"I drove myself. I wanted to talk to you alone."

Jerome pointed to the seat next to him, and he sat after she did. "How did you know I was here?"

"Because you're always here." Maxella touched his hand. "That's what I want to talk to you about."

"Well, I guess that's true. What do you want to talk about?"

"I know you love my daughter, and I love you so much for that. My daughter is fighting for her life, and you have spent the past three weeks here day and night. Now it's time for you to start fighting for your life."

"I don't understand what you're saying."

Maxella drew in a deep breath. "Everyone knows how much you love Nicky. You don't have to try to prove it. So you need to listen to the woman who carried her in her body for nine and a half months, then had her little lips attached to her breast for another nine months while I nourished her. Watched her grow and learn to walk, talk, spell and read. So you see, no one can be closer to the woman lying in bed seven of the intensive care unit. You need to get on with your life. We don't know if she will wake up in an hour or a year, if at all."

Jerome was stunned by her candor. "Mom, don't say that."

"I hate myself for saying it. But it needs to be said. You need to get up from here and go home. Start with a shower, shave and haircut, and then pick your babies up from school, make them a good dinner and watch TV with them—or better yet, read to them from their favorite book. Let them know that on that day back in October, they didn't lose two parents. Tuck them into bed, and then you go climb into that big ole expensive bed of yours, pull those covers up and get a good night's rest. Then get up tomorrow morning and start it all over again."

Jerome only stared.

"My daughter would be so disappointed in you. You've lost sight of what your goals were together. You are a team—if one of you can't carry the ball, then by God the other is supposed to pick it up. Baby, it's not going to be easy. But it's necessary."

"You're right, Mom. I just feel so guilty anytime I leave or sleep or anything that takes me away from her."

"Remember, I said if I'm telling you it's okay, then no one else had better even think otherwise."

Jerome laughed. Maxella Devereaux was often referred to as the gray-haired mafia. She made things happen, and no one dared argue with her. She was the president of the homeowners' association, and she ruled with an iron hand. She was involved in city politics and challenged government officials up to the White House. No one would ever think to second guess her for the advice she had bestowed upon her only son-in-law. "I can see her again in about twelve minutes. I'll go after that."

"Listen to yourself. Twelve minutes. How many times have you seen her already today?"

"Five."

"This next visit in—what is it now?—eleven minutes belongs to her mother, because her husband is going home."

"Yes, ma'am." They hugged each other long and tight.

"I need a shower, huh?"

"Lord, yes, boy. I always talk about how good you smell. You are sho' nuff making a liar out of me lately."

Jerome gathered his cell phone and jacket and stared down at the woman he'd known all his life. "I really want to thank you for giving me permission to live. I've wanted to die since the moment I saw her that afternoon, which seems so long ago."

"It's going to be all right, baby. We're all here to help you do your job when you need it. But this is your job. *You* need to handle it."

Jerome hugged her once again and headed for the elevator. A war of thoughts raged in his head. He had no idea what to do next. Then he remembered Maxella's instructions. Shower, shave and haircut. As he pushed the down button the words "first day of the rest of my life" tiptoed through his brain.

45

"We're here to see Captain Frederickson." Two men in dark suits stood at the front door of Station 27.

"Are you with the IRS?" Mychel asked sarcastically, eyeing them up and down.

The shorter of the two reached into his breast pocket and pulled out a badge. "Internal Affairs, Ms. Hernandez."

"How do you know—" Mychel cut herself off. "Oh, my name tag. You can wait here while I summon the captain for you." She opened the door wide enough to allow them entry. "Please have a seat." She pointed to the guest chairs near the entrance.

She disappeared through the gray door that led to the equipment bay.

Lloyd appeared almost immediately. "Good morning, gentlemen." Lloyd extended his hand.

The shorter of the two took his hand. "I'm Officer Daniel Wollenski, and this is my partner, Ted Letterman."

"Please have a seat over here." He led them to the seats near his desk.

"May I offer you some coffee?"

"Nothing, thank you. We'll get right to the point. We've received notification from headquarters that there have been a few unexplained incidents here at this station on your shift," Letterman began as he opened a thin file.

"I'd say more than a few. I shared a very large file with Chief Marlborough. I can get you a copy of the incident reports if you like." *Here we go,* Lloyd thought to himself.

"I believe we have the complete package." Wollenski spoke this time. "Our file at the office is of considerable size. This"—he lifted the manila legal folder—"file contains only our notes."

"Then what can I do for you?"

"I just have a few questions for you and your crew. We trust we'll have your full cooperation," Letterman said without expression.

"Inspector Letterman, there is nothing that I want more than for this to be resolved. We haven't had anything happen recently. And if it is over, thank God. But this fool needs to be caught."

"We're very glad to hear that. That answers my first question. So once you filed the formal complaint the incidents stopped?" Letterman appeared to be in charge.

"You know, Inspector, I hadn't thought about it, but you're right. Nothing has happened since then. We've been so busy around here. We've had some temporary replacements because Winters's wife was severely injured a few weeks back."

"In your summation in the complaint you stated that you thought it to be someone in the fire service. On what do you base this accusation?"

"Purely on access to the fire station. No outside person could possibly have done the things this person or persons have done."

"Do you have any suspicions about whom it might be?"

"Not a clue."

"Were all of your crew accounted for when these incidents took place?" Wollenski piped up.

"What the hell are you asking?" Lloyd had to reign in his anger. "If one of us is doing this? You're crazy!"

"Captain, understand we can leave no questions unasked," Wollenski answered very matter-of-factly.

Practicing a breathing technique he'd recently learned in counseling, Lloyd responded slowly. "I'm only going to say this once, so make note of it, record it, burn it into your brain: There's no one on C Shift at Station 27 that has anything to do with these stupid pranks bordering on dangerous acts that were reported to Chief Marlborough."

"What precautions have you taken since you filed the complaint that might explain why the incidents have ceased?"

"We haven't done anything any differently. We've followed to the letter of the law all the new procedures instituted post nine-eleven. So instead of looking at us, you need to focus your energy elsewhere. We haven't been negligent, and we most certainly haven't been malicious."

"Why do you think your shift has been singled out?" Letterman served.

Lloyd considered his words carefully. "Because, Inspector, we're a one hundred percent minority shift. We have a near-perfect record, and someone is pissed off about it."

Wollenski was making notes. "Why would someone be angered by your good record?"

"Inspector, there is no rational explanation for ignorance."

Wollenski looked up from his note taking. He stared a long moment at Lloyd. "Well, it seems there is nothing further to be gained from you at this time."

Letterman stood. "We do plan to return and speak with the rest of the crew in the near future."

"Why can't you talk to them now?" Reducing the intimidation factor, Lloyd rose as well.

"We're done here for the moment." Without another word the two turned and left.

46

"They think they're so special, wasting taxpayer money exercising while on duty. Well, let's just see how good they can handle a little fifteen-forty-weight motor oil." The man spread a thin coat of the clear substance on the bar of the dumbbells.

"What an appropriate name—dumbbells for fools. They think they're so superior. Walking around flexing all those muscles like Mandingo warriors. Well, I'll show them."

It felt good to be back at the helm. He felt in control again.

He'd been out of sorts since his trip to New York to find his fallen comrade. No one even knew Jimmy Doherty. He had wanted to ask him how he could work under such stressful conditions. No white man should be forced to work with so many blacks, browns and women. When he went to the prison they couldn't find the pseudo firefighter who'd been arrested for starting fires. It had been a total waste of time—time he could have used to plan the destruction of C Shift at Station 27.

He moved down the steps stealthily. He picked up his bag and slipped out the door as quickly and quietly as he had arrived.

47

"You know, one of these times ole Jackson McKinley is really going to have a heart attack." Austin backed the paramedic unit into the equipment bay.

"Yeah, every time he and Mrs. Mc get into it he has chest pains. Reminds me of Fred Sanford," Mychel said.

"Who's Fred Sanford?"

"Don't tell me you never watched *Sanford and Son*?" Mychel quipped.

"Ooooh, Fred Sanford."

"Yeah. I think of that show each time we go on a run to the McKinley house. It was kind of ironic it was the big one that came and got Redd Foxx."

"On the real. Want to spot a brother while I lift a few weights?"

"Give me a minute and I'll change into some workout gear. I could use a little work myself." Mychel slammed the door of the unit and headed for the dormitory.

As she slowly removed her uniform, her mind wandered to Jerome. She did miss him so. She'd called, left several messages on his cell and home phone, but he hadn't returned any of her calls. Her e-mails had gone unanswered. In general conversations, the others in the crew had said they hadn't heard from him either. The captain was the only person who'd had any direct contact with him. Unit 27 held little appeal without firefighter Winters.

She changed into a sports bra and sweats and headed to the workout room on the second floor. When she arrived, Austin, Andrew and Marshall Fitzpatrick, Jerome's temporary replacement, were discussing the pros and cons of cable versus satellite.

"Don't you think one of the men should spot him, Mychel?" Marshall asked innocently enough.

"Oh, man, don't you know? She's one of us."

"Go to hell, St. Vincent."

"Marshall, we spot for each other all the time, but thanks."

"You ready?" Mychel asked without looking in Andrew's direction.

"I *stay* ready, so I don't have to *get* ready," Austin boasted.

"Whatever," Mychel teased. "Come on before the bell rings again."

Austin slipped on his gloves and lay on the weight bench. Mychel stood over him, ready to protect him if he needed it, a position she'd taken many times in the year and a half she'd known her partner. Austin took a deep breath and prepared to lift the dumbbell from its cradle, grabbing it firmly with both hands. He lifted it the five inches to clear the rack. As he moved over his chest, he felt it slipping. The more he struggled to tighten his grip, the less control he had over the weight.

Spotting his troubles immediately, Mychel reached for the barbell. Her small, strong hands tightened around the bar, but as she lifted she, too, lost her grip. Marshall and Andrew observed and moved in to assist her. The three of them struggled to control the one hundred-seventy-five-pound weight.

What happened next was a blur. The more they gripped, the more elusive control became, until the dumbbell landed on Marshall's right femur with a bone-chilling crack.

48

"I can't believe it—I have to wait three months to see you?" Glynda leaned back in her office chair. "How long can you stay?"

"That's why I can't get there until February. I wanted to stay for two weeks." Dawn's glee transcended the distance.

"Oh, snapdragon, girl! That's wonderful. So that will give me plenty time to fix a sistah up. And you know what?" Glynda said, sitting up straight.

"Whoa, slow your roll. I'm not coming out there to get fixed up. I just want to kick back and relax. Get my Jacuzzi on."

"Girl, puh-leeze! All of these foine brothas in Southern California, and you don't even think I'm going to try to help you get your swerve on. I don't think so. But what I was going to tell you before I was so rudely interrupted was there is this huge red-and-black ball put on by the Stentorians, an African-American firefighters' organization, for Valentine's Day every year. Can you imagine two or three hundred brothers dressed to the nines and smelling good? Gurl, the eye candy alone is worth the price of admission. Lawdhamurcy! I may have to leave Anthony at home because you don't take sand to a beach or . . ."

". . . a sandwich to a buffet!" Dawn finished her sister's thought with a laugh. "Gurl, you know full well you won't be going anywhere without Anthony Sanders."

"You're probably right. But you *are* going. I'll line up a few prospects and do the evaluation process before you get here. Narrow it down to the top three."

"Gurl, this is not a business deal. It's a date."

"And take it from someone who knows, dating is serious business." Glynda smiled as she thought of fourteen days with her sister. The extra time to plan would give her plenty opportunity to clear her calendar and possibly take at least part of the time off. "So, how's everything on the eastern front? What drama has befallen our sisters this week?"

"Collette isn't speaking to Renee."

"Lucky Renee. What happened now?"

"I shared the conversation with Renee that I had with Estelle, and she decided to give her a call. After all it's been more than long enough to get over whatever. So Renee just called to say hello and tell her she'd like to have an invitation to her retirement party. She made the mistake of telling Evileen. All hell broke loose."

"Lord, she needs to get over herself. How can one woman harbor so many ill feelings? Life is way too short. Daddy's death should have taught her that."

"Gurl, your sister needs a remedial course in life. Speaking of life, how was your visit with Nina?"

"It was really great, just too short. The conference was a little more demanding than she had anticipated so we didn't get to spend quite as much time as we would've liked. But the best part was she was downtown not far from where I worked, so we had lunch almost every day."

"Did she say anything about Edwina?"

"Chile, that's all she talked about. That poor woman is fit to be tied. But I knew when I met her at Daddy's funeral she had some challenges."

"Challenges? You mean problems, don't you?"

"See, you're so wrong." Glynda laughed. "I think Nina has been so lenient on her to compensate for what she feels she missed out on as a child."

"Poor decisions have tentacles that reach out for generations. What're they going to do?"

"They put her hard-to-manage butt in military school."

"Military school? For girls?"

"Apparently so. She literally went off kicking and screaming. She's not talking to her parents. It's just a mess. I felt so sorry for Nina. She carries a really heavy burden. She hasn't been burden-free her whole life. She's a sweet woman. It's amazing how she can look so much like Collette and be so totally different. I saw it even more this time."

"Ain't that the truth! Well, big sis, if I'm coming to L.A. to get my swerve on as you put it, I'd better pack my clothes and move to 24 Hour Fitness. I love you. I'll call you this weekend when the minutes are free."

"Sounds like a plan. Anthony and I are having a Calgon weekend. Lots of movies, popcorn and bubble baths. I love you, too." The sisters hung up, and Glynda turned to her computer. She received three notifications for new e-mail.

The first one was the monthly reminder that billable hours were due into accounting by the fifth working day of the month. The second was from her assistant, the forward queen. The third one was from a sender she didn't recognize.

If you think you have a case with the firefighters you're wrong, "dead" wrong. I'd hate to see that pretty yellow suit get red stains on it. Back off!
We'll be watching.

Instinctively Glynda looked around her office. Who'd sent this threatening e-mail? She hadn't left the building all day. She'd brought her lunch and eaten in the office lunchroom. She hadn't been to court or to visit a client. Suddenly she felt vulnerable and, for the first time in her legal career, scared.

49

"Nicolas! Get in here and wipe up this milk you spilled!" Jerome yelled into the den as he stood in the midst of a domestic catastrophe.

The dishwasher was too full to slide the bottom tray in. There was a red substance running down the front of the refrigerator. Something crunched under his feet with every step he took. Christian sat in the high chair with a spaghetti crown and a snot mustache.

"If I tell you again, I'm going to come in there and neither one of us is going to leave smiling."

"Daddy, Christian spilled the milk, so why should I have to mop it up?" Nicolas whined.

"Because if you do, I'll let you live."

"Jordan should have to help," Nicolas sulked. "He's just sitting here watching *Cosby*."

"Both of you turn that TV off and come in here now." There was something in their father's voice that made them know action was the only reasonable response.

"Dang, I wish Mommy was here," Jordan said as he kicked the air.

"You know what, Jordan?" Jerome heard himself for the first time and realized he bordered on an abusive tone. He lowered his voice and walked to the doorway where his sons stood. "Me, too."

Stooping down so that he was eye level with them he began in a much calmer tone. "I wish I wasn't so bad at all of this. Your mother made it look so easy. Everything was neat, clean and in order. I try really hard, but I have no clue what I'm doing. I need your help. I need you to do a little something extra to help your dad out. Can I count on you?"

The boys hugged his neck, and Nicolas began to cry. "Daddy, when will Mommy come home? I miss her."

Jerome went to his knees, leaning back on his feet. He thought back to the day at the hospital a week ago and remembered how much he'd appreciated Maxella's raw honesty. "I wish I could answer that question. But the truth is no one knows. She could wake up and be fine tomorrow or it could be a year from now."

"I heard Uncle Desmond talking to Grandpa, and they said Mommy could die." Jordan sat on his lap with one arm around his neck.

"She could die. But we pray every night that she doesn't. We just have to learn to do the things for ourselves that we always depended on her to do. Now we are going to start with the laundry. I want you to go upstairs and get all of your dirty clothes and take them to the laundry room. I'm going to get your brother out of the high chair and meet you upstairs in five minutes. Okay?"

Very seriously, Jordan looked into his father eyes and said, "Okay, Dad. We can do this."

Hugging his number one son, he laughed from the bottom of his soul for the first time in what seemed like an eternity. "Yes, we can."

"Now go get your clothes, and then I want you to take a shower," Jerome yelled after them.

"Well, little man, you're going to have to pitch in, too. This whole spaghetti to the head thing is going to have to stop. Do I make myself clear?" Jerome hugged him, adding spaghetti to the many other stains from the night's dinner preparation.

Jerome took him over to the sink and scraped the spaghetti with meat sauce from his curly dark hair into the sink. He wanted to take the spray attachment from the Delta faucet and hose him down, but he thought better of it. He wet a paper towel and cleaned his hands and face. Only shampoo could help his hair. Jerome let him slip from his arms to the floor and told him to go help his brothers. He'd planned to try to pick up the kitchen but the task seemed too overwhelming, and he decided to just go upstairs and help the boys, get them settled for the night and return to hurricane harbor when the boys were asleep. *Spend time with them. Make sure they know they didn't lose two parents that day.* Maxella's words echoed in his head. Just as he reached for the light switch the phone rang. He looked where he knew the cordless phone should have been and remembered he'd taken it down when his mother called. Now, what was he doing at the time? He was making salad. He retraced his steps and found it under a pile of brown lettuce leaves.

"Hello," he rushed, trying to answer before the phone rolled over to voice mail.

"Hey, Jerome. This is Mychel."

Speechless, Jerome held the receiver to his ear.

"Hello? Are you there?"

"Yeah, Yeah. I'm here, Hernandez. What can I do for you?" He was surprised at how cold his voice sounded.

"Look, this is just purely a coworker calling to check on you. Lloyd told us you were holding down the fort alone, and I just wanted to call to give you a word of encouragement. I know it must be a little better than difficult for you."

"It's a challenge, but we're making it okay. How are things at 27?"

"You don't need to hear about our nonsense. We—"

"Dammit!"

"What's wrong?"

Before he could answer, the smoke alarm sounded. "I have to go, Mychel. I forgot I put cookies in the oven and now they're burning. Gotta go. Bye."

When Jerome opened the built-in oven, smoke billowed up the wall. His first instinct was to grab the fire extinguisher, until he realized there were no flames. He reached in to get the cookie sheet with no oven mitt. It took the pain several seconds to reach his brain, but when it did, he sent the cookie sheet with its charcoal disks sailing across the room.

He rushed to the refrigerator to apply ice to his thumb and forefinger. As he opened the freezer, the half-frozen cherry Hi-C that was going to be Popsicles came crashing to the floor. The camel's back was broken—this was it. He left this room of the house that was obviously possessed by demons.

Climbing the stairs, he didn't know a human being could be so tired. His day had started with him and the boys oversleeping. He burned the oatmeal, and when he arrived at school he realized Christian's tennis shoes didn't match. How in the world did Nicolle manage all of this, keep the house spotless, work full-time and remain the sexiest woman to ever breathe in two millennia?

As he reached the second-story landing, a football caught him in the gut. "I thought I told you to gather your dirty clothes so I can wash them." Jerome wanted to yell, but it would have taken way too much energy.

Instead he moved first to Jordan's room. It was not possible this much damage could have been done in the four weeks his mother had been gone. It looked like an eight-point earthquake had struck.

"Boy, what happened in here?" Jerome began picking underwear, socks and pajamas from the floor.

"I kinda haven't picked anything up lately. Mom checked my room every day, so I knew I had to pick it up. But you haven't done laundry since she's been in the hospital. You just keep going to Wal-Mart and buying more underwear," Jordan said humbly.

"Lord, I'm scared to look in your brother's room. Well, help me get this stuff to the laundry room. I'll do better I promise."

"Why don't you call Miss Carmen?" Jordan asked innocently enough.

Jerome thought long and hard for a moment before asking, "Who's Miss Carmen?"

"She cleans the house."

"What?"

"She comes and cleans the house."

"How often does she do this?"

Jordan shrugged his shoulders. "I just know she does."

"I'll be—" Jerome laughed. "What does she do?"

"Laundry, change the beds, vacuum."

"Where can I find her phone number?"

Jordan only stared.

"I'm sorry. I guess you have no clue, huh?"

"Yeah, Dad. How would I know that? I hardly ever see her. I was home sick once when she came. That's why I know about her."

There was hope for Jerome. There was someone who would come in and turn the house right side up. He just had to find her phone number. At this point it didn't even matter how much she charged. "Let's get moving. I'm going to your brother's room next. God only knows what I'll find there."

When they finished fifteen minutes later, there were three arm-fuls of clothes, two bowls, a cup and five saucers recovered. Jerome took the clothes to the laundry room and started the washer. He stuffed as many pieces as he thought was reasonable, added three cups of detergent, turned the settings to heavily soiled and hot.

Jordan wasn't quite sure what was wrong with the steps he'd just seen, but he'd never seen his mother do the laundry exactly that way. Jordan followed his father to his brother's room where Nicolas hung over the top bunk with his torso swinging freely. Much to Jerome's pleasant surprise Nicolas's room was a far cry from the dis-aster he'd encountered in Jordan's domain.

"Where're your dirty clothes, young man?"

"In the hamper in my closet." Nicolas flipped off the bed back-ward.

"In the hamper in my closet," Jordan mocked.

"Daaaaaad? He's making fun of me!" Nicolas whined.

"You're always so goody-goody. I hate you." Jordan started for the door.

"Get back here and you two stop it." Jerome searched the closet for dirty clothes, but found only a small collection of underwear and school uniforms. "Where's the rest of your stuff?"

"What stuff?" Nicolas looked at him, confused.

"The rest of your dirty clothes. This can't be all after almost a month."

"Yep, that's it."

"Do you change your underwear every day? Like after you shower?"

With a puzzled look, Nicolas gazed back at him. "You didn't put any clean ones on the bed so I just put the same ones back on."

"Boy—" The doorbell interrupted him. "Lord, let this be one of your grandmothers."

Jerome took the handful of dirty clothes and dropped them in the laundry room with Jordan's and ran down the stairs to the front door. So sure it was the cavalry, he never looked through the peep-hole. He opened the door with enthusiasm. "Lord, am I glad to see you."

"Well, are you now?" Mychel Hernandez stood there, smiling.

50

"What the hell do you mean, you didn't tell anyone about this? This person obviously has been following you. I can't believe you!" Anthony paced the family room.

"This is why I didn't want to tell you. I knew you were going to get spastic on me." Glynda nervously toyed with the fringe on the burgundy pillow. "This only tells me that I must be close to uncovering something. I've got them running scared." She pleaded her case. "I'm a civil rights attorney. People don't like me. I'm lucky this is the first threat I've ever received."

"Well, your civil rights lawyering days are numbered. There is no way I'm going to allow my wife to work a job where she gets threats."

"Allow?" Glynda leapt to her feet. "You don't allow me to do anything. I love what I do, and if I die because of it, then so be it. I won't cower because they don't have the balls to stand up to me."

"Do you hear yourself? You're not a Tuskegee Airman, police officer or firefighter—you're a lawyer, and not even a criminal lawyer. You sit behind a desk and occasionally go to court."

"I know you're not trivializing what I do!"

"Of course I'm not. But I'm really pissed that you got a threat and didn't tell anyone, and that you're going to continue to pursue this case. You're not even being paid. Glynda, I love you. It's my job to protect you. I won't stand idly by and let you travel more than a hundred miles a day open to attack. You have to understand the kind of people you're dealing with. There are people getting hurt. The last guy hurt was a white guy, but you know he wasn't the intended target. Just by the nature of prejudice these people are crazy. The whole reason I have a job is because there are people in the world who hate every American. Not that you or I did something to them personally, but they hate what we represent."

Anthony's demeanor changed. He was warm and loving. "Please let me call some people I know in the protection business. If they're watching you like this e-mail implies and they see you with a bodyguard, even if it's only for a few days, they may back off."

"Honey, I'd feel silly with a bodyguard."

"Feeling silly is far better than feeling dead, don't you think? Promise me you'll call into the office tomorrow and tell them what happened and see what they suggest. That will give me time to contact the brotha I have in mind."

Glynda looked at the floor. In her heart she knew he was right. But if you want to run with the big dogs, you can't be scared to get off the porch.

51

"What are you doing here?" Jerome asked, stunned.

Mychel smiled. "When I heard the smoke detector go off, and then you were gone, I tried calling back, but the voice mail picked up immediately. I got worried."

Jerome moved his body to block the doorway. "You shouldn't be here."

Mychel sighed and shifted her weight from left to right. "Look, let's call a truce. I'm here as your friend and coworker. I called Austin, and he's on his way, too." She peered into the house. "From the looks of things, you could use a friend," she said as she peeped around him looking at toys in the foyer.

"We're doing fine here. I've got everything under—" Just as he was about to say "control," there was a loud crash and a blood-curdling scream that came from upstairs. Without thinking he darted up the stairs, leaving the door open.

Mychel smiled and walked in, closing the door behind her. When Jerome arrived at the source of the noise, he found Christian sitting in the midst of trophies and books, with the shelving lying on the floor near the window and Christian contently playing with his brother's trophies.

Jordan and Nicolas had both gone off to take a shower and left their two-year-old brother unattended. The best Jerome could surmise, Christian had climbed up the chair onto the desk trying to reach his favorite model car, and his weight had toppled the shelf. Nothing was broken, most important Christian. Lord knows he needed to take a domestic engineering/parenting class. Fighting fires and saving lives was like unemployment compared to this job.

"Come on, little man." Jerome picked him up and kissed him. "I need to give you a bath and wash your hair. Then do you want me to read you a story?"

Christian nodded his head yes. Since Jordan and Nicolas occupied the two small bathrooms, he took Christian into the master bathroom and began running water in the oversize Jacuzzi tub. As he turned on the water it reminded him of the night he and Nicolle had spent just a few short weeks before, which now seemed like a lifetime ago.

After a thorough washing from head to toe, Jerome dried Christian and realized he hadn't brought a diaper or pajamas with him. He wrapped him in the towel and took him to his room. He smoothed baby oil over his body and put on his diaper. When he went to pull pajamas from the drawer, there were none. Sighing deeply, he remembered the laundry he'd put in the washer. Nothing for Christian. He found an undershirt that was too small, but it would have to do for now. He sat with him in the rocking chair and read his favorite SpongeBob SquarePants book. Christian was asleep by page three.

Jerome gently laid him in the crib and covered him. He gathered the dirty clothes and headed for the laundry room. As he passed Nicolas's room, he heard his two older boys talking quietly.

"I really miss Mommy." For the first time Jerome noticed Jordan's voice cracking.

"Yeah. Me, too."

"Dad's cool. But he's just not good at taking care of us."

"Did you taste that spaghetti? Man!"

"I know why Chris put it on top of his head."

"But he's really trying. We need to help out, too."

"Yeah. I guess I should clean my room."

Jerome's heart smiled. He moved on to the laundry room. When he opened the washer he knew there was a problem—pink suds filled it to the top. "Dang." He pulled the clothes from the tub of the washer and everything was either red or pink. Jordan wasn't going to be feeling like pink underwear.

The sound of the vacuum cleaner shocked him, and he suddenly remembered he'd left Mychel at the front door. He dropped the clothes and rushed down the stairs. He immediately noticed the foyer was cleared. As he turned the corner he saw that the mail from the past week had been neatly stacked in three piles. Walking down the hall, as he approached the family room he saw that everything had been picked up and Mychel was vacuuming.

"What the hell are you doing in here?" Jerome was livid.

"Look, you left me on the porch like a stray cat, but you left the door open. Now correct me if I'm wrong, but you needed some help. I don't want anything, except to be your friend."

"I just don't think you should be here."

"I'll just finish this and go. I don't want there to be any problems." Mychel sounded defeated.

"I can do that." Jerome stated flatly.

"Sure you can." Mychel waved her hand, causing Jerome to look around the house. "You've done such a great job already."

Despite himself, Jerome was forced to laugh. FEMA should be called in to declare this entire house a disaster area. "It's pretty bad, huh?"

"Ya think?"

"I'm going to find the housekeeper's number and get her to come by."

"Please, just let me help you get the kitchen squared away, and when the boys come down for breakfast they'll have a nice surprise." Mychel softened her voice and struck an innocent pose. "I know I've come on strong in the past. But I just want to be your friend. Nothing more."

Against his better judgment, Jerome's resolve wavered. "Okay, friends." He extended his hand, and she smiled and took it. She shook it firmly.

The two went to work. Mychel finished the den, and together they tackled the kitchen. She was careful never to get in his way. She reloaded the dishwasher, and miraculously most of the dishes fit. She hand-washed pots and pans, after which she cleaned the stove. He cleared counters and returned spices to the cabinets.

Jerome was amazed that he and Mychel were contemporaries yet she was so much better skilled in the kitchen. There was something very special about women. God had made them different than men. They could manage multiple tasks at the same time. How did they do that?

Within forty-five minutes the kitchen was restored to predisaster mode. Mychel had worked up a sweat and grabbed a bottle of water from the refrigerator. She went to catch her breath in the den while Jerome mopped the floor.

Ten minutes later Jerome emerged from the kitchen and fell back in his favorite chair, letting out a sigh of relief. Mychel had made herself at home and was watching *Law & Order.* Jerome looked at the floor and chose his words carefully. "I just want to thank you for helping me restore a little order. I guess things were a bit out of control."

Check.

With a very relaxed laugh she said, "A little?"

They both laughed.

"I'd better get going. I'm just glad I could help. If you need me for anything, anything at all, just call."

They both stood and slowly walked toward the door. "By the way, what happened upstairs?" she asked.

"What do you mean?"

"The big crash that made you leave me on the porch with the door open."

"Ohhhh. Christian pulled a shelf down, but it obviously didn't hit him. I guess it scared him. By the time I was upstairs he was sitting in the middle of the floor playing."

Well, Christian Winters, thank you very much, Mychel thought to herself. She said, "I'm just glad everything turned out okay and I was able to help."

"What ever happened to Austin?"

"Austin?"

"Yeah, you said he was on his way."

"Oh, that. He called and said he'd have to take a rain check. Something came up." Mychel almost blew it.

"That's my boy. I bet it did. Thanks again."

Mychel reached up to hug him, and then decided not to.

Seeing her hesitation, Jerome reached down and hugged her. She kissed him lightly on the cheek. "Remember if you need anything, just call."

"I promise I will."

Checkmate!

52

"Tell me what's on your mind—and don't even think about lying," Nellie said softly as Lloyd effortlessly maneuvered the Infiniti Q45 through rush hour traffic.

"I was just wondering how I could go on for so many years thinking I was giving you all that you needed and in reality I missed the mark."

"Your focus was different. It was all about making it for you. If I haven't learned anything else in these eight weeks in therapy, I know it was my responsibility to speak up to get what I wanted. If I needed more, I should have asked." Nellie never looked at him.

"Do you think therapy is helping? I leave that place so beat up at times."

"It's made me reconsider the divorce."

Lloyd turned to look at her. "What did you just say?"

"Watch it!" Nellie pointed at the car that cut him off. "I said, it's made me reconsider the divorce."

"I think I need to pull over."

"Don't be silly. We can talk about it when we get home, if that's better for you and means you're not going to kill us."

Lloyd couldn't believe his ears. All during the counseling sessions he felt he was hammering one nail after another in the coffin called their marriage. "What brought about this decision?"

"A lot of things, actually—the counseling for the most part. But a thousand other little things, like you bringing home flowers every week for the last thirty years. Do you know how many women don't get one rose petal?"

Lloyd stole another look at Nellie. "Go on."

"But I think it's mostly Jerome and Nicolle. They had the perfect life, and now it's been shattered. I don't want to destroy something, though not perfect, that we've spent a lifetime building."

"Does this mean we can stop going to see this woman every week?"

"No, it does not! We promised to commit for thirteen weeks. We're going to stick to it."

"Okay, okay." Lloyd felt like jumping up and clicking his heels. "This calls for a celebration. What do you want to do?"

"I want to go home with my husband." For the first time since the conversation began, Nellie turned and looked at Lloyd. They'd been celibate for eight weeks. She was going nuts. There was no better way to celebrate than to knock some lamps off tables and pictures off the wall.

53

Jerome pulled the midnight-blue Audi A6 into the visitor's parking lot of the hospital. He'd been driving Nicolle's car since the accident. He'd washed the exterior a few times but hadn't touched the inside, trying to preserve the White Diamonds fragrance she always wore, which faded more and more with each passing day.

He turned off the car's ignition. The CD continued to play, and Gladys Knight's voice filled the car. Her words spoke perfectly to his heart: *There's a hole within my heart that can't be filled since we're apart.* He opened the door, and the music stopped.

He'd tossed and turned all night. He'd finally found the number for the housekeeper, who had come and cleaned the house. His mother had shown him how to do the laundry. Nellie had cooked and frozen several meals for him and the boys. He by no means had the domestic situation under control, but he was improving daily.

Today he was nervous. He was going to talk to Nicolle about going back to work. He was losing his mind just staying around the house. He needed to get back to solving other people's problems instead of concentrating only on his own.

He'd learned to treasure the time he spent talking to Nicolle. He was convinced she could hear him. He told her about the boys and their schoolwork, his mishaps in the house. He shared whatever was in his heart. The nurses still hadn't relaxed the five-minute rule, but they would let him in every thirty minutes unless the unit was particularly busy. He'd seen patients come and go. Some got better, others didn't. He felt blessed that Nicolle continued to hold on. As long as she held on there was hope she'd come back to him.

He finally got out of the car and made his way to the surgical intensive care unit. The patient information receptionist and security personnel on every shift knew him by name. He took the elevator to the seventeenth floor. When he stepped off, he passed two of the nurses from the unit who were entering the elevator.

"Hi, Mr. Winters. How are you?" Bonnie, a petite blonde with a warm smile and caring eyes, asked.

"Hanging in here, Bonnie. How's the Mrs.?"

"Nothing new. But I know she's waiting to hear your voice."

"Well, her Big Daddy's here! Have a good lunch. I'll probably be gone when you return. Got a busy day with the boys."

"Then we'll see you tomorrow." Shauna, the sistah from Birmingham, Alabama, with the kindest heart he'd encountered in a long time, said.

The elevator doors closed, and he walked the ten steps to the SICU phone. He called and announced himself. The doors opened and Maureen stood waiting to greet him. "Hi there, Mr. Winters. She's waiting for you."

"Thank you, Maureen. I can't wait to see her either," Jerome teased. Maureen had started this same dialogue after about a week. Though Nicolle was listed as critical, her condition had stabilized. The nurse looked as though she was three days past retirement. Her raspy voice said if she no longer did now, she had smoked for a lot of years. Jerome liked her best.

Jerome walked the hall to bed seven's entrance. His boo looked so thin. His ears ached to hear her call his name. His arms longed to hold her. He slid the chair across the room. He bent down and kissed her very still lips. He'd give his soul to have her kiss him back. He kissed her again, this time on the forehead. He slowly sat down next to the bed.

"Hey, Babe-ski. Today is Wednesday, and it's overcast and a little chilly. They say it may rain tonight. But you know Fritz hasn't been right in a long time. Nicolas got an A on his English test. He's very proud. He insisted I bring it to you and read the teacher's comments." Jerome pulled the folded paper from his back pocket. " 'Great Job, Nicolas. Welcome Back.' The teachers have been very lenient with them while they've been adjusting to you being . . .

being away. Jordan's voice is cracking, and he's so funny. I try not to laugh, but sometimes I just can't help it. I know if you were there you'd hit me.

"There's something I need to talk to you about, Nic. I've been home with the boys a few weeks now, and we're adjusting. My mom and yours have been coming by and helping, and now the house-keeper and I have it going on. I'm taking good care of your house until you get back. Nic, I need to go back to work. I hope you won't think I'm not still grieving, because I am. I just need to be back at the firehouse. I need to help other people with their problems. Man! I wish you could tell me it's okay. I wish you could give me some kind of sign. I know you understand." Jerome dropped his head and whispered. "Please tell me you understand."

Jerome leapt from the chair when there was a loud sound behind him. As he sought out the source of the noise, he found Nicolle's vitals chart on the floor.

54

"Are you out of your mind?" William Marlborough yelled into the cell phone. "What are you thinking, sending her e-mails? I don't give a cat's hairball what is already in place. You'd better back off. I might not be able to save your bacon this time. The politics are different here in L.A., and I won't jeopardize my job for you."

"How—"

The chief cut him off. "You shut up and just listen. Back off. Do I make myself clear? People have been hurt. Your last prank backfired, and one of us was hurt. If you keep this up, I'll call the police myself. You've lost your mind this time. Don't force my hand—you won't like the cards I play." He hit the End button without another word. He held the button down until the small screen went blank.

The man stared at the phone. What in the hell was William talking about, "one of us was hurt"? He hadn't done anything except follow the lawyer woman, hoping to scare her off. After all, he only wanted to protect his friend. He couldn't have these colored people cause him problems like they did in Texas. William Marlborough had been his friend since high school. Marlborough had protected him from bullies and his abusive foster parents. It was now his job to protect him. But he'd done nothing to hurt anyone.

How had his friend found out about the e-mail he'd sent to that nigga woman? She must have run to that troublemaker, Frederickson, and he immediately called William to complain.

Well, he'd just have to teach her a little lesson.

55

"Does somebody up in here need rescuing?" Jerome Winters felt alive as he stepped through the door of Station 27. In the five weeks he'd been gone, his life had changed so much that he no longer even recognized it. He felt like a bystander looking through a picture window at someone else's existence. But here, in this building where the equipment was still red and the floors and walls still gray, he felt like his old self.

"Well, well, well. Look what the cat dragged in! Had enough loafing around?" Austin extended his hand to shake Jerome's, but Jerome grabbed him, giving him a warm brotherly hug.

"Yeah, soap operas and bonbons have gotten old." Jerome laughed.

"Welcome back, man! We have had some lame folks through here while you were gone! You know we got the tightest crew in the LAFD." Andrew hugged him.

"I don't know about all that. B Shift would stand to argue that point. But, nonetheless, welcome back, Winters." McInerney shook his hand. Their relationship had taken an upward swing since the time they cleaned up the handiwork of the Menace. They wouldn't be considered friends, but they each had a newfound respect for the other. Jerome knew his words were reflective of his true feelings.

"Welcome back." Captain McDonald smiled and shook his hand. "We're out of here. I just have to tell you that everything we ran on last night was bizarre. So just be forewarned."

"How's Nicolle, man?" Austin asked softly, not knowing exactly how to broach the subject.

McDonald and McInerney both stopped and turned to listen. They, too, didn't know how to ask. Lloyd had told them all she was still critical.

Jerome seemed to suck all of the air from the recreation room. "Nothing's changed. She's still in the coma. But we're believing God that she's going to come out of it. And be as good as new."

"My wife and I have told our church, and they have prayed for her every Sunday since it happened," McInerney added, much to everyone's surprise.

"Thank you, man. That's really good of you." Jerome struggled to force the words out over the lump forming in his chest.

The thickness of the quiet weighed heavy on the room. "There's no need to thank me for doing what it is we're supposed to do." McInerney turned to leave.

"But it's really appreciated. There's nothing more any of us can do but wait and pray. I sure have missed Mrs. Gonzales's burritos. What's for breakfast?"

The C Shift crew laughed. "You've been eating your own cooking, huh? No burritos, but someone brought a flat of muffins from Costco. They're da bomb if you heat them in the oven for ten minutes," Andrew volunteered.

Jerome went to the kitchen and poured a large mug of coffee. As he was placing the muffin in the oven, Mychel arrived.

"Jerome!" Mychel ran the length of the recreation room, passed the dining table and stopped short, composing herself. She hugged him very siblinglike and said, "No one told me you were coming back today."

"Yeah, I couldn't stay away any longer." Jerome hugged her back without apprehension. "I want to thank you again for what you did. The boys noticed when they came down for breakfast."

She smiled, tilting her head. "What else are friends for?"

"I just really wanted you to know that I appreciate you."

" 'Nuff said."

"So, where's our commander this morning?" Jerome asked as he checked the muffin.

"I think he had a meeting downtown again. So much has been happening since you've been gone. But we were sworn to silence until you returned." Austin joined him in the kitchen for a cup of coffee.

"What's been going on?" He had Jerome's undivided attention.

Andrew and Mychel brought Jerome up to speed on the events that had occurred during his absence.

"We have to come up with a plan to catch this guy or at least point the investigators in the right direction. Are the police involved?" Jerome warmed his coffee. Just then, a call came over the radio.

"Station 27, domestic dispute with injuries. LAPD on scene." The dispatcher's voice was a sweet melody to Jerome's ears.

"Well, people, they're playing our song. Let's go!"

Andrew and Austin took the pole, while Jerome and Mychel descended the stairs.

The paramedic and engine were rolling out of the station in less than one minute. The synchronization had returned to Station 27 C Shift.

The man sat in the El Camino, watching as the fire truck and paramedic unit rolled on the call.

So Winters had returned. He felt safe in reinstating his plan. He hadn't wanted to take a chance on hurting another one of the brethren.

It was one thing to rescue them on the job, but why had that foolish man come to the aid of those clumsy buffoons? Now that the shift was back intact he had a few more tricks up his sleeve.

But for now he had to get to his job. He didn't want to rouse any suspicion on his shift.

He'd come too far to blow it now.

56

The team finished treating the victims and began packing their equipment. Within just a few minutes they were headed back to Station 27. Jerome backed the engine into the driveway and decided to leave it outside.

"Captain McDonald was right. Looks like we're in for the bizarre today. I was rather proud of you, St. Vincent. You've matured a bit since I've been gone."

"'Cause he's fiendin' on that lawyer lady. She told him he was too juvenile." Mychel busted him out.

"Glynda Sanders? She's married."

"Whatever, man. Don't listen at Hernandez. I just happen to think she's really a cool lady. I don't want to get with her or anything." Andrew looked at Mychel with disdain.

"For whatever the reason, I'm pleased to see a more mature you. Ahh. Cap is back. I'll meet you upstairs. I'm going to go into his office and have a little talk with him."

"Later. And it's good to have you back in the driver's seat, man." Andrew and Jerome slapped hands in midair as they went in different directions.

"What's a brother got to do to get a welcome back from his captain?" Jerome asked as he entered Lloyd's office.

Lloyd rose and extended his hand. "Man, am I glad to see you! It's been rocky around here since you've been gone. But I refused to let any of this worry you while you were dealing with so much at home."

"I sure could have used the distraction. The gang was filling me in this morning before the run. What is HQ doing about this?"

"I met with I.A. again this morning. We've gone over a list of possible suspects about a hundred times now, and the list isn't changing. They've done a psychological profile, and they've come up with a white male between the ages of thirty and forty who has tried countless times to join the department and failed."

"Oh, so they've narrowed it down to, say, a quarter of a million suspects?"

"Exactly. That could be anyone. They've really spooked Glynda, but she refuses to quit the case."

Jerome took a seat next to Lloyd's desk. "What exactly happened to her?"

"Thank God, there hasn't been any direct contact, but whoever sent her this e-mail was watching her. Told her what she was wearing. Told her to drop the case."

"But does she even have a case?"

"No. Until we prove this is happening because we're black, it's just a criminal investigation."

"But doesn't this prove our point? If it wasn't racially motivated, the person would have nothing to fear from Glynda being on our team."

"That was my exact argument this morning. But I must say they are taking all of this a little more seriously now. They have filed a report with the LAPD aside from the death of Casper and the tire slashing. Your replacement that got hurt with that barbell caper has had surgery twice."

"How ironic that the first person to be hurt is a white guy. Is he going to be able to come back to work?"

"Ironic, indeed. But I know full well one of us was the target. Yeah, I'm sure he'll be fine."

"What can I do to help? I need to have my hands in something to keep my mind off my problems." Jerome hung his head and sighed. "This thing is wearing me down, Lloyd."

"I know it would have to be. It was good to have you and the boys over for dinner last night. Nicolas confided to Nellie when he was helping her with the dishes that your cooking is getting a little better." Lloyd smiled.

"Oh, so now Brutus doesn't turn his nose up at it?"

Lloyd laughed. "Something like that. You know we'd be delighted to have you over more often."

"As much as I love Nell's cooking, I've got to do this for my boys and for me on my own. I've matured as a man in the past thirty-three days. I was a good husband, make no mistake about that, but I depended on Nicolle for everything. I didn't have to remember where I put stuff because she remembered for me. I know now that I hardly did anything around the house except take out the trash, and I haven't even done that in the past couple years because Jordan and Nicolas handle that now. I don't understand why this has happened to me, but I'm starting to see some good coming from it."

"I don't know what to say. I guess you weren't in my boat, but we were on the same lake."

"Station 27, reported Dumpster fire in back of liquor store at corner of Florence and Vermont." The alarm sounded, and both men were on their feet.

57

I t was the first break he'd had all day.

His new boss was getting on his nerves. He didn't like the new time and mileage logs. It would be more difficult to make little stops over at 27 if he had to account for every minute and mile.

He hadn't set a fire in a long time, and it felt good to watch the flames lick the air.

A crowd was starting to form. Everyone wanted to watch a hero.

He checked the stopwatch on his wrist. He'd saved for months to buy this timepiece because he needed to log those people's response time to the second. It was no secret they were second-rate and lazy. He had to prove it to headquarters. If he showed the chief what misfits they all were, it would make him a hero, and he was sure he could get a special dispensation so that he could wear the blue uniform.

This crowd should be watching him. He should be their hero.

58

Mychel tossed fresh romaine lettuce leaves in the large metal bowl before mixing in croutons. Austin was in command of the barbecue grill just outside the kitchen where steaks were cooking to perfection. "Winters, can you check the baked potatoes?"

"How do I know what I'm checking for?" Jerome asked innocently as he approached the oven.

"Dang, man, even I know when a potato is done," Andrew interjected from the recliner where he watched *SportsCenter*.

Mychel smiled inside as she thought of herself in their kitchen, teaching her husband how to cook. "Just take a fork, slip it in nice and easy. If you meet no resistance, it's done." Was she really talking about a potato?

"Ahhhhh, dang. What y'all talking about in here?" Austin carried a tray of perfectly grilled steaks.

"Miss Hot Pepper over there *says* she's talking about potatoes," Andrew answered for them. "Sounds like a little innuendo to me!"

Jerome stared at her.

"Oh, big word for someone with such a little—"

The alarm sounded and interrupted their little exchange. "Station 27, chest pains, eighty-three-year-old male, 110 Wall Lane."

"Stick our steaks in the oven, Captain," Austin yelled as he and Mychel ran for the paramedic truck.

Jerome and Andrew followed them down the pole. The firehouse doors rolled up, and they were out in less than a minute.

He was across the street watching.

Setting the fire earlier in the day had gotten his blood pumping.

He had no definitive plan, but felt the urge to do something—anything to let them know he was still in charge. He stared at the building as pure loathing rose in his chest. How dare they have his job? He was about to get out of the car to check his toolbox in the bed of the El Camino when he saw movement on the second floor.

His heart began to race. He closed the door and stared more intently. He hadn't been mistaken. The captain had remained behind. He began hitting his head on the steering wheel. He'd almost blown it. Though it wasn't necessary, Captain Control always rode along on rescues. He turned the key in the ignition and pressed the pedal in the floor. The El Camino jerked and sped off, burning rubber.

Lloyd stepped out onto the patio to check the grill coals. He heard the screeching of tires, looked up and saw the El Camino leaving in quite the hurry. There was something familiar about the vehicle, but he couldn't place what it was.

He pulled into the carport and slammed on the brakes.

His breath was quick and his temples throbbed from the force of the blood rushing through his body. He slammed his fist into the steering wheel again, cursing himself for his carelessness. He got out of the car, not bothering to cover it.

How would he have explained to the captain showing up at the station at this late hour? He ran up the flight of stairs two at a time. His hands trembled as he fumbled to get the key into the door.

Once inside, his pulse lessened and the ringing in his ears ceased. He opened the refrigerator and pulled a Miller Genuine Draft and popped the cap. He took a long swig and didn't bring the can from his lips until it was empty. The alcohol rushed to his brain. He could feel himself calming down.

He could never let his zeal again cloud his judgment—there were too many who counted on his success.

59

The November morning was unseasonably cold for Los Angeles.

Jerome had dropped off the boys at his parents', and his dad was taking them to school on the last day before the Thanksgiving holiday. He never remembered getting the Wednesday before Thanksgiving as a holiday when he was in school.

He made the Manchester exit off the Harbor Freeway. Since Nicolle's accident he no longer talked on the phone in the car, and he didn't hear his cell phone ring. His phone was in his bag in the backseat.

As he pulled into the parking lot of Station 27, McInerney approached his vehicle, looking distressed. *What has the Menace done now?* Jerome thought. McInerney motioned for him to lower his driver's side window.

"Hey, man, what's up?" Jerome eyed him suspiciously.

"The hospital just called. They need you to get over there right away." McInerney was flushed and talked quickly.

"What did they say?" Jerome put the Durango in reverse as he talked.

"They just asked for you, said they tried you at home and on the cell phone. They need you to come to the hospital right away."

"Oh my God." Jerome felt his stomach drop.

"I'm getting off—do you want me to drive you?" McInerney asked, seeing the apprehension in Jerome's face. "I don't want you to get into an accident."

"No. I can handle it." Jerome was backing out of the parking lot as he spoke. "But thanks, man."

As Jerome disappeared around the corner, Mychel made the left into the parking lot. McInerney was walking toward the station when she lowered her window and called to him, "Where's Jerome going off to in such a rush? Isn't he going in the wrong direction?"

McInerney stopped and turned to answer. "The hospital called. They wanted him to get there as soon as possible."

Something inside of Mychel quickened. "What happened? I hope it isn't bad news."

"Lord, I hope not, but I don't know. They just said get the message to him if we could."

Mychel parked the car and rushed inside. She was the first to arrive on shift. She was hoping Lloyd could fill her in. She was so tired of playing the dutiful friend. Offering to help with this or that because that's what friends do. She wanted to make him feel like a man again. She headed for the dormitory; she needed some time to think of her next move now that Nicolle was out of the way.

Jerome maneuvered the SUV through the morning rush hour traffic, taking every opening no matter how small, as an opportunity to inch just a little closer to Nicolle. The ride seemed to take years when in reality it was only forty minutes since he left the station.

He unbuckled his seat belt, opened the door and exited the car in one motion. He ran up the stairs through the electric doors, past security and patient information without stopping. All sorts of thoughts ran through his mind. None of them good. He didn't remember the drive over. He'd made the journey to the hospital so many times now that he could do it in his sleep. Not since the day of the accident had he done it with such apprehension.

He should have called his and Nicolle's parents. But those precious seconds could mean the difference between seeing Nicolle alive one last time and not. As he waited for the elevator he considered taking the stairs but decided against it. Even he wasn't faster than an elevator climbing seventeen stories.

The elevator doors opened, and everyone seemed to move in

slow motion. When the car was finally empty, Jerome stepped on and pressed the button for his floor. Four other people joined him, each wanting a different floor.

The last person finally got off on the tenth floor. He expressed his way the last seven floors. David and Maxella Devereaux were entering the elevator as Jerome stepped off. There was a gleam in their eyes that didn't register with Jerome immediately.

"Mom, Dad, what's happened?" Jerome grabbed his mother-in-law's shoulders.

"Son, we were just coming to look for you! Nicolle's having some movement! She moved her left hand. God is truly good." Maxella began weeping.

Relief washed over Jerome as his body relaxed. "Oh, thank God. When did this happen? I was just here yesterday afternoon before I picked up the boys from school."

"Just before we arrived. The nurse was in changing her I.V. bottle and noticed. She still hasn't woken up, but this is such promising news. They notified the doctor and she's on her way."

Maxella opened her arms, and Jerome gladly fell into them weeping. Through his sobs he managed, "Oh my God, Mom, maybe she'll be all right."

"Look at me, Jerome. I know she's going to be all right. She has a long road ahead of her, but neither she nor you will be traveling it alone. Now I want you to dry those tears and let's go see my baby."

Dave Devereaux smiled at his wife and said, "I don't think they'll let us all in to see her."

"Well, we'll just have to see about that." Maxella marched off in the direction of the SICU.

60

"D r. Fulton, how is she?" Jerome rushed toward the doctor as he stood talking to a colleague. "My mother-in-law told me she moved her hand."

"I'll talk to you later, Jim." Turning his full attention to Jerome, Dr. Fulton said, "Mr. Winters, this is indeed encouraging news. We're waiting for Dr. Hale to arrive to order more tests. But the movement gives us hope. She's not out of the woods yet, however."

Dave and Maxella caught up to Jerome. "Dr. Fulton, can we see our daughter? I know if she can just hear our voices again it will make a difference," Dave asked.

Looking deep into the eyes of a grieving father, Dr. Fulton said, "Only one at a time and for five minutes each. We're going to bend the rules this one time and let you go in one after the other. But you know the rules are one person per hour." He smiled as he returned his pen to his white lab coat.

Grabbing his hands, Maxella kissed them. "Thank you, Doctor. Thank you so very much. My husband's right. If we can just talk to her, let her know we're all here, it's going to make all the difference in the world. And we'll obey the rules. I promise we will."

"I think you want to see your daughter?" Dr. Fulton joked. "Please follow me."

Obediently they fell in line like ducklings as they went off to the SICU.

Maxella turned to Jerome and said, "You go first."

"Are you sure, Mom?"

"Of course I'm sure, but hurry up," she teased.

Jerome walked the few steps to the doorway that led to bed

seven, God's perfect number. He slowly opened the door. As he took the steps toward the bed his heart began to race. The thought of his wife coming back to him shot volts of joy throughout his body. His hands shook as he reached out for her.

"Hey, Babe-ski. I've been missing you like crazy. I think I miss your laugh the most." Jerome was so overcome with various emotions he didn't know where to begin. "It's so infectious. The boys are doing really well with all of this. They're doing great in school. Though you know Nicolas had a million reasons why he shouldn't be in school at all. They get out today for a five-day weekend to celebrate Thanksgiving. But of course you know that. You know everything. You always made everything look so easy. I've learned to appreciate every little thing you do. And I promise, when you're back taking care of everything, I'm going to do a lot more to help you. Your parents are taking really great care of the boys while I'm at work. I take them home when I get off."

Jerome dropped his chin to his chest, trying to stifle the pain he felt. "There's something blue in my soul without you, Nic. I feel so empty and cold inside since you've been in this place. Did you know that a person's world could stop spinning?" Just above a whisper and between sobs, Jerome poured his soul out onto the snow-white sheet. "Everyone's telling me I have to be strong, but what's the point if you're not here to be strong for? I need you to come back to me, baby. Please, please, please, come back to me, Nicolle."

The nurse tapped lightly on the window. When Jerome looked up she pointed at her watch. He acknowledged her notification and turned back to Nicolle. He brought her hand to his lips as he said gently, "Baby, I have to go. They only give me five measly minutes and they go by like a second. Your mom and dad will be in right behind me. Just keep fighting. You're going to beat this thing."

Jerome leaned over to kiss her forehead. He wondered if she'd heard him. And if she heard, would it make a difference? His soul felt heavy, weighing down his steps as he slowly moved toward the door.

"Are you okay, son?" Dave asked quietly.

"Far from it, Dad. I don't know how much longer I can keep this up."

"As long as you need to. You remember all those pretty words you said at that event seventeen years ago that cost me so much money?"

Frowning slightly, he said, "You mean our wedding?"

"That's the one. Well, this is what they meant. You know, better or worse, sickness or health. Well, you got yourself a package deal here."

"Dad, I'm not even thinking about bailing. I just feel like I'm coming apart. I can't take care of the house and the boys the way Nicolle did."

"How do young folks say it? It's all good, son. Just keep on keeping on."

As the two men talked Maxella walked into Nicolle's room with authority. She lightly touched Nicolle's face. "This is your mother talking to you. Nicky, you've laid here long enough. It's time to wake up so that you can get on with the business of living. It'll take you a little time, but you're going to be as good as new. Your daddy and I are going to be there to take good care of you. We'll—"

Suddenly Maxella began to weep. She fell to her knees at her daughter's bedside. Her husband reached her before anyone else could even make it into the room. He tried lifting her from the floor, but she refused to budge.

"Leave me here. I'm not leaving my child. I belong here with her."

"Come on, Mother. You know we promised Dr. Fulton we'd obey the rules." Dave tried to soothe her.

"But a mother belongs with her child. Lord, why has this happened to my baby?" Maxella wailed.

"I'm sorry, Mr. Devereaux, but we're going to have to ask you to take your wife back to the waiting room." The nurse tried to help him lift her from the floor. Her resolve, more than her weight, made their task next to impossible.

Jerome stood helplessly by and watched the commotion on the floor. He'd dealt with more than his share of families who refused to let him do his job to save their loved one. But now he couldn't move. He saw them but was unable to respond.

"Leave me alone! I'll get up when I get good and ready."

"Mother, shhh. You're going to disturb the other patients!" Dave chastised.

"I don't care about anybody else. This is my child lying here at death's door."

"Mrs. Devereaux, if you don't leave, we'll have to call security. Please don't make me do that!" the nurse pleaded.

Suddenly there was a rattling of Nicolle's bed, and all in the room turned to see what was causing the movement. It was Nicolle shaking the bed railing.

"Oh my God!" The nurse abandoned Maxella and ran from the room.

Jerome moved across the room without touching the floor and was at Nicolle's side almost instantly. "Baby?"

"Oh, thank you, Jesus!" Maxella scrambled to get off the floor.

"My baby's back. Oh, my baby girl is back!" Dave rejoiced as he helped his wife up.

The nurse returned with Dr. Fulton and another doctor in tow. "I'm sorry, but you are all going to have to leave for now."

"I'm not going anywhere." Maxella folded her arms and stood steadfast.

"Mom, come on. They need to attend to her. Nicolle may be waking up." Jerome gently moved her toward the door. "They'll call us as soon as we can return."

Jerome's words betrayed the hope in his heart. He wanted more than anything to stay, to hold her hand and kiss her lips. He slowly walked with Maxella and Dave into the hallway. The three turned to watch the medical team go to work checking Nicolle's eyes, blood pressure and reflexes.

The special SICU team rushed back and forth using few words. Dr. Fulton barked orders and everyone obeyed them. Nicolle was awake. Though she didn't say anything, her eyes were opened and focused. She looked from one to the other as they had gathered around the bed. She now watched with a bewildered look on her face at the team as they moved about the room doing various and sundry things to her body.

61

Shauna Perkins, who had been Nicolle's nurse since she was brought to the unit following surgery, stuck her head out of the doorway. "You all may want to go wait in the family lounge. We're going to be quite a while—maybe an hour or so. We'll come get you when you can come back to see her. I'm so happy for your family. It's apparent to all of us how loving and dedicated you are."

"I'm not going anywhere!" Maxella folded her arms and planted her feet firmly on the floor.

"Now, Mother, there's nothing we can do standing here. And quite frankly, seeing them sticking and poking my daughter is getting to me. Let's go to the lounge, and I'll get you some coffee and orange juice." Dave touched her arm and spoke softly.

"Mom, he's right, and I can call my parents, the boys at school and Lloyd. This is truly a beautiful day, and all praise belongs to Him." Jerome, too, tried to convince Maxella that moving to the family lounge was best.

With a streak of stubbornness that had been her most memorable trait since birth, Maxella still refused. Dave shot Jerome a glance that said "Let me handle this."

"Well, Mother, you stand right here as long as you like. Jerome and I will be in the lounge having coffee."

"Do whatever you have to do. I'm not moving!" Maxella snapped.

Dave looked at Jerome and winked. "Let's go, son. Do you think they have some of those bagels left?"

"It's still early, they may." Jerome played along with his father-in-law.

"You just going to walk away and leave me standing here, Dave?"

"Maxella, they've told us to go to the lounge. This is what they do. We need to trust them. Now, are you coming or not?" He extended his hand.

"I just need to get some coffee. That's the only reason I'm going."

"I know, Mother."

Jerome shook his head and smiled. Nicolle was her mother's daughter. This was a snapshot of his future. He liked what he saw.

The trio slowly walked toward the family lounge. When they arrived, Jerome poured each of them a cup of coffee and served Maxella a Danish before he settled in at the desk to start making phone calls. The first call was to his parents. They were heading for the hospital immediately. His next call was to the school. He spoke with the principal, and she was going to get Nicolas and Jordan out of class so they could call him and he could give them the news personally.

Jerome's insides quivered in anticipation of what the doctors would tell him. He'd prayed without ceasing, and he'd believed. Now his precious Nicolle was back.

He dialed the station. Lloyd answered on the first ring. "Fire Station 27, Captain Frederickson speaking."

"She's awake." Jerome felt like screaming it from the mountaintop, but the words came out in a whisper.

"Excuse me?"

"It's Jerome. Nicolle's awake. It just happened. They called me because she'd had some movement earlier."

"Oh, man! That's fantastic. I'll call Nellie and tell her. I'm sure she'll be right over. You know I'd come if I could. How is she?"

"We don't know yet. They are running all kinds of tests. Doc Fulton said it would be about an hour. Her mom and dad were here when she had the first movement, and we were all in the room when she woke up."

"Oh, wow. God is awesome. Just letting you see His miracles. Have you told the boys?"

"Mrs. Bundy is pulling them from class so they can call me and I can tell them myself."

Lloyd had tried to convince Jerome in the past that he should have let the boys see their mother no matter what her condition, but Jerome had flatly refused. "Are you going to let them see her now?"

"Yes, now they can see her."

"Man, I'm so happy for you, for the boys, for all of us!"

"I'm going to go in case the school is trying to call."

"Of course, and I'll call Nellie. I'm going to call for a replacement."

"I'll be in later."

"No, you won't. Stay with your family, praise God and prepare for a huge Thanksgiving celebration, and we'll expect you back on Sunday."

"Thanks, Cap." Jerome hesitated and then to his best friend he said, "I couldn't have made it through this without you."

"Sure you could have, but thank God you didn't have to. Talk to you a little later today." Lloyd hung up first.

Almost the instant he replaced the handset in the cradle the phone rang again. Jerome snatched it from reflex. "Hello. This is Jerome Winters speaking."

"Dad?" Jordan's cracking voice made it sound like two syllables.

"Jordan!" Suddenly Jerome felt a dam of emotion breaking free. He struggled to maintain his composure. "It's your mom. She's awake!"

"For real? Can I come see her?" Jordan was so excited his words tripped over one another.

"Yes, of course you can." Jerome took very deep breaths. "I'll come pick you up now. Let me speak with your brother."

The next sound Jerome heard was an apprehensive Nicolas. "Hello." His voice was barely audible.

"Hi there, Nick. Are you okay?"

"I'm just scared. When they got us out of class and told us to call you, I thought Mommy died."

"Oh, no! Just the opposite, son. Your mom woke up. Isn't that great news?"

"I want to see her. I want to come see her now!"

Jerome was beginning to wonder if his decision to shield them from the pain of seeing their mother in a coma had been a wise one. "I'll be there shortly to pick you up. I'm leaving now."

"Hurry up, Daddy." Nicolas didn't wait for Jerome to respond. In his mind the longer his father talked on the phone the longer it would take him to get to the school.

"Son, rather than you drive all the way over and back, ask your folks to pick them up." Maxella munched a banana nut muffin.

"She's right, son. You're so shaken right now the less drive time you have the better," Dave cosigned.

"This sitting and waiting is driving me nuts," Jerome protested.

"You've waited six weeks—another hour isn't going to kill you. Get a muffin and come sit next to your mother-in-law. Tell me the first thing you're going to say to her when you see her."

Jerome laughed as he remembered that Maxella Devereaux's immediate solution to any problem large or small was a quick prayer and consumption of a few fat grams. "I'm not hungry, Mom."

"You need to eat something. I see your hands trembling. You eat a little something and you'll be surprised at how quickly that'll go away. Now, don't argue with me."

"Yes, ma'am. As soon as I call my parents."

Jerome's father answered on the second ring. "Hi, Dad. I'm glad you haven't left yet. Could you go by and pick up the boys from school? They want to see Nicolle."

"Of course, we can. It's about time you came to your senses. Cecelia's just about ready. We're leaving as soon as she gets her coat."

"Okay, Dad. Please hurry." There was something urgent in Jerome's voice that touched his father.

"I'm on my way, son."

His new boss was really ruining his plans.

She wanted to change the stations he serviced. How dare she? Why would they put a woman over his department? He didn't give a good horse's ass how much military experience she had. What could a woman possibly know about what he does? When he'd taught the blacks a lesson, the women would be next.

He hadn't done anything since the night Lloyd Frederickson had almost caught him. He looked at the white board on the wall in the tiny kitchen, at the list of his plans and checkmarks that signified his success.

There was still much to be done.

How could he justify being at Station 27 if it was taken out of his rotation? In frustration, he picked up the coffee mug from the table and threw it against the wall in the living room. Brown liquid splattered onto the wall and the badly stained sofa that doubled as his bed as his cup broke into several pieces.

He needed time to think, and the voices in his head were too loud today.

loyd took the steps two at a time, his heart light with the news he'd just received. As he walked through the recreation room, he saw Mychel vacuuming and Andrew mopping the kitchen floor. "I see you've been trained well."

"Yeah, he's finally getting into shape." Mychel shut off the vacuum and wrapped the cord around it to put it away.

Lloyd laughed and moved to the dining table. "Where's Austin?"

"I think he's cleaning the equipment bay. What's up, Cap? You look kinda serious." Andrew put the mop in the bucket and walked over to the table.

"It's really good news from Jerome. I wanted to tell everyone together."

"I'll page him." Andrew went to the phone on the wall next to the kitchen, picked up the phone, hit a few buttons and said, "Fitzgerald, front and center to the rec room. Cap wants to have a meeting."

Mychel's heart stopped. She approached the table where Lloyd sat. She didn't dare appear too anxious.

Austin entered and the team gathered around their leader, who prided himself on dangling information like a horse trainer with a carrot. Mychel was impatient. "Well?"

"Winters called from the hospital. Nicolle woke up this morning."

"Oh, Cap, that is fantastic news!" Andrew walked over and slapped hands with Austin.

"Wow. I'm not a praying man usually, but I have been saying a few words for her." Austin seemed subdued by the news.

Mychel knew she needed to react. But how could she pretend

she was happy? "I know he's relieved. How is she?" From experience she knew just because Nicolle woke up didn't mean she'd be okay or even live.

"They don't know yet. But this is going to be a wonderful Thanksgiving around the Devereaux-Winters table, I can tell you that. I've called for a replacement. Jerome won't be in for the rest of the shift," Lloyd said, standing. "If a fire call comes in before the replacement gets here, we'll get backup."

Mychel's curiosity was getting the best of her. "So, did he say anything else? What's her prognosis?"

As Lloyd headed for the back step, he turned and looked Mychel in the eyes. "We're not sure about anything just yet, but I'll be sure you're one of the first to know."

Mychel wasn't sure what his inference was, but she let it go. She'd just have to wait to see. Now all she could seem to hope for was that Nicolle would be an invalid. She and Jerome both knew he needed a whole woman in his life.

63

Montgomery and Cecelia Winters arrived on the seventeenth floor with their three grandsons. The boys ran from the elevator without knowing exactly where they were going. Jerome heard them before he saw them. Christian ran and jumped into his waiting arms. Nicolas and Jordan rushed to him and grabbed him around his waist.

"Can we see Mom now?" Nicolas asked first.

"Not yet. They're still running tests. The nurse came out about an hour ago and said it will be a little longer."

Maxella sat on the couch with her arms extended. "Come give your grandma some sugar, boys."

Montgomery and Cecelia caught up to the boys. Jerome hugged and kissed his mom, then hugged his dad. "Have you seen her yet?" his mother asked as she wiped lipstick from his cheek.

"Not yet. It's a hurry up and wait thing. She's still undergoing tests. I don't know if they will let all of us see her."

"I'll be surprised if they let us"—Dave pointed back and forth between him and his wife—"ever."

"Oh, hush up, Dave. It was all that ruckus that woke her up."

"What happened?" Cecelia sat next to Maxella on the couch.

"Let them tell it, I was showing out in Nicky's room. They wanted me to leave, and I didn't want to."

"I can't see how that's such a big deal," Cecelia said, taking a cup of tea from Montgomery.

"Come on now, Mother. Tell it like it really happened," Dave taunted.

Cecelia looked from Dave to Jerome and then back to Maxella. "I'm confused."

"Well, she was a little boisterous with her request to stay put. She actually had a mini sit-in." Jerome laughed as he relayed the story.

"Oh, so just Maxella being Maxella?" Montgomery sat across from the ladies next to Dave.

"Pretty much." Dave chuckled.

"I don't know what you find so humorous." Maxella folded her arms in protest.

"Come on now, Mother. You know . . ." Dr. Fulton entered the room and all fell silent.

"How is she, Doctor?" Jerome moved to meet him halfway across the room.

"I think we should talk privately." Dr. Fulton turned, pointing toward the door.

"That is my child in there." Maxella jumped to her feet so swiftly she shocked everyone. She moved to within inches of the doctor's face. "I want to know what's wrong with her, and I want to know now!"

Dr. Fulton looked to Jerome for permission to speak. Jerome nodded, saying, "No one of us loves Nicolle any less than the other. You can speak freely."

"First, I need to explain again what happens when a person is in a coma for an extended period. How a person recovers depends on what part of the brain was injured. If a person is in a coma for a week, then you can expect that their recovery will take a week to ten days."

Jerome interrupted the doctor. "Are you saying that it will take Nicolle six to eight weeks to recover?"

"Yes, pretty much. But it goes far beyond that alone. As I stated, it depends on what part of the brain was injured. In Nicolle's case it was her right frontal lobe. In the pathology post-trauma it was determined she sustained a blow to the head by hitting the passenger-side window. It was like she turned to look for an escape route."

"Did Inspector Grissom do it?" Jordan asked innocently.

Dr. Fulton turned to look at him, puzzled. "Inspector Grissom?"

"Sorry, Doc. He's talking about *CSI*. It's his favorite show. It's what he wants to do when he grows up," Jerome answered.

"Oh, I see." He turned his attention back to the boy. "Are you Jordan or Nicolas?"

Jordan seemed surprised Dr. Fulton knew his name. "I'm Jordan."

"Well, Jordan. Inspector Grissom is in Las Vegas. We have our own investigators here in Los Angeles."

"Kewl." Jordan seemed satisfied with his response.

"There are several functions controlled by that part of the brain. But the one we're most concerned with is her memory, particularly her visual memory."

"What does that mean?" Maxella moved back to the couch and sat on the edge.

"There's a strong possibility she won't recognize you. Her speech is slightly impaired, but that is mainly attributed to her vocal cords being dormant for so long. When she saw her reflection, we asked her who it was, and she said 'Aunt Alice.' "

Maxella gasped and put her hand to her mouth. "That's my sister. She's been dead more than twenty years, but Nicky looks exactly like her."

"That explains a lot, then. When we asked her name, she said 'Nicolle Devereaux.' " Dr. Fulton paused, searching each adult's face. "And her age—fifteen."

Jerome shouted, "What are you talking about? She doesn't know that we're married?"

"I'm afraid not. Not at this moment. But don't get too upset. She's been awake less than four hours. Her memory could fast-forward and catch up in a matter of a few days."

"Or?" Montgomery posed the question.

"Or, she could start life over at fifteen. But with therapy that's highly unlikely."

"When can we see her?" Cecelia posed the question.

Before Dr. Fulton had a chance to answer Maxella asked, "And can we all see her?"

"She's actually sleeping again. She's very tired, as is expected. Her vitals are very strong, and although there's some atrophy, her muscular movement and reflexes are very good."

"So when can we see her, Doc?" Maxella was insistent.

"I'm getting to that, Mrs. Devereaux. I just want to explain what we're doing currently and what we have planned for the next few days."

"I'm sorry, Dr. Fulton. My wife's just a little anxious, as you can well understand."

"I don't need you to apologize for me like I'm not here. I want to see my child now."

Jerome saw the need for intervention. "Dr. Fulton, can we just see her for a moment, even if she is sleeping? I promise we won't disturb her." Jerome shot a glance to his mother-in-law.

"What?" Maxella played innocent.

Everyone, including Dr. Fulton, laughed. "What I was going to tell you is that if her vitals remain strong and consistent overnight, we'll move her tomorrow into an acute care room where the family can go in together. We'll just insist you not overtax her. She'll go through scores of tests over the next week. As soon as her physical condition is no longer acute, we'll transfer her to a rehabilitation facility. That's far more conducive to getting her back home to you and returning her to the life she had."

"So when can we see her?" Maxella wasn't giving up. "And which of us can go in?"

"I'll leave that decision up to Mr. Winters. I must warn you that you must not push too hard for Mrs. Winters to remember. You don't want to disorient or upset her."

Mr. Devereaux took offense at the doctor's words. "Why do you think we'd do anything to upset my daughter? We want her to get well as quickly as possible."

"I know you'd do nothing intentionally, but when a patient doesn't remember, families tend to push just a little too hard. It's perfectly understandable. I'll come back shortly and let you know when. I just ask that you be patient for a little longer."

"Hmph. That's easy for you to say," Maxella mumbled.

64

"Why didn't you put this back where it belonged?" Mychel yelled at Austin when she did the inventory after a rescue run.

Austin threw his hands up in a surrender motion. "What's eating at you? You've been pissy at me all day. Whatever it is, I promise you I didn't do it!"

"Maybe she's ragging, man!" Earl "the Squirrel" Murray, Jerome's shift replacement, teased.

It was no mystery why Murray was a floater: a firefighter, EMT or paramedic who had no home. No one shift could tolerate his arrogance, egotism and general bad attitude more than occasionally. But hands down there was no person you'd want on a fire with you more than Murray. He had a sixth sense that few could parallel.

"You betta back off of me, Murray. Because if I'm 'ragging,' as you put it, then I'll be justified for wrapping my fingers around your throat and squeezing until your eyes bug out and no jury will convict me." Mychel slammed the equipment compartment of the paramedic truck.

"Whoa, Miss Thang, Big Daddy knows you want some of this. You're just fighting the inevitable. Let's just do our thing. Get it behind us and move on," Earl teased.

Mychel pushed past him, shoving him aside. "Get out of my way."

Earl looked at Austin and said, "See, man, I told you. She wants me."

Laughing in his face, Austin said, "Yeah, I know. Just like I want West Nile. Come on, wanna shoot some hoops out back?"

"You don't want a piece of me. You better get pretty boy to double-team me, that's your only chance." Earl pretended to dribble and shoot.

"Just get your tennis shoes, fool."

Mychel had gone to the dormitory to think through her situation with Jerome. What could she possibly do to make Jerome see that he needed to be with her? Since that night at his house he'd been far less hostile, friendly even. She couldn't lose that. She'd worked too hard to get here. How dare Nicolle wake up now? She'd planned to make pumpkin pies for him and the boys as a Thanksgiving treat.

She fell facefirst into her pillow and screamed. There had to be a way to make her plan work. She just had to think it through. She flipped on her back and laid in the quiet of her room for she didn't know how long. She wasn't sure when her attraction turned from the chase to an overwhelming desire. Jerome represented everything she'd ever wanted in a man. His physical attractiveness was no longer her motivation. She needed a man like him in her life. One who was strong and assured, yet loved and respected a woman, a characteristic that had been elusive in relationships gone by. She deserved a man like Jerome Winters, and she couldn't let Nicolle stand in the way of what she deserved. Her concentration was broken by the sound of a crash followed by the sound of a man's anguished cry.

She jumped up and ran in the direction of the cry. Lloyd met her in the equipment bay and they ran to the yard together. Andrew was pinned under Earl. Austin struggled to get the backboard off him.

"What the hell happened here?" Lloyd demanded.

Trying to balance the board without hurting Earl any further, Austin yelled at Mychel, "Give me a hand!"

The sight of the two on the ground had momentarily immobilized her, and her natural instinct took a backseat to amazement. She quickly moved to assist Austin and they effortlessly lifted the backboard off Earl.

Austin extended his hand to Earl to help him up. Blood trickled from Earl's lip. Other than that he didn't look any worse for wear. They both turned to help Andrew up. Andrew's arm looked contorted under his body.

"You all right, man?" Austin asked both of them.

Earl touched his lip and head. "I think I'm okay. Nothing feels broken." Turning to Andrew, he asked, "What about you?"

"Other than your big ass knocking the wind out of me, I think I'm okay. What happened?" Andrew was dusting himself off and feeling his arm.

"I dunked, and the next thing I knew you were trying to get intimate with a brotha. But of course I was on top." Earl made jokes to cover up for the disorientation he felt.

"Look at this!" Mychel was examining the broken backboard. "This has been cut clean. You didn't break this."

Lloyd's heart sank. The Menace had struck again. "Y'all sure you're okay?"

"Yeah, Cap. I'm okay. Probably have a bruise or two tomorrow. But it's not going to affect my ability to eat turkey on Thursday." Andrew flexed his arm again.

"You?" Lloyd's question was directed at Earl.

"Nothing to sweat. Just a drop or two of blood. Nothing a man can't handle."

"I'm going to need you both to complete a report. I'm going to call I.A. They're taking my calls these days. They'll probably send someone out to talk to you before the end of the shift."

"What's different now, Cap?" Austin followed Lloyd back into the station.

"They've finally opened a full-scale investigation into the Menace problem. The D.A.'s office, detectives—the whole nine yards—are involved. There'll be some new security procedures instituted. All of this is taking more time than I'd like, but I'm pleased it's happening."

"Why are we just hearing about all of this?" Mychel snapped.

"I wanted to be sure exactly what will be happening and when. I didn't want you to think they were still yanking our chains."

"And how do we know they aren't now?" Austin asked.

Earl looked from one to the other. "What are y'all talking about? A menace?"

"What happened out there on the court was no accident. We've been having problems for months now. Just one thing after another," Andrew added.

"Who'd do such a thing? That's crazy." Earl's normal cocky behavior had given way to genuine alarm.

"That's what we're trying to find out. But to answer Austin's question—trust me, I know. I've been in meetings even on my days off, strategizing ways to capture this fool."

"I'm so sick and tired of always being on pins and needles, not knowing what will go wrong next." Mychel went to the utility sink to wash her hands. "Around every corner you're wondering if something has been booby-trapped."

"I know. But believe me, I'm working as hard as I can to get a resolution. I just hope it doesn't come too late."

65

The Winterses and the Devereauxs took turns pacing the floor of the spacious lounge. Christian napped on the sofa next to Grandma Maxella. Nicolas and Jordan took turns playing games on the computer. Dave and Montgomery read the *LA Times*. Maxella chatted with Cecelia. It was Jerome's turn to trace the pattern in the gray carpet.

"Son, why don't you sit? You're making me dizzy," Cecelia admonished her son with love.

"I can't. I want to see Nicolle. What is taking so long? It's been almost three hours since the doctor was in here."

Just as the words escaped Jerome's lips, Shauna Perkins walked in. "Mr. Winters, you can see your wife. She's awake. Drs. Fulton and Hale are with her. There's also Dr. Stanton. She specializes in patients who've awakened from long-term comas. You ready?"

"What about the rest of us?" Maxella was on her feet.

"Mrs. Devereaux, we'll let you know when you can come in. We're going to start with Mr. Winters. If seeing him doesn't upset her, we'll try another visitor."

"You'd better try real hard, missy. I don't want to cause a scene, but don't think I'm afraid to do so."

"Maxella, please let them do their job." Cecelia grabbed her hand.

"Let me go. CeeCee, I mean no disrespect, but your son is standing right here. That's my child in there. I've been separated from her for six weeks. I think it's time we got reacquainted."

Cecelia hadn't been offended by her lifelong friend's words. Instead she humbly sat back and let her handle her business. Because she was right—if it were Jerome, only someone who walked on water could stop her from doing whatever it took to see him.

Jerome moved to Maxella and took her hands in his. "Mom, I'll only stay a few minutes. If she's up to it, I want the boys to see her, and then I promise you'll be next."

Tears formed in the corners of Maxella's eyes. "Please hurry," she whispered.

Jerome kissed her cheek. "I promise." He turned to the nurse and said, "Let's go."

Jerome followed the nurse to the SICU. Dr. Fulton was at the desk conferring with a very tall and slim African-American woman in a tailored suit. He assumed she was the specialist the nurse had mentioned.

As Jerome approached the desk, Dr. Fulton turned toward him. "Mr. Winters, I'd like for you to meet Dr. Stanton. She has become your wife's primary care physician. She's a neurologist who specializes in patients who've awakened from a long-term coma such as Nicolle's."

"Mr. Winters, very nice to meet you. Unfortunately, when I meet the family of my new patients, it's not under the most pleasant of circumstances. First, I want to give you my card. Either I or one of my associates, who'll be thoroughly familiar with every aspect of your wife's history and care, will be available twenty-four hours a day, three hundred sixty-five days a year. We never close. In the first few days you'll have lots of questions and they might not necessarily come up during office hours. When you call this number, you get someone in our office and not a service."

"That's quite impressive, Dr. Stanton." Jerome looked from the card to her and back again. "I promise not to abuse it."

"That's impossible, Mr. Winters. Secondly, we have just become partners in facilitating a speedy recovery for Nicolle. And I think as partners we should be on a first-name basis. My name is Millicent. My friends call me Mimi. I expect after today we'll be friends."

Jerome was speechless.

"Lastly, I will always be honest with you. If there is something I don't know, I will tell you. As good as I am, I'm not God, and there are many things that are out of my very capable hands. I will ask you to do the same. There may be difficult questions for you to answer, but I will always need the most forthright answers. Have I made myself clear?"

"As spring water."

"Good."

"Can I see her now?"

"I'd like to talk with you first. Please come have a seat in the office." Mimi led the way. Dr. Fulton and Jerome followed dutifully.

She sat at the desk, crossed her very shapely legs and leaned forward. "This is what we know so far. Nicolle is quite alert when she's awake, but she tires very easily. This is totally normal. We've asked her a series of questions. She thinks she's fifteen and that she's in high school. From reading the profile you've provided over the past six weeks I understand she's known you since she was a toddler."

"Actually even before that. But our earliest memories are of when we were three."

"If what you've told the other doctors is true, you have a rock-solid marriage and are very much in love. Because of the strength of your relationship our hope is that when she sees you it will jar her memory and she will fast-forward to the present. But we have no guarantees. Now, this is the first test of your complete honesty. Since she knew you at fifteen, I must ask you, will she have any unpleasant memories of you from that time?"

Insulted, Jerome retorted quickly, "Absolutely not! There have never been anything but good and even better memories between us."

"I'm going to have to trust you, Jerome." Mimi was an amazing woman, and Jerome couldn't help but admire the way she commanded respect in the most unassuming manner. "One final thing—if you're visiting with her and she starts to get upset and I tell you to leave, do not mince words, turn yourself around and walk out of the room. I'll be more than happy to discuss with you after the fact what I think may have happened. But at that moment my only concern is not upsetting her. Are we on the same page?"

"Doctor, you seem to think I would do something to impede my wife's progress. Since we've known each other all of five minutes I'm going to let that slide for now. But don't ever assume anything but that I'd walk the Sahara or swim the Black Sea for that woman in bed seven. If I go into burning buildings for people I don't know, what do you presume I'd do for those I love?"

"Good. You've passed the first test." She stood and said, "Let's go see your wife."

This woman is a piece of work, Jerome thought. But if this is what it takes to bring Nicolle back, then so be it. "Okay."

Mimi led the way. She walked with the same authority with which she spoke. When they approached Nicolle's bed, she slowed her gait, turned and looked at Jerome. "Ready?"

"Ready."

"Wait here until I call you, okay?"

Reluctantly Jerome agreed. "Okay."

"Hi, Nicolle. I brought someone to see you." Mimi spoke in a soft gentle tone. She beckoned for Jerome to join her.

Nervously he slowly walked to her bedside. "Hi, Nicolle. How're you feeling, baby?"

Nicolle moved her head back and blinked several times. She seemed to be focusing, then she smiled broadly and said, "Hi, Mr. Montgomery. You sure are dressed funny. Is Jerome with you?"

He'd been sitting in his car watching when the backboard fell onto those loafers.

Taxpayers would thank him. It just wasn't right that they played ball in the middle of a workday. At what other job outside of the NBA could a person get paid for bouncing a ball up and down the court?

He devised a plan to outsmart that new manager. He'd just falsify the time sheets. No one looked at the time or even what he did for that matter. He'd simply write down that it took longer than it actually did on the days he had plans for Station 27.

66

"Thanks for letting us know about this latest incident, Captain Frederickson." The Internal Affairs inspector's attitude had made a one-eighty.

"I have everyone involved completing a report," said Lloyd. "I'll fax them over to you as soon as they're complete."

"I just wanted you to know we've placed the requisition for the cameras. They should reach the chief's desk by week's end. But the holiday may delay it a couple days."

Lloyd felt a sense of pride that his persistence had paid off. The department was finally taking the steps they should have taken from the beginning. The old adage "Better late than never" gave him little solace. "I understand. If I don't talk to you again before Thanksgiving, you have a good and safe one."

"You do the same, Captain."

Lloyd hung up the phone and turned his attention to the e-mail. There was a message from the chief.

Captain Frederickson,

Please be advised this office is taking measures to guarantee the safety and security of Station 27, more specifically C Shift. The security office will notify you with planned changes regarding access to the facility in the next few days.

Please take this correspondence as our commitment to resolving the compromise of safety for you and your crew. Official correspondence will be forthcoming from this office.

Sincerely,

Chief Marlborough

Well, well, well. This came pretty close to an apology in Lloyd's book. He couldn't wait to share the news with Glynda. Now that the department was forced into action, they had essentially won a battle. Though the war raged on, Lloyd felt they had to celebrate each little victory.

There was something about this very talented professional young woman that made him miss his daughters. He'd decided his vacations in coming years would be spent in Italy and Seattle. He couldn't make up for lost time, but he could start from today forward being the best father he knew how to be.

"Isaac, Townsend and Parker," the pleasant voice sang.

"Glynda Naylor-Sanders, please." Lloyd smiled as he spoke.

"With pleasure."

Glynda's secretary picked up on the first ring. "Glynda Naylor-Sanders's office."

"Is she in?"

"Oh, hi, Captain Frederickson. She's away from her office this afternoon. Can I have her call you?"

That she recognized Lloyd's voice always made him smile. "You bet."

"I've got your work and cell number right here. Which do you prefer?"

"Either works."

've opened an official investigation. I cannot, more important will not, do anything to cover for you any longer. You've compromised this office and the entire department for that matter. I don't give a rat's turd what our personal agenda is—anyone who wears this uniform is a member of an elite group.

"You need to consider my debt to you paid in full. If you think you need to make my secret public, then so be it. But you won't hold me hostage with it any longer. You could have killed someone."

"What the hell are you talking about, Bill? All I did was follow that lawyer woman. I sent her an e-mail but never even talked to her. I never got close enough to kill anyone."

"Look, I know you're the one sabotaging C Shift at 27. I've been getting the e-mails from you. You think I don't know it's you?"

"I haven't sent you any e-mails!"

"Stop trying to deny it. You and that brotherhood of yours are nothing but a modern-day Klan. I feel as much disdain for these black folks taking over as the next true Americans, but we have to face the facts. They're here to stay. Some of them are actually kinda good at their jobs."

"I want you to shut the hell up and listen to me closely. I haven't done anything but try to discourage that Glynda Sanders woman from filing a civil rights suit. Nothing more. I don't know anything about sabotage at Station 27. Look, I would never betray you. You've kept my hocks out of jail more than once."

"The civil rights thing has died on the vine since the department put the investigation on the front burner. Frederickson has been right all along. There is foul play on their shift."

"Then there is nothing more I need to do with the Sanders woman. I give you my word. I have done nothing else."

Marlborough sat back in his chair and took a deep breath. If Burns wasn't behind the activity at 27, then who was?

68

Jerome stared at Mimi and back at Nicolle. "Baby, I'm Jerome."

"No, you're not. Stop teasing me, Mr. Montgomery. Did Jerome put you up to it?" Nicolle laughed faintly.

Looking at the doctor for guidance, Jerome was encouraged to keep talking to her. "How do you feel?"

"I'm really tired. The doctor said I had an accident, but I don't remember being in any accident. My arm doesn't move right."

"We're going to start physical therapy tomorrow if you have a good night," Mimi added.

"So, Mr. Montgomery, where is my mom and dad? Why are you here instead of them?"

"Umm. Umm, I was in the neighborhood and just thought I'd come by to see how you're doing. They're here now, and I'm going to go out so they can come see you." Jerome choked back tears.

"Okay, I want to see Mom. The nurse said I've been asleep for a while."

"Yeah, you have. I've missed you a lot, Nicolle."

"Did Jerome miss me, too?"

A lone tear rolled down his cheek and onto his Hard Rock Cafe–Paris sweatshirt. "He's missed you like you can't even imagine."

"Why are you crying, Mr. Montgomery? I feel okay other than my arm and being tired. I want to go back to sleep now."

"Mr. Winters is going to leave now, Nicolle. He'll be back to see you later, if that's okay."

"It's fine, but I really want to see Jerome." Nicolle tried to turn over, but her body was too weak to respond. Before Jerome could leave the room, she had fallen asleep.

Jerome turned and quickly walked from the room without a word to Mimi. He needed to get some air. The sounds of the unit suddenly became magnified, and he couldn't hear his own thoughts.

Mimi followed him into the hall. "Are you okay, Mr. Winters?"

He looked at her coldly. "You're kidding me, right? I've loved that woman since we played in the sandbox together. Do you know I've never made love to another woman?" Jerome never gave her a chance to answer. "I've held my breath for forty-one days, Dr. Stanton. Today, I thought I could finally exhale only to discover that Nicolle thinks I'm my father. And you have the nerve to ask me if I'm all right?"

"I need you to remain calm, Mr. Winters. You're getting upset and that will do none of us any good. This is actually a good start. She does have some memories. I want her mother and father to come in to see what her reaction is, but she needs to rest for a bit. Don't lose hope, Jerome. Give it a chance. Great things have happened here today."

Jerome walked away without another word. He couldn't determine if he liked this woman or not. One minute he thought she was great and the next he loathed her. As he walked back into the visitors' lounge everyone accosted him at the same time. He felt so defeated. This was not at all what he had expected.

Maxella ran to him and grabbed his hands. "How's my baby?"

"She thinks I'm my father."

The adults looked from one to the other. Cecelia went to her son and hugged him. "I'm so sorry, Jerome. How long do they think she'll be like this?"

"They have no idea. It wasn't supposed to be this way!" Jerome turned so that they couldn't see his tears; his effort was futile.

"Daddy, when can we see Mommy?" Nicolas stood in front of him with accusing eyes.

Jerome squatted so that he was eye level with Nicolas. "I'm not sure. When I saw your mom a few minutes ago she was having trouble remembering things. She may not remember who you are."

"That doesn't matter. I know who she is. I haven't seen my

mommy in a long time. I don't want to wait anymore." Nicolas never broke the eye contact.

"Me, too, Dad."

Now that he had their hopes up, he still didn't want them exposed to her possible rejection. If she thought he was his dad, who would she think her sons were?

Maxella walked over to them. "Jerome, I want to see and talk to Nicolle more than anything, but I'll give up my turn so these boys can see their mother. Maybe seeing them will snap her back to the here and now."

Jerome looked up at Maxella and then over to his own mother and then to the two patriarchs. Their eyes all said the same thing: It's time. "I'll speak to the doctor. She wanted her to rest for a bit before Ma-Ma and Pa-Pa went in. So I'm sure it will be the same for you," he said, looking at his sons.

"I think this would be a great time to go have some dinner. Your mommy is resting, and I personally am famished," Maxella said to her grandkids as she moved toward the door. "Anyone going to join me?"

At best he'd have a turkey potpie today.

There were no invitations for him to join family and friends for a bountiful feast.

He paced the distance between the kitchen and the living room. It had never seemed this small to him before.

When the city made him a hero, and the chief was forced to make him a firefighter, he'd be able to afford a bigger place. In the meantime he had to find a way to fill his time. What was he going to do with four days off? C Shift didn't return until Sunday.

There was a meeting with the new boss on Monday. What could she possibly want to discuss with him? She didn't know or understand how important his job was.

Without him there was no Los Angeles Fire Department.

69

"Happy Thanksgiving. I'm Dr. Stanton, but you can call me Dr. Mimi. I've been taking care of your mother since she woke up from her very long sleep. She is doing much better. In fact, she's doing so good that we've moved her to a room where everyone can visit her at once for as long and as often as they like. We just can't make her too tired. Do you have any questions?"

Nicolas looked at his dad, his brother and then to Dr. Mimi. "Can I see my mommy now?"

The doctor laughed and answered, "You surely may."

At the doctor's suggestion Jerome hadn't seen Nicolle since she'd thought he was his father. The doctor also insisted that the boys wait until this morning to visit their mother. When her parents had visited on Wednesday, she'd recognized them but wondered why her dad's hair was so gray. Maxella, with the benefit of L'Oréal Feria #205, looked the same as she did twenty years before. Nicolle had rambled on about the junior prom and how excited she was. She asked the doctor several times if she'd be released in time to go.

"Let's go, gentlemen." Mimi led the way down the hall to the elevator. "We must go down one more floor. It will only be a few more minutes."

The remainder of the short journey was in silence. Jerome was as tense as a tightrope at Barnum & Bailey Circus. He was so afraid Nicolle would reject the boys and they would be devastated.

Mimi led the way as they stepped off the elevator. They walked several feet down a long hallway and turned the corner. Nicolle's room was the second one on the left. When Mimi stopped in front of the door she looked at the boys and smiled. "I'm going to talk to her for just a minute to introduce you. And then I'll call you over to her bed. Okay?"

"She's our mother. She knows us already!" Jordan snapped.

That's my boy, Jerome thought.

"Remember, she was asleep for a long time and may have forgotten. Don't forget she hasn't seen you for a month and half," Mimi explained.

It had been six weeks and one day almost to the minute since that fateful day when all life had changed. Jerome wondered how much longer he could maintain a brave front. "Boys, it's going to be just fine. I promise." Once again Jerome held his breath.

Dr. Stanton knocked lightly and opened the door before Nicolle had a chance to answer. "Well, good morning, young lady. I heard you drank all of your breakfast this morning. If you keep that up, we'll be able to get this needle out of your hand by tomorrow and solid food by Sunday. Would you like that?"

"I sure would. I'm so hungry."

"That's a great sign. I've got someone here who wants to see you." Mimi motioned for the boys to come forward.

"Jerome!" Nicolle was grinning at Jordan. "I knew you'd come. Daddy said you couldn't come right now. But I knew you wouldn't stay away," she rambled on in excitement.

"Mommy, my name is . . ." Jordan began, but Dr. Mimi indicated he shouldn't say any more.

Nicolle looked at Nicolas, frowned and said, "Desmond Devereaux, it's about time you came to see your big sister."

The boys looked to their father with pain-filled eyes. Jerome wanted to run to them and pull them from the room. Mimi cautioned him to stay put. Jordan took Nicolas's hand and said, "I think we'd better go now. We don't want to make you too tired."

In the hallway, Nicolas began to cry. Jordan was visibly angry when he spoke. "Dad, why did Mommy think I was you?"

"Remember, Dr. Mimi told you that your mommy is a little confused. She just needs a little more time for her thinking to be clear."

"I want her to know me now!" Nicolas shouted.

70

The spread on the dining room table was fabulous.

Cecelia Winters had taken her pent-up frustration to the kitchen and let it loose. The house smelled of turkey, dressing, candied yams, greens, macaroni and cheese, baked rolls and, of course, peach cobbler.

She'd spent two days slicing and dicing. When the doctor had refused to let the boys see their mother until she was moved to the acute care floor, Cecelia had stormed out of the hospital. She didn't, or didn't care to, understand all of the rules. She just knew that her daughter-in-law needed to be around the people who loved her. She was tired of other people making decisions that were affecting her family.

Her royal highness, Dr. Stanton, had moved Nicolle from the SICU unit the evening before and had agreed the boys could see their mother on Thanksgiving morning. Jerome had buffed and spit-shined them, and if Cecelia's calculations were correct, they should be approaching the hospital right about the time she slipped the peach cobbler in the oven.

Maxella and Dave arrived just before noon bearing wine and dessert. The stress of the past weeks had drawn lines in Maxella's face. The makeup she wore did little to conceal the toll all of this was taking on her.

The mothers worked effortlessly in the kitchen while the dads kicked back watching football.

"Do you think she'll ever be the same again?" Maxella didn't look up from the cornbread mix she was whisking.

Cecelia dried her hands on her apron and walked over to where

Maxella stood. "For all that is within me, I wish I had an answer for you. You know since Nicolle was born, she's been like my daughter. She has been wonderful for my son. I know that every night and morning I pray that she'll be made whole."

"I guess that's all any of us can do. What time will Jerome and the boys be back?" Maxella poured the mixture in the pan.

"If it goes well, around two. If it doesn't, they could be walking through the door any minute."

Cecelia opened the top of the double oven and basted the turkey. The back door opened; Jerome and the boys walked in.

Maxella and Cecelia shot each other a glance. "How're my boys doing? You hungry?" Cecelia asked, trying to add cheer to her voice.

Nicolas rushed past her. "No."

"Me neither," Jordan answered as he followed his brother.

Maxella slipped the cornbread into the bottom oven, wiped her hands on the apron and turned to Jerome. "Since that boy first cried he's been hungry. What happened?"

"Dr. Stanton went through all the preparation motions with them, and Nicolle was sitting up. She'd eaten breakfast. She looks so much better. Her color has come back, and she was smiling. She looked like my best girl."

Cecelia stopped dinner preparations and moved across the kitchen to stand in front of her son. "What happened, Jerome?"

"She thinks Jordan is me and Nicolas is Desmond when we were teenagers." Jerome stared at the floor. "All she talked about was me—well, I guess I should say Jordan—taking her to the junior prom. I feel like yet another door has been slammed in my face."

Maxella's hand went up to her mouth. "Lord Jesus!"

Cecelia got in his face and spoke through clinched teeth. "Boy, I don't want to ever hear you talk like that again. If I counted all the windows God opened after doors were closed, I wouldn't have time to do anything else all day. It's all in the believing. You talk the faith talk, now you betta lace up your Nikes and start walking the faith walk."

There were those words again. *It's all in the believing.* "Why did you say that, Mom?"

"Because it's not like you to be defeated. You never let anyone or anything get the best of you. Nicolle needs you to keep believing she's going to get better."

"I mean, those exact words, 'It's all in the believing'?"

Cecelia looked perplexed. She really wasn't sure why she said it. "Hmph. I don't know."

Нe stormed out of the department meeting and never saw the two men watching him.

Who did this woman think she was? He had been with the department for almost fifteen years, and no manager until now had ever challenged him. She'd stood before the more than two hundred men and told them she was hired to make the department run more efficiently. She'd spouted on and on about her years in the military and her numerous awards and commendations, like he cared.

The first and most sweeping change was that the firehouse assignments would rotate every three months and no one mechanic would service a station twice in a row. That was insane. How could he carry out his plan? He'd worked so hard and meticulously, and the coup de grâce was just on the horizon.

He needed time to think. He rushed from the headquarters building and into the midday sun. The sun blinded him and gave him a headache instantly. The voices in his head screamed, making the pain bounce around.

Inspectors Wollenski and Letterman looked at each other and smiled. The meeting had been a setup. Their investigation had narrowed down those who had access to the fire station to the various crews. When that investigation yielded them nothing but dead ends their attention turned to the vehicle maintenance crew. While suspicious action alone did not a guilty person make, it truly narrowed the field of possibilities.

n the weeks that followed, Jerome's applecart was never quite set upright. Nicolle's physical condition improved rapidly, and ten days after she awakened, Dr. Stanton signed the orders for her to be moved to a rehabilitation facility, where she would undergo intense physical therapy.

Jerome visited her on his days off, and she still greeted him as his dad. As Christmas approached, Jerome sank deeper and deeper into depression.

"Hey, Dad, whatcha doin'?" Jordan and Nicolas walked into the kitchen while Jerome sat at the table staring into space with his hand wrapped around a cold cup of coffee.

"Hey, Jordan, Nick. Where's your brother?"

"He's asleep, Dad," Nicolas answered with a hint of sarcasm. "It's almost midnight."

"Yeah, I guess it is." Jerome stood and walked over to the sink to pour the coffee down the drain. "What're you two doing up?"

"We couldn't sleep." Jordan sat down at the table and began toying with a paper towel. "We've been talking, and . . ."

"And?"

Nicolas walked up behind Jordan's chair. "It's almost Christmas and there's no tree, no presents, nothing."

Jerome looked from one to the other. "What are you saying?" He didn't want to let on that he was in no mood for the holidays. He also knew that his feelings of depression had nothing to do with his sons' desire for at least gestures toward a merry yuletide season.

"We're saying that we miss Mom, too. But we also want to have Christmas. We want a tree. We want presents."

"You know, you're right. When you get out of school day after to-morrow we'll go and get a tree. We'll pull the decorations from the garage and have a house decorating party. How'd you like that?"

"What about presents? Mom always asks us for a list right after Thanksgiving." Jordan felt a little more confident in his demands.

"Then you're about three weeks late!" Jerome forced himself to laugh. "You'd better get those lists to me like yesterday."

They each pulled a piece of notebook paper from their pajama pocket and handed it to him. "We've been waiting for you to ask for them," Nicolas said, proud of being prepared.

"Tell me something. How do you feel about your mother not knowing who you are?"

Nicolas looked more like Nicolle every hour. "I miss her being my mom. I don't like her thinking I'm her brother. Will she ever know I'm her son?"

Now it was Jerome's turn to avert his eyes. "I wish I knew. Dr. Mimi says she could wake up one day and we could be back to today."

"But what if she doesn't? Will our mom be gone forever?" Jordan's words cut his father deep.

"It's almost like she died." Nicolas spoke so soft it was barely audible.

Jerome's initial reaction was to chastise Nicolas for even thinking such a thing. But how many times had those same thoughts tiptoed through his mind, yet he didn't have the heart to verbalize them. "As long as she's alive there's a chance she'll come back to be the way she was. So we just have to keep loving her and believing God will fix her mind."

"Daddy?"

"Yes, Nicolas."

"What happened to the man that hurt Mommy?"

Jordan piped in. "And what about Miss Daphne?"

Taking a deep breath, Jerome sat down across from his boys. "He's probably just fine. He had a broken leg and that should be healed by now. Miss Daphne is doing really good, too. She's back to work. She wasn't hurt as bad as your mom. Why do you ask?"

Jordan sat in the chair at the head of the table between his brother and his dad. "Because sometimes I wish he was dead or it was him that couldn't remember, since it was his fault that Mommy and Miss Daphne got hurt. Are you going to sue him?"

Jerome chuckled. "What in the world do you know about suing anybody?"

"Judge Judy, People's Court, Judge Joe Mathis—that's all people do is sue each other. And since Mommy can't go herself, I figured you'd go."

"Well, yes. The man who hit your mother and Miss Daphne will be sued. Whether or not it ends up in court will remain to be seen. But none of that can happen until your mother gets better or . . ." Jerome let the words hang in the air.

"Or what? She dies?" Nicolas asked.

"Your mother won't die from this accident. That part is pretty much recovered. Her brain injury has healed to the point it is no longer a danger. What I was going to say was, or stays the way she is."

"Oh."

"Hey, you guys need to get to bed. It's a school night, and I have to work in the morning." Jerome stood.

The boys did the same and walked out of the kitchen. Before they had left completely, Jordan turned and said, "Thanks, Dad."

"For what?"

"Being honest with us. Not treating us like little kids."

Jerome looked down at the two Christmas lists and then back at his very mature son. "No, son, I need to thank you for giving me a reality check. Good night. I'll be up in just a few minutes."

Jerome looked around the kitchen after he put his cup in the dishwasher. He'd gotten much better at maintaining the house. With the help of the housekeeper, who came in once a week, everything was neat and in place most of the time.

He turned off the lights and headed up to his empty room for one more night. The doctors said Nicolle needed at least another three weeks of therapy. She was walking much better, and she could now control her left hand well enough to throw a ball. Her physical progress was remarkable, to use Dr. Stanton's words. But what was he going to do when he brought home a teenage girl?

72

It was unusually quiet for a New Year's Eve. The day had been uneventful, with only one rescue call. Jerome didn't know if that meant as the night wore on they'd become insanely busy or that they would usher in the new year quietly.

Austin and Andrew had decided to grill ribs and chicken. Everything smelled heavenly. Jerome had soaked corn on the cob, husk and all, in salt water for six hours, and now it steamed on the grill. Nellie had sent homemade banana pudding, and Jerome's mother had made greens. Lloyd made his world-, well at least city-, famous baked beans. Mychel wrapped homemade tamales.

"Man, I'm so glad to hear Nicolle will be coming home in a week or so. I know it's been a long row to hoe for you," Austin said as he stirred his secret barbecue sauce.

"But you've hung in there. You held it all together. I don't know if I could have," Andrew cosigned as he headed to check the meat on the grill.

"You do what you gotta do. I'd never lived alone. I went from my mama taking care of me to Nicolle doing the same thing. The first time I washed clothes, my son wore pink underwear for weeks. I almost set the kitchen on fire. But now it's all pretty good. The boys are helping and I'm teaching them to be self-sustaining. We're all learning together."

Mychel listened but didn't have anything to contribute to this conversation. She thought for sure that by now her man would have caved and come running to her.

Lloyd brought a pan of beans to the table. Austin entered with a large tray of ribs, chicken and corn. Mychel retrieved the potato salad from the refrigerator and the pitcher of homemade lemonade. As the clock struck nine, C Shift of Station 27 gathered around the table. Lloyd blessed the food, and they began to dig in.

"So, if you weren't working tonight, what would you be doing, lover boy?" Austin posed to Andrew.

"I'd be getting ready to take some honey out for an expensive meal—probably Morton's—then to some happenin' party and have her in my bed by one A.M."

"Yeah, right," Mychel mocked. "You think you're all that, don't you?"

"Baby, I don't have to think it. Women tell me daily. I just do what I can. So many honeys and so little money."

"Someday you're going to have to reap these oats you're sowing," Lloyd managed between bites of ribs. "There's a price that's paid for everything. You're out there writing them checks, you betta hope the Bank of Ass has enough to cover them."

"What about you, old man, what would you be doing? Lemme guess—in church."

"Actually, Nellie and I would be in church. Do you have any idea why there is a watch night service?"

"Of course I know," Andrew said cockily. "I'm not a heathen. People go to give thanks for a new year."

"You're right. Now, that's why they go. But do you know how it started?"

"Oh, here we go. Let me guess. A black firefighter?"

Lloyd laughed, sat back and wiped his mouth.

"Uh-oh." Austin scooped more potato salad on his plate. "Once again my man has stepped into it blind."

"See, son, that's your problem. You're too self-righteous. Think you know everything. Back in 1865, on December thirty-first, all the slaves gathered at churches to wait and *watch* for midnight because, you see, at twelve-oh-one on January first, 1866, we became legally free."

Andrew was humbled. "No stuff?"

"No stuff. So that's why we go to church on New Year's Eve. We go because our parents, grandparents and great-grandparents did."

"Cap, I didn't know that." Jerome licked barbecue sauce off his fingers.

"Most don't. I make it my business to find out why we do what we do."

"What about you, Mychel?" Austin asked.

"Probably be at home with a bottle of wine and a good book."

"It's hard to believe a fine woman like you wouldn't be out celebrating with someone very special." Jerome turned to look at her.

Why can't you see I should be celebrating with you? Mychel thought, then said, "He just hasn't awakened to his burning need for me yet." She stared at Jerome until he looked away.

Her comment didn't go unnoticed by the others. Lloyd turned to Austin to break the tension. "What about you?"

"I do the barbecue thing for some of the fellas. We play bid whist and get real toasty. Then sleep it off and wake up to black-eyed peas, chitterlings and football."

"A true bachelor." Jerome laughed.

Without thinking Austin said, "And you know this? What do you do?"

Jerome winced. "Hmph. In years gone by Nicolle and I have had some of the best nights of our lives. We tried going out to parties, but we really preferred to be alone. So about ten years ago we abandoned the notion of trying to please others and decided that New Year's Eve belonged to us. One year we rented a camper. It was a full moon, and we lay outside in sleeping bags watching the stars. We went out at about ten thirty. We talked and drank cognac and talked some more. Just before midnight Nicky pointed at the sky and said, 'Wasn't the moon over there when we first came out here?' I looked and sure enough the moon had changed positions. At that moment we realized we were watching the Earth rotate. New Year's Eve has been special to us for as long as I can remember. This is my first year without her."

"You've had to work on New Year's Eve before, haven't you?" Andrew dug down into an ear of corn.

"Oh, yeah. But even those years she always made it special. I'd find a note in my bag. We'd be on the phone if I wasn't on a call. See, when I say we've never been apart, I mean even when we were kids. Our parents celebrated New Year's Eve together every year, so of course we were together, too."

"Wow, that's deep."

Mychel couldn't stand it any longer. "Anyone want more lemonade?" She felt her heart being squeezed by Jerome's every word.

She had no takers. Without meaning to, Jerome had brought everyone down. They finished the meal in silence and began to clear the dishes. Austin cranked up the Wave After Dark. The smooth jazz station was sure to set the mood straight.

The five of them quickly cleaned up the kitchen and then they went off to do their own thing.

Jerome went to the equipment bay and began polishing the truck. When he finished he sat on the back-end bumper staring into nowhere. He glanced down at his watch, a gift from Nicolle. Thirty minutes till midnight.

"Can I help you with that?" Mychel startled him.

Turning to look up at her he said, "With what? I'm all done now."

"I meant the burden you're carrying." She sat down beside him.

"It's that obvious?"

"A little child could see."

Looking at the floor, Jerome felt a lump forming. "I thought I hid it all so well. Tonight is just getting to me. I miss her so much."

"I understand." Mychel chose her words carefully. "You need to do something to get your mind off her."

"I don't want to stop thinking about her."

"I didn't say stop thinking about her. Just do something to distract yourself."

"Like what? No matter what I do, it reminds me of the hole in my soul without her."

Mychel suddenly got up and disappeared behind the paramedic unit. The next sound Jerome heard was the end of Luther Vandross's "A House Is Not a Home," Nicolle's favorite Luther song. Pain radiated through his body.

Mychel returned to sit next to him. "Now, isn't this a little better?" Mychel smiled at him. "A little music and good company should help."

"This is her favorite song."

Just her luck! "It's almost over. The night has been quiet."

"Yeah, it has. I wish the bell would ring. Then at least I would be thinking about something else for a time."

The song ended, and the Kirk Whalum tune "All I Do," with Wendy Moten's strong vocals, filled the air. The upbeat tempo made Mychel snap her fingers. "Now, this is more like it. Let's dance."

"Naw, but thanks."

"Ah, come on." Mychel stood and pulled him by the hand. "It's almost midnight. You know what they say?"

"What's that?"

Still pulling on him, Mychel ribbed, "Whatever you're doing or feeling at midnight is what you'll experience the rest of the year. So maybe just a little movement will get some happy enzymes moving through you. I hate to see you like this."

Finally Jerome gave in and joined her on the makeshift dance floor. He couldn't remember the last time he'd danced. He couldn't remember the last time he felt anything but pain.

Even at Christmas he'd only gone through the motions. He'd finally shopped for the boys and their grandparents. He spent so much more money than Nicolle ever would have, but the boys were ecstatic. He bought Nicolle a sweetheart diamond necklace and had Jordan give it to her. They were keeping up the facade and it became a little more difficult every time he and the boys went to see her. She made no connection with Christian at all.

Dr. Stanton was optimistic and said she saw improvement in her daily. Jerome, on the other hand, saw none. He had discussed at length with her doctor and his in-laws if he should bring Nicolle back to their house or if she should go be with her parents for a while. He felt she belonged with him.

Jerome had never danced with Mychel before. She had a natural rhythm and moved with grace and style. She unclipped her hair, and it fell midway down her back. Jerome had never seen her as beautiful, until this moment. Mychel's movements and the awesome tempo of the song worked magic on his feet, and he began dancing. It felt good.

The Wave eased right into the Kim Waters tune "You Know That I Love You," and they moved right into the cha-cha.

There could be no more perfect song, Mychel thought as she let the music sink into her body and soul.

Jerome was caught up, and they began laughing. He worked some of his best moves on her, and she was no slouch. "Do you salsa?"

"Every chance I get."

"You're a very good dancer," Jerome said, slightly winded.

"It's in my blood. My mother went into labor on the dance floor. She and my dad won lots of Spanish hustle dance contests. Hey, you're not half bad yourself."

"Well, you know I have that dark gene. That's the one with the rhythm in it."

They laughed even more, throwing off their movements. When the dance tune ended they had both worked up a sweat and sat back on the bumper of the truck still laughing. Lawrence Tanner's sweet baritone voice announced there were only ten minutes left in the year. Why did they have to play Marvin Gaye's "Let's Get It On"? It was a two-generation favorite of the Winters men. He vividly remembered watching his dad dip his mom on the dance floor to sensual sounds of the instant classic.

"You look sad again."

"I'm sorry. This is not the best song for me to hear right now. But thanks for the dances. I never thought I'd have any fun tonight."

"What else are friends for? You've done amazingly well, considering." Mychel was very cautious. She had to hit while he was vulnerable, but too quickly and she'd blow it. "You've managed to balance the job, home, the boys and it seems all is under control."

"It sure doesn't feel like it. I'm a lot better, but nothing even close to how efficient Nicolle is . . . was. You know what I'm trying to say."

"Yeah, I understand. When will she be coming home?" Mychel had overheard him talking to Lloyd that she may be going to her parents instead. Perfect.

Jerome answered quietly. "I don't know."

Yes! Mychel moved closer to him and rubbed his arm. "I'm so sorry."

"Yeah. Me, too. She should be released from rehab in a week or so, but I'm not sure if it's a good idea for her to come to our home since she thinks she's fifteen." He looked down at her hand on his arm. He knew he should move it, but he didn't.

All at once the sound of numbers being shouted in reverse caught their attention. Mychel and Jerome stared at each other as the New Year's Eve anthem "Auld Lang Syne" began playing.

"Happy New Year, Jerome."

"You, too, Mychel."

It suddenly became very awkward. *It's now or never,* Mychel thought.

She leaned over, reaching up to kiss Jerome. He leaned into her, and she closed her eyes. As their lips grew closer, he felt her breath on his nose.

Jerome Neville Winters. He jerked away as he heard a strangely familiar voice.

"I'm sorry. I can't do this." He stood abruptly and disappeared through the doors to the dormitory.

The next sound Mychel heard was the slam of the door, and she knew that was her future.

73

Jerome almost ran into the dormitory area. When he finally made it to his room, he rushed in and slammed the door. What in the hell was wrong with him? How had he let Mychel get so close?

He fell onto his bed facedown and began weeping. *Lord, please forgive me. Please show me what to do,* he prayed.

You are not alone.

Jerome turned over and bolted up in the same movement. He was accustomed to moving quickly, but this time it wasn't a fire bell. He heard the same voice that had called his name as he almost kissed Mychel. He looked around the room, but he saw no one.

Why was this voice so familiar? As he paced the small room the quiet grew louder and louder. He pulled a small CD case from his bag and searched for some music to soothe his frayed nerves. Kenny G's *Duotones* always worked, but as he looked through the case he remembered he'd left it in the CD changer. He didn't want to risk facing Mychel again, so he looked for another. He flipped the plastic sleeves and stopped when he saw Yolanda Adams's *Mountain High . . . Valley Low.* He pulled the CD from the plastic protector with urgency.

He placed it in the player and skipped to number seven. The beautiful voice of the queen of inspirational gospel made him close his eyes.

Alone in a room, it's just me and You.

The song did little to comfort him. He'd almost kissed another woman, while his wife lay in a hospital. He was losing his mind. He was hearing voices. There was something about that voice that not

only scared him but was very familiar, yet it wasn't the voice of anyone he knew. It wasn't his mother or mother-in-law. Who was she?

A soft knock made him jump. He didn't respond.

"Jerome, please, let me in. I'm sorry. I just got caught up in the
moment. Please, Jerome," Mychel pleaded through the closed door.
Silence.

Mychel stood on the outside of the door with her forehead
pressed against it. She knew she'd pushed too hard, too soon.

The fire alarm rang. *I guess it will have to wait.* Within an instant
she was firefighter/paramedic Mychel Hernandez with nothing on
her mind but getting to the scene of a multiple gunshot wound.

He was depressed about the changes in the department and their
impact on his plans, and at midnight he lay in the dark, awake.

The voices were so loud in his head that he hadn't been able to
concentrate on much the past few weeks.

He'd taken a week off as sick leave after his reassignment, to help
clear his head and assess a new plan. He'd show them all they
couldn't stop him. He had a new plan, one that would make them
all sit up and take notice.

Yes, all he needed was opportunity, and sooner, rather than later,
it would present itself.

74

"We've had him under surveillance for all this time and nothing." Inspector Ted Letterman blew on the steaming-hot black coffee as he paced. "Do you think we could have been wrong about him?"

"I can feel it in my gut. I know like I know you need to get laid that's he's our man," Daniel Wollenski ragged.

Ted took offense. "What makes you think I ain't gettin' none?"

"Rosie Palm and her five sisters don't count."

"Man, forget you!" Ted threw a paper clip at him. "Maybe that feeling of yours can be eased with a little Metamucil. This man has done nothing to confirm your suspicions. I admit I was convinced, too, when he left that meeting. Maybe we go back to the drill sergeant and get her to switch him back?"

"Naw, too suspicious." Wollenski slammed his hand down on the desk so loud it made Letterman jump. "Partner, you're brilliant!"

Letterman tried to play off that he'd been startled. "You act like that's headline news. Of course I am. But what brilliance have I displayed this time?"

"We have the maintenance manager call him into the office, give him some line about the person she'd put on his old locations isn't doing a good enough job and she's been getting some complaints. She needs his help to get things straight."

"He'll eat it up because his replacement was a minority, Hispanic guy."

"I think it'll work. According to the psychological profile, he thinks he's so much smarter than we are, and he dares us to catch him. He's also so hell-bent on discrediting any minority that he won't think anything about his replacing the Hispanic mechanic."

"Yeah, it'll be more like an 'I told you so' kind of thing."

"Precisely."

The two smiled with a sense of satisfaction. The cheese had been placed in the trap. Now all they had to do was wait for the mouse to come take a bite.

75

Jerome stood at the window, watching the winter storm drench his city. Rain came down in sheets as he looked out onto the perfectly manicured lawn.

The noise behind him caused him to turn to see his wife, standing without the assistance of a cane. Her left side was still measurably weaker than her right, and she dragged her leg only slightly, but the sight of her standing, dressed in a beautiful pantsuit her mother had purchased for her trip home, sent waves of emotions through his heart. "Nicolle, are you ready to go?"

"Yes, Mr. Montgomery. I'm ready. Are my mom and dad coming?" Even the pitch of Nicolle's voice sounded twenty years younger.

Jerome ached to shake recognition into her. "No, they're at home planning a special welcome-home feast for you. Everyone is very excited."

"Is Jerome at school? Is that why he's not here?"

"He's, um, he's here in spirit."

"I just wish he could have come. I've missed him. I think we missed the junior prom. Tell me the truth, Mr. Monty. He didn't take another girl, did he?" Nicolle's eyes met Jerome's, and she frowned.

"Never, Nicolle. He'll never dance with anyone else, I promise you." Jerome wanted to run to her and scoop her up into his arms. She had thinned since the accident, and she still always looked tired to him. He'd heard healing takes a lot of energy.

"I guess we can call Kathleen to come get me."

Jerome was zipping up her bag when he heard the name Kathleen. He looked up, startled, and asked, "Who's Kathleen?"

"Oh, she's a temporary nurse today. My regular nurse is off. She's really the nicest lady."

As soon as Jerome heard the name, he knew whom the voice belonged to that he'd heard the week before on New Year's Eve. It was the woman who'd been in the SICU that first time he'd gone to visit Nicolle. He hadn't mentioned that night to anyone and had avoided Mychel like she had smallpox. They barely spoke outside of the performance of their duties. He did have to commend her though—when that fire bell rang she was all business. On a fire, he never had to worry if she had his back.

Jerome almost wanted to run into the hall to find this Kathleen woman. There was no way it was the same person. But how and why had he heard her voice again?

His curiosity was satisfied when the short, slightly built woman with the bright smile and penetrating eyes bounced into the room. She looked different, but her voice was the same. She greeted him like an old friend. "Mr. Winters, I know you must be quite happy to have Nicolle coming home today. It's been a long road, but she's made amazing progress. You see, like I told her this morning, it's all in the believing. Ain't that right, missy?"

"Yep. Miss Kathleen told me that God sends angels to guide and protect us, that all we have to do is believe. She said that I had a lot of people believing for me when I couldn't do it for myself."

Jerome stared at the woman. Her eyes met his, and he saw a glow behind her. He looked at Nicolle, who seemed to notice nothing. He opened his mouth, closed it and then opened it again. The glow faded, and Kathleen patted the back of the wheelchair. "I think it's time for you to go home, Miss Nicolle."

Jerome was having trouble forming words, and his thoughts were jumbled. The past months had taken their toll on him both mentally and physically; however, he still thought he had a foothold on reality. But hearing more than seeing Kathleen had shaken him more than he cared to admit.

"Mr. Winters, I'm going to be wheeling Nicolle to the front door. You can go and pull the car around front." Kathleen smiled and pointed toward the door.

Jerome wondered what would happen when Nicolle saw their

SUV. In her head it was 1984 or 1985. He was driving a 2002 vehicle that hadn't even been engineered then. Would she notice that everything was different? Would that help her to come back to him?

"I'm having a party, Miss Kathleen. My mom and dad are giving me a welcome-home party. I'm so excited." Nicolle turned to look at Jerome. "Will any of my friends from school be there?"

"Not this time. This is just for your family and really close friends." Jerome was doing his best not to lie to his wife.

"Well, that's fine. I guess I've been gone so long it would be good to see everyone in the same place at the same time."

"Everyone is really looking forward to it."

"Why didn't Miss Cecelia come with you, Mr. Montgomery?"

"She's helping your mother get ready for the party."

Nicolle seemed satisfied with the answer, at least for the moment. She'd asked on many of his visits in the past why his mother hadn't come with him. He'd made one excuse after another. Nicolle would always look at him with questioning eyes. After Cecelia's first visit, during which Nicolle hadn't recognized her, Jerome's mother thought it best to stay away.

"I'll meet you out front." Jerome picked up Nicolle's two bags and headed for the door. The doctors, the Devereauxs and he had agreed Nicolle would first go home to her parents, with Jerome and the boys visiting often. He knew this was a giant step forward, but he wanted his wife back. He wanted to hold her, kiss her and feel her soft body under his. He shook the images from his mind and headed for the parking lot.

76

"Can you believe I've been here for ten days already? This is really getting good to me." Dawn ran the iron over the black silk blouse she was to wear over the black lace bodysuit Glynda had talked her into buying.

"You can always move here. Gurl, they are importing nurses on contract, we're so desperate." Glynda applied lotion to her body as she sat on the vanity bench. "I love having you around. I just hate I had to go to work for a few days. I'd really planned to spend the whole time with you. But I work so far away, I can't just drop into work."

"Don't you even give that a second thought! My brother-in-law has taken really good care of me, and I've enjoyed this immensely. And can we talk about the outlet malls for just a moment? Gurl, I think I need a new suitcase," Dawn mused. "Speaking of Anthony, where is he?"

"He's in the guest room. He said he'd give us some getting-ready space. He told me to let him know after we had on our makeup, then he'd start getting ready. Ain't that nothing. He's actin' like it's going to take us a long time to get ready or something."

The sisters laughed because they both knew it to be the truth. They had shopped for days looking for the perfect outfits to wear to the big dance. It was like they were back in high school. Anthony had left the room many times saying he was in giggle overload.

"What time are we leaving again?" Dawn held up the black top.

"It's going to take an hour and some change to get there, so no later than seven. I want you to get there in time so you can scope out the door. Can we say eye candy?"

"I know that is correct! But tell me again, why are we doing this? I live three thousand miles from here. Why do I want to meet a man in California?"

"You just want to have some fun, meet some decent men. Build your confidence a little. Maybe if you meet someone tonight, you can squeeze another date in before you leave, make a few phone calls when you get home and bam! You're back out here to visit. There's a method to my madness."

"You've really thought this thing through, haven't you?"

Turning away from the vanity mirror, Glynda looked seriously at her sister. "Dawn, I miss you. I get so lonely for my family at times. I know Renee will never pick her family up and move. I don't *want* Collette to move, and now that Daddy's gone, you have nothing holding you in Baltimore."

"I do love it here. That's a huge decision, though, Glynda." Dawn had stopped putting on her bra and was staring at her sister she loved and liked so much.

"I'm not asking you to decide right this minute, but if you meet someone here that you hit it off with, that will give you just a little more incentive. Plus, you know Anthony works at the base."

"Gurl, you need to stop it!" Dawn laughed as she continued dressing.

After much preparation and making Anthony wait for twenty minutes—even though he'd started getting ready an hour after the Naylor sisters—they had finally left Antelope Valley headed to the Hyatt Regency in downtown Los Angeles for the Stentorians' red-and-black Valentine's Day ball.

77

As the valet opened Dawn and Glynda's door, at the same time their eyes gazed upon a sea of beautiful, well-dressed African-Americans that filled the air with an array of exotic aromas.

The sisters stood waiting while the valet prepared the ticket to give to Anthony. From behind, Glynda heard a friendly and familiar voice.

"Ms. Sanders, it's great to see you again." Glynda turned to see Andrew's smiling face.

"Andrew. How nice to see you as well."

"You look simply marvelous this evening." He turned to Dawn. "And who is this lovely lady?"

"Andrew St. Vincent, meet my sister Dawn Naylor."

He took her hand and held it for a long moment, staring into her eyes. He finally smiled and stammered, "Hi, um, I'm, um, Andrew."

"I know." Dawn laughed. "Glynda just said that."

Embarrassed, Andrew looked at the ground. "Oh, yeah, she did." Andrew regrouped. "I see that extreme beauty runs in the Naylor family."

This time Dawn was embarrassed. "Glynda's the beautiful one."

"Then obviously you're not seeing what I'm seeing. Are you ladies here alone?"

"No, they're not." Anthony walked around the car extending his hand. "I'm Anthony Sanders."

"Ahhh, Glynda's husband." Andrew shook his hand. "Very nice to meet you. That's quite a lady you've got there. She's set me straight a time or two."

"She is something else. Good to meet you, man." Anthony arched both his arms and said, "Ready, ladies?"

Dawn and Glynda looped their arms through his and began to walk away. "It was very nice to meet you, Andrew."

Andrew was struggling to come up with something clever and playerlike when he remembered Glynda's advice. Be genuine. "Excuse me."

The three turned, and Glynda spoke. "Yes, Andrew?"

"I don't mean to pry or be rude, but I know Ms. Sanders is with my man here. Dawn, are you here with anyone?"

Dawn looked at Glynda as if to ask for permission to speak. When her sister said nothing, she finally answered, "My sister and her husband."

Andrew's smile lit up the night sky. "Then please save a brotha a dance."

"I'll be sure to do that, Andrew." Dawn blushed and turned to walk into the lobby of the very posh hotel.

Andrew watched her very ample hips cause the sheer panels of her black ensemble to take on a personality all their own. Her perfume hung in the air around him. He was sure he hadn't had a drink yet he felt intoxicated. He looked down at the ground and laughed to himself, thinking of his favorite movie, *Bringing Down the House*. The scene where Queen Latifah entered the restaurant and Eugene Levy saw her descend the stairs replayed in his head. All he could say was, "Shazzam!"

As the Naylor sisters stepped into the grand ballroom, Dawn gasped. There were at least five hundred African-American people in this room, dressed to the nines, and the room was not even a quarter full. The decor was tasteful and elegant. Black and red, her favorite color combination, decorations with hearts everywhere put her in a romantic mood.

"We have VIP seating. Captain Frederickson has a table, and we're his guests. He said his table is number eleven." Glynda looked around the room.

"Well, this is table two fourteen. I'd assume it's closer to the stage." Anthony gently moved Glynda in front of him.

The couple started to move forward without realizing that Dawn stood looking around the room with the same awe as Dorothy when she arrived in Oz.

"Close your mouth and come on," Glynda teased her.

Dawn laughed and caught up. They maneuvered through the tables, looking for number eleven. "You know, I thought I'd attended some pretty classy events with the Black Nurses Association, but that was like the county fair compared to this. Who put this on again?"

"The Los Angeles City and County Stentorians. Can you believe all of these beautiful black people?" Glynda said as her eye caught table eleven. "Over there." She waved to Captain Frederickson. "They're already here."

"Because Mrs. Frederickson didn't change her hair, dress and shoes three times," Anthony chided.

"How do you know? They live closer," Glynda retorted, laughing.

As the group arrived at table eleven, Lloyd rose to greet them.

"Glynda!" Lloyd grabbed her hand and kissed her on the cheek simultaneously. "And you must be Mr. Sanders?" Lloyd shook his hand.

"Anthony, please, sir."

Lloyd extended his hand to Dawn. "And who might this beautiful young lady be?"

Dawn was struck speechless at how much Lloyd reminded her of Edward Naylor. Glynda had warned her, but she was not sufficiently prepared. She took his hand and suddenly found herself fighting back tears. "I'm Dawn Naylor."

"I've heard so much about you. I feel like I know you already. This is my wife, Nellie."

Glynda greeted her first. "It's a pleasure to finally meet you, Mrs. Frederickson."

Nellie remained seated. "Same here, dear. Lloyd has said so many nice things about you."

"Please, everyone, have a seat. My entire shift will be here except for Jerome Winters."

"Oh, how's his wife doing?" Glynda sat next to Nellie with Anthony on her left, and Dawn sat next to him. "How long has it been since the accident?"

"Nearly four months. She's at home with her parents. She's around eighty percent physically back to normal, but she's lost about twenty years of her memories," Lloyd told them.

"It's so sad, but I know they'll pull through. Nicolle is a fighter," Nellie said, taking a sip of white wine. "Dawn, Lloyd tells me you're from Baltimore. I love the Inner Harbor, and there is no crab cake in the country like in that town."

"Yes, and I agree. I haven't traveled a whole lot, but I have to tell you, I don't eat crab anywhere but at home."

"I can't believe I could be this lucky." Dawn turned quickly to see Andrew standing behind her.

"Why, Andrew, what a pleasant surprise." Dawn looked up into his blue eyes. *Lawdhamurcy, this boy is foine!*

Andrew moved around to face her. "I assure you, the pleasure is all mine. May I sit here?" *Hmph, hmph, hmph, this sistah got it going on. Don't blow this, St. Vincent!*

Okay, please don't let me be imagining that this young, finer-than-expensive-wine brother is flirting with me. "I think this table is reserved for Captain's Frederickson's guests."

Lloyd was amused by the exchange between the two youngsters. He was afraid if sparks flew any harder one of them was going to hit him and singe the little hair he had left. "Miss Dawn, Andrew here *is* one of my guests. He's on my shift."

Thank you, Jesus, Mary and Joseph! "Oh, wonderful. Then by all means, please be seated."

Conversation around the table was lively and punctuated with laughter. The room filled quickly as the dinner hour approached. Each of the gentlemen purchased bottles of wine, and their glasses were never empty. Shortly before their table was served Mychel and Austin joined them.

They didn't come as a couple but had arrived in the hotel lobby at the same time. After the introductions Austin filled his and Mychel's wine glasses.

Dinner conversation was plentiful, and before the coffee was served they all felt like old friends. Andrew was very attentive to Dawn, and with the first chord of dance music they were on the floor. As the rest of them watched, Dawn Naylor and Andrew St.

Vincent made magic on the dance floor. They looked like they'd been dancing together for years. Andrew spun and dipped; Glynda was stunned at her sister's grace.

"Your sister's quite beautiful, Glynda," Nellie said as she sipped her, everyone had lost count, glass of wine.

"Nellie, I've been telling her that for as long as I can remember." Glynda was pretty tipsy, too. "All she does is work, work, work. This trip out here has been so good for her, and tonight doesn't owe her a thing. Thanks so much for inviting us, Lloyd. Was someone else supposed to join us?" Glynda asked, pointing at the two empty seats.

"I was hoping that Jerome and Nicolle could have been here. I didn't give away their tickets. It's been a tradition with us for the past ten years. So this is for the ones who ain't here." Lloyd held up an almost empty glass of Long Island ice tea.

Anthony laughed and raised his glass of club soda. "Captain, who's driving you home tonight?"

"Just gotta push an elevator button, son. But don't think I didn't notice you doing the right thing."

"Y'all need to be out on that floor. This deejay is slammin'. Andrew's such a good dancer." Dawn fell into her chair, out of breath, and reached for the water glass.

"It takes two." Andrew was staring into Dawn's eyes. *I wish I could ask Glynda if I'm doing this right,* he thought. *Dawn's so much fun. I just need to play it cool.* "Dawn's right though. Y'all need to get out there on the floor. The music is bangin'."

"Glynda, will you come with me to the ladies' room?" Dawn asked as she patted sweat from her brow and cleavage.

"Excuse us."

Anthony and Lloyd stood. Andrew watched them and followed suit. The sisters disappeared through the crowd.

As they stepped into the bathroom, Dawn turned around and hit Glynda. "Guuuuuurl, why didn't you tell me about Andrew?"

Grabbing her shoulder, Glynda said, "Ouch! What's there to tell? He's a smart-ass rookie who thinks he's God's gift to women."

"Andrew St. Vincent?"

"Gurl, you have always had the worst judgment when it came to men. All these decent brothers in here and you hone in on playa-playa." Alcohol always worked like sodium pentothal.

Dawn looked hurt. She wanted so much for Andrew to be someone she could try for something special with. There was so much chemistry between them.

"Plus he's, like, twelve."

Dawn lashed out. "Who cares how old he is? I like him."

"Then have a great evening with him. Dance until you have blisters. Hell, even get your groove back if you want. But don't give him your heart, Dawn, promise me."

Dawn put her hands on her hips. "You act like I don't know how to control my feelings."

Glynda mocked her pose and just stared at her until they both started laughing.

"Okay, okay. So maybe I do have a few issues in that area," Dawn admitted.

"A few? But you know I love you and only want you to be happy. If this boy toy is going to make you happy, then go for it. Just keep your heart out of it. Now let's go pee. I hear the cha-cha slide!"

78

Jerome sat on the patio and enjoyed the crisp February night. Maxella and Dave had them over for dinner every weekend since Nicolle came home from rehab. The boys were watching television, and Nicolle was helping Maxella in the kitchen with the cleanup.

Nicolle had been at her parents' for more than a month. Her left hand and leg were almost back to normal capacity. She kept saying she was ready to go back to school. Her daily therapy was being reduced to three times a week. She just thought Jerome was her dad's best friend from down the block, Montgomery Winters.

He'd finally gotten a good routine down. Jerome was proud of how well he took care of the boys and their home. He managed to accomplish it all with only triple the time and effort it would have taken Nicolle. He laughed to himself. With much prayer and soul-searching, he'd came to be at peace with all that had happened.

There was nothing anyone could tell him that would make him doubt that Kathleen was his guardian angel. He believed she could appear in another form at any moment. But he also knew she was always there watching over him.

Dave joined him on the patio and lit up a cigar. "You okay, son?"

"You know, Dad, for the first time since any of this happened, I believe I *am* okay. I'm at peace, and I believe with all that is within me Nicolle is going to be just fine. She'll be back as my wife and the boys' mother. There was a great lesson in all of this for me. I had the perfect life and took it all for granted. Never again."

"I know Maxella and I probably haven't told you, but we're real proud and happy how you've hung in there. You're a good man. My daughter was very lucky to fall in love with you."

"Dad, I'm the lucky one. I've been so naïve. I assumed everyone had what we had, and I was so foolish to think it would last forever. I believe I've always been a good husband, and Lord knows that has been my goal. But when Nicolle comes out of this, and she will, I'm going to be so much better."

There was a colossal noise coming from the den right inside the patio doors. Dave and Jerome rushed into the house to find Jordan and Nicolas scrapping in the middle of the floor. Christian stood by crying. Nicolle and Maxella rushed in from the kitchen just as the antique Tiffany lamp crashed to the floor.

Jerome took three steps toward them when he heard Nicolle scream, "Jordan and Nicolas, I'm going to whip your behinds but good for this. Look what you did to Grandma and Grandpa's lamp!"

Jerome stopped cold in his tracks. Jordan and Nicolas stopped fighting. Christian stopped crying. Maxella started screaming, "Oh, thank you, Jesus, thank you, Jesus." She fell to her knees and began weeping.

Jerome ran to Nicolle and picked her up and spun her around, kissing her all over her face.

Nicolle struggled. "Put me down, Jerome. What's wrong with all of you?"

What was unfolding before their eyes became apparent to the boys. Jordan and Nicolas ran to embrace their mother. Christian, not really sure, did what his brothers did. "Mommy! Mommy! Mommy!" It wasn't easy to tell which of the boys was talking. They were all over their mother.

"Will someone please tell me what is going on?" Nicolle's voice had returned to that of the normal mature mother of three.

He knew that his boss had no idea what she was doing.

Now, maybe, they could see what he could see. He would show them.

He'd been back at 27 for six weeks, and as much as he'd wanted to get back to his mission right away, he'd waited. He didn't want anything to look suspicious.

But now it was time.

He rose early that morning. He showered, shaved and dressed

with care. He trimmed his hair. He needed to look good for the television cameras.

Now *he* was going to be hero.

He'd tried to tell, but no one would hear.

Today, they'd all have to listen.

79

"Good morning, all." Jerome bounced into the station with his feet barely touching the floor, thirty minutes late. "I'm sorry I'm a tad tardy. But I think you'll forgive me, Cap." Jerome was actually giddy.

"What is up with you? Did you hit the lottery?" Austin asked as he poured coffee. "Dang, it's going to be hard to live with you and St. Vincent today."

"Well, I don't know about Andrew, but I've got awesome news."

"Do tell." Mychel looked up from the newspaper. *He's leaving Nicolle. No, wait, only I'd think that was awesome news.*

"Nicolle's memory returned on Saturday night."

Lloyd jumped up from the table, spilling coffee, and ran to Jerome to embrace him. "Why didn't you call us?"

"I would've left you a message at home, but I knew this was your special Valentine's weekend. It could wait until I got here today, because she's back forever. She moved back home yesterday and we had our own celebration."

Andrew walked to him, hugged him and slapped his hand. "Man, that is nothing less than tremendous. I'm so happy for you." He hugged him again.

"She still has therapy. She has really bad headaches, and she doesn't remember everything. But she remembers us, and I just can't ask God for any more than that."

Mychel rose from her seat and walked away from the group. She turned to Jerome and said, "I'm really happy for you, Winters." She disappeared down the stairs.

Andrew grabbed a Red Bull from the refrigerator while the other men refilled their coffee cups. Jerome was too hyped to sit.

"So, St. Vincent, what's up with you?" Jerome took a long swig from the black mug.

"Don't listen to these clowns." Andrew seemed embarrassed.

"Well, the way I see it, Andrew here has met the future Mrs. St. Vincent," Austin quipped.

Jerome turned and looked surprised. "Word?"

"Naw, man. I met this really nice woman at the dance. She's mature and beautiful, refined and got her own thing going on. She laughs and has a quick wit."

"Uh-oh. That laughter and wit will get you every time," Lloyd teased.

"So what makes her so special?" Jerome asked.

"She's just different than anyone I ever dated. When we left the dance, I took her to Manhattan Beach, and we parked and watched the waves crashing onto the beach. It started to rain. We just watched it and talked. I got her some coffee from the Kettle, and we talked some more. Then I drove her back to her sister's place in Quartz Hill, which by the way is da bomb!"

Lloyd hung on to Andrew's every word. "I'd imagine Glynda's house to be just beautiful."

"Whoa, whoa. This is Glynda, the lawyer's, sister? Man, that's like family. You can't be playin' around in the family." Jerome began pacing. "We all know your objective."

"Hit it and you're out," Austin added.

"This is different, I swear. I didn't even try anything on Saturday night or yesterday."

"You already had a second date?" Jerome asked.

"Yeah, she leaves on the red eye on Tuesday headed back to Baltimore."

"Just don't make me beat you down, my brotha. Cuz I will," Lloyd said, only half joking.

The shriek of the fire alarm brought the camaraderie to an abrupt end. "Stations 27 and 36, fire at 8111 Kirby. Hotel structure. Victims may be trapped. Explosion followed by smoke and flames reported."

All four of the men were on the first floor before the dispatcher finished talking. Mychel was outside the paramedic wagon stepping into her turnout gear when they arrived. The others quickly followed her lead and were in the trucks and rolling out of the station within one minute.

He sat across the street and pulled into the flow of traffic behind the paramedic wagon. Yes, today they would all see.

Station 36 pulled on the scene within thirty seconds of 27. The four engine companies, two trucks and one emergency squad all went to work under the direction of Battalion Chief Isaac Graham. Captain Lloyd Frederickson and his crew were charged with search and rescue.

"Winters, St. Vincent, grab the hose and take the second floor. Hernandez and I will take the first floor. Fitzgerald, you man the truck. Let's move!" Lloyd barked.

Jerome and Andrew headed to the second floor where blinding, thick, black, toxic smoke filled the stairwell of the small pay-by-the-hour hotel. There was no way to know if everyone had escaped. When they arrived on the second floor it was amazingly clear, yet extremely hot. There was hardly any smoke and no flames to be seen. The hallway was lined with unusually large picture windows. It was assumed the force of the explosion had blown out the glass.

Something about the situation wasn't feeling right to Jerome. Adrenaline had replaced the blood in his veins as his sixth sense kicked in. Three feet behind, Andrew carried the hose, keeping cadence. "St. Vincent, use the line to blow the smoke and heat gases out the window."

Water splashed their face shields as Andrew sprayed the ceiling and forced the gases out the window.

Suddenly St. Vincent dropped the hose and water sprayed on the floor. Jerome turned to see why St. Vincent was no longer spraying the ceiling. In slow motion he saw the helmet light falling to the floor. Moving swiftly to where Andrew had fallen, Jerome quickly pressed the button that activated his microphone to summon help.

"Man down! Man down! Man down! I need some help up here!" Jerome yelled into the device mounted on the collar of his jacket. "Second floor rear. Man down!" Jerome crouched low to the floor. "St. Vincent! Man, what's wrong?"

In his head he was cautioning against the panic that lost lives. He removed his gloves and felt for Andrew's pulse—faint, but beating. Precious seconds ticked away. He could see the flashlights as the rescue team from the first floor climbed the stairs. He pressed the mic: "We're straight ahead. He's unconscious. Hurry!"

Jerome's ears rang as his pulse raced. What the hell happened to Andrew? He slowly turned him to his right side. His oxygen tank was empty, but no alarm had sounded! *Oh my God, he has no air!* "We need air! His tank is empty!" Jerome screamed into his mic.

As the rescue team reached them Jerome could feel the heat increasing even through his gear. In his ear Jerome heard an unfamiliar voice announce the air tank was on the way.

"Let's move him toward the stairs," Mychel said as she put her arms under his armpits and began dragging Andrew like he weighed fifty pounds. Lloyd moved around to Andrew's feet, and just as he was about to bend down he saw it. The red ball of flames was rapidly moving in their direction. Lloyd's and Jerome's eyes met. A split-second decision had to be made. There was no time to make it down the steps carrying Andrew. There was only one way out. They had to jump out of the window. Microseconds passed as Lloyd calculated the risk of jumping out of the window with Andrew versus tossing him from the second-story window.

Somewhere between milliseconds, Mychel joined the thought process. With a few steps to the window, Lloyd and Mychel tossed Andrew out of the window feetfirst and immediately jumped out behind him. Jerome had only cleared the window by a foot when a large fireball exploded into the night sky.

Jerome felt like he was falling in slow motion, and his entire thirty-eight years flashed before him. In reality it was less than a second before he landed. Showers from the hose rained down on the pile of bodies as Jerome stared up at the flames shooting out of the window from which they had narrowly escaped death.

As Jerome lay on his back, he wondered if he was having an out-of-body experience because he felt no pain. He heard orders being barked from below him as his conscious mind began to function. He turned to his right, and at that instant realized he was lying on top of other people. He rolled, becoming aware he was not on the ground but on the canopy that led into the entrance of the hotel. He felt someone under him began to squirm just as he saw the ladder.

"You all right? This thing is going to give any second—there's an air mattress below if it does. Do you think you can climb down the ladder?" His face was familiar but Jerome couldn't recall the fire-fighter's name.

"Yeah, man. I think I'm okay. Does this mean I'm not dead?" Jerome asked in all seriousness.

"You are very much alive, my man!"

"Thank you, Jesus!" Jerome yelled.

"Indeed!"

"Get off me." Jerome recognized the voice as belonging to My-chel.

As Jerome rolled off, he felt himself falling again. This time, the firefighter on the ladder tried to catch him but missed. He fell ten feet and landed on the air mattress. Two rescue workers rushed onto the mattress and moved him to the ground clear of the canopy.

Austin approached him immediately and began checking him. "Anything hurt? Do you feel any pain?" He moved a penlight back and forth in front of Jerome's eyes.

Jerome moved Austin's hand out of the way. "Get that thing out of my face. I'm fine." Everything was coming into focus, and Jerome remembered Andrew was out of oxygen. "You gotta check St. Vincent! He was out of air."

Above them was a ripping sound and screams from the onlook-ers. As Austin tried to move Jerome clear he turned onto his side just in time to see the bodies of his friends fall onto the air mattress.

The rescue team on the ground rushed to check Lloyd, Andrew and Mychel. Jerome struggled to get up as Austin applied pressure to his shoulders to restrain him. "They got him. My job is to make sure you're okay." Austin made eye contact with Jerome and said with authority, "Don't make me strap you to a backboard, man."

Jerome began to relax as he realized his friend and colleague was only doing what he was trained to do. Austin felt Jerome's arms, legs and rib cage all while asking if he felt any pain.

With exaggerated impatience Jerome said, "Look, man, I'm fine. Now let me up so I can help with the others."

Austin shook his head and reluctantly helped Jerome up. When Jerome stood he was a little woozy but didn't let on to Austin. They both quickly moved to the other side of the canopy where Lloyd, Mychel and Andrew were lying on the ground.

Water showered down on the teams of two as they worked on each of the fallen firefighters. Jerome didn't know where to go first. He chose Andrew. "What can I do to help?" he asked Sean.

"It's all under control, man. Are you sure you shouldn't be checked out yourself?" Sean, the paramedic from Truck Company 12, looked up momentarily.

Avoiding Sean's question Jerome asked, "How is he? He didn't have any air in there."

"He's doing good. He wasn't deprived long. He's responsive, but I think you need to go back over there and let Fitzgerald take care of you."

Jerome never answered Sean. He just moved to where Lloyd was. Jerome laughed as he listened to his friend and wondered if he'd sounded as ridiculous.

"Look, I'm fine. Just let me up from here so that I can help the others," Lloyd protested.

"Captain, I think you have a fractured rib. You have tenderness in that area. I'm sorry, but you cannot move. Please don't make me call the battalion chief over here," Alexandria Richardson, a veteran firefighter/paramedic, warned.

"Now, you know better than that." Jerome leaned over him. "Stop being such a pain in the butt, Cap."

"What are you doing up?" Lloyd winced slightly as he spoke.

"I checked out okay. After all, you broke my fall," Jerome teased.

"How're Hernandez and St. Vincent?"

"He's doing okay. They're giving him O_2 and he's responsive. Doesn't appear to be any broken bones."

"And Hernandez?"

"She's my next stop. You relax. Let us take care of you for a change." Jerome started to leave.

"Winters?"

"Yeah, Cap?"

"We got really lucky in there."

Luck had nothing to do with it. It had to be Kathleen. "Someone's guardian angel was doing her job." Jerome smiled and went to check on Mychel.

Mychel's face was contorted, and Jerome knew that meant the little giant was hurt. "How ya doing?"

"What do you care?" Mychel asked with hostility.

"Don't do this, Mychel. You know I care about you as my friend and, most of all, as the one who had my back in there. Your quick thinking saved us all. By making the decision to toss Andrew out of the window, we were able to follow your lead, and now we're all safe. You're one of the best firefighters in this department, and you're one hell of a woman."

For the first time in all the time Jerome had known Mychel, he saw tears in her eyes. Somehow he didn't think it was from the pain caused by her fall. He turned to the emergency medical technician that was working on her. "How's she doing?"

"Possible ulna or radius fracture. Other than that she's one very lucky young lady, having the two of you fall on her. We're still checking her out. But all seems well, considering."

Jerome turned back to Mychel. "You think you bad, don'tcha, kid?"

She only smiled.

He stood among the crowd, watching as the four bodies fell from the second-story window. He wasn't sure if the force of the flames had pushed them or if they had jumped. With any luck, they'd all be dead. He'd carefully orchestrated the fire in a room he'd rented.

He'd been renting rooms periodically, for a few hours to overnight, for the past two months, preparing for this night. With a history of staying at this fleabag, it wouldn't cast any suspicion on him when the fire started.

While that group of slackers drank coffee and lollygagged around the station, he'd exchanged that half-breed's air-supply tank for an empty one and disabled the alarm. His plan had been flawless.

He smiled with a real sense of satisfaction. The only step left was to make an anonymous call to let them know it was the incompetence of St. Vincent that had caused this tragedy. A tap on his right shoulder interrupted his revelry.

"Dear, it's really nice to finally get to meet you." Antoinette passed the yams to Dawn as the St. Vincent family partook of some of her best fixings. "You've made a great difference in my son's life."

"Mom, you're embarrassing me." Andrew blushed. "Could we please change the subject?"

Jules toyed with the pork roast. "I guess everything is back to normal over at 27 since they caught that lunatic."

"Lunatic indeed. It's so hard to believe someone could be so distorted by hate that they would come up with such an elaborate scheme to seek revenge." Andrew stared at his father.

"Son, I need to apologize." Jules put down his fork. "You tried to tell me, but I refused to believe that prejudice still existed in this day and age. In the back of my mind I've known things were not as good as they should have been, but I was hoping they were better than they actually are. I hope you can find it in your heart to forgive me."

Andrew sat quiet for a moment, caught by surprise with his father's rare display of emotion. He stared from his mother to Dawn before speaking. "Dad, I'm just glad things turned out as well as they did. There's nothing to forgive. Mother told me you went to meet with the chief after I talked to you. So I know you did what you thought was best. I think we've all learned from this experience."

"I should have been more of an advocate for the rights of minorities. I could have had a powerful voice, but I chose to remain quiet and just let things happen around me, hoping it would never be deposited on my doorstep. But I was wrong, almost dead wrong."

Dawn touched Andrew's arm as she witnessed the exchange between the man she loved and his father. "Mr. St. Vincent, may I add something?"

"Please, dear, speak up," Antoinette said.

"When my father died, I learned a very valuable lesson. I believed him to be perfect and flawless. We tend to do that to our parents. But on the day when my half sister showed up and I realized I'd been cheated out of a lifetime of love, I understood at that moment that the past can never be changed. All we can do is make the future as bright as *we* want it to be. Don't waste another moment worrying about what you could or should have done. Concentrate on what you're going to do from now on."

Jules nodded his head as he washed down Dawn's words with a glass of vintage cabernet. "How did you get so wise in such a few years?"

"I had the best teacher of all. I just wish my sisters could figure it all out. We're missing the best of everything while harvesting the worst of a few things. My sisters Renee and Collette are too proud to ask me not to move to California or to even admit they will miss me. We've let my father's grandest hope and fondest dream die with him, that we be a close and loving family."

Andrew smiled proudly at Dawn, and his heart warmed as he thought of how much she'd come to mean to him.

As the St. Vincents prepared for bed, Antoinette sat at her vanity table holding her hairbrush. "Andrew seems serious about Dawn."

"Well, it's the first one he's brought home to meet us. So I'd say that's a little serious. She's a fine young woman. Pretty smart, too."

"Indeed." Antoinette fell silent as Dawn's words rebounded in her head. *Don't waste another moment worrying about what you could or should have done. Concentrate on what you're going to do from now on.* She was making a call to her sister, Margaret, at Rutgers University in the morning.

EPILOGUE

The assistant district attorney slammed his briefcase closed just as Lloyd and Glynda approached him. He smiled with the satisfaction of knowing Timothy Martin wouldn't be causing any trouble for minority firefighters in Los Angeles—or any other department or city—for the next fifteen to twenty-five years.

Martin's defense attorney had failed to get the judge to agree his client was suffering from mental defect as a result of verbal and physical abuse at the hand of his Nazi-sympathizing father. If his testimony was to be believed, he'd tried and failed to be hired as a firefighter fourteen times before he finally gave up. He actually believed he'd passed the test but was passed over so that the department could hire people of color and women. His attorney presented evidence that he in fact had one of the lowest average scores of anyone taking the test during the hiring rotation in which he'd applied. Though it was apparent this man suffered from a very warped sense of right and wrong, the judge felt he was competent to stand trial and was well aware of the havoc he'd wrought on the C Shift of Station 27.

Lloyd extended his hand. "Thank you, Mr. Johnston. You did a fine job. Justice was served here today."

"I agree. If you ever get tired of prosecuting, I think my firm would be very interested in talking to you," Glynda said, offering her congratulations as well.

"Thank you both. But no thanks are necessary. People like this fool make all of us"—Johnston rubbed his finger on the back of his hand, indicating Europeans—"look bad. I took this case very personally. I know this one success doesn't even come close to solving our race relations issues, but at least you can sleep better at night,

Captain Frederickson. I'd also like to thank you for not lying down when no one would listen. It's because of your insistence that he's been put away for a very long time."

"We won't take up any more of your time. Remember to call us if you want to get into private practice." Glynda smiled as she turned to walk away.

Lloyd shook his hand and followed Glynda. When they were in the hallway he paused a moment. "How about some dinner?"

"Thanks, but Dawn's arriving at five thirty."

"She's really going to make that move?"

"Yes, and I couldn't be happier. She and Andrew seem really happy, but she still plans to take it slow. She says any man can seem perfect from three thousand miles away. She said just because she can't see doesn't mean she's blind."

"Smart girl, but then I'd expect no less from your sister. I've seen a real change in St. Vincent since he met Dawn and had that near-death experience. Don't know which one caused it, but that boy has a little potential now." Lloyd chuckled.

"Well, the only thing I know is he has caused my sister to smile a lot and think she's all that and a bag of flaming hot chips. She's moving out here with me despite Renee and Collette trying to rain on her parade. So I ain't mad!"

"I bet you are happy. Nellie and I leave a week from Saturday for Rome. We're going to spend two weeks with Victoria and then leave there and go see Portia in Seattle for a week. She's so busy that's all we could get her to commit to. But we may just go on over to Vancouver for a few days. It's going to be our second honeymoon." Lloyd beamed.

"So you're taking a month off work? I'm so proud of you!" Glynda hugged him.

"Yep, yep. I'm really trying to make some changes. This trial was my last official act. I'm passing the baton. Let some of the youngsters take up the gauntlet. And you'll never guess who's gotten really active in the cause?"

"Andrew St. Vincent?" Glynda laughed.

"I was about to ask how you knew. But, I guess a little pillow talk, huh?"

"Indeed."

"The boy has turned out to be downright radical. He's going to be really good at recruiting other youngsters."

"I hate to run, but I have to meet Anthony at the OB at three thirty."

"You look radiant, by the way. Pregnancy really agrees with you."

Glynda touched the basketball shape on her stomach and smiled. "We're really happy. Anthony Edward Sanders is due for his debut December first. Dawn plans to move before I deliver so she can take care of us."

"That sounds like a plan to me. You take care and I'll see you at the shower on September twelfth." Lloyd kissed her on the cheek and they parted, each feeling blessed for knowing the other.

As Lloyd walked out into the hot August sun, he looked to his left. He could see the top of the building that housed the fire department headquarters. The past few months the department had met with sweeping changes after Chief Marlborough stepped down following allegations of his involvement in a secret society operating within departments around the country. The mayor had appointed a temporary chief, who seemed fair and a very progressive thinker.

For the first time in a very long time, he felt good about those who were in charge, and he liked going to work. Mychel had made him proud when she passed the captain's test and was waiting for her own assignment. She had scored number one in all of Los Angeles City and County. She had visions of chiefdom dancing in her head.

Indeed, his life was getting better every minute of every day. He dialed Jerome's number to tell him the good news about the outcome of the trial.

Nicolle answered on the first ring. "Hello?"

"Hey, Nicky. How're you feeling?"

"Hey, Lloyd. I'm doing just wonderful. I saw the doctor last week, my headaches are almost completely gone, and there are so few things I can't remember that I don't even get frustrated anymore. So I'd say I'm just about perfect."

"Now you know your uncle Lloyd just loves hearing that. Is your husband around?"

"No, but you can catch him on his cell. He's picking the boys up from school and taking them to the movies."

"I'll do that. What do you want us to bring you back from Italy?"

"You know I always want the same thing, a Hard Rock Cafe shirt, and maybe some real Italian wine."

"You got it, sweetie. Bye-bye."

Nicolle smiled as she hit the Off button. She felt the love of her family and friends more and more each day. Though she was well on her way to a full recovery, she still tired easily. She decided she'd lie on the couch for a few minutes before preparing dinner.

She stirred slightly before opening her eyes. When she awoke, Jerome was leaning over to kiss her forehead. She smiled up at her husband and asked, "What time is it?"

"Eight thirty." Jerome kissed her again gently. "Are you feeling okay? You never even heard all the noise the boys were making when we got home."

"I've been working really hard on that new account. I stayed up pretty late last night. I still hate sleeping alone when you're at work, you know." Nicolle pulled herself up on the couch. "I love having my own business, but it sure is more work than I ever thought it would be. I'd never work this hard for someone else."

"You don't have to work at all. We have more money now than we ever dreamed we'd have. Why don't you just sit back and enjoy it? God knows you earned every cent of that settlement."

"I could ask you the same question. Why don't you just quit? You can stay at home, start a business, take a year or two off. Whatever you want."

"I don't go to work because it's a job, baby. I go because it's a calling. This is what God put me on earth to do. You know what, Nic?"

"What, honey? You look so serious."

"I thank God every single day for you coming back to me. I thought I was blessed before all of this happened, but I just didn't know how much."

She leaned forward and kissed him, then wrapped her arms around him, pulling him close to her. She'd shed so many tears in the past six months, both in and out of therapy, that her tear ducts should be dehydrated, but somehow more came. "I should be the grateful one. You took care of me and the boys and the house. As difficult as all of that was, you never stopped believing I would come out of it. You kept the home fires burning even when it looked like the flame had gone out."

"You know what we learned the first day in the fire academy?"

"What's that, baby?"

"When a fire is almost snuffed out, all you have to do is stoke it and just keep fannin' the flames."

In May 1999, shortly after I'd begun the thirty-eight-week road trip to promote the self-published edition of *The Shirt off His Back,* a firefighter friend encouraged me to attend a conference being held in Little Rock, Arkansas. I gladly accepted the invitation, and nothing could have prepared me for the very warm reception I received from the South Central Region of the International Association of Black Professional Fire Fighters. During my first book tour I was introduced to the most wonderful group of individuals in any one profession. Understanding the power of the gift God has given me, I decided after my second conference in the fall of 1999 that I had to write a book—a story that told of the rich and rocky history of black firefighters, who still in the new millennium faced challenges because of their race.

I interviewed firefighters, paramedics, emergency medical technicians and dispatchers for hours. But I also sat quietly among them in hospitality suites at various conferences over the years (I haven't missed a conference since I attended my first one) and observed. I began to recognize that I was in the presence of something very special. The more I observed, the more enamored I became of the firefighters. Being in the presence of these brave, selfless people has forever changed the way I view life. My love and respect for them is so strong that not a fire truck or rescue unit passes that I don't whisper, "There go my boys."

I believe with all my heart that to whom much is given, so very much is required. Therefore I wanted to give a little something back to those who have inspired me to write *Fannin' the Flames.* I wanted the men and women of the fire service who've taught me what a true calling is to feel a part of this project. The call went out in the form of an essay contest in which the winners would be featured in this book, and many responded. It was so difficult to choose the winning essays because they all said the same thing: they love what they do. After several attempts I was finally able to find something extra special about Pamela Harris's and Jamal Johnson's entries. As you read their essays I hope you'll feel the same and agree that they are but two of the thousands of very special people who risk their lives every day for us all.

A childhood photo, in which I stand with my older brother, a firefighter, clothed in my father's firefighting gear, best captures my seemingly predestined career path. For seventeen years, my father, a Vietnam veteran, fought fires for the Detroit Fire Department, and for nine years, my older brother has been fighting fires for the same department. This is my second year as a firefighter working side by side with him.

While fighting fires is a major part of this job, our days are also filled by such incidents as rescues from auto accidents, uncovered manholes, the aftermath of a tornado, performing CPR and hazardous waste removal. There are only two types of emergency responses: police or fire service. And like our brothers and sisters in blue, we are bound to respond to an emergency situation even when we're not on duty.

As rewarding as the firefighting and rescue work is, I find that children bring so much enjoyment to this job. I often volunteer to give engine house tours and make school visits. With wide-eyed amazement the children always ask how they can learn to do what I do.

There is an unexplained sense of family among all of us firefighters. We help one another not only on the job, but also in our personal lives. There are surely jobs that pay more with a lot less risk, but I just can't imagine doing any of them. It's not just a duty, but also an honor to be a firefighter serving the people of Detroit.

—*JAMAL K. JOHNSON,*
Detroit Fire Department, Engine 55, Ladder 27

've always dared to be different. Before I became a firefighter I served in the United States Navy as a medic, taught school and became a grandmother. My only regret is that I wish I'd become a firefighter sooner. I've worked at stations where I was the only female as well as the only Black, so I have known the harsh and ugly side of the job, but the love I have for my work has kept me strong during those times and continues to do so now. I serve as director of an adult day care center, and one of my greatest rewards comes from my work with senior citizens. Speaking to schoolchildren about fire safety and to young women about my job and its many rewards are also very nice perks.

I remember how my oldest son, Ahmad, reacted to my news of joining the fire service. He said, "I guess it is no different than my running down the football field into a wall of guys waiting to crush me! Just do your best and don't let your fear get the best of you." Those are the words that kept me going after his death at the age of 22 of a massive heart attack. It doesn't matter how young, strong or driven we may be, we have no control over what life has in store for us. Because of all that Ahmad gave me in his short life, I knew there was nothing I couldn't accomplish. So at forty-plus years of age, I became a firefighter!

I've come to realize that life can be very short and you better be about the business of living right and doing all you can to be happy. My sanity was tested during the period of my son's passing. My saving grace was my other two children, Kamya and Chris, along with another of Ahmad's blessings: my granddaughters Ryhen and Se'Aira. Because of them and Ahmad's love of life I knew there was only one choice, for me "TO KEEP LIVING." My job with the fire department will continue to benefit from my experiences.

—*PAMELA HARRIS, Firefighter/EMT,*
Lincoln Heights, Ohio, Fire Department, Station 58

Parry "EbonySatin" Brown is the author of the best-selling novels *The Shirt off His Back* and *Sittin' in the Front Pew,* the nonfiction work *Sexy Doesn't Have a Dress Size: Lessons in Love,* and appears in the anthologies *Proverbs for the People* and *Love Is Blind.* She is a motivational speaker and radio talk-show host with a special love for privileged-challenged children.

You can visit Parry's Web site, www.parryabrown.com, or e-mail her at ebonysatin@parryabrown.com.